EXQUISITE PLEASURE

Without a word, she led Charles up the stairs to an empty room. She knew what she was doing; yet it was like the dream she'd had long ago when she had felt she was merely standing aside and watching her own movements. She knew what she was doing was wrong—wrong for her and Charles at least—but she also knew she was going to do it.

She led him to the door and, still without speaking, she locked the door and removed her dress. He took her in his arms and crushed her to his chest. His body was so large and warm and rough against her smooth flesh. Like his cloak had been. He kissed her lips, her neck, her breasts, and she understood what the Duchess had said: she was too old not to have known the pleasures of a man. Blanche was learning what those pleasures were.

UNDYING LOVE

WE HOPE YOU
ENJOY THIS BOOK
IF YOU'D LIKE A
FREE LIST
OF OTHER PAPERBACKS
AVAILABLE FROM
PLAYBOY PRESS,
JUST SEND
YOUR REQUEST TO
MARILYN ADAMS,
PLAYBOY PRESS,
919 NORTH
MICHIGAN AVENUE,
CHICAGO, ILLINOIS
60611.

In Love's Own Time

Janice Young Brooks

PLAYBOY PRESS
PAPERBACKS

INTRODUCTION

When Blanche saw that the folded parchment bore Pierre's seal, she knew what the letter said without opening it. Margaret had died. Blanche took the letter to the great hall and settled herself before the fire to read Pierre's shaky handwriting.

She was right. The letter told of Margaret's last hours. Pierre said that he had stayed by her deathbed only out of duty. He said that the pretty girl he had once loved had died many years before and the bitter old woman whose death he was reporting was someone else to him. But that was because Pierre never really knew Margaret or understood her, Blanche thought. Pierre had loved what he wanted Margaret to be, not what she was.

As Blanche sat before the fire, the letter in her lap, she knew that already there were scholarly monks in England setting down chronicles of the terrible times when so many had died under the opposing banners of red rose and white rose. Certainly the cloistered scholars would write about Margaret, for she had caused those wars, but what would they say? That Margaret of Anjou was born in 1430, died in 1482, married Henry the Sixth of England, and bore him a son?

Facts—little shells of information locking up the bursting emotions within them. But how could they ever tell what Margaret was like? What she did to those who had loved her and the many more who had hated her and, like Blanche, watched their lives be twisted and channeled by Margaret's whims?

Pierre's letter said he had stayed with Margaret out

of duty. Duty! How much of my life was spent in duty to Margaret, Blanche thought. How much I sacrificed for a promise made so lightly, when I was too young to know what I was promising.

Blanche leaned back and closed her eyes . . . remembering.

BOOK ONE

CHAPTER ONE

Blanche opened the wooden shutters of the narrow window and surveyed the scene in the courtyard below. A light snow had begun to fall and the tournament had ended. People were making their way back through swirling snow to the comparative warmth of the castle. The squires were lugging armor, shields, and spears. The women, duchesses and serving maids alike, scurried along, pulling hoods closely about reddened cheeks. Everywhere Blanche looked she saw the daisy emblem, the emblem of her half-sister, Meggie. No, not Meggie anymore. Now she was Margaret —Margaret of Anjou, Queen of England.

Soft flakes of snow melted against Blanche's face, mingling with the tears and glistening in her golden hair. The end of childhood, Blanche thought, and at the end, a kingdom and husband for Meggie and for me—nothing. Worse than nothing—a long, dreary existence counting out the days and years in a convent. A familiar feeling of suffocating panic swept over her. For the hundredth time she thought desperately, There must be something else for me—some other place in life.

The worst part was that Blanche couldn't tell anyone how she felt. Meggie was too wrapped up in her own hopes and René seldom listened to what anyone said unless it was clever or amusing. How could Blanche tell anyone that she had no calling for the religious life? René would simply have told her that this was the fifteenth century and she was French—did she think she could behave like some kind of barbarian English peasant and just turn her back on the civilized way of doing things? And he would have been right. There was no other place for her but a convent.

She slammed the shutters and went to the fire that sputtered and hissed at the other end of the room. She sat on the floor and, carefully folding back her outer skirt, dried her face on one of her petticoats. It's not even my own fault, she thought angrily. I'm not to blame for being born a bastard. Even *that* wouldn't have made marriage impossible if Meggie hadn't married a king. Now Blanche was suspended between two worlds. It was unfitting for a queen's sister to marry a commoner even if the sister was the daughter of a kitchen maid. And it would be equally unfitting for her to marry into the nobility *because* she was the daughter of a kitchen maid.

Blanche was about to give in to the impulse to cry again when she heard voices in the hall. She hurriedly stood up and tried to compose herself. The door opened and Margaret entered and walked slowly to the middle of the room. With the slightest nod, Margaret indicated that her ladies might remove her elaborate headpiece and furred outer cloak from her slender shoulders. Margaret stood poised and still, small chin uplifted proudly while the women fussed about her.

Margaret was a beautiful girl with dark eyes and hair, set off by pale, flawless skin. She moved with easy grace, and if her manner was somewhat cold and imperious, people were generally too taken with her beauty to notice the chill.

Finally she said, "You may go now. I would like to be alone with my sister." She held the statue stillness until the last of the ladies had gone; then the womanly dignity fell away and she and Blanche were merely two fifteen-year-old girls with a few moments to spend together without pretense. "Blanche, where have you been? Father has been looking for you. Weren't you at the tournament?"

"René wanted me? Whatever for?" Blanche asked, momentarily forgetting that Meggie didn't approve of Blanche's calling their father by his given name.

"You'll see. I think he is with Suffolk now. They ought to be back from the tournament soon." Margaret lifted a small gold frame from the shelf next to the mirror. A tiny, ill-colored picture of King Henry of England stared out at her. "There must not be any good painters in England. I wonder what he really looks like. Do you realize, Blanche, that I have been Queen of England for eight days now and I've never seen England or my husband and I won't for months yet? I hate proxy weddings."

"But it was a beautiful wedding just the same," Blanche said, "and it would not have been safe for King Henry to come to France in person. Not while this war is still going on."

"I know. But still, if there had to be a proxy groom, I wish it had been someone younger and more handsome than Suffolk—not that I don't appreciate Suffolk," she added hurriedly. "I owe him the crown I'll wear. If he hadn't negotiated the truce and betrothal, I'd still be wondering how Father would ever find me a husband. There are few kings who want dowerless princesses."

"There are men who are not kings," Blanche said, trying not to sound sarcastic. "Pierre de Breze would marry you." She managed to say it lightly despite the fact that she had fancied herself in love with Pierre de Breze since she was a child and he had never noticed her.

"Oh, Pierre." Margaret dismissed him with a shrug.

"He is a good man and handsome, Meggie. He's always been in love with you. You would probably be wed to him by now if this marriage had not been arranged."

"In truth, Pierre *is* handsome. But he is so plodding and dull."

". . . and marrying him wouldn't make you a Queen of England," Blanche added, wondering what right she had to complain. Pierre was a nobleman who wouldn't marry a bastard anyway.

A page knocked at the door and announced that René had returned from the tournament and would like to see Blanche. "Meggie, what does he want now?" Blanche asked again.

"Come along and find out," Margaret answered. "I'll come with you."

Blanche wasn't in any hurry to talk to René. He probably had changed his mind about which convent he was sending her to, and knowing him, it was likely that he had based his decision on something like which order wore the most stylish habit.

When they entered René's chamber, he was painting. He had an easel set up with a half-finished work. He was standing back admiring it and whistling to himself. "Ah, girls, you both look lovely. How do you like this?" he asked. Without waiting for an answer he went back to work and motioned absently to Blanche to come closer. "Are you ready to go to the convent?"

"There is very little to get ready. All I need to take along is my dowry and you must provide that," Blanche said bitterly.

"Ah, the dowry—there's been a little problem with that."

"I'm not surprised," Blanche said so coldly that René put down his brush and looked at her. He stared for a moment, then laughed.

"You know me too well, my dear. You see, I hadn't exactly put the money aside earlier, and now with Margaret's wedding and all the expense connected with it, well—I'm a little short of money——"

Blanche crossed her arms and said, "So now I suppose I must go into the convent as a charity case. I will have the same status as any other poor peasant girl whose family had abandoned her. How could you do this to me?"

"No, no—that wouldn't be fitting for a daughter of mine. I have found another solution. I have been discussing this with the Duke of Suffolk—"

"It was my idea," Margaret interrupted and took hold of Blanche's arm affectionately.

"Yes, but I made the arrangements," René said pettishly. "I've talked it all over with Suffolk and you are going to be your sister's lady-in-waiting."

Blanche stared at him in disbelief. "Meggie, is this true?" she asked, turning to her sister. "Could this really be true?"

"Yes, won't it be nice, the two of us getting to stay together?"

"But it can't be," Blanche protested. "I heard the marriage treaty discussed. Meggie, you aren't allowed to bring any attendants with you. You are supposed to have only English women in your household."

"In theory, yes," René said, "but I got Suffolk to agree to an exception since you are so young and Margaret had her heart set on taking you along."

"Don't be silly. You got him to agree because you didn't know what else to do with me," Blanche said bluntly, "but I don't care. Meggie, I thank you with all my heart. I can't begin to tell you what this means to me." In spite of herself, she began to cry.

"That's enough of that," René huffed. He didn't like emotional scenes in which he didn't play the sympathetic lead. "Margaret is to leave tomorrow. Can you be ready?"

"I could be ready in half an hour, if necessary. I could walk out the door right now, just as I am, if I had to."

"Then get along and pack," René said, dismissing them and going back to his painting.

Outside the door Blanche threw her arms around Margaret and hugged her. "Meggie, I am so grateful. I'm afraid there is nothing I can ever do for you to equal what you've done for me today."

"Yes, there is," Margaret said, grasping Blanche's hand. "Please promise me something."

16

"Anything, Meggie. What's wrong?"

"I don't know, Blanche, but I'm frightened. I'm going to another country to live my life with a man I've never seen. Please promise to stay with me."

"Of course I'll be with you. You know I'm going along as your lady-in-waiting—that's with you."

"I know, but promise you'll *stay* with me."

"I'll stay with you."

"Forever?"

"Forever."

"No matter what happens?"

"No matter what," Blanche said.

"There is something else. People tell you more than they tell me. What do you hear about King Henry? What do you suppose he is like?"

Blanche hesitated, picking her words carefully. "Well, they say he has the Plantagenet looks, though he's not as comely as his father, and that he dresses very plainly. Of course, none of the English know how to dress," she added with an inbred French scorn of English fashion which even she was unable to overcome.

"Go on," Margaret prodded. "What else do you know about him?"

"I hear he is very pious, but I wouldn't let that worry you," Blanche said. She didn't want to tell Margaret *how* pious King Henry was, partly because she didn't know if it was true or just gossip.

"Worry? What do you mean? Why should that worry me?"

"No reason at all, Meggie. Anyway, how pious could a man be in the same room with you?" Margaret looked as though she was about to ask more

17

questions, so Blanche seized her arm and said, "Meggie, you're all ready to go and I have to get all my things packed tonight. Would you like to help me?"

Margaret stiffened slightly and Blanche said, "I'm sorry. I keep forgetting you are a queen now, not just my sister. May I have your leave, your majesty?"

It was going to be difficult to think of Meggie as Queen Margaret, but Blanche was determined to do everything right since she had been given a second chance at life.

In the morning Margaret's entourage were ready to begin their long journey to England. Everyone was excited to be leaving, none more so than Blanche, who was nearly light-headed with relief. René surprised them all by riding along for a ways. Although he had officially turned his daughter Margaret over to the Duke and Duchess of Suffolk, he protested that he could not yet bear to part with his favorite child. Blanche was sorry he came along, for although she understood his fickleness and his vanities, she loved him and was loath to prolong the pain of parting.

René knew that eventually he must turn back. He continued to entertain the company with frivolous jests until the last minute. Finally they came to a halt. René bade farewell to the visiting English and then to Blanche. "Goodby, little girl. You didn't belong in a convent. Take care of your sister. Make her laugh sometimes." Then he went to Margaret. He took her hands in his and the entire company was silent. They waited respectfully to hear what parting words of advice René of Anjou had for his beloved daughter.

18

But he had none. Father and daughter stood frozen, hands locked for long minutes. Tears welled in Margaret's eyes and silently spilled over. René kissed a spot on her hand where a tear had fallen, then quickly turned and mounted his horse. He rode off without speaking, without looking back. Blanche almost had to smile. So typical of René—the love of the dramatic. He would tell the story of his parting to all his friends, emphasizing how noble, how bereaved *he* was, so that he could be petted and made a fuss over. Everyone would lose interest in the story pretty soon and then he would stop telling it and stop thinking of Margaret. Blanche wondered how she could understand the man so well and still love him.

Blanche comforted Margaret after the parting and was joined in her efforts by the Duke of Suffolk's wife. Her name was Alice Chaucer and she was probably the best friend that Margaret was ever to have. Alice was plump and kind and completely without vanity except on one small point. Her grandfather had been a minor official in the English court and had written poetry and tales about an imaginary group of religious pilgrims. The girls had read some of the tales. Blanche had roared with laughter at Master Chaucer's view of people. Margaret, however, had thought the stories coarse and Blanche's laughter unseemly. Lady Alice was inordinately vain about her relative. It was her only worldly vice.

The trip through France lasted all winter, partly because of Margaret's popularity. Romantics saw in her a fairy-tale princess. "Poor little hinny," whispered toothless old women watching them pass, "leaving her

dear papa to go live in such a nasty cold country."
They wept at her leaving and got their feet stepped on
trying to get close enough to touch the hem of her
cloak.

More realistic souls saw her as an ideal political
pawn. "With a pretty little piece of France like that
in his bed, King Henry won't have no need to come
over and bother us no more," muttered hard-bitten
old soldiers who had spent their entire adult lives fighting off the English. They rejoiced in her going. Margaret's entourage stopped at every town along the way
to bid farewell to romantics and cynics alike who stood
in the icy mud to see the young Queen of England
pass.

Margaret could have hastened the moment when she
would reach her new country, and Blanche wondered
why she didn't until one night Margaret confided that
she was concerned. She said she knew that there was
more to marriage than love poems and long, meaningful looks. There was a physical relationship and she
was half afraid, half eager to experience it. "It might
be very nice, but it might not be. Then what?" she
asked Blanche.

Blanche told her, as usual, "Don't worry." Blanche
couldn't imagine worrying about that side of life. *Her*
only concern was that it was an aspect that she would
probably never have the opportunity to know. And
yet how nice it would be to walk hand in hand with a
handsome man, to feel the warmth of a hand on her
shoulder, to know the feeling of soft lips and a rough
beard against her face. The love poems she heard always made it seem that it was the meeting and joining

of souls that made love true. But Blanche suspected that the joining of bodies, of senses, might be important, too. She said nothing to Margaret of this; she was afraid Margaret would think her common and vulgar. But even if I never know the touch of a man, at least I won't be buried alive in a convent, Blanche thought.

By March they were nearing M'antes. An English soldier rode out to meet them with an invitation from the Duke of York, who hoped that her majesty and her entourage would allow him to express his respects to the Queen at a feast the next evening. Blanche turned to Alice Chaucer and said, "This Duke of York—isn't he in charge of the English armies in France?"

"Yes," Lady Alice replied. She seemed bubbly and excited at the prospect of dining with the Duke of York, but Blanche noticed that Alice's husband, the Duke of Suffolk, was glaring at the soldier who brought the message with an even fiercer look than he usually wore. Blanche wondered why.

Blanche had observed that people seemed to think that their social inferiors couldn't hear; consequently she learned a great deal about the Duke of York from the English people with whom they were traveling. She filled in the blanks with carefully casual questioning of one of Lady Alice's maids. She knew, of course, that England had been trying to take over France for many years and it had looked as if they might succeed until Joan of Arc turned the tide in favor of France. The English were still trying to pretend they might win, but it was hopeless.

Richard, Duke of York, the man who was to be their host, had been appointed Governor of France several years before. He had been very young at the time and hadn't wanted the appointment, but had gone anyway at the urging of the King's Council. Against great odds he had done a good job for England and managed to push the French army back a safe distance from Rouen.

Blanche got most of this information by reading between the lines of what she was hearing, for it appeared that there was much jealousy of York among the English. There was a great deal of tension in the air just now about the appointment of another English nobleman, the Duke of Somerset, to a post that somehow conflicted with York's. Apparently the men had always been enemies, and there was a great deal of taking sides going on even among Margaret's entourage.

Blanche wasn't happy with what she was hearing. It sounded to her as if England's nobility had long been divided into two factions—and strong factions at that. She didn't know where King Henry stood in this matter. She hoped that he was the kind of enlightened man who had the wisdom to maintain his own power by playing the sides against each other. Her greatest concern was that Margaret would involve herself. Blanche wasn't sure that Margaret knew enough to take the right side.

Margaret broke into her thoughts as they rode toward M'antes. "This man who is to entertain us is a kinsman of my husband, Blanche. Did you know that? Probably just another smelly old soldier. At least he won't have the sense to notice how worn my wardrobe has become."

"You would look lovely even in rags, Meggie."

"Oh, well, we will soon be in England and everything will be all right. I shall have new clothes. Do you realize I have been married for almost five months and have yet to meet my husband? I feel as though we have been traveling for years."

They arrived at M'antes that night and the next morning they felt the first welcome hint of spring. Margaret had her hair washed and Blanche brushed it dry in front of a sunny window. Naturally their threadbare gowns couldn't be washed—only linen undergarments were able to withstand lye soap and water —but everything was hung out to air. They arrived at the castle at M'antes looking, feeling, and smelling better than they had for months. As they rode into the courtyard, Blanche glanced around idly, wondering which of the ragged English soldiers was their host.

"Welcome, your grace. Richard of York at your service," said the one well-dressed man in the crowd as he stepped out to greet them. He had a broad smile, which revealed straight white teeth. His face was boyish and handsome with soft brown hair that fell across his forehead. Blanche glanced at Margaret and was appalled. Margaret was staring at York as if stupefied. York went on, "I'm afraid we are ill-equipped to entertain ladies here. We had hoped your party would pass through M'antes earlier, but you seem to have brought the spring air with you. If I may say so, your majesty, it is fitting, for you are as lovely as a spring flower yourself."

He was talking to Margaret as if she were a pretty child, but Blanche could see that Margaret was not thinking as a child.

23

"Thank you sire. We are honored to be here," Margaret said in the coyest tone Blanche had ever heard her use.

The ladies were helped from their horses and led through the courtyard by the handsome Duke of York. They entered the great hall, where fresh, aromatic rushes were spread on the floor and silver goblets lined the tables. "Is the Duchess not dining with us tonight?" Margaret asked in a sugary voice. York took the question at face value, but Blanche knew that the real question being asked was, "Is there a Duchess of York?"

"The Duchess is in England. Her rooms were badly in need of repair, so she went home to visit her family while the work was being done. My wife, Cecily, is the youngest of her father's twenty-three children and it's hard to get her away from her doting brothers and sisters. She's still the baby to them." He said it with such fondness that it almost hurt Blanche to hear him, for she feared that no man would ever speak of her in that way.

"Twenty-three children? My lord, surely you jest," Blanche said.

"No, truly. Her father married twice and fathered almost two dozen young. Of course, my Cecily is the best of the lot. Excuse me just a moment," he said, stepping away.

Margaret gripped Blanche's elbow and hissed, "Pray to every saint you know that King Henry be just like him." As far as Blanche was concerned, if the saints could arrange for every man in the world to be like the Duke of York—or Pierre— it would be fortunate, to say the least, but she was sorry to hear Margaret express the opinion. She was also surprised to realize

24

that it was the first time she had thought about Pierre for days.

The Duke of York returned with another man. "Your Majesty, allow me to present my kinsman, Richard Neville, the Earl of Warwick." Warwick was handsome, but the effect of his exaggerated perfection of feature was almost distasteful. His eyes were deep blue and of frightening intensity. His beard was carefully tended and thick for such a young man. His dark hair looked like a silk helmet. There was something so malevolent, so coldly arrogant in his look that Blanche drew back involuntarily. She later learned that Warwick was but twenty years old, but he seemed much older—perhaps not older, but one of those people to whom age does not pertain.

Margaret must have felt the same awe and fright of him as Blanche did. He approached her, bowed low over her outstretched hand and spoke in fluent French, "We are honored by your presence, Your Majesty." Margaret pulled her hand back as if she might hurt it and replied in icy English, "Sire, I am no longer a French princess, I am the Queen of England. I prefer to be addressed in English."

Warwick drew back as if struck. He was still smiling, but it was a painted, strained smile. His blue-black eyes narrowed dangerously. Margaret didn't seem to notice Warwick's reaction. Blanche thought Margaret hadn't meant to offend him—she found him disconcerting and made use of an opportunity to show York how grown up and regal she could be.

Margaret was to wonder afterwards why Warwick hated her with such destructive intensity. Many years later when Blanche reminded her of this incident, Margaret didn't remember it. She said Blanche was silly to think a man could generate such life-long hatred on the strength of such a trivial remark. But Blanche believed it was true. Warwick would never forget an insult, particularly one from a foolish girl who was his queen. He nursed and brooded over it for years.

There was a superb dinner and minstrels and dancing afterwards. Blanche was annoyed to see Margaret behaving quite giddily. But from what Blanche could overhear of the conversation, York was more interested in talking about the work he was having done at the castle than in complimenting Margaret. "There is a lake in the field behind here," he said after the minstrels had finished. "The men have cleared the area around it and the women who are here with their husbands have planted flowers. It is quite lovely. Perhaps you and your ladies can return tomorrow and see it."

"I should like very much to see it now," Margaret said sweetly. Apparently she thought there might be pretty compliments forthcoming during an intimate little stroll on a spring evening.

"Would you really be interested?" York asked doubtfully. "It's getting dark." There was a touch of panic in his voice. "Very well. Warwick, would you take the Queen and some of her ladies to see the lake? I have some dispatches I must make if you will excuse me, Your Majesty."

Margaret stiffened and Warwick looked rebellious. Blanche was embarrassed for Margaret's sake. The Queen had, after all, tried to lure York out into the dark and he had rejected her—rebuked her!

26

They all took the now obligatory stroll around the little lake. Margaret looked as if her legs were splinted at the knees. In the half-light and dreary setting Warwick seemed even more frightening. His speech dripped with lazy sarcasm and there was something sleekly sinister about his very posture. His nostrils flared as if there was a bad smell in the air that had nothing to do with the lake. Blanche felt a chill run through her at the sight of him silhouetted against a muddy sunset.

They stayed that night, as they had many times during their journey, at a nearby convent. Margaret and Blanche and Lady Alice Chaucer were sharing a small, clean room that normally served as some sort of storeroom. The abbess had seen to it that the room was freshly whitewashed and had beds with clean straw mattresses.

Blanche looked around the room and thought, I shall leave here in the morning and never come back. I shall be free to live outside walls. She knew she would probably never have a husband or family of her own, but neither would she be walled away from even observing life like the women who lived at this convent as nuns. Once again she felt a surge of gratitude to the sister who had saved her from that fate. Life with Meggie wouldn't be easy. Meggie could be haughty and selfish, but life with her would be interesting, at least.

Blanche helped Margaret remove her heavy dress. Margaret was silent while Blanche unwound her hair and began brushing it. "I have a husband now and *he* will take me for moonlight walks, won't he?" Margaret asked unexpectedly. Blanche didn't know whether to laugh or cry. It was such a naive remark from a girl who was now a queen, and an unusual admission from Margaret that she had been acting very foolishly. Blanche had never known Margaret to admit a mistake, not even in an indirect manner.

Soon Lady Alice returned, and Margaret and Blanche crawled into their beds. Blanche pulled the coarse covers up to her chin and began her favorite daydream about Pierre de Breze. She was beginning to tire of it, though, for Pierre's face was getting harder to recall.

"Lady Alice," Margaret said, "I'm glad you are to serve me and I shall ask a great deal of you, starting now. As you know, my fortunes have always seemed to be tied to France. Father insisted that Blanche and I learn to speak English, but we were taught little about the English people. I shall rely on you to instruct me and to help me."

The Duchess must have been surprised at this burst of talk, since Margaret had been very quiet and self-contained throughout the journey. "Your grace, I shall be delighted to be of any help that I can."

"Good," Margaret said, sitting up in bed and pulling her knees up to serve as a chin rest. "We shall begin tonight. Pay attention, Blanche," she said, unnecessarily, for Blanche was insatiably curious. "I know nothing of your Duke of York, Lady Alice. Tell me about him."

Alice smiled knowingly, making Blanche sure that she had observed Margaret's ill-fated flirtation with York earlier in the evening. "I'm not sure I can do that very well—you see, my husband doesn't get along very well with the Duke of York and I don't know that

I'm a very good judge. You know how silly men can be."

"That is why your husband pleaded illness and didn't go with us to the feast tonight?" Margaret asked.

"I suppose so. I don't really know what it is between them. I think the Duke of York is a fine man myself. I believe they had words over York's appointment to this French post."

"He's quite young for such authority, isn't he?" Margaret asked.

"Nay, I think not. York isn't nearly so young as he looks. I think he is more than thirty. He's been here in France for years. They say he does a wonderful job of anything he does"—Alice laughed—"but they don't say it in front of my husband."

"I understand York is King Henry's kinsman," Margaret said. "In what manner are they related?"

Alice sighed deeply. "Oh dear, where to start?" She thought for a minute, then said, "About a hundred years ago, when this war with France was starting, there was an English king called Edward the Third and he had many sons. The oldest one was called the Black Prince, but he died before his old father, so when Edward the Third died, the Black Prince's son, a boy named Richard, became king . . . Richard the Second."

"I remember hearing about Richard the Second," Blanche interrupted. "He was a bad king, or so they said, and his cousin Henry something—Bolingbroke, wasn't it—became king." She was proud to get the chance to show off that bit of information. It was one of the few facts she knew of the tangled Plantagenet genealogy.

"Yes," Alice said, "Bolingbroke became Henry the

Fourth. He was the son of John of Gaunt, the Duke of Lancaster. Lancaster was another of the old King Edward the Third's sons."

Margaret looked a little confused. "You mean this John of Gaunt was a younger brother of the Black Prince?"

"That's right. You see, Richard the Second and Henry the Fourth were first cousins. Their fathers were brothers. And Henry the Fourth was your husband's grandfather."

"Where does the York branch of the family come into this? From another son of Edward the Third? A younger son?" Margaret asked.

"Yes and no," Alice replied. "There was another brother who was born between the Black Prince and John of Gaunt. His name was Lionel."

"But Lionel must not have had any children," Blanche said.

"Yes, he *did*. That's why I mentioned him. The Duke of York is descended from Lionel and also from another brother, the youngest of the sons."

Margaret suddenly sat up very straight. "What are you saying?" she asked sharply. "Do you mean to tell me that the York family is descended from an *older* son than the Lancaster family, King Henry's family?"

"Yes," Alice said meekly, as if she had unwittingly let out some secret. It took even Blanche a moment to realize what Margaret was upset about.

"Then the York family has a better claim to the throne than the Lancasters?" Margaret said accusingly.

"No, no, well—maybe, if you wanted to look at it

that way—but the Yorks don't see it like that. Not *this* Duke of York anyway. It seems to me that his father and grandfather got into some trouble pressing such a claim, now that you remind me——"

"How much trouble?" Blanche asked.

"They were beheaded," Alice admitted. "But *this* Duke of York isn't like that. He's a loyal subject."

"Lady Alice, I've become very thirsty," Margaret said. "Do you think you could manage to get me a little glass of wine this late?"

"I would be glad to," Alice said, hurrying to do an errand that suited her far better than giving history lessons.

"Why wasn't I told about this?" Margaret said to Blanche as soon as the door shut.

"I suppose because no one considered it important," she answered.

"Important! Why, of course it's important. Can you imagine there being an older branch of the King's family? And to allow one of the Yorks to hold such a high post!"

"Calm yourself, Meggie. This is silly. You are worrying about the order of children born generations ago. I'm certain no one but you is upset about it. Surely the English nobility all know about it and seem to regard it as of no consequence." Blanche was tired and irritated with Margaret for carrying on about this.

"Well, *I* certainly regard it as dangerous. It is insane to allow that man to hold such an important position."

Blanche snapped, "You are just angry because 'that man' snubbed you." As soon as the words left her mouth she was sorry.

31

Margaret grew rigid. "Nobody snubs a queen! And I do not need advice from servants' bastards."

Blanche stared at her, stunned beyond speech. They had argued as girls, of course, but Margaret had never referred to Blanche's birth in any but the lightest and most sympathetic terms. Blanche felt as if she had been hit in the face with something heavy and sharp. She managed to whisper, "Yes, your majesty," and make her way to blow out the candle that lit the room.

Blindly she groped for the door and, finding it, fled down the long hallway that opened onto the nuns' kitchen garden. Even in her nearly mindless distress she managed to skirt the neat rows of seedlings and ran out across the adjoining field until she could no longer catch her breath. She flung herself onto a pile of leaves at the foot of a large tree and wept until she was nearly ill.

She was so wrapped up in her unhappiness that it took her a minute to realize that she was not alone. Someone was patting her shoulder and saying in a soft male voice, "There, there, don't cry. Please don't cry. It will be all right."

She hadn't the energy left to be surprised. She just sat up and went on sobbing. The stranger pulled her gently against his shoulder and let her cry there. Finally she began to come to her senses and realized that she was sitting out in a field in the middle of the night with a perfect stranger. She was wearing only a nightshift and not even a pretty one. She pulled away from the man. "Please excuse me, sire." She hiccuped. "I have mussed your cloak. Would you please direct me to the abbey?" she said, getting to her feet. Oddly enough, she had no fear of this man; it never crossed her mind that he might do her harm. There was something reassuring about him, as if he carried his own atmosphere of trust. She could see him but dimly. All she could tell was that he was young and had dark, curly hair. He was wearing some sort of uniform.

"You aren't a nun, are you?" He sounded shocked at the idea of a nun being loose in her nightshift.

"No, I am part of a group of travelers," she said, for she could not bring herself to even mention Margaret's name or title. All the pride she'd had in being the Queen's lady-in-waiting had vanished.

"Please allow me to escort you to the abbey," he said, wrapping his cloak around her shoulders. In her disordered state of mind she thought it an almost affectionate gesture. But what could inspire affection in the sight of a nobody like me with red eyes and hiccups? she thought critically.

When they reached the abbey, Blanche managed a whispered, "Thank you."

To her surprise he answered, "Thank *you*."

"Please wait, your cloak," she said, holding it out to him.

"No, you are still shivering. Leave it with the abbess and I will get it tomorrow." Suddenly he was gone in the darkness.

Blanche crept into her room. Margaret appeared to be sleeping, but fitfully. Blanche started to fold the rough, warm cape and changed her mind. She wrapped it around herself and slept.

CHAPTER TWO

Margaret wakened before Blanche, and if she noticed the cloak, she said nothing. Blanche arose and briskly set about her duties. She shook out her dress and brushed the Queen's suede riding boots. She braided Margaret's hair and wound it tightly, maybe a little too tightly, around her head. Margaret said nothing about the night before and neither did Blanche, but their roles were strangely reversed. Blanche was cool and respectful and formal, while Margaret was obviously trying, in her own rigid way, to make amends. Though she could never bring herself to apologize, she was doing so in her own way. She kept saying things like, "Do you think I should wear this ribbon in my hair, Blanche? You have much better taste than I in such matters. I can never tell what will look well as you can," and "I do hope they have some quail here we may take along for the midday meal. I know how you like quail."

Normally Blanche would have been warmed by Margaret's thoughtful attitude. But today she was both angry and indifferent. Angry for the words Margaret had flung at her the night before and indifferent because her mind kept drifting back to the mysterious young man under the tree. Alas, like Pierre, this young man would never enter her life again, but the memory of his kindness would remain to comfort her. When Margaret and Alice left to eat the morning meal, Blanche refolded the cloak. How good it felt—rough and yet soft—a very masculine fabric. Reluctantly she took it to the abbess' cell and explained that it had been loaned to her and that a young man would be calling at the front gates later for it. The abbess did not ask the name of the young man, which was fortunate, for, of course, Blanche did not know.

They were to depart later in the morning, so there was much to do. Everyone gathered his belongings and ate heartily in preparation for the ride ahead. Rather than eat in the hall, Blanche went into the kitchens and asked for a plate of cakes and some ale to sip while she packed Margaret's things. She still felt the need to be alone.

Eventually all was ready. The last chests were loaded on wagons and the saddles securely cinched. They rode out the front gates of the abbey after distributing small gifts among the abbess and sisters. As Blanche had expected, the Duke of York and his retinue were there waiting to bid them farewell. Blanche was too involved in her own thoughts to pay much heed to the confusing crowd of departing guests and well-wishers until a familiar face came into view. The young man with the cloak! He was standing next to the Duke of York.

Blanche hadn't gotten a good look at him the night before. Her tears and the watery moonlight had prevented that, and yet he looked just as she thought he should. He was slender, but not too much so. His fair skin and clear blue eyes contrasted beautifully with his dark, curly hair, which he wore just a little longer than fashion demanded. There was something finely wrought about his appearance, something sensitive but without a trace of weakness.

Margaret stopped so that the Duke of York would have to come to her. "We regret your departure, your majesty," York said, "but England is awaiting your arrival and will rejoice at the sight of you. My men and I wish you Godspeed."

"I thank you for your kind words and hospitality, sire," Margaret said, her voice shaking slightly. Blanche could tell that she was still upset about the previous evening.

"If I may be so bold as to make a request of you?" York asked.

"What is it?" Margaret said curtly.

"This young gentleman," York said, indicating the man in the cloak, "is Sir Charles Seintleger. He is a member of my staff and has received word that his father is ill. Perhaps he could return with you to England."

Margaret looked at the man speculatively, at his cloak especially, then at Blanche, who colored slightly. "We would be honored," she told York and turned to Seintleger. "Sir Charles, I would like you to meet my sister, Lady Blanche."

Blanche was astonished. Margaret had never introduced her as anything but a member of the family, exact relationship unspecified. Margaret must have been sincerely contrite to publicly call her "sister" and to elevate her to the status of "Lady" Blanche. Naturally, that wasn't official and it was rather silly of Margaret, but it was a touching gesture.

Blanche rode beside Margaret as they inched their way through the crowd. "Thank you, Meggie," she whispered.

"Thank heaven!" Margaret exclaimed. "If you had called me 'your majesty' once more, I would have screamed."

The day's ride was especially long for Blanche because she knew that Sir Charles Seintleger was riding behind her. What a beautiful name, she thought, not clunky and Saxon. Seintleger with the French pronunciation—it rolled off the tongue. He must be a member of one of the old Norman families who had gone to England with William the Conquerer so many years before. She sat very straight and tried to bounce and wiggle as little as possible just in case he should happen to glance her way.

Blanche was pleased that she had taken care to put on her best clothes that morning. At the time, she hadn't admitted to herself that she had any hope of seeing him again. She had put on a white chemise with wide bands of fine Flemish lace at the hem and sleeves and told herself all the time that it was foolish to dress up for nothing. Over the chemise she had put a dove-gray cote-hardie, which laced tightly up the front. She laced it even more tightly than usual. The neckline was low and showed off the lines of her firm young breasts. Even Margaret had commented on how nice Blanche looked.

In the late afternoon they had reached another abbey. The ladies were all seen to their quarters and the gentlemen went to lodge in a nearby monastery. Blanche watched Seintleger ride away. "This is ridiculous," she told herself, "I am only the bastard daughter of a serving woman. Seintleger was kind to me and I am making a fool of myself. Any decent man would have offered me his cloak if only to spare himself the sight of that wretched old nightshift. Any normal individual would have done his best to get me back into safekeeping just to prevent me from becoming a menace, wandering about all red-eyed and puffy-faced. There is nothing more to it. I am going to remain the unmarried companion of my half-sister all the rest of my life."

It was a hard thing for a girl of fifteen to face, but there would be compensations, she told herself. She would never have to worry about the fate of children she might have raised. She would never have to bear the pain of parting with a husband going to war. She would never need fear dying in her youth of childbed fever. She would never have to accommodate herself to the whims of a man—only to Margaret's whims. But these compensations seemed empty and worthless to her now.

She came out of her unhappy reflections and noted that Margaret was unusually quiet. "Don't keep worrying about him, Meggie," Blanche said, "Everything will be fine when we get to England."

Margaret smiled wanly. "It's not just that, Blanche. My birthday is a few days hence and I shall be expected to dispense alms along our route." Blanche had forgotten about that, not her sister's birthday, of course, but about the tradition of queens giving gifts to the poor on their birthdays.

"What shall I do?" Margaret asked. "I've not enough gold to even buy wool for dresses for myself. How shall I give gifts? Everything I have with me is itself a gift to me and I would insult the givers if I disposed of any of it."

"Didn't Father provide you with any gold to bring along? No, of course not. Why need I ask? Could you borrow some money from Lady Alice? I'm sure she would be glad to help you out."

"No, she has already mentioned that she and Suffolk are in reduced straits until they can return to collect their rents from their tenants."

"What about the Duchess of Somerset?" Blanche asked.

"I couldn't bear to expose my poverty to the Duchess of Somerset," Margaret said, and Blanche could see her point. The Duchess of Somerset, whose husband was reputed to be a great enemy of Richard of York, was a remarkably malicious and sharp-tongued woman. Listening to her, Blanche had picked up much of her information, information that had to be strained and sifted before it could be believed. She was a strange-looking woman as well—sallow and sour of expression, with mud-colored hair pulled back so tightly that her eyebrows always seemed to be fighting to get loose from their moorings.

"I see how you feel, but her husband is one of the negotiators of your marriage settlement. No doubt she already knows more of your affairs than you know," Blanche said.

In the end, the Duchess of Somerset became the guardian of Margaret's silver serving vessels in return for enough money to distribute coins along the way. Margaret decided to try getting along with the Duchess.

There was much she would need to know about the people she would be meeting in England, and Lady Alice, though a dear soul, was not nearly as good a source of information as the Duchess of Somerset. She was a born gossip, and though, like all gossips, she heard only the worst about everyone, she was quite willing to share all she knew or thought she knew.

So Margaret humbled her considerable pride and borrowed from the Duchess and received, along with the money, the information that Richard of York's father had been beheaded for treason during the previous reign. He had raised a rebellion against Henry the Fifth, the present King's father.

"What is the matter with the English that they allow the son of a traitor—a condemned traitor to the crown —to go free and hold office?" Margaret stormed. Blanche had learned her lesson and said nothing, though she wished to point out that the son was not the father. "Certainly this York," Margaret sneered the name, "must hold some grudge against the son of the king who beheaded his father." Then she became smug. "I'm sure my husband has some very clever reason for allowing this situation and undoubtedly he will explain it to me after I get to know him."

Perhaps she is right, Blanche thought. Perhaps I'm not as good a judge of character as I would like to believe. But York seems kind and innocent. Margaret wants to think he is dangerous only because he insulted her by rejecting her attentions.

On the day they expected to reach Rouen they stopped for a midday rest in a lovely clearing by the road. After eating their fill of bread and cheese and meat pastries, everyone was loath to get back on horses, so they rested a bit. Blanche went off into the woods to rinse her cup in a stream that she could hear bubbling nearby. She was sitting on the bank enjoying the fresh, green smell of new growth when a voice said, "May I join you?"

"Please do," she said as calmly as she could.

"Is it better now?" Charles Seintleger asked.

"Is what better?"

"Whatever you were crying about that night."

"Oh, yes. Much better. It was nothing, really. I had just gotten my feelings hurt and we are all rather easily irritated from our long journey."

"Was it a man who hurt you, Lady Blanche?" he asked.

"No, it wasn't a man," Blanche said. Was it her imagination or did he really look glad to hear this? ". . . and please don't call me Lady Blanche. My sister spoke in jest. I am merely Mistress Blanche. I have no title."

"It seems to me an unkind jest," he said, "but in truth, I am glad you are not Lady Blanche."

Blanche knew that he must understand her position. Since she was the Queen's sister, yet untitled, it should be obvious that she was illegitimate. "Why are you glad?"

"If you were an exalted, highborn lady, you would not lower youself to speak to me and we could never be friends. But it is presumptuous to think that you would be my friend anyway."

"Not at all. I should like it very much, but it is I who am unworthy. My mother was——"

42

"Your father is René of Anjou," he said, deliberately cutting off her confession. "Your sister is my queen. I am honored to be in your presence."

At that moment a trumpet sounded to signal their imminent departure. "We had better return," she said, "lest we be left behind."

"That would suit me," he said, offering his hand.

Once or twice during that afternoon's ride, Blanche could not resist looking back, and every time she did, his eyes met hers and he smiled at her. When they arrived at Rouen, Margaret was asked to delay for a few days before making the last leg of the journey through France. It was a beautiful city and since it was still in the hands of the English, many of the group were delighted to have the opportunity to visit with family and friends. The next day Margaret was invited to tour the town with Lady Alice and Suffolk. Blanche asked to be excused. Charles Seintleger had offered to escort Blanche on a tour of her own. She took special care of her hair and even borrowed some of Margaret's oil of rose.

Charles took Blanche first to see the place where the heretic Joan of Arc had been burned fourteen years before. Blanche had been but a babe at the time, but only the year before she had heard René mention Joan's role in changing the tide of the war. They went to the cathedral where Margaret's husband had been crowned King of France. "But kings of France are crowned at Paris, not Rouen," Blanche protested.

"That's right," Charles admitted. "But when the English were claiming to rule France, they couldn't get to Paris through the opposition, so they held their ceremony here. It wasn't valid, of course. It was just a bold venture that failed."

"That doesn't sound very loyal," Blanche said. "You yourself are one of the Englishmen who want to rule this country."

"No, I am an Englishman doing his duty to his overlord, the Duke of York. I don't believe we have any reason to be here. Neither does York. England is the finest country in the world and would profit more by keeping the peace with France than we are likely to profit by continuing this war."

"You talk like a merchant," Blanche said.

"That's because I am. My ancestors were tool traders, still are. But now my father is very wealthy and has a title, so people pretend that they don't know we are in trade."

"But you are a soldier."

"Yes, my oldest brother will run my father's business, I shall represent the name of Seintleger in the army, and my younger brother, George, is in the Church."

"You are going home to see your father, are you not?"

"Yes, but he has been ill for a long time and I doubt that I will get there in time." He said it calmly. A man who can face the truth, Blanche thought.

"I am sorry for your sake that we travel so slowly."

"I am far safer traveling slowly with the Queen's party than I would be trying to traverse France by myself. Besides, the company is much better."

They walked for several hours; then Blanche hurried back. She wanted to be there before Margaret so that she would not question her whereabouts. Blanche didn't want to have to lie to her sister and yet she didn't want to confide in her, either. Blanche felt rather ashamed of herself for even pretending to believe that there might be any future between herself and a wealthy English knight.

The next morning they were on their way at last for the coast of France, where a ship, the *Cokke John,* had been waiting since September. Blanche had no more opportunities to talk with Charles. She and Margaret boarded the ship reluctantly. Neither of them had ever seen the sea before, much less set out upon it. Margaret said little and only Blanche guessed how nervous she was.

They left behind the soft spring breezes of France for cold, foggy Channel winds. By the time they were too far out to sea to make any attempt to retreat, the winds had become a full-blown storm. Inside the ship, the passengers became sick and the fetid atmosphere quickly became unbearable. The craft, which had seemed so enormous and stable when they boarded, rolled and pitched and groaned in harmony with the groans of the seasick cargo. Blanche was in a cabin below with Margaret. True to her personality, Margaret was gritting her teeth and pretending she was in full control of herself. Blanche tried to emulate her example, but finally realized if she didn't get at least one breath of fresh air, however wet and windy, in a few seconds, she would be ill. Without a word, for she didn't trust herself to open her mouth, Blanche rushed out of the cabin and up the narrow ladder that led to a door on deck.

She pushed against the door, but it felt as though someone was leaning on it from the outside. She frantically pushed harder, and suddenly the door was yanked open by the violent wind which had been holding it shut. She kept her grip on the door and hung there for a moment. The deck swarmed with sailors adjusting sails and tying down equipment. The men slid on the wet decks and shouted unintelligible orders over the howl of the storm. The ship suddenly rocked in another direction and Blanche lost her footing. Somehow she kept her hold on the door when her feet went out from under her, and she was struggling to pull herself up against gravity gone mad when she heard Charles's voice dimly through the howl of the wind. "Get below, you fool!" he shouted and, yanking her to her feet, propelled her roughly through the door and slammed it behind her. Weak and trembling, she half climbed, half fell down the stairway and made her way back to her cabin—all notions of seasickness forgotten.

She went back to Margaret's tiny cubicle. She was already terribly shaken, but when she saw the Queen, her heart leaped. Margaret was sitting bolt upright in the corner, keeping her balance with outstretched arms braced rigidly against the walls. She was so white, and her eyes so large and staring, that for a second Blanche had the awful thought that she might be dead and somehow impaled there. As Blanche staggered toward her, Margaret bent her head and retched. She vomited until there was nothing left in her stomach, then she kept on gagging and retching. The little room had become a nightmare. Their clothing was fouled and their hair was wet with sweat. The ship ceased its violence for a few moments and Blanche used the precious time to strip off both Margaret's clothing and her own. She got fresh shifts from a trunk. When she had both Margaret and herself both decently covered, she pulled and carried Margaret out of the room and called for help. No one could hear her, or if they could, any reply was lost in the sound of the storm. Blanche dragged Margaret along the narrow, dark hallway until she found another tiny room like their own, which was unoccupied.

Blanche got Margaret into the room, which had a clean bed, and dumped her on it. There were some clothes strewn about from a travel case which had broken open. Blanche quickly rummaged through and found a petticoat. She ripped it into strips and tied the strips across the bed to keep Margaret from falling out. She appeared to be barely conscious and obviously hadn't the strength to take care of her balance.

Within an hour the storm had subsided slightly, and other passengers were beginning to stagger about. One yellowish-green face after another peeped through the door to inquire, "How fares her majesty?"

And to each of them Blanche said, "She is better, I think, and resting now." Blanche knew it to be a lie. Margaret was still as white as one dead and was tossing against her restraints, mumbling nonsense. Blanche didn't want to alarm anyone or cause embarrassment if it was simply the aftereffects of seasickness, so she waited until Charles came to the door of the cabin. Blanche was gratified that he asked about her condition before he inquired about the Queen's.

Blanche said quietly, "I am well, but I am worried about my sister. Could you fetch the ship's doctor?"

"I can't," Charles replied. "The doctor went on deck to help an injured sailor. Both the doctor and the sailor were swept overboard."

It wasn't until that moment that Blanche fully realized that a storm at sea was not merely an unpleasant experience; it could have meant all their deaths. If she had lost her grip on the door when she tried to go on deck, she might have been swept into the sea with the others. She began to tremble and then, to her everlasting disgrace and utter humiliation, she got sick. Right there in front of Charles.

And that finest of men simply led her back to the other narrow bunk in the small room and gave her a damp cloth for her face. He waited until he was sure she was all right and departed. As he got to the door, Blanche said in a weak voice, "Charles, whatever do you see in me?"

"I can't imagine," he replied with a smile to match her own.

They landed at Porchester the next day. The rain had slowed but not stopped entirely, so that they all disembarked wet and thoroughly unattractive. Fortunately the King had not known when they were expected to arrive, so they were spared the indignity of a royal welcome in their wretched state. Margaret was a little better but still pale and weak. Suffolk had to carry her off the ship. As a measure of her condition, she didn't take any interest in trying to make herself look nice, just in case the King should be there. Again they spent the night in an abbey, but had little rest before they were on their way again the next morning. This time they went by barge to Southampton. Most of the group had recovered enough to enjoy themselves in spite of a chill drizzle. Groups of people huddled together along the way to get a look at their new Queen. Margaret smiled and waved at them and seemed to be taking some strength from their cheers, but Blanche could tell that she was under a strain and she confessed later that her head was aching fiercely.

Just before they reached Southampton, Charles drew Blanche aside. "I received word in Porchester of my father," he said. "He still lives, but there is little hope of recovery. I shall be leaving your party as soon as we reach Southampton to hasten to him."

"We shall all miss your companionship," Blanche said, fearing to express the depth of her feelings.

"I shall miss you, Blanche. But I shall be back in London as soon as possible and perhaps we can then discuss . . . well, our future."

"Our future?" Blanche said, hardly believing her ears.

"I should not have said that. It is too soon to press my suit, but please think of me while I am away."

Blanche wondered if she would be able to think of anything *else*. Blanche had no other chance to see Charles. There was so much to be done and she was still worried about Margaret's health. She found to her relief that the abbey where they were to stay was cozy and pleasant and had a reputation for catering to sick travelers. There was a large herb garden where the nuns grew mustard, foxglove, and belladonna for poultices and medications. The sisters were experienced in treating illness. She told Margaret of their good fortune.

"I'm not ill," Margaret protested, "just tired and excited. I need rest. I'll get into dry clothing and rest awhile and I'm sure I'll feel better. Don't worry about me, Blanche."

They got to the abbey and Margaret had a nap. She had just awakened when Lady Alice tapped at the door and, with a very silly giggle, said that there was a messenger from King Henry who desired audience with the Queen. Blanche accompanied Margaret to the waiting room and could tell from the slowness of her gait that she was still unwell. The messenger was an unkempt individual with sawed-off hair and bad teeth. He knelt before Margaret and lisped, "A message from King Henry to his most beloved spouse."

Margaret looked at him sharply for a moment before taking the parchment. Blanche wondered why King Henry had chosen such a loutish messenger. The man looked vaguely familiar—perhaps a relative of one of the nobles they had met during their trip. Margaret took the note and sat down to read it. Blanche read it over her shoulder. It was disappointing. It was simply a formal welcome. There was nothing personal in it, merely the sort of greeting one would send to any important visitor. The messenger stared at Margaret as she read. His eyes were doglike with admiration and his mouth drooped open slightly, revealing stained teeth.

There were a number of other people in the room. They all seemed unusually curious, watching Margaret as if they were anticipating an interesting reaction to the letter. The messenger spoke again. "Your grace, King Henry regrets that he is unable to join you until Parliament adjourns and London is made ready to receive you. He begs to know if there is anything that you need."

Blanche could tell that Margaret was formulating a lengthy and sharp reply. She couldn't blame her. Considering how far they had all come through winter weather, certainly the King could get away to travel a few miles to meet his bride. Apparently Margaret decided against airing her views, for she just said, "Yes, please explain to his majesty that my wardrobe is inadequate and ask that a dressmaker be sent while I await him."

The messenger made no reply and Margaret said, "You may go now." He left the room, forgetting to bow to her at the door. Blanche thought it unforgivable. Margaret got up and went to the window. Blanche stayed close to her, as she seemed to wobble a bit. "It's terribly hot in here, is it not?" Margaret said, touching the throat of her gown. Actually it was quite cold. The room was deathly still. Everyone stood about smiling foolishly, even Suffolk, who almost never smiled.

"What is the matter with all of you?" Margaret snapped.

Lady Alice bustled forward. "What did you think of that messenger, your grace?"

"Messenger? Messenger! Why should I think *anything* of the messenger?" she demanded.

"Because the messenger was King Henry himself," Lady Alice chirped.

Margaret groped for a chair. "Oh," she said. It sounded like a gargle.

Lady Alice burbled on, "What a fine surprise! King Henry always says you can get a true idea of a woman's

51

beauty by watching her read a letter. Isn't that clever of him? I'm surprised that you didn't recognize him. He looks just like that little picture you had. Oh, yes, that picture got lost, didn't it, your grace? Your grace —oh, dear, quickly, somebody bring some water. The Queen has fainted."

Within hours of the disguised King's departure, a real messenger was hastily following him to London to request the King's physician be sent to attend Queen Margaret. She had been slow to revive from her faint, and when Blanche and the sisters undressed her to put her to bed, they found red spots on her legs and arms. The abbess was called and immediately diagnosed Margaret's illness as smallpox. King Henry's physician arrived and agreed.

Word was sent to King Henry's Council and they kept a close eye on the King. The members of the Council feared that with his undeveloped sense of self-preservation he would attempt some chivalric nonsense, such as flying to her side to comfort her. Small comfort he would have been. If King Henry should contract smallpox and die, leaving neither brothers nor sons for the crown to pass to, there would almost certainly be civil war, and civil war following the long war with France might be a death blow to England.

King Henry retired to pray—and pray—and pray. For days he hardly got off his knees. He found dozens of reasons to blame himself, and in spite of constant assurances that his young bride was only suffering a mild case of the affliction, he continued to whip himself into a frenzy of guilt and remorse. His great-uncle,

Cardinal Beaufort, came to tell Henry that his new wife's beauty was unaffected. There had been no pox on her face. Henry lifted his own tear-stained face and said, "Dear Uncle, what care I for these things of the flesh?" but there was a gleam in his watery blue eyes. "All my prayers are that her life be spared and her soul safe. I blame myself entirely that this punishment for my sins should have fallen upon her. I should never have married."

"Nephew, stop this." Cardinal Beaufort had been listening to this sort of thing from Henry for years. Beaufort told his friends that Henry's first words as a baby were the Lord's Prayer. "Queen Margaret is quite all right. She was only slightly ill, and if you ever listened to anyone, you would have known it."

But it was useless. Henry's head was bent again and he was muttering yet another prayer. Cardinal Beaufort shook his head and left the room. He had another appointment with the King's treasurer. The Queen had requested a dressmaker and Beaufort had to help find a way to squeeze yet more money out of the negative balance in the treasury.

Taking care of Margaret helped Blanche keep her mind off Charles. It was hard to be lonely when she was so busy. Having smallpox at that particular time was a blessing for Margaret, too, in a way. It gave her time to readjust her mind to the turn her life had taken. Blanche was rather surprised by this. She hated to admit it, even to herself, but she knew Margaret to be a spoiled girl and half expected that she would storm and weep and demand to go home after seeing what she was married to. It would have done her no good, of course, but still Blanche was pleased to find that Margaret had the sense to recognize that there was no choice but to make the best of her situation.

In a short time the King's physician decided that Margaret had recovered sufficiently for the dressmaker to begin her ministrations. The dressmaker, Mistress Chamberlayne, and her army of feminine helpers moved in and began sewing. Mistress Chamberlayne was a born general, ready to face the foe armed only with thimble and needle. The nuns' modest quarters were piled high with cloth of gold, brightly colored English wool, delicate linen for shifts, sable, miniver, and jeweled buttons. Margaret was caught up in the bustle and seemed happier. Once, during a fitting, Mistress Chamberlayne smacked her on the bottom and told her to stand up straighter and Margaret just smiled and stood as she was told.

It was fun for all the women, watching a lovely new wardrobe take shape, for neither Margaret nor Blanche knew at the time that part of King Henry's jewels now reposed in Uncle Beaufort's vault in security for the large loan that was financing the clothing. The government treasury was too poor to afford to clothe the Queen. After a week of feverish stitching, Mistress Chamberlayne pocketed her scissors, pulled out her troops, and peace was restored to the abbey.

Final preparations for another wedding were being completed in London. Since Margaret and Henry had been legally married in Anjou, with Suffolk standing proxy, there was no real need for a renewal of the vows in England. But in such cases another wedding was usually performed anyway because the people of England, who were expected to be loyal to the new Queen, liked to see her wedding. Margaret didn't object, for she loved pomp and ceremony and feasts and it gave everyone an excuse to get dressed up (and then get drunk, in many cases). Blanche kept hoping that Charles would be able to return to London during the festivities, but the days went by and he did not.

Margaret waited in Southampton while London dressed itself up to greet her. Although she had not been officially welcomed to England, she received a stream of important visitors. It was not fitting for a queen to be alone with a visitor, especially a man, so Blanche always sat a little way off, busying herself with her needlework and listening while pretending not to. Margaret introduced Blanche as her sister, and Blanche found that she was being treated a little more respectfully in England than she had been in Anjou. Blanche thought of herself as neither pretty nor ugly, but was beginning to think that she was so ordinary as to render herself almost invisible to most people. She didn't mind, however, for it caused people to talk in front of her as if she weren't there at all and consequently she learned many interesting things. The circumstance suited her, for she was a naturally curious person.

One of Margaret's first visitors was Cardinal Beaufort. Margaret and Blanche both liked the sturdy, freckled old man immediately. He never criticized King Henry, of course, but neither did he try to praise him. He called Margaret "niece" and took her for a walk in the abbey's orchard. He helped her forget about Henry for a while. Later, sitting over glasses of chilled wine, he helped Margaret and Blanche get a few more threads of the Plantagenet genealogy straightened out.

Beaufort knew the truth of Blanche's "sisterhood" with Margaret and he specifically invited her to join them while he told about his family. He told how his father, John of Gaunt, the Duke of Lancaster, had married a beautiful heiress who died during the plague. Gaunt then took as his mistress Katherine Swynford, the young widow of an obscure knight. Katherine had raised John of Gaunt's children from his first marriage (including Bolingbroke) along with the illegitimate children (including Cardinal Beaufort) she had borne John over the years. The illegitimate Beauforts and the legitimate Lancasters had grown up as a close family. The Duke made another political marriage, but finally, when the children were grown and the second wife died, he had shocked the court by marrying his mistress of twenty years, Beaufort's mother. By that time Richard the Second was King of England and not yet married. Since John of Gaunt was Richard's closest living relative, that made Katherine Swynford the highest ranking lady in England for a while. Beaufort's laughter echoed through the abbey as he told of the upheaval among the prominent high-born ladies who had shunned his beautiful mother for twenty years and then had to bow to her. Blanche wondered if there was a lesson in that for her.

The Beauforts and Lancasters had remained close in the turbulent years since then, Cardinal Beaufort told them. They had stood together when, after John of Gaunt's death, Henry the Fourth, or Bolingbroke, as

Beaufort referred to his half-brother, had seized the crown from his cousin, Richard the Second.

The only rift in the two branches of the family seemed to involve Humphrey of Gloucester, King Henry's uncle, whom Margaret remembered primarily for having opposed her marriage. Cardinal Beaufort's manner was cold when Margaret asked about Duke Humphrey, so she changed the subject.

The next visitor was Duke Humphrey himself. He was the King's full uncle, so Margaret wasn't exactly rude to him despite the fact that she had set her mind against him. During the initial negotiations for the marriage, René had mentioned repeatedly that Duke Humphrey was objecting to the arrangement. Though Humphrey's motives were purely political, Margaret had viewed it as a personal affront. Later she mentioned to Blanche that the Duke of York had called Duke Humphrey a friend and Margaret had decided that York's friends were not to be her friends.

Blanche felt sorry for Duke Humphrey. He seemed old and tired and was obviously trying hard to be amiable. But the interview with Margaret was cool and brief despite his efforts. Blanche started to say something to Margaret about her behavior after he had left, but Margaret gave her such a cold look when Blanche opened the subject that she changed her mind. She is a queen now, Blanche had to remind herself. The days of bickering with one another as equals were gone forever.

The next guest was Cecily Neville, the wife of Richard, the Duke of York. She was on her way, with her children, to rejoin Richard at M'antes. Since Margaret had convinced herself that she disliked York, she was fully prepared to dislike Cecily as well. As far as Blanche could see, it was plain jealousy on Margaret's part, but Margaret would never have admitted it even to herself. Margaret intended this meeting with Cecily to be as chilly as her meeting with Duke Humphrey had been, but Margaret, like most people, found it impossible to resist Cecily's charm. Cecily was in her late twenties; she was an energetic, bubbling young woman who glowed with motherhood.

She brought her children with her. Young Edward was three and Edmund two. They were stocky, blond little boys full of energy and merriment. The oldest child was a girl named Anne, already a saucy little six-year-old version of her mother. The youngest, Elizabeth, was not yet a year old and resembled only other fair English babies. Cecily was very proud of all of them. Unlike most ladies of elevated rank who gave birth to children and then let servants and tutors raise them, Cecily preferred to raise them herself.

Margaret and Cecily spent an hour or so going over Margaret's new wardrobe, then they and Blanche ended the afternoon scrambling around on the floor playing with the children. Young Edward of York sat down by Margaret and showed her the carved wooden soldier he had with him. "My papa made this," he told her proudly.

Margaret hesitated only a second, then said to Cecily, "Edward is a good boy and he has a fine English name. I'm told that King Henry is fond of the name Edward. Perhaps when God wills that I should bear a son, we will name him Edward also. Someday he would be Edward the Fourth and our Edwards could be fine friends."

Cecily agreed.

King Henry's Council decided that in view of the Queen's recent illness, it would be folly to subject her to the unclean air of London right away. As usual in the early spring, there had been a few isolated cases of plague reported. It had been almost a full century since the worst plague epidemic, which had wiped out nearly a third of England's population, but still it was a constant threat. The Council agreed that it would be unwise to risk exposing the young Queen to any danger, however slight, until she had fulfilled her duty to provide England with an heir. What would happen if she should die? Henry might get some mad idea about devoting himself entirely to the religious life. He had seemed on the verge of that sort of thing before he saw the picture of Margaret that brought about the betrothal. The Council shuddered collectively at the thought of what complications would ensue about the succession if King Henry were to remain childless.

Humphrey of Gloucester, as the King's full uncle, was the heir apparent, but he too was childless, and beyond that there was heated disagreement as to the probable line of succession. The Beauforts felt that Edmund Beaufort, the Duke of Somerset, who was Cardinal Beaufort's nephew and only surviving male relative, should be next in line. After all, the Beauforts *were* Lancasters, like King Henry, even though the family had originated out of wedlock.

Others felt (as Margaret feared) that the Yorks had an even stronger claim to the throne than did King Henry himself, and Richard of York should certainly be recognized. But right now the question was academic. King Henry was young and reasonably healthy of body, though his mind wasn't quite adequate. And now he was getting married to a young woman who would certainly bear children. As things stood, King Henry could be manipulated, and although there was a lot of politely disguised jockeying for ascendancy over the mild monarch, English affairs were proceeding evenly so long as there was hope for a peaceful succession eventually.

So arrangements went on for the wedding ceremony to be held at Titchfield Abbey, a few miles east of Southampton. Getting Margaret ready for the wedding started the day before. The servants dragged a large tub into her room. Blanche and the other ladies filled it with steaming water and rose petals. A fine aromatic oil was added to the water. When all was ready, one of Margaret's wedding gifts was unwrapped—a bar of fine Spanish soap made from olive oil and herbs. There was a seat built into the tub and they made Margaret sit and soak in the hot, fragrant water until she complained that she was nearly cooked. Her long hair was washed, brushed dry, and rubbed with rose oil until it shone.

Very early the next morning the final preparations were begun. First were her undergarments. They were of cotton and Margaret was proud of them. Not many people this far north in the world had ever seen cotton fabric, not even the richest nobles. They were gifts from

France. Next came a delicate linen shift and layers of lace-trimmed petticoats. Three of the ladies then lifted Margaret's dress over her head.

The dress was of a deep blue velvet and had a very full skirt with a long train. All over the fabric, pearls were sewn in daisy designs with filigree gold disks for centers. The dress was magnificent. It would last Margaret all her life and be passed on to her eldest daughter someday. It was, like all good garments, made with generous seams so that it could be let out for pregnancies or to fit a larger woman. It had a deep neckline, exposing more of Margaret's bosom than most English ladies customarily exposed, but Blanche assured Margaret that fashion followed the Queen, not the other way around. The dress buttoned up the back. Buttons were a new idea, imported from the strange lands that had been discovered far to the east of civilization. Many older women were suspicious of them. Each button on Margaret's wedding dress was a different jewel in a gold setting.

Around Margaret's slender waist was a wide band embroidered with large red roses. There had been a problem with that. The first belt had been done with white roses until someone told the ignorant underscamstress that white roses were the emblem of the house of York! Red roses were the symbol that the Lancasters used. The white silk was picked out and red silk used.

Finally Margaret's hair was brushed again and braided into a thick rope, which was wrapped in a chignon on top of her head. A precious handful of gold dust was sprinkled over it and the pearl-encrusted band was put on that circled the braid and covered the rest of her hair. Then she added the rings, bracelets, and necklaces that completed her costume. One more drop of rose oil between her breasts and behind her ears and she was ready.

Blanche wept at the sight of her. She had never seen anyone so very beautiful, and to think that she was marrying someone who was so—so different—from what she had hoped. As Margaret neared the abbey the crowd cheered and tossed spring flowers at their pretty new Queen. She seemed to have her feelings in hand and was able to smile and actually look happy about her fate. Blanche was wondering about this transformation when Margaret whispered something to her that helped explain.

"Do you remember the time, when we were girls, that we hid in the pantry and listened to the kitchenmaids?" she said with a smile. Suddenly the memory flooded back to Blanche. She and Margaret must have been only seven or eight years old and were curious what the servants talked about among themselves. They had hidden in the pantry along with the bugs and listened.

"Ah, that Jean," one of the cooks had sighed. "He's a damn fool in the sunlight, but he's such a lusty buck between the blankets. It's the only thing that keeps me from bashing in his head." The girls had nearly exploded with suppressed laughter, for Jean was one of the grooms and made up in girth what he lacked in teeth. They crept back to Margaret's room and discussed the scrap of information, comparing it with what they had observed about the dogs and cats in the stable until they felt they had a pretty clear idea of the exact nature of the relationship between the sexes. It was a delightful and hilarious discovery.

So that was what was on Margaret's mind. "Do you remember what your Uncle Charles says about ugly men?" Blanche asked. King Charles was always saying that ugly men make the best lovers. Margaret and Blanche were convinced that he said it only because he was so ugly.

"He might be right, you know," Margaret said with a wide smile. Blanche hoped so. If Margaret could not fall in love with King Henry in her head and heart, perhaps he would have the skill to awaken her body. Maybe that would be enough.

As they neared the abbey Blanche looked around the crowd for some sight of Charles Seintleger. She didn't really expect him to be there, but what harm in hoping? But he wasn't there. She supposed he was still at his father's home.

King Henry's appearance was a pleasant surprise. Cardinal Beaufort had insisted that he dress respectably for the occasion. Henry would undoubtedly have preferred a rough brown monk's habit to the rich brocades, but Cardinal Beaufort hadn't allowed him the choice. King Henry didn't look too bad, if he just kept his mouth shut and concealed his teeth. At least he had a proper haircut. Margaret actually smiled at him as she got out of the coach and willingly took his hand to ascend the steps.

The ceremony was brief. King Henry gave Margaret a wedding ring set with an enormous ruby. It was a beautiful ring and Lady Alice whispered to Blanche that the ruby had been given to Henry by Cardinal

Beaufort on the occasion of Henry's coronation as King of France years before. In light of the fact that Henry had never made good his claim to the French throne, the great stone seemed to Blanche to be slightly ill-omened. She learned later that the primary reason for selecting that particular stone, however, had been practical rather than symbolic. It was one of the few good jewels that King Henry had left. Most of the others had been pawned, mainly to Cardinal Beaufort, to keep England's treasury afloat.

Margaret and Blanche were surprised to find that the wedding dinner was quite subdued. Previous experience with wedding dinners had led them to expect several hours of gluttonous eating, lewd joking, and prodigious drinking. What's the matter with these thin-blooded Englishmen? Blanche wondered. She could tell that jokes were being told and enjoyed, but in far corners of the hall and very quietly. Strange, the English who celebrated the proxy wedding in France didn't act like this, Blanche remembered. It must have been King Henry's dampening influence. He was quiet and remote. He prayed silently (and rather ostentatiously, Blanche felt) before partaking of each course of the dinner.

Margaret and Henry were to spend the night in a nearby manor house. Henry rose and asked Cardinal Beaufort to say a closing prayer. Beaufort, who had been laughing with a group of men at the opposite end of the hall, reluctantly set a large mug of ale on the table and intoned a blessing on the assembly. Blanche chuckled to herself at his effort. He was definitely slurring the prayer. She didn't know whether he was hurrying to get back to the joke that Henry had interrupted or if he was just a little too full of ale.

Most of the group continued in the merriment. A few of the lords and ladies, including Blanche, were to accompany and attend the King and Queen in the ceremonies preparing them for the marriage bed. Some of the ladies attending Margaret, including Lady Alice, had indulged in more spirits than usual with the result that getting the bride ready for bed was a drawn-out giggling sort of party. They laid aside the heavy blue wedding dress and royal jewels and dressed Margaret in a delicate white nightshift, the pride of Mistress Chamberlayne's needlework. It had long, flowing sleeves and a round neckline gathered on a silk ribbon that could be easily loosened. It draped itself to Margaret's high-breasted young figure almost as if wet. It might have been woven by angelic spiders, it was so lacy and thin. Margaret's pink nipples showed faintly through. Some of the older women looked at her a little enviously, as if they wished they were as young and desirable as the Queen.

Finally one of King Henry's gentlemen knocked at the door to ask if the Queen was ready. Lady Alice and Blanche went with Margaret to the chamber where the great high bed waited for her. Blanche embraced Margaret before she left. Margaret responded with a trembling smile.

Margaret stood alone, hearing only the beating of her own pulse in her ears. She could feel that her face was flushed and knew that she looked prettiest when her color was high. She stood rooted, not knowing what to do, but King Henry entered the room just then. He turned and bolted the door behind him and then walked slowly to Margaret. She put out her hand to take his. Without a word he led her to the side of the large canopied bed. To Margaret's astonishment, he released her hand and knelt beside the bed. Not knowing what else to do, she knelt beside him.

Henry's prayer was long and barely intelligible. His Latin had a heavy, unfamiliar English accent and Margaret's state was not, at that moment, attuned to prayers. She did catch some references to Saint Paul and the phrase "sins of the flesh."

As abruptly as he had begun praying, Henry stopped. He stood up, pulling Margaret along by the elbow. He stared at her breasts and touched his palms lightly against the now erect nipples that were making lumps behind the fabric. Margaret was excited by his touch, but shrank from the wild look in his eyes.

Suddenly he was fumbling with the silk ribbon at her neck. It came loose and the shift fell off her shoulders and down to the floor. She looked at it lying around her feet. She heard a gasp, a strange animal gurgle, and looked up. Henry was staring at her naked body. He was bent forward slightly, his mouth open. He was breathing in short, loud gasps and his hands were moving in time to his breath. His fingers were folding and unfolding in a quick rhythm. Margaret realized that her sexual excitement had turned to fear. This wasn't what she had expected at all.

At the moment that she started to draw back, one of the clutching hands shot out and grabbed her left breast. The grasp was hard and painful. She was unbalanced and found herself being flung backward onto the bed. She saw Henry pulling up his own nightshift in the second before he threw his body on hers. She was terrified. She tried with all her strength to turn her face to the side and attempted to push this strange moaning, heaving body off her own. But even in her terror and inexperience, it wasn't long before she realized that there was something wrong. The moans were turning to whimpers. Henry's hands were no longer clutching, they were trembling.

The worst was over and nothing had happened. Her marriage was unconsummated. All she had to show for the nightmare were bruises. She felt his grip loosen and she quickly rolled away. As she jumped from the bed, her knees buckled and she fell to the floor, scrambling for her discarded shift. Her hands shook so violently she could hardly hold it in front of herself. Henry looked at her with tears running down his face. All she could think was, He is crying—I suffer this and *he* is crying. She felt a convulsion in her chest and throat that suddenly spewed out as laughter, the cackling and uncontrollable laughter of hysteria. Her knees went weak again and she sat down on the cold stone floor, laughing.

She heard Henry whining, "Oh, my beloved, don't do this to me. This is God's will—'tis God's will," and she laughed all the harder. Eventually the laughter subsided and turned into quiet tears. She realized that she was cold and naked and exhausted. Henry was on the far side of the bed with his face turned away. She stood up and put her shift back on, pulling the silk ribbon tight and double-knotting it. She crawled under the covers on the very edge of the wide bed and closed her eyes.

Margaret slept fitfully and woke at dawn to the sound of a muffled voice. She remembered where she was and why and shuddered involuntarily when she realized that the voice was Henry's—praying again. She slipped out of bed and put on the warm robe that Blanche had left on the chair in the corner the night before. By the time she had it fastened, King Henry had finished his prayer. Margaret had mastered her emotions of the night before, and so, apparently, had Henry.

"Good morning, madam," he said stiffly. "I have informed the servants that we shall attend Mass shortly and then return here for breakfast. I hope that is satisfactory to you. I didn't wish to disturb your sleep to inquire."

"That will be quite satisfactory," Margaret lied. She had never liked attending Mass with the first rays of the sun. She stepped to the door. "My ladies and I shall dress and meet you in the chapel presently."

"Good," Henry replied. "I understand the chapel here is quite old and attractive."

Thus, with a few words spoken and thousands left unspoken, King Henry and Queen Margaret declared a personal truce in their relationship that would last for many years. From that day on, whenever they had to share a bed, King Henry would wait until the servants had left the room, then would get out of bed and sleep on the floor. It suited him as well as the hairshirt that he wore under his robes of state.

CHAPTER THREE

Blanche was nearly sick with sympathy when Margaret confessed what had happened on her wedding night. Margaret seemed like a being without hope of happiness except in the trivial pursuits of daily life with the court and her ladies. But knowing Margaret, Blanche felt that she would find little satisfaction in such a life. Margaret was born to carry great passions, and if she could not love a man, Blanche feared that Margaret might turn instead to passionate hate, certainly of King Henry, possibly of men in general.

Two days after the wedding, Blanche's concern for her sister was dimmed by events that touched her own life more deeply. She was cutting some linen for an altar cloth with Lady Alice when a page came to announce that there was a priest asking to see her. She hurried along, wondering why a priest should seek her out. She was taken aback for a moment when she saw him. He was very young, and at first glance, she thought him to be Charles Seintleger, then realized it was a younger man.

"Please forgive me for intruding upon you without an invitation, mademoiselle," he said gravely, "but my brother Charles asked me to see you on his behalf."

"Where is Sir Charles? Is he unwell?" Blanche asked with some alarm.

"He cannot come himself. He is well but sick at heart and begged that I speak with you. . . ." The young man seemed unable to go on.

"Please, speak freely. Something is the matter. I can tell that. Fear not telling me. I am not a maiden to swoon," Blanche said as heartily as she could.

"Mademoiselle, my brother is married," he said with a rush.

Blanche nearly went back on her word. She felt her knees weaken, but caught herself. "Do you mean newly married?" she asked. The priest nodded dumbly. "Then please give him and his wife my good will when next you see him. It was kind of you to let me know." What else could she say?

"Please, mademoiselle, you make me feel like a child. You are so brave. I have dreaded this meeting, for Charles told me how kind and beautiful you are and how he loved you," he said miserably.

"I am sorry that you are distressed," Blanche said. "There is no reason to be. As Charles might also have told you, I would have made an unsuitable match, and though I have the greatest admiration for Sir Charles, there was nothing spoken between us of love or marriage. Nor was I expecting any such bond." That was a lie, but it salved her pride a bit to say it to the priest.

"Please, you do not understand . . ." he began.

"I understand quite well. There is no need for you to further inconvenience yourself in this matter. If you will call at the kitchens on your way out, I will arrange that some food be prepared for you to take on your return journey."

"But Charles asked me to tell you . . ."

"There is no need to tell me anything else," she said, her voice beginning to break. "You must excuse me now, please." She fled from the room, unwilling to be seen any more by those soft eyes so like Charles's.

She told herself she should not have been upset. After all, it was just what she should have known would happen. And yet, she had allowed herself such dreams, such hopes for a future with a man whose very touch made her want to laugh and cry at once. She was in no worse position than she had been a few months before —before Sir Charles Seintleger had found her sobbing in a field outside an abbey. And yet, a few months before, a future as a solitary virgin had been acceptable. Now the prospect of such a life was so bleak that it made her stomach knot and her vision blur with acid tears.

She'd had no real right to believe it would be any different. And now Blanche and Margaret, unhappy in their separate and similar ways, would grow old together. What a desperate thought. Blanche said nothing to Margaret—and Margaret was so self-absorbed with her own unhappiness she didn't notice that there was anything wrong with Blanche.

The next weeks were long and terrible for Blanche. Eventually her optimistic nature began to reassert itself and she started to see life as something besides her own sorrow. The English court was very stiff and formal, especially in comparison to the happy-go-lucky way René of Anjou had conducted court. But when King Henry was not present, the many young people were as gay and pleasant as privileged young men and women anywhere. Blanche made many friends and found herself in rather different circumstances than she had anticipated. Though it was no secret that she was not full sister to the Queen, either the English tended to forget the exact relationship or they simply didn't care. Blanche was therefore accorded more courtesy and privileges than she had expected and began to worry less about her status.

Margaret managed to deal with her disappointment as well. She became a little more distant and was sometimes quite cold to people, but that was her way of protecting her feelings from further harm. She too had found some special friends. One of her favorite people was Cardinal Beaufort, and Blanche was glad that Margaret visited him so often, for she accompanied Margaret on these visits. Cardinal Beaufort was kind to Margaret and particularly nice to Blanche. He seemed to feel a keen sympathy with her because his parents had not been married, either, at least not until he was grown.

They went to visit the Cardinal often at his home near London, for he was aging and in poor health. Margaret was such a frequent visitor that he had redecorated the room where they most often sat to Margaret's tastes. Blanche and Margaret went to visit him one day two years after Margaret's wedding.

"But, Margaret, certainly you realized that it was bound to come out sooner or later. You can't expect that much land to change hands during a war without anyone noticing." Cardinal Beaufort's voice had lost its hearty, booming quality and his sturdy frame looked wilted, but his mind and tongue were as quick as ever.

72

Under the terms of the marriage treaty that Suffolk had arranged with the King of France and René of Anjou, the province of Maine was now being turned over to the French and there was a great deal of public rumbling about it in England.

"Of course I knew it would come out. It's just that the way Humphrey of Gloucester tells it, it sounds like treason and makes me look so bad," Margaret said from behind her needlework.

"Margaret, don't let's be silly over words and loyalties. It *is* treason in a way. English royal marriage treaties are supposed to have the approval of Parliament."

"Parliament!" Margaret snorted the word as if it were an obscenity. "What is the matter with England that they let everyone else rule but the King?" It was a favorite complaint of hers.

"As I was saying," Beaufort interrupted sharply, "marriage treaties are supposed to have the approval of Parliament even if it means simply telling them about it after the treaty is signed—but not several *years* after."

"But that's not treason," she objected. "Treason is disloyalty to the King. Henry approved the treaty."

"Nevertheless, giving back conquered territory to the enemy is not generally done."

"Do you mean to say that *you* consider it treason?" Margaret asked.

"Margaret, I told you not to be foolish. I was in on the plan from the beginning. In fact, Suffolk and I discussed it initially in this very room as soon as Henry became so taken with the idea of marrying you. It's

73

just that I want you to understand how other people see it—especially when they hear Gloucester's version."

"What's to be done about it?" Blanche ventured. She didn't have Margaret's capacity for enjoying intrigue and yet, in this case, even Blanche could see the need for action. With a weak king like Henry, Gloucester could stir up enough discontent to cause a rebellion and the crown was not well equipped to deal with a rebellion. In the first place, such action was costly.

"Gloucester must be silenced, of course. I haven't decided yet how. My nephew, Somerset, is due here for a visit. He may have some ideas. In the meantime, I have a few thoughts I'm considering. I erred once before with Gloucester."

Beaufort didn't elaborate, but Blanche and Margaret knew what he was talking about. They had heard the story from Lady Alice. Humphrey, Duke of Gloucester, had married a strange woman named Eleanor Cobham years before. Being so close to a throne had been too much for her. She consulted with Gloucester's chaplain and a friend of the chaplain, one Margery Jourdemain, about the future. Eleanor Cobham was later found guilty of witchcraft (this was Cardinal Beaufort's doing). Eleanor claimed at her trial that she had only wanted to see into her future, not control it. But the chaplain and Mistress Jourdemain, who was more commonly known as the Witch of Eye, claimed that they had helped the Duchess of Gloucester make wax images of King Henry, which she then melted down bit by bit on the theory that as the wax melted, so would King Henry's life ebb away.

Cardinal Beaufort had made no attempt to implicate Humphrey directly in the plot, feeling that it was unnecessary. The chaplain was hanged for treason; the Witch of Eye was burned to death; and Eleanor Cobham, the Duchess of Gloucester, had to walk through the streets of London barefooted for three days and was then taken away for life imprisonment.

For all the trouble he had gone to, Beaufort's plan had backfired. Humphrey of Gloucester was popular with the people, and instead of alienating his friends, the trial of his wife had gained him sympathy. Besides, it hadn't kept him quiet for long. The trial had been barely five years before, and though Gloucester had retired from public affairs for a while, he was now making himself heard again.

Blanche had been especially interested in the story, for Alice kept insisting that Eleanor Cobham really was a witch—that she was able to see into people's futures. Alice believed it sincerely, and though Blanche wasn't convinced, she would certainly have liked to meet the lady. Lady Alice said Eleanor was still confined and was moved around from one castle to another from time to time.

Blanche's thoughts were interrupted by Beaufort saying, "Margaret, you are right about Gloucester being a danger, but you are upset for the wrong reasons."

"What do you mean—the wrong reasons?"

"You are angry for purely selfish reasons. It doesn't matter if people don't like you personally. But it's far more important for them to honor *you* as Queen than it is for most queens."

"Why do you say that?" she asked.

"My dear, I haven't time left for coyness. You know

perfectly well why. You aren't just a queen; you are King of England as well, or you will be when I am gone. Your Henry is the royal equivalent of the village idiot. If he were a common peasant he would have been relegated to cleaning up behind the village dung cart."

"That's a little harsh, isn't it?"

"I'm too old to be patient with him anymore. He's well-meaning, I'll grant that, but even as slow-witted as he is, he should be able to figure out that a king must rule, not just reign," Beaufort said.

"But you tell him what to do and your decisions are for the country's good."

"Margaret, do you think I'll be around to tell him what to do for the next thirty years?" His voice lowered. "I'm an old, old man. I've lived in the reigns of five kings of England. Even my physician admits that I haven't long to live."

"Don't say that, Uncle," Margaret implored.

"It's true, my dear. You will have to take my place in the affairs of this country. I've been trying to prepare you for this since your wedding. Somerset and Suffolk aren't as smart as you, but they are crafty and loyal to you and more experienced in diplomacy. They can be of great help if you use them wisely, but in the end, you must be the ruler."

"I'm afraid you're right, Uncle," Margaret said, putting down her needlework and walking to the fireplace to warm her hands. "You know, I always imagined myself living a quiet, cultured life such as my father created for himself. Painters, musicians, tournaments, warm breezes from the south, and someone else to make all my decisions." Her tone was merely wistful, not bitter. "Do you remember our plans, Blanche? How we would stay up late at night and imagine what it would be like to be grown?"

Blanche remembered. They were pleasant dreams, but they were Margaret's dreams. In them Blanche was part of the background scenery with no life of her own except what she reflected of Margaret's. But Blanche was used to this trait in Margaret and had accepted it and could love her in spite of it. Besides, Margaret's attitude was right. Blanche had no life of her own.

Cardinal Beaufort laughed. "Oh, to be young enough to remember what your dreams were—and you with your life still ahead of you. And yet, I seem to have a vague recollection of daydreams of becoming Pope."

"But you nearly were," Blanche said.

"Nearly isn't the same thing. I don't think, looking back, that I would have been happy so far from England. Besides, I'm useful here, probably more useful than I would have been in Rome. But this is getting me away from something I want to talk to you about, Margaret." He drew himself up to deliver a lecture. "I am fond of Edmund Beaufort. After all, he is my nephew and the heir to the throne after I'm gone . . ."

"What about the Duke of York?" Blanche interrupted innocently, knowing how they both felt about him. It was one of the bonds between Margaret and Cardinal Beaufort. They both looked at Blanche as if she were jesting, and said nothing in reply.

". . . as I say," Beaufort continued, "I wouldn't want Edmund on the throne. To be Duke of Somerset is enough for him."

"I know what you are getting ready to tell me—again," Margaret said.

"You should know. I've told you often enough be-

fore—you must get your husband back into your bed!"
Cardinal Beaufort was the only person besides Blanche
who knew of Margaret's and Henry's sleeping arrangement. Others suspected, but only Beaufort knew. He
didn't know what had happened that first night and
hadn't asked, probably because he knew Henry well
enough to guess. Beaufort was considerably more distressed about the situation than Margaret. "You will
never produce a son this way and it is imperative that
you do so." He turned to Blanche. "My dear, you have
more influence with her than I do—can't you convince
her?" Blanche just shrugged; she didn't wish to be
drawn into this particular discussion.

"But, Uncle," Margaret said, "I'm not yet twenty.
There is plenty of time."

"Maybe for you, but not for me. I want to know before I die that you have a son and that he has your
traits and not Henry's."

Margaret looked at him. Blanche dropped her needle-
point. The idea that Margaret might bear a child like
Henry had never occurred to either of them. "You don't
suppose our child could have Henry's . . . disposition?"
she asked.

"Who can tell? I've never been able to account for
why Henry is as he is. His French grandfather was
mad, as you know. But his mother, Queen Katherine,
always seemed all right. In fact, she was so normal that
I thought her quite dull. She showed very poor judgment after Henry's death, but understandably, I suppose. She fancied Owen Tudor and she was forced
into a very lonely existence for a young woman. Strange
—all those little Tudor bastards turned out normal."

Everyone knew the young men he referred to. Jasper and Edmund Tudor were nice enough young men about the same age as Margaret and Blanche. They were a little difficult to understand, with their Welsh accents, but well liked. The older boy, Edmund, had a look of perpetual, sickly youth. He coughed often but gently, as if ashamed of his delicate health. Edmund seemed to love being with King Henry, his half-brother. He liked to go wherever the King went except to Mass, where his cough seemed loud and obtrusive.

The younger brother, Jasper, seemed to be much older because of his robust health. He was handsome in a sandy, freckled way. He seemed to radiate energy; his walk, his ready smile, everything about him bespoke well-being. But he was a very private person. His speech was so overly courteous that he always seemed to be keeping a personal distance between himself and everyone else.

Blanche had always felt that she and Jasper might have had much in common. He seemed to be an observer of life, capable of loyalty to someone despite his flaws. But perhaps that was reading too much into a few brief meetings. Maybe Jasper's aloofness was the result of feeling that he personified his mother's scandalous behavior. That, too, was something Blanche could understand. Jasper seemed to be more interested in protecting both his sickly brother and his royal half-brother than in making friends with other young people at court.

"Yes, I have always felt that if there were any need for family support, the Tudors would make themselves very useful," Beaufort said.

Margaret took his hand in hers and smiled. "Uncle, you worry overmuch. I have never known you to dwell so on imaginary troubles. Henry won't need his half—brothers' help. There will be no trouble. I will have fine sons someday. Now, stop fretting."

"I'm sorry, my dear, perhaps with my own death hovering over me I am taking everyone else's problems too much to heart."

"Come, Uncle, walk me to my carriage. I must be getting back to Windsor. Oh, look, there is a group of horsemen coming over that hill. Could that be Somerset?"

The old man squinted against the sun. "I believe it is. He will be presented to you at court tomorrow. Would you like to stay a little and meet him informally first?"

"Yes, of course," Margaret said. She and Blanche were interested in getting the chance to see Somerset in person. They had already formed a rather unfavorable impression of him from remarks made by his wife. The Duchess didn't seem to mind not seeing her husband for two or three years at a time, but she filled the time while he was gone by prefacing most of her remarks with, "My Lord Duke always says . . ." and "According to my husband . . ." Blanche had remarked that the Duchess thought the Gospels were Matthew, Mark, Luke, and Somerset.

"I would like for you to wait and meet him, Margaret," Beaufort said. "We shall have much to discuss during his visit. We will have to decide what to do about Gloucester before he does any serious damage to the treaty with France. It shouldn't be too hard to get

Henry to agree to whatever we plan. His Uncle Humphrey is about the only person in the world he doesn't like."

"I know. He's even fond of Richard of York," Margaret complained. "He actually says he admires the man."

"If it weren't for his family relationship and his friendship with Gloucester, you would admire him yourself," Beaufort said. Blanche wondered if Beaufort knew that there was more to Margaret's fanatic dislike of York, for Beaufort was generally a perceptive man.

"I would not like him under any conditions!" Margaret said.

"Margaret, you must learn to assess both friend and enemy fairly. If you allow yourself to see only one side of anyone, you might make serious misjudgments."

"You sound just like Blanche," Margaret said with a pout that Blanche thought was terribly unbecoming. "Blanche can always see both sides of everything."

"Then Blanche is a wise young woman. By the way, there are some things I need to discuss with Blanche. Margaret, if you wish you may wait here. I will bring Somerset to you. Blanche, will you come to the courtyard and wait with me?"

Blanche assumed rightly that Beaufort wished to discuss the ladies of the court with her. There were always fifteen to twenty wives and daughters of the nobility in attendance upon the Queen. They lived at court for periods of several weeks to several months at a time and then others would take their places. As chief lady-in-waiting to Margaret, Blanche was always in attendance and in charge of keeping track of who else was there. It was her job to see that everyone got a chance to wait upon Margaret and she was also responsible for the daily schedule and good behavior of the younger girls. Lady Alice Chaucer filled the same function with the older, more important women. When Lady Alice was gone the Duchess of Somerset took charge.

"Blanche, there are a number of young men who are becoming rather powerful and important to York. I don't wish Margaret to know this, but I do have some suspicions of his ambitions and I think it might be wise to have the women of some of these families at court as . . ."

". . . as hostages," Blanche finished for him.

"My, how worldly you are, my dear," Beaufort laughed. "Very well, 'hostages,' if you like. I will have my clerk make a list of the women I have in mind. You will handle the invitations to attend the Queen and see to it that they stay at court as much as possible. They are to be well treated, extremely well treated, for if this dispute should divide firmly into sides, as it might well do if Margaret remains childless, it is always prudent to have friends among one's enemies. Ah, here is my nephew. . . ." Beaufort broke off as the horsemen rode in through the gates.

Blanche immediately backed away and returned to Margaret's side. They watched Beaufort's meeting with Somerset from a window. Somerset was about forty, with sparse hair and spindly legs, but dressed like a peacock. He wore a flowing cape, which he kept flinging aside lightly as a vain woman does long hair. His skinny shins were encased in tight blue hose and his pointed shoes hardly interfered with his self-consciously swaggering walk. His voice, shrill and loud, pierced the air. "Dear Uncle, you are looking wonderfully well."

Beaufort said something. Somerset looked toward the window where Margaret stood and bowed low—an excessive gesture, Blanche thought contemptuously. He repeated the act when he entered the room a few moments later. He seemed to like doing it; it showed off the rich fabric of his expensive cape. "My wife has written to me of your beauty, your majesty. But I see now that the written word can hardly do you justice," he said.

Beaufort looked on, half amused, half annoyed. "Edmund, you may pay the Queen fancy compliments when you are presented at court. We have more important things to discuss now. You are aware of Gloucester's attempts to stir up discontent over the return of Maine and Anjou to France?"

"Yes, yes . . ." He stopped and stared at Blanche pointedly.

"This is Queen Margaret's sister, Blanche," Cardinal Beaufort explained. "You may speak quite freely in front of her. No doubt your wife has mentioned her in her letters," he said dryly.

"Yes," Somerset drawled doubtfully. The message came through that he had never heard of Blanche. "Well, now," he said briskly, "about Gloucester. I have heard nothing else since I landed in England. A pity he feels the need to complain. I believe we can effectively convince him to stop."

Blanche suddenly understood why the Duchess didn't

mind having him gone for so long at a time. There was something slimy about him.

Margaret must have felt it, too, for she suddenly said, "My lords, I must return to Windsor. Please excuse me. I will arrange to discuss this with you later."

Later that evening, Blanche received her list from Cardinal Beaufort. Most of the names meant little to her, but the last two on the expensive parchment made her heart stop for an instant—Lady Jane Seintleger and Lady Ursula Seintleger. Sister and wife of Sir Charles Seintleger.

CHAPTER FOUR

Lady Eleanor Cobham, once Duchess of Gloucester, stood at the window embrasure watching a horseman ride away from the castle. He wore the emblem of the Duke of Buckinham, while she, Lady Eleanor, wore no emblem, no colors save the grayish-brown homespun dress of the prisoner. Her clothes weren't uncomfortable or inadequate, only plain. Her meals were well cooked and nourishing, but served on earthenware plates instead of the silver and gold vessels she had so quickly become accustomed to as Duke Humphrey's wife. She was once sister-in-law to a king. A few years of solitude had aged her, but in spite of a scattering of premature gray hairs, she still had traces of the fey beauty that had fascinated and sometimes frightened people.

The horseman was out of sight before she went back to her chair by the fire and picked up her sewing. She was waiting for Joan to return. Joan was Eleanor's servant, or at least she had been once. Now she was a voluntary companion, but it made both women more comfortable to think of Eleanor as the Duchess and Joan as the servant. Joan had recognized the rider in Buckingham's colors as her cousin Harry. She had rushed down to the great hall to see what news he had.

After a while Joan was back at Eleanor's door. She was pale and distressed. She hung back from speaking and stood by the door, looking at Eleanor. Eleanor gave Joan a quick glance and went on stitching. "You don't have to tell me, Joan. He is dead," she said matter-of-factly.

Joan burst into tears. "Yes, madam," she sobbed.

"That simpering King Henry let someone talk him into killing my husband," she said calmly.

"Well, not exactly," Joan sniveled.

"Sit down and tell me what your cousin said."

So Joan told the story as she had heard it from her cousin, who had been there. King Henry had summoned Parliament to meet in February at Bury St. Edmunds. Most of the King's party had already assembled there when Humphrey of Gloucester arrived. As Gloucester entered the city, he was met by the treasurer of the King's house and another gentleman of the King's household. They had a message from King Henry. ". . . that forasmuch as the foresaid Duke of Gloucester has labored in that fervent cold weather, it is the King's wish that he should take the next way to his lodging and go to his meat." In other words, he was not to appear at the meeting of Parliament; he was not to ride about the town showing himself to the people; he was to go directly to his rooms and wait for his fate.

Humphrey read the message and nodded a resigned acquiescence. He signaled to his retinue that they were to go to their lodgings for the time being. But Humphrey didn't make it to the inn immediately. He got lost in the winding streets and ended up in a narrow, dark lane of dismal houses and shops. He hailed a toothless old man who was sitting in a doorway busily picking his nose. Humphrey asked if this street had a name.

The old man hobbled near, hoping for a handout. "Aye, sire, it has a name. 'Tis called Dead Lane."

Humphrey slumped a bit in his saddle. "So be it. 'Tis aptly named." He took a silver coin from the purse at his belt and tossed it to the old man.

Humphrey and his company finally found their way to the inn in time for their midday meal, which they consumed in gloomy silence. As they were leaving the dinner hall, there were noises in the courtyard, sounds of a large group of men dismounting. In a moment Humphrey found himself facing the Duke of Buckingham. With Buckingham were the Marquess of Dorset, the Earl of Salisbury, Viscount Beaumont, and Lord Sudeley, an impressive array of Beaufort-Suffolk adherents.

They had come, Buckingham said, to place him and twenty-eight of his retainers under arrest for treason. He was not to leave his lodgings until he was summoned. Much to their disappointment, he made no protest. "I see," he said. "I shall gladly remain here, as I am weary and unwell. Now, if you will please excuse me, gentlemen, there is much I must do before I rest. Please summon a scribe for me. I must make some additions to my will."

"You'll have no use for a will," Buckingham said maliciously. "A condemned traitor's goods are forfeit to the crown."

"Do you presume, sire," Humphrey fired back, "to instruct me in the laws of England? Do you forget that I am uncle, brother, and son to kings of England?"

Buckingham had the good grace to look embarrassed.

"You forget also that I am not a 'condemned' traitor. According to that parchment in your hand, I am an

87

accused traitor. I shall not be condemned." Without another word he walked proudly out of the hall. Buckingham and his cohorts were left to gather what shreds of dignity they could and make their departure. None of them could quite look the others in the eye.

But for Humphrey this minor showing of the Plantagenet temper marked the last of his spirit. He died the next day in his room at the inn, with only a few faithful servants to hear the death rattle.

"Was it poison?" Eleanor asked. She had finally laid aside her sewing and sat staring at the wall.

"No, madam, Harry says not. He says Buckingham and Suffolk were frantic when they heard of his death. If it was poison, they didn't seem to know about it. They thought he might have taken his own life."

"No, Humphrey was not a man to take his life, but he might have let it slip away without grasping at it under the circumstances."

"Harry says the townsfolk were fair upset when the word got out. They figured Duke Humphrey had been done in and they raised such a fuss that King Henry's Council had the Duke's body displayed in the town. They gave out it was so people could pay their respects to the King's uncle, but it was really to show that there wasn't no marks on him. That's what Harry says."

Eleanor resumed her sewing. "There are ways to murder without marking," she said in a knowing tone that caused Joan to shudder.

"I know how you loved Duke Humphrey," Joan said. "I can't fathom how you can take this news so calm."

"Because it isn't news. I already knew he was dead.

I didn't know how or where, but I knew. I have known since the day and hour he died."

Joan was fascinated and yet frightened of this. "Do you really know things like that about other people?"

"Not always." Eleanor sounded a little frightened herself. "Usually it is only about people I love or hate. I do know there has been another death, but I don't know who it was. Four days ago I felt it."

Joan scrambled to her feet so quickly that she tipped over the stool she had been sitting on. She crossed herself instinctively. But Eleanor's thoughts were not interrupted by the clatter or the gesture. "My lady," Joan whispered, "I was about to tell you—my cousin Harry left London three days ago. The day before he left, Cardinal Beaufort died."

Eleanor appeared at first not to have heard; then a wisp of a smile came to her lips.

"Good," she said quietly.

The deaths of Gloucester and Beaufort had a strange effect on Margaret. She changed subtly in a way that Blanche especially disliked and feared. Beaufort had told Margaret that afternoon that she must someday take over the reins of government and suddenly the day had come. It was as if Humphrey's death had given her the first taste of blood, even though the plan had misfired somewhat. Margaret had hated Humphrey. Now he was dead. It was that easy.

Blanche was Margaret's constant companion even when Margaret was in conference with Suffolk and Somerset. The two men had come to regard Blanche as nothing more consequential than a wall hanging.

Margaret seldom referred to these discussions when she and Blanche were alone and never asked her sister's opinion. Given other circumstances, Blanche would have been upset by this, for she was aware that Margaret was making mistakes in judgment. But Blanche was far too concerned over her own forthcoming meeting with Charles's wife and sister to take any action. Not that her opinion would have moved Margaret to anything but anger.

Margaret was far too willing to exert the power that had been thrust into her hands. Her first impulse was to use her influence against Richard of York. York's commission in France had long since expired, but on the advice of Cardinal Beaufort, he had been officially "forgotten." That left him in France doing the hard work and financing a losing war and yet he could be replaced at a moment's notice with no explanation needed.

The situation could have gone on indefinitely, but Margaret was anxious for a confrontation. She seemed compelled to show him her power. And she had Somerset urging her on.

Blanche thought Somerset's motives were quite transparent, but Margaret didn't seem to be aware that he was manipulating her to his own ends. Somerset wanted to be king someday. He was King Henry's closest relative and would be heir apparent except that the Beaufort family's claim had one great, gaping flaw. Many years before, when Henry the Fourth had legally legitimatized his father's Beaufort bastards, he had added the condition that neither they nor their descendants should ever be eligible for the throne. It was a sort of "conditional legitimacy." That would seem to have ended the question, but Edmund Beaufort, Duke of Somerset, didn't seem to regard it as the last word. He frequently said (privately, to be sure) that any conditions arbitrarily decreed by one king could be superseded by another. He did have enough sense not to mention this idea to Margaret just yet. For all he knew, she might yet produce a child; then there would be no question of who would be the next king. But the end result of Somerset's daydreams of glory was that he hated York as much as Margaret did and they would both join any scheme that was to York's disadvantage.

King Henry's opinion? He didn't have one, or at least no one ever bothered to ask him. He had other things on his mind, such as it was. He had been terribly upset over his Uncle Beaufort's death. It wasn't so much that Beaufort had died, it was that Beaufort's death had so closely followed the death of Gloucester. "Don't you see, madam," he tried to explain to Margaret, " 'twas God's displeasure at my decree against Gloucester. I know you told me he was an evil man and a traitor, but I had no right to try to take his life. None but God has that right. That is why God took my beloved Uncle Beaufort from me."

"You had *every* right," Margaret argued. "You are the King of England and he was a traitor. Besides, he died of natural causes and so did Cardinal Beaufort."

"It was not the act, but the intent, by which God has judged me," he answered stubbornly.

Margaret gave up. She had learned that it was impossible to argue with Henry. He could be easily manipulated in most situations, but on the rare occasions

91

that he had an opinion, he was absolutely unshakable. Margaret went back to her plotting with Suffolk and Somerset and left Henry to grapple with his soul by himself.

"There is no place on earth where a man can be more easily forgotten, madam, than in Ireland. Filthy savages there," Somerset muttered to Margaret one afternoon. "York could be sent there."

Margaret thought for a moment and a slight smile of satisfaction crossed her face. "Yes, that would be well. It would be an enormous insult to him, of course. Do you think he might be so discontented that he might do . . . anything?"

"What could he do, madam? You could give him the lieutenancy of Ireland; it is theoretically an honorable post. Bestow some lands on him for his trouble and what can he do about it?"

It occurred to Blanche that bestowing more lands on the richest man in England was not a wise thing to do if the object was to weaken his position, but no one asked her what she thought, so she kept it to herself.

"Yes, I think you are right," Margaret said. "But it is essential to catch him by surprise. He will have to be recalled, and we do not want any hint of the Irish lieutenancy to come to his ears in advance. On what pretense shall we recall him?"

"Ah-h-h," Somerset said, leaning back and smugly examining his fingernails as if the answer was written upon them. "That had occurred to me and I confess that a plan has crossed my mind." Blanche shivered with revulsion.

"And has it crossed your mind to tell *us* your idea?" Margaret said, emphasizing the royal pronoun.

"Certainly, certainly," Somerset said quickly, sensing that he had pushed her too far. "It is but a poor plan that I thought might find favor with your majesty." The switch from arrogant to fawning caused him no apparent discomfort. "The Duke of York has for years been trying to get a place on the King's Council, and if we let the word be circulated that his recall is for the purpose of appointing him, he would be here on the fastest ship available."

"Very well. 'Tis an adequate plan. Let it be done," Margaret said, dismissing him. As he left the room, Margaret shuddered slightly, then looked at Blanche in a manner that could almost be interpreted as apologetic.

"Are you sure this is right?" Blanche asked hesitantly.

"Yes!" Margaret answered curtly.

For the next few days Blanche was so busy she forgot both Margaret's behavior and her own problems. A number of ladies had left the court to make room for the women on Beaufort's list. Such projects took considerable time. Women who had not previously been to court had to be allowed several months' notice in order to assemble an adequate wardrobe and make travel arrangements. The women who were leaving invariably left behind some trinket or article of clothing and even, in some cases, a servant or two who could not be found at departure time. Weeks later a passing messenger would leave word that Lady So-and-So forgot her red taffeta petticoat and would like it sent along next time someone was going to Kent. By that time the red petticoat had usually been cut down to fit someone else or had found its way, via the kitchens, to a future as curtains in a farmhouse. Blanche was presently involved in a veritable torrent of communication with an elderly lady-in-waiting who had lost her silver-backed hairbrush and was hinting, rather bluntly, that Blanche had deliberately stolen it and was planning to sell it to the Evil Forces who were always trying to cast spells upon her. Blanche was beginning to feel that if the Evil Forces had *not* gotten hold of the hairbrush, they were missing a good thing.

As each party arrived, Blanche met them. She tactfully sorted out the ladies who knew proper etiquette and court procedure and took those who didn't in hand for some lessons. The younger girls were often homesick and cried for the first few days. Some continued to get lost at regular intervals for weeks after they should have known their way around. Sometimes the lost girls would turn up in the arms of some wholly unsuitable young man and this would keep the others entertained for some time.

The women who lived the closest to London naturally arrived first, and Blanche was deeply immersed in getting these first arrivals situated when a page rapped at her door. "Lady Jane Seintleger and Lady Ursula Seintleger present their compliments and wish to see you at your convenience."

Blanche hurried to the great hall to meet them. She passed through the minstrels' gallery to get to the stairway and stopped for a moment to survey the scene below unobserved. It was easy to pick them out of the bustle. They had the misplaced look of newcomers. From above, it was hard to tell anything about them and Blanche had to abandon her surreptitious post and face meeting these two women who knew the man she had once loved so much better than she did.

They did not see Blanche approach, and she had a few seconds to observe them. They were a study in contrasts. One girl was as petite and perky as a winter bird. She had the appearance of a person who had spent her entire life wanting to go to court and didn't intend to let a single word or gesture that occurred in the entire castle escape her. She had flaming red hair with wispy little curls that had crept out of her head-dress. Her eyes were clear blue and she was dressed unusually well for someone who had not been at court before. The other girl had much the same qualities, but they just didn't work right. Her hair was reddish, too, but rather like red mud. Her complexion was blotchy rather than clear. Her eyes were a watery, washed-out blue, and though her clothes were rich and fashionable, they were obviously new to her and uncomfortable because they didn't fit quite right. She had lovely teeth, but they looked as though they belonged to a much larger person.

Above all, this girl looked frightened and unhappy. No matter what her previous feelings about these young women were, Blanche couldn't help feeling a wrenching pity for the awkward young woman who was sitting tentatively on the edge of a traveling trunk and nibbling uneasily at her nails. At the same time, Blanche had an immediate dislike of the prettier girl. Maybe it was simply because she was so very pretty and so boldly confident in a situation that reduced most newcomers to jelly. Maybe because she assumed that the girl was the person who had taken her place in Charles's heart.

"Welcome," Blanche said with a heartiness she did not feel. "I am Blanche, Queen Margaret's sister. Her majesty has asked me to meet you and see you to your rooms. She will greet you herself later today."

The pretty girl studied Blanche greedily, as if she were a sight the girl intended to write home about later and wished to memorize every detail of her appearance. "We are pleased to meet you," she said. "I am Jane Seintleger; this is my sister-in-law, Ursula." Ursula had gotten up and was regarding Blanche uncertainly.

As Blanche and the two newcomers wound their way through the halls, Blanche pointed out features to them and they chatted, or at least Blanche and Jane chatted—Ursula trailed along gawking. In spite of herself, Blanche felt that both girls would be well liked at court. Jane was witty and enthusiastic about everything she saw. Blanche's liking for Ursula was tinged a little with pity. She seemed to be a pleasant, placid young woman thrown into circumstances that she hadn't chosen and didn't know quite how to deal with. Her face was sad and lonesome-looking.

"You will each share a room with four girls," Blanche explained. "Each group takes turns in rotation as principal companions to the Queen. You will help with her wardrobe, assist her in preparing for bed at night, wait upon her at meals, and be present and available to do anything else she might ask of you. This may include running errands, taking messages, or planning masques or entertainments, though at this court such activities are rare." Blanche always felt honor-bound to add this remark so that the starry-eyed girls who expected a royal court to be a constant round of festivities would not be misled. At some courts, such as Blanche's father's court at Anjou, they would not have been disappointed.

"This is one of the suites," Blanche went on, pointing out the doorway to their right. "One of you will be here and the other will be assigned to the rooms to your left. Unfortunately, the Duchess of Buckingham's coach has broken down and she will not be leaving for a day or two. Until she leaves, one of you must share my room." Blanche found to her surprise that she was eager to get to know these women better even though her common sense told her she would only inflict more pain on herself by being friendly with them. She would be constantly reminding herself of Charles. But in the back of her mind she felt that to know someone who had a claim on Charles would be a little like having a small part of him.

Jane and Ursula seemed to be engaged in a quick, silent conversation that needed only eye contact; then Ursula nodded. Jane, obviously used to being the spokesman of the pair, said, "Ursula will stay with you and I will stay here." Blanche settled Jane in her room and instructed the page to send their trunks and clothes presses to the proper quarters.

Conversation with Ursula was difficult. She seemed weary of trying to be proper in circumstances that were foreign and uncomfortable to her. She spoke very quietly. Blanche had to make a deliberate effort to catch her words. Blanche helped her unpack some of her things when her trunk was brought up. "Are you betrothed, Ursula?" Blanche asked, hoping to induce Ursula to open up and talk.

The girl's face lit up for the first time. "I am a wife, Mistress Blanche. My husband is Sir Charles Seintleger." She said it with such pride, such loving intimacy, that Blanche was almost embarrassed that anyone would so reveal her inner heart in one sentence. But another feeling was stronger in Blanche—relief. As much as she hated to face it, Blanche was terribly relieved that it was Ursula—shy, homely Ursula—who was Charles's wife. In an instant Blanche was deeply ashamed of herself for the emotion.

Ursula was a nice girl and as much in love with Charles Seintleger as Blanche had been. How nasty to take pleasure in her undesirability, Blanche told herself. It wouldn't have mattered if Ursula was hunchbacked and had a harelip. She is Charles's wife and I am not, Blanche thought bitterly. He chose her, not *me*. That is that.

". . . you must have met him," Ursula was continuing. "He traveled to England with her majesty's party from France three years ago. He was with the Duke of York and had to return when his father died."

"Yes, I think I do recall such a gentleman," Blanche said. "Where is he now?"

"He is back with the Duke of York in France, but I believe he will be coming here with the Duke next month." For a moment Ursula was almost pretty. Her face radiated love for her husband, and it made Blanche feel small and sly and ugly to know that she loved the same man who was this girl's whole life and mind. Blanche remembered all the times she had thought of Charles's wife so hatefully, thinking her a cold, beautiful woman who had stolen Charles from her out of spite. How wrong she had been and how she felt now, realizing all over again that she had not gotten over her pain. She had simply buried it deeply in her soul and now, after the years since she had last seen his handsome face, the very sound of his name made her catch her breath.

"Come, it is almost time for the evening meal. You shall accompany me and meet the others," Blanche said.

After she had eaten, Ursula seemed to come out of herself a little. She mingled with the other young women and, though her laughter sounded a little forced, she seemed to be enjoying herself. It was a pleasant evening and Queen Margaret took her ladies into the gardens for a stroll after they had eaten. Ursula and Jane were presented to the Queen, and while Ursula made little impression on Margaret, Jane was charming and vivacious, and after the formalities were over, she proved to be an entertaining conversationalist. She told the ladies about their adventures on the way to court. She acted out their groom trying to lead the way in spite of trousers which kept slipping. She pulled sour faces that made them all see just what the poor man must have looked like attempting to be dignified in wayward garments. She had a gift for copying the speech of country people. Blanche could see that Jane was going to be a court favorite. But there was some elusive, unnamable quality about Jane that Blanche didn't like. It bothered her that she couldn't figure out what it was.

Queen Margaret was chatting with Lady Alice, and Ursula was swallowed up by a group of young married ladies. Blanche was sitting on the grass, brooding over her own vain soul. She was asking herself the same question she had been asking since she first realized that Ursula was Charles's wife. "Why her and not me?" Could it be her illegitimacy? Even as sensitive as she was about it, Blanche knew it made no difference to Charles. He certainly acted as if he genuinely cared for her and had even hinted at more that last time they spoke. She had seen many girls fooled by men who pretended interest in them, but Charles had never forced his attentions on her or tried to take advantage of her. Possibly all the girls who were led on by men thought the same way. But then why had he sent his brother to tell her of his marriage?

Blanche had thought it all out before. The only conclusion she could reach was that she was a fool. It wasn't a new idea; it had just become stronger since the arrival of Jane and Ursula.

And so she sat, getting grass stains on her best dress and feeling thoroughly sorry for herself. Presently Jane Seintleger sat down beside her in a billow of yellow skirts. The contrast between Jane's red hair, cream complexion, and saffron dress was breathtaking. Jane said nothing for a moment, but studied Blanche pointedly. "Charles told me you were both beautiful and capable. He was right."

Blanche could say nothing. She was utterly shocked. So Charles had told his sister of their relationship. Blanche sat speechless, unable to form into words the questions that were tumbling over each other in her mind.

"Saint George said you would not listen to him," Jane went on.

"Saint George?" Blanche asked blankly. Did this sane-looking girl think she spoke with saints?

"My brother George. The priest who visited you after Charles and Ursula were married," Jane explained the family nickname.

Blanche nodded. A long silence stretched out between them. There was much they had to say that neither of them wanted to speak of first. Finally Jane broke the quiet. "I have grown up with Ursula and I love her. I would not have her hurt." She got to her feet and smiled pleasantly to Blanche before moving away.

Blanche didn't know what to say. This newcomer was issuing her an ultimatum. Blanche could not and would not hurt Ursula. Ursula had won the battle for Charles without even knowing there had been a war. Why should Jane speak to Blanche thus? Then Blanche realized what it was she disliked about Jane: Jane hated *her*.

Blanche thought it all out again that night and came to what she thought was a sensible decision, if only she could hold herself to it. She had no connections with the Seintleger family except for the responsibilities she had toward all the young women under her supervision. She must learn to thrust her feelings for Charles out of her life and simply do her job as far as Ursula and Jane were concerned. She could not avoid seeing Charles when he arrived, but she would regard him with the same polite indifference she felt toward the husbands of the other ladies-in-waiting.

It was an easy decision to make—the only sensible way to behave—but it would be hard to carry out. Blanche told herself she was a strong individual and would be able to do what she thought was right.

Margaret's plan to hasten the Duke of York to England to claim his place on the King's Council had worked. Even in the midst of her personal concerns, Blanche was deeply troubled about what might result from the trick. York was being lured to England with a promise of an honor which he deserved long ago simply by virtue of birth if not merit. What would happen when he found it to be a sham? Margaret thought herself clever in the way of politics; Blanche thought she could not hope to compete with men whose country and families had been steeped in deadly intrigue for generations.

Blanche did not discuss this with Margaret, of course. Though they were together a great deal of the time, there had been a subtle drawing apart. The change in the relationship was mainly because of a change in Blanche. Knowing love and the sorrow of lost love had changed her, but that was only part of it. There were positive reasons, too. She had work to do besides just sitting and sewing and making small talk with Margaret. She had proved to herself and others that she was a capable person. Though this did not match the satisfaction she might have had with

Charles, it was some comfort. She believed herself to be enough liked at court and often received pleasant compliments from people who had nothing to gain by flattering her. She truly enjoyed the daily domestic tasks that fell within her ken.

But it seemed that Blanche could do nothing to make life easier for Margaret. The Queen had retreated further into her shell of aloofness. Blanche watched her looking sad and small and tired and her heart ached for her wrong-headed sister. Later Margaret was to do evil, unforgivable things, but only Blanche would know how she became that kind of person. Blanche suspected that Margaret knew that the men who claimed to be her advisors and friends were only using her to further themselves.

And Margaret must have known that Blanche disapproved of the way she was conducting her life, though naturally Blanche never openly expressed her doubts. Sometimes while she was talking with Somerset or Suffolk, Margaret would catch Blanche's eye and say lightly, "Dear Blanche thinks I'm silly."

There was a frantic atmosphere at court. There were more Yorkist sympathizers than Lancasterians present. Sympathizers! Blanche came to despise the word. She didn't feel that very many people were genuinely sympathetic to either Richard of York or Suffolk in their silent battle to be King Henry's heir if Margaret didn't produce a son.

Finally the ship that carried York arrived at Portsmouth. York's meeting with King Henry was planned like a great pageant. It was to take place in the great hall at Windsor. Fresh rushes were strewn on the floor.

The best tapestries to be found were hung on the clammy stone walls. Henry and Margaret's thrones were set up on the dais and everyone was invited to be there to observe the play. For that is what Margaret intended it to be, a play—a farce wherein the main actor didn't know the lines.

"Fair cousin," Henry greeted York after the formalities were done. "I welcome you to England. You have labored well on our behalf these years in France."

"My only wish is to serve my King and country, my lord," York answered easily. Blanche watched York and Margaret during this exchange and was struck with how often men improve with age, how seldom women. York was even handsomer than he had been when she first saw him in France. And Margaret? Margaret was still very beautiful—there was no one who could deny that—but she looked older and harder.

"Your devoted service to us is invaluable and we shall ask more of you," Henry said to York.

"I am always at your command, your majesty," York answered.

"My Council and I have considered your talents and given much thought and prayer to what your position should be."

York stood there smiling slightly. He, like the rest of them, was impatient, but the formalities had to be observed in the proper order.

". . . and God has seen fit to guide our thoughts," King Henry said, lifting the parchment he had been holding. He began to read: "Forasmuch as our most beloved kinsman and subject Richard of York, also titled Earl of March, Lord of Wigmore, Clare, Trim, and Connaught, has so nobly and faithfully served us in all his duties and responsibilities, we pray that upon the first opportunity he assume and execute the duties of Lieutenant of Ireland for a period of appointment of ten years. . . ."

York's smile disappeared. His face reddened as he glared at Suffolk standing next to Henry. Suffolk looked bland and disinterested. Margaret smiled placidly. King Henry droned on: ". . . and inasmuch as our said liegeman Richard of York has so faithfully served us in the execution of his duties in the past, we do require and exhort him to accept as token of our great love of him the following castles and estates . . ." (the listing of payment for accepting this exile). Henry's voice went on, detailing estates, titles, and duties. Blanche was watching York's face and saw the tension in his expression suddenly relax. He has thought of a way to combat this, she gloated, and felt guilty, for her heart's loyalty should have been with her sister and Queen, not this handsome man. But still she was excited and anxious to see what he was going to do.

". . . and ask our most blessed Lord's mercy and bounty. Given under our privy seal at Winchester in this year of our Lord 1448." Henry's lisping voice finally stopped.

There was a heavy silence before York spoke. "I am most pleased and honored that your majesty has seen fit to make these gifts and honors to your humble servant, but," he added doubtfully, "I know so little of the conditions of Ireland. There surely must be someone better qualified than I to manage the affairs of that country." Certainly he didn't think it would be that easy, Blanche thought.

"Nay, cousin, we have earnestly prayed and well considered this matter," King Henry said. So skillfully had Margaret and Suffolk planted the idea that King Henry truly believed it to be his own. This attitude of York's verged on refusal and Henry wouldn't be refused when he thought God had directed him. "We most heartily feel that you are the best person to be our representative in Ireland."

York's smile widened and he said convincingly, "I'm pleased at the honor you have bestowed by appointing me to this post." He went so far as to bow over King Henry's hand as if overcome by gratitude.

Margaret and Suffolk exchanged alarmed glances as if to say, "What is he doing?" York suddenly assumed a look of dismay. "But, your majesty, I have left so many things undone and untended in my years of absence. My overseers tell me that my estates must be attended to. They say that the crops are not being harvested on time and the village churches are falling into disrepair, and now your majesty has graciously granted me responsibility for more lands—" he lowered his voice reverently "—and more Christian souls. These things should be attended to before I depart again for a long absence."

Blanche almost laughed with pleasure at seeing someone deliver such a master stroke. It was the mention of neglected churches that did it, of course.

"My dear cousin, I understand the importance of these matters," King Henry said. "If only more of England's great landholders realized their duties to the souls and temporal welfare of their subjects . . . There is no reason for you to make haste to Ireland. Look well to your affairs and take as long as you need."

"But it might take quite a bit of time," York said with lines of dismay around his eyes.

"We shall be glad for you to remain in England for as long as you think is necessary. Now, if you wish, I would like to share with you the plans for the colleges that I am having built."

"I should be delighted, sire." York flashed a devastating smile at Margaret and Suffolk before he turned and left the room with the King. There was a deafening cheer that went up in the hall as York exited.

Margaret rose stiffly, and as Suffolk took her arm to escort her from the hall, Blanche heard her mutter through clenched teeth, "Damn him!"

Margaret was a fledgling at intrigue and had just floundered to earth on her first solo flight. She had overlooked an important fact. If she could manipulate King Henry easily—so could anyone else who took the trouble.

Blanche avoided Margaret for the rest of the day, for she knew that the Queen would be in nasty spirits and Blanche was honestly exhilarated at the coup York had delivered. She could not have hidden her feelings, so she stayed away from Margaret.

She stayed away from *everyone* the next day. She pretended a headache and thus spared herself the pain of seeing Charles and Ursula reunited. She could not bear the thought of seeing them look into each other's eyes with love and shared secrets. To think of them together that night—sharing a bed, kissing, touching one another—caused her real pain, a hurt that constricted her heart. It was a truth she must learn to face. But how could she? She would be certain to see him before the week was over, but she wasn't ready yet. She had to stiffen her resolutions to be unmoved. Late in the afternoon Margaret, having heard Blanche was ill, sent her physician to attend her. Blanche feigned a quick recovery lest her pretended illness attract more attention to herself than she desired. She went to dinner, though she could not touch her food. She forced herself not to cast her eyes about to see if Charles was present in the noisy crowd, but she knew he was. Some sense she had never been aware of before told her clearly that he was near.

She left the hall as quickly as she could after the meal, but it was not quickly enough. She had almost escaped when Ursula's familiar voice hailed her and she turned to see Ursula hurrying toward her, pulling Charles along by the hand. "Blanche, this is my husband," Ursula said with pride. "Charles, this is Blanche. She is the Queen's sister and has been most, oh most, kind to me here."

Blanche stared at him, unable to say anything at first. He, like York, had aged in the intervening years, and with age his face had gained in comeliness and character. He was no longer a boy; he was a man now and had something in his expression that had not been there when Blanche first knew him. Then she realized it was lines of experience, of pain suffered. She wondered if he had suffered some injury in his service to the Duke of York. Blanche's heart was beating so fiercely that she could hardly swallow and she wondered that her breathing wasn't obviously labored. Charles stared at her, a message in his look, a message she could not read the sense of, only the intensity.

Ursula watched them and finally said, "I thought perhaps you two had already met when the Queen first came to England." She said it softly with a questioning look that had nothing to do with the words she was speaking.

She must not know my thoughts, Blanche told herself sharply. "I believe perhaps we did," Blanche said, trying to sound natural.

"Blanche!" Ursula said, "you look faint. I heard you were ill today. You should have asked me to bring your dinner to you."

"Yes, I do feel a little tired," Blanche mumbled, seizing on the excuse Ursula had inadvertently offered her for her strange behavior.

"Let me take you to your room," Ursula said. "Charles, I will return after I see Blanche safely to bed."

Blanche nodded to Charles and turned away. Charles stood as one in a trance, watching the two women move away from him.

Blanche stayed in her room again the next day. She waited until she thought everyone had finished dining that evening, then crept almost furtively to the kitchen. She was ashamed of herself for acting like a silly child, but her good intentions to surmount her emotions were not holding up. After eating a little bread and sipping some wine left from dinner, she slipped out into the courtyard to get a little fresh air, thinking it might magically clear her head. The air was cool and astringent and she felt her eyes watering. Suddenly, without realizing what she was doing, she was leaning against a wall, silently sobbing. It came over her quickly and unexpectedly.

A voice came out of the darkness. "This is where we started," Charles said. He gathered her in his arms and she responded to his touch in a way she thought herself incapable of. She returned his kisses with a passion she had never dreamed existed in her own practical nature. She heard herself saying, "I love you, Charles . . ." over and over like a litany. Then suddenly she regained her senses. She pulled away from him and smoothed her hair and tried to wipe the salty tears from her face. She could say nothing, but turned away from him. His strong hands grasped her shoulders.

"Don't go, Blanche," he said softly. "I have waited these years to see you, to touch your hair. Sweet Jesu, you have grown so very beautiful." There was a catch in his voice that set off Blanche's tears again.

"Why, Charles, why?" she sobbed. "Why did you marry her when I loved you so?"

He looked at her, puzzled. "But I sent Saint George —I mean my brother—to explain. Jane wrote to me that he had talked with you, but that you would not send any message. I thought you didn't care."

"Explain what?"

"Why, explain about Ursula, of course. Please,

walk with me in the garden and let me tell you."

"No, I can't. It doesn't matter now. It's past and we should not be together."

"I must at least tell you. If you really love me, let me have just a few more moments of your life to explain to you."

They walked hand in hand into the gardens, now flooded with moonlight and rose scent. They found a bench to sit on and he stared at her for a long time before speaking. "When I reached my home after I left you, my father was nearly gone," he began. "He could still speak, though, and he told me he had arranged for my betrothal with Ursula. I objected, but he would not, or could not, hear me. With this war going on in France, the piracy in the Channel has become rife and many of our wool shipments have been lost. The family business was suffering and Ursula's father was a rich man, willing to give a large and badly needed dowry. My father had already used the dowry, in fact, before telling me of the transaction.

"Only a month before I got home, Ursula's father had died of the fever. Her mother had died long ago and she had no brothers. Ursula herself had been very ill and my family had nursed her back to health. You see, there was no choice. Even if I had not been morally obligated to honor the contract my father had arranged, Ursula's money was already gone and there was Ursula herself—she had no one to go home to. She had no one at all."

"And she loved you," Blanche added.

"Yes," he admitted sadly. "Yes, she loved me and

depended on me." He was silent for a moment, then added, "I must be honest with you, Blanche. I . . . I do love Ursula, too, in a way."

Blanche drew back and he went on hurriedly, "Don't misunderstand. It doesn't have anything to do with my love for you. It doesn't diminish my feelings for the woman I would have chosen for myself—still would choose, if I had a choice. But I love Ursula in a different way. She depends on me and she has, you must know, many good qualities. She is an excellent wife. It is not her fault that I have no passion for her."

"Then we are agreed," Blanche said, "nothing must hurt Ursula. You see, I too am very fond of her and would not have her come to sorrow. Let us go back now, before we are missed." She said this with a cheerfulness she did not feel. Charles held back for a moment as if to say something more and yet they both knew there was nothing more to say.

The next day the Duke of York left. Sir Charles Seintleger and his wife, Ursula, went with him. Blanche left early that morning on a totally unnecessary errand to Southampton so that she would not be available to say goodby.

CHAPTER FIVE

Almost two years had passed since Richard of York had been politely exiled to Ireland and yet he was still in England. He and his young kinsman and advisor the Earl of Warwick had been conferring at York's favorite castle, Fotheringay. They had come to a decision and called for refreshments. In a moment there was a knock at the door.

"Enter," York called to the serving maid. But it wasn't the maid who entered; it was York's wife, Cecily.

"Your drinks, sires," she said with mock coyness as she curtseyed.

"Have care, Cis, lest you overbalance and roll across the room." York affectionately patted her pregnant belly.

Cecily put the tray on the table and sat down with Richard and her nephew Warwick. "You two have been shut up in here exchanging secrets all week. I thought mayhap a maid might overhear more than a wife."

"Cis," Richard said, "can you be ready to move to Ireland in a month?"

"What!" She tried to spring from her chair, but her bulky body prevented that kind of move. "Oh, Richard, what has happened?"

"Now, Cis, stop floundering around in that chair and listen." Richard smiled and waited until she had leaned back.

Cecily took a deep breath and said in a low voice, "I'm calm. Now, what is all this about? I thought that you were going to keep on stalling about going to Ireland until you could get King Henry to change his mind. What has gone wrong?"

Warwick had been silent during the exchange, but now spoke with unexpected venom. "How can you change a man's mind when he hasn't got one?"

Cecily looked sharply at her bitter young nephew. It wasn't that she hadn't thought the same thing for years, but not many people would state it so bluntly even in a small, trusted circle. Warwick had a capacity for saying very little but rocking people back on their heels when he did speak up.

"Crudely put, cousin, but unfortunately true," York said. "You see, Cis, I've wasted all this time with King Henry, trying to talk some sense into him. I talk all day and Queen Margaret apparently talks all night. That may be why she has not yet a babe." He winked at Cecily. "But by morning, I'm back where I started. The Queen tells him that Somerset and Suffolk are his most important allies and supporters. I try to hint that they well may ruin him and the realm. He really hasn't the ability to weigh the two opinions, so he takes her word.

"It's not only that he can't decide, he just isn't interested. He doesn't realize it's important. All he wants to talk about is that college he's building—Eton, he calls it. God's teeth!" Richard groaned. "I've seen those plans so many times I know them backwards."

Cecily was making an effort to stay calm. "Please,

Richard, don't ramble—I don't want to hear about Eton."

"Nor do I, ever again," Richard teased.

"Why do we have to go to Ireland? What has happened to make you change your mind?"

"Nothing has happened yet, Cis. That's just it. I think a storm is brewing and I think it's wise to take cover before it breaks."

"A storm?" Cecily asked. "Over you?"

"No, over Suffolk and Somerset. Suffolk primarily, but they are a pair. What blacks one, blacks the other. I've been trying to convince King Henry that Suffolk is poor counsel, but getting nowhere. Now I think Suffolk has gotten himself in so much trouble that Parliament is going to dispense with him and I won't need to convince the King of anything. That is the key. I'm sure it is coming and I want to be as far as possible from Parliament so Queen Margaret can't accuse me of plotting against her friend Suffolk."

"But you haven't been plotting against him—exactly," Cecily said uneasily.

"Not exactly?" York laughed. "That is the beauty of it. All my poor plots have been for naught. Suffolk has brought all his trouble upon himself. Every bit of it. It would seem that he has finally offended everyone except the King and Queen. His enemies have discovered that he has no friends left. His enemies are no longer a majority, they are almost an entirety."

Cecily looked to Warwick for confirmation, but he was glaring at his glass of wine and nodding to himself. "I guess I've been in the nursery too much of late," Cecily sighed. "What has Suffolk been doing?"

"Nothing different from the usual, it's just all coming out into the open," York said. "Like that treaty he made to return Maine and Anjou to France." The lightness had left his voice. "Damnable treason! He didn't consult anyone and even got Parliament to officially 'forgive' him in advance for any mistakes that he might make. Mistakes! He meant all along to sign that secret treaty. When I think of the English blood that soaked that soil, just to give it back to France . . ."

Warwick's deep drawl cut in: "All to buy that dowerless French whore." He didn't look up from his glass.

There was a silence while Cecily drew a long breath. York braced himself for the explosion he could tell was coming. "Richard Neville!" Cecily spat out. She used his name instead of his title only when she was really angry. "Queen Margaret is not, as you so delicately put it, a 'French whore.' I visited her and that nice sister of hers when they first came to England. Queen Margaret was pleasant enough, just shy. In fact, I rather liked her." Cecily looked apologetically at York. "Oh, I know, she doesn't seem nice now and she's making things terrible for us, but still I can understand." She saw York's exaggerated expression of doubt. "Well, I *can* understand. If I had come to another country and found myself married to someone like King Henry, I would have grabbed for the nearest available support and Suffolk has certainly made himself available. It's a shame she didn't listen to her sister, Blanche, though. She seemed to be an unusually sensible person." Cecily had lost her fire and Warwick obviously wasn't paying any attention to her. He was twirling his glass of wine and meditating on the carving around the ceiling.

"After all"—Cecily turned to York—"how was a girl like Queen Margaret to know that my Richard is the smartest man alive?" She struggled up and went over to settle herself on York's lap.

Warwick rose and strolled to the door. Richard called to him. "Warwick, please ask that young Edward be sent in here. He is coming of an age. I would tell him of this decision and the reasons."

The Duke of York and his family left England in July with their children and servants. Young Edward, who had once shown the Queen his toy soldier, was now seven years old. He was officially the Earl of March. Edmund, a year younger, was Earl of Rutland. Unborn George was still making his mother awkward. Once having made the decision to leave, Richard of York seemed almost anxious to go. Cecily was unhappy at the prospect of leaving England for ten years. "Our children will grow up to be foreigners in their own country," she lamented.

"Don't worry, Cis," York assured her, "we will be back long before any ten years pass. I am the work-horse of the government and they will need me back." He turned to the brooding young Warwick, who planned to accompany them to the boat. "I trust you to be my eyes and ears in my absence. Try to control your tongue and be privy to all that happens at court."

Two years passed for Blanche without word of Charles. Then Jane returned to court with news of him. Blanche thought she had hardened her heart to the old hurt, but she was wrong. Charles was with the Duke of York and Ursula had suffered a miscarriage and been very ill.

Margaret had spent the two years harping on the injustice of Richard of York dawdling in England, though even she tired of the subject from time to time, for he was doing nothing—absolutely nothing—to excite criticism except that he was still in England and not Ireland.

Blanche was more concerned with the activities of the Duke of Suffolk. She knew that the people at court were getting more and more distressed about conditions over which he had control. There was much open criticism of him, and once she had come upon dear, placid Lady Alice crying because of some slight she had received because of her husband's unpopularity.

The treasury of England, which was decidedly unhealthy when they first arrived in England, had now become depleted. Even Blanche's meager requests for the necessary funds for administering the Queen's household were questioned in painstaking detail and she seldom was allotted more than half what she asked for. Taxes were raised repeatedly and yet there was less money. It was going *somewhere*. Most people felt that Suffolk knew where and wasn't telling.

Even Margaret took Suffolk to task about his administration of the treasury. But he offered her such glib and complicated answers to her questions that she had no idea what he was saying. It was a clever way to deal with her and showed that he understood her well, for Margaret fancied it an admission of stupidity to confess that she didn't understand something on the first explanation. She sat and nodded intelligently while he spouted nonsense. It made Blanche furiously angry with both of them. Once she told Margaret that she thought Suffolk had actually said nothing, and Margaret said defensively that Blanche simply didn't understand and besides, the Queen's sister wasn't required to understand. From then on Blanche kept quiet.

Blanche worried, too, about King Henry. She seldom saw him anymore; no one saw much of him. His daily round consisted of prayers, meals, prayers, planning his colleges, more prayers, and sleep. He did not like to be in groups of people and seemed to dislike any sort of gaiety or entertainment. Blanche never saw him laugh and saw him smile only during Mass. During meals that he took with the court he kept his eyes on his plate or on Margaret at his side. He never seemed to quite remember who anyone was from one meeting to the next.

Margaret had come to terms with him by generally ignoring him, or when she couldn't, speaking to him as one would to a rather dull child. Their discussions consisted mainly of comments on the food they were served or the weather or what religious observances should occur on upcoming holy days. When there were legal matters that required his signature, she and Suffolk would explain the matter to him in simple (and often inaccurate) terms and he would sign. But he didn't like being taken away from his prayers to sign papers and that suited Margaret and Suffolk quite well.

Parliament was about to convene and there were rumors that action would be taken against Suffolk. This angered Margaret afresh. "What kind of country

is this that merchants may give orders to their King?"
she raged. "The King's word should be the only law.
How dare they assume that they may usurp the King's
right to appoint his advisors?" Blanche thought that if
it hadn't been sad, it would have been amusing, for it
was Margaret who had usurped the King's rights; and
in any case, with a King like Henry, any passing black-
smith could have made wiser decisions with more
enthusiasm than the King.

Blanche had taken great interest in the workings of
the English Parliament, which was indeed unique, and
tried to explain to Margaret, but it only made her
angrier. "So you betray me, too. You wish these goldsmiths and carpenters to rule."

"Parliament is not just goldsmiths and carpenters.
That is the Commons and they haven't nearly the power
of the House of Lords."

"Commons! Lords! A pack of traitors, ungrateful
traitors, that's what this wretched Parliament is. The
French wouldn't put up with this. We wouldn't allow
it for a moment."

"We?" Blanche questioned. "*We* are not French,
Margaret, not anymore. You are English now."

"Ha!" Margaret said, as if it clinched her argument.

On the day before the fateful Parliament was to begin meeting, Blanche saw Charles again. He was rattled
and hurried. He wasted no time on pleasantries. "I am
to Ireland, Blanche, and I fear for Ursula's health. I
have no right to ask anything of you, but I am here
to ask anyway. Please let Ursula stay here with you
while I am gone."

"Of course," Blanche said. She would have done

anything he asked, and Ursula's company was not unpleasant. In fact, she had missed her. "But why to Ireland? Is the Duke of York sending you there?"

"No, I am going with him."

"He is finally going to Ireland? But why after all this time? My sister has all but given up interest in trying to send him there."

"May I speak freely to you?"

"You must know me well enough to be assured that I can keep your words to myself." She was a little hurt by his doubt.

"I know. Yes. But you are the Queen's sister . . ."

". . . and I am loyal to her, but she has never wanted my advice and I have gotten over the urge to give it to her. Please, what is happening?"

"I'm not sure . . . that is, I don't think York is sure. He says that England is a pot ready to boil over and he wants to be well out of the way of blame when it happens."

"How long will you be gone?" Blanche asked.

"I have no idea. It might be years or only weeks. I won't leave Ursula here for too long. She has not been well and I have no idea what living conditions I will find in Ireland. As soon as I am able I will send for her."

"I will take good care of her in the meantime . . ." Blanche had time to say before he kissed her. Was this to be her life? she wondered—one bruising kiss every two years?

The next morning Charles brought Ursula to court. Blanche was shocked at her appearance; her clothing hung on her thin figure, she looked tired and wan, but she did not complain and made an effort to be a cheerful companion. Blanche settled into a pattern of taking care of Ursula, trying to build up her frail strength, and watching the political situation with growing alarm. It wasn't long before York's predictions of Suffolk's downfall came true. The English situation in France had gone from bad to worse since Anjou and Maine were returned to France. Fighting had resumed in several places and the English were losing all that remained of their French possessions.

The court heard a frightening story in late January of 1450. The Duke of Somerset was ready to set out across the Channel and his sailors were waiting at Portsmouth to be paid in advance of their departure. They were already angry when Suffolk's treasurer, Bishop Moleyns, Keeper of the Privy Seal, showed up at the port. When the sailors learned that Moleyns didn't have nearly enough money to pay them their full wages, they were incensed. It was well known that Moleyns and his friends had themselves never felt any economic pinch. When Moleyns, a stupid man at best, began to shout abuses at the sailors who demanded their pay, the gathering turned into a riot. They murdered Moleyns in the street.

This was the first open outbreak of the common people against Suffolk and Somerset's policies and it frightened Suffolk, though Blanche had the awful feeling that Margaret was exhilarated by the conflict's coming into the open. Suffolk went before Parliament at the end of the month and tried to get another blanket forgiveness for anything he might do in the future. It had been unusual for such a condition to be made once; it was impossible now. In fact, requesting it was Suffolk's undoing.

He gave a speech at Parliament, enumerating his own virtues, and he hastily blamed the Commons for the "odious and horrible language that runneth through your land" against him. He was hated for his conceit and deceptions, but the word "your" finished him off. It was as if he were admitting to foreign sympathies and placing himself above and apart from the English. Humility might have been to his advantage, but Suffolk was incapable of humility.

The Commons thought it over for four days (which showed remarkable restraint), then demanded that Suffolk be imprisoned for treason and corruption. It was not a general sort of accusation. They listed specifics. According to the House of Commons:

> Suffolk was responsible for the secret and treasonable treaty with France . . .

> Suffolk had planned to marry his son to Somerset's niece in preparation for getting rid of King Henry and putting either Somerset or the children on the throne . . .

> Suffolk had advised the King falsely on finances of the realm and had given the government's money to his friends rather than paying the soldiers' and sailors' wages . . .

> Suffolk had placed greedy and corrupt friends of his in important sheriffs' positions . . .

The list went on and on.

Margaret was furious. She couldn't see what had gone wrong. Blanche, however, thought that the only reason Suffolk had prospered in the past was because Beaufort had allowed him to. But Cardinal Beaufort was dead now, and Suffolk possessed a fatal combination of traits—unrestrained pride and ambition, but none of the humility needed to temper such characteristics. Blanche had seen Beaufort act as self-effacing as the lowliest woodcutter's apprentice when it suited his ends, and so he had thrived. Suffolk was doomed.

The Commons presented the indictment to King Henry and demanded that it be acted upon. "A demand from the Commons!" Margaret snorted. "How dare they tell the King what to do?" She was angry about the accusations and even angrier because she could not ignore one nagging doubt in her own mind. It was one of the few times she confided her true feelings to Blanche. "The very idea that Suffolk and Somerset had conspired to replace Henry!" she stormed.

"Do you think it might be true?" Blanche asked, feigning innocent curiosity.

"No, of course it's not true." She was quiet for a long moment, then said, "Do you think it could be true?"

"I know nothing of such matters, but I do recall that they kept the betrothal of the children very secret and I wondered why at the time."

"Yes, that is so. I remember being surprised when it came to my ears, and when I questioned them about it, they changed the subject. They are both far wealthier than I, and possibly between them they have more power," she brooded.

"Perhaps you have allowed them too much power," Blanche suggested.

"Nay, they are good men. This is simply a trick to make me doubt my own council and I shall not play into the hands of my enemies by even considering it," she said resolutely. "Besides, I have convinced King Henry to declare an end to the Commons' investigation of Suffolk and refer the matter to the House of Lords. There will be no more trouble."

"Has the King the right to do that?" Blanche asked, knowing that according to English law, he did not.

"Of course, Blanche, don't you understand yet? The King has the right to do anything he pleases."

Blanche fought back the urge to tell Margaret how utterly wrong she was. It would have done no good and would only have made her angry again. The great flaw in the plan was apparent even to Blanche—the peers of the realm hated Suffolk as much as or more than the Commons. The most powerful lords of England traditionally made up the King's Council, but for years this duty had been purely nominal because Suffolk had usurped the nobility's authority to advise the King. Although the Council still legally existed and even met occasionally to decide the trivial matters allowed to them, neither Suffolk nor the King attended their meetings or paid much attention to any of their decisions.

This was the body of men that Queen Margaret thought would *save* Suffolk.

The House of Lords determined that the only charge that would result in Suffolk's death was a charge of treason and that the only thing that would rid England of Suffolk's influence was his death.

Margaret was beside herself when she realized what

was happening. "These men are his own kind of people," she said, perplexed and angry. "How can they suggest that he should die?"

"They aren't really his 'own' people, Margaret," Blanche corrected. "Suffolk is not old nobility. He hasn't a single drop of royal blood. Almost every man in the House of Lords is a great-nephew or third cousin of one English king or another. They are all related to each other in some way, at least most of them are. Suffolk isn't related to anyone there. That's only part of the reason they hate him."

"Well, they shall not have his head. I have discussed this with Henry and everything will be taken care of tomorrow."

"How will everything be taken care of?" Blanche asked, afraid of what crazy scheme Margaret was involved in now.

"Never mind, you shall see."

The next morning Blanche sought out a young knight who was her friend and had previously proved a valuable source of information. Blanche sent him to find out what was happening at the House of Lords. He returned in the early afternoon. "The King sent an announcement that Suffolk's punishment was to be a five-year banishment from England," he reported.

"Only five years? And they wanted his head! How was the announcement received?"

"Very badly. There were many men standing in the streets and alleys shaking their fists and grumbling. They are surprised and angry that King Henry would be so lenient when they demanded death," he said.

Blanche had often relied on this young man to run

such errands for her and they had an understanding. He told her the truth and she kept his confidences to herself. "What else are they saying?" she asked, sensing that there was something he was thinking about holding back.

"They say, begging your pardon, milady, that it is because of the Queen. They call her names and say she has cast a spell on poor King Henry."

"Don't worry, I shan't ask you what names," Blanche said. He smiled. "Thank you for telling me."

It boded ill. Blanche didn't think that the English would let their quarry be snatched from their jaws this way. There was no legal recourse for them to take and she felt sure someone would find a more violent solution. She could only pray that Margaret would be spared whatever happened.

Blanche felt a pang of pity for Lady Alice as well. She was such a dear, simple soul and had never done anyone harm. She loved England and her husband and Blanche greatly feared that she would lose both. It isn't fair to her, Blanche thought.

Suffolk left England with all his movable possessions —money, furniture, and family—loaded in two ships. They made their way across the Channel toward Calais. As they neared Calais, a pinnace was sent ahead to ask official permission to land. It was simply a formality; Suffolk was confident that he would be welcome. The pinnace did not return.

While Suffolk and his captain were discussing their next move, a large ship was moving nearer and nearer. They could finally identify it as the *Nicholas of the*

Tower, the pride of the English warships. It was commanded by Henry Holland, Duke of Exeter, High Admiral of the English fleet.

The great warship sailed to the side of Suffolk's miniature fleet. A sailor called to them from the *Nicholas,* "My lord Exeter wishes to speak with William de la Pole, Duke of Suffolk. Be prepared to come aboard, sire."

Lady Alice plucked at her husband's sleeve. "My lord, must you go on board that ship?"

Suffolk looked surprised and said stiffly, "Certainly, my dear, why not? I imagine Holland only wants to offer his support."

"But those sailors look so rough and mean," Lady Alice said.

"I have outwitted my enemies in both houses of Parliament, madam. Don't you think I can deal with a few sailors?"

"But it was the sailors who murdered Moleyns," she blurted out.

Suffolk paled, but drew himself up and said haughtily, "Moleyns was not a gentleman."

Suffolk summoned his captain and explained that Holland would probably desire to escort him personally to Calais. He wished the captain to take the two small vessels into the harbor, where he would meet them later. But as Suffolk's boat pulled away, Lady Alice could see her husband boarding the *Nicholas* and hear the sailors' shouts drift across the widening gulf. "Welcome, traitor!" they were shouting.

Lady Alice knew that he would not meet her at Calais.

Suffolk was kept for the rest of the day and night

in a tiny, dark cell in the bottom of the ship. This room was usually used to confine the unruly drunks and it reeked of stale vomit. Suffolk spent his time there fighting down nausea and rats. They were a belligerent and invisible army in the dark cell. He was not frightened, just indignant. When he got his chance to be heard, he would certainly straighten Holland out.

By morning the laughter and drunken obscenities overhead had died down and Suffolk found himself being led onto the dawn-bright deck. Blinking and squinting in the sun and trying to maintain his dignity, he heard Holland's voice behind him.

"Traitor! Turn and face your jury."

Suffolk saw only Holland and his officers. Holland's heavy face was red and angry. "We have held trial this night and found you guilty of treason most foul and dastardly," Holland said.

"How dare you! You have no right . . ." Suffolk began.

"You have sold our heroic dead in Maine and Anjou for a penniless princess, you murdered good Duke Humphrey for daring to expose your villainy, you stole from the coffers of your gentle King to line your own purses. You call yourself a gentleman, so you shall die in the manner of a gentleman traitor—by beheading." A sailor stepped up to Suffolk and held before him a sword—old, rusted and blunt—very, very blunt.

Suffolk stepped back in horror from the sword and the leering sailor. He realized that there was no way to move these men, but he could and would die like a true knight.

The sailors grabbed him and dragged him to the

block they had set up on deck. He tried to move with slow dignity, but they pushed and prodded and tripped him. They shouted obscenities and spat on him. Holland, who had never before tolerated such behavior from his crew, turned aside and stared out to sea.

Suffolk's head was forced down onto the block, and before he had time to compose himself, the rusty sword struck. But the sailor wielding it was not used to handling swords and missed his target slightly. The sword glanced off Suffolk's head, cutting the scalp and slicing through his ear. He had only a painful second to draw breath before the second blow fell. This time the sword hit his neck, but was too blunt to sever it completely. The head rolled forward and Suffolk's death scream spurted out with the blood from the great pulsing arteries in his neck. His lifeless body convulsed and thrashed and his blood sprayed the spectators.

"Bloody bastard don't want to part with 'is 'ead," one sailor shouted.

" 'E might as well. Ain't no pretty little queen gonna want 'im round lookin' like that," the ship's wit called back.

It took the inept executioner with the blunt sword three more butcher blows to finish beheading the Duke of Suffolk. They stripped the blood-soaked doublet off his body and took turns trying it on. They ripped off the rest of his clothes and left the naked, headless corpse on the deck, congealing in its own blood, while they set sail toward the shores of Kent. In a few hours they threw the gruesome trophies overboard.

Two days later a fisherman at Dover went down to

the edge of the sea to check his nets and found Suffolk's body. A few miles along the coast two small boys out for an adventure found a head among the rocks. It had been badly battered, but there remained traces of disdain on the bloodless features.

When word reached court of Suffolk's death, Margaret dismissed her ladies and spent the day alone. Every time Blanche entered the Queen's rooms she found her sister either weeping or pacing angrily. During one of the weeping sessions she said, "How has this happened to me? I'm married to an idiot and now I've lost Cardinal Beaufort *and* Suffolk. They tried to help me. Now only Somerset is left and he is in France. I'm all alone. I'm so alone in this cold country full of people who hate me. People didn't hate me in Anjou. Why do they hate me here? I'm young still—shall my whole life be so empty?"

There was nothing Blanche could say. Margaret didn't expect her to have the answer anyway. Besides, it rather hurt Blanche's own feelings. Margaret wasn't alone in a strange land—Blanche was with her. She could have advised Margaret better than Suffolk had if it had ever occurred to Margaret to listen to her.

The next time Blanche passed through, Margaret had cried it out of her system and changed her attitude. "I haven't time for self-pity," she told Blanche. "I miss Suffolk only as an ally, not as a friend. I need to get Somerset back here and I need to get a message to Alice. Suffolk's enemies may be unkind to her. I shall ask her to come here and stay with us." Margaret went to the door leading to the sitting room that adjoined her suite. There was a pretty, gray-eyed girl of thirteen sitting by the window, trying to catch the fading afternoon light on her sewing.

"Mistress Woodville," Margaret said.

The girl dropped her sewing and made a quick curtsey, "Yes, your grace."

"Elizabeth, I wish to send a letter to the Duchess of Suffolk, but my eyes are very weary. I shall let you copy it out for me and we shall see how your hand-writing is progressing." Margaret quite often asked little personal favors of the girls in her care. It made them feel important to be singled out for special attention from the Queen. Margaret could endear herself to women, Blanche had often thought. It was a pity that Margaret didn't cultivate the same talent for getting along wih men. It would have done her more good.

"Thank you, your grace," the girl answered in a slow, quiet voice. Elizabeth Woodville obviously adored Queen Margaret and considered it an honor that the Queen should be interested in her studies.

As they sat down to begin the letter, Margaret said, "Elizabeth, I understand you are betrothed to Lord Grey's son. I have seen him at court. He is a very handsome young man."

"Yes, your grace. Our parents have drawn up the contracts. Of course, we shan't be wed for a while." A delicate blush spread up her cheeks. "My mother says I'm not old enough."

"And you think you are?" Margaret laughed. "Don't rush things. You are your mother's firstborn and she is not overeager for you to be grown." Margaret was remembering herself at thirteen, only seven years ago, eager to be wed, imagining a handsome, romantic husband. "Now, remember what I told you about turning the parchment properly to achieve comely writing," she went on.

Margaret's mind was obviously more at ease and so was Blanche's. They both hoped that Suffolk's death would placate the people's discontent and there would be less turmoil when it was all forgotten. Then Margaret could devote herself to such leisurely pursuits as helping this pretty, pleasant girl with her lessons.

But they were wrong. As the news of Suffolk's death spread through Kent, where his body had been found, it set off heated reactions. The common people had hated Suffolk, the merchant's grandson who had lorded over them, but his death hadn't satisfied them, only whetted their appetite for reform.

CHAPTER SIX

Richard of York and his son, Edward, were practicing archery. York spent many hours every day working on the affairs of Ireland and had quickly become popular with the Irish. They considered him fair in his judgments, and his conservative, cool-headed attitudes tempered the hot-headed opinions of the Irish lords whom he had been sent to govern. But no matter how much work he had to do during the day, he always found or made time to be with his sons, particularly his favorite, Edward.

It was such an occasion today. There had been messengers riding in every day from the Earl of Warwick with garbled messages of upheaval and revolt in London, but York was calmly introducing Edward to a longbow. It was a special longbow. It had been made especially for Edward and it was large—not as large as the ones that real soldiers used, but far larger and handsomer than most eight-year-old boys ever got to use. But then, Edward himself was far larger and handsomer than most boys of eight years. He was the essence of the Plantagenet heritage. He was already as tall as his mother and had the wavy blond hair and transparent blue eyes of his illustrious ancestors, but Edward had more. His face was square and strong, and though there was still a childish plumpness about him, it was clear that he would soon be an extremely good-looking young man.

"Now, Edward," York was explaining, "I didn't want you to grapple with the strength of this bow until I felt you had mastered the skills with a smaller bow. I think you are ready now. Get the target set up in front of the far wall," York called to a servant, "and keep everyone well away! This is his first try."

Edward planted his large feet firmly and began pulling the strong, waxy cord. It was even harder to do than he expected. He gritted his teeth and squinted his eyes. His bow arm trembled with the effort. He managed to pull it nearly all the way back before releasing it. The arrow whistled across the courtyard and shattered against the wall an arm length to the right of the target. There was a second or two of silence before Edward's laughter rang out. "You see, ladies and gentlemen," he said with mock formality to the crowd of onlookers, "when my lord father tells you to stand clear, he means you had better get a fast horse."

Everyone laughed with him. Edward's down-to-earth wit made him the darling of the household as well as the pride of his parents. Richard of York threw an arm around the boy's shoulders and they started to go in when one of the sentries in the watchtower called down, "My lord, there is a group of horsemen riding hard up the road."

"More of Warwick's messengers?" York called back.

"Aye, sire. They're flying his colors. I think it's the Earl himself."

"Warwick here? Edward, run in and tell your mother to have rooms prepared for Warwick."

"Yes, sire." Edward turned to go.

"Edward, after you tell her, put your equipment away and join Warwick and me in the tower room. You shall hear whatever he has to say firsthand."

Edward's face glowed. "Thank you, sire. I shall be there."

"What is the child doing here?" Warwick asked when he entered the tower room.

"He is not just a child, Warwick. He is my son. He is fast growing to manhood and 'tis time he take his place in our councils," York said.

"It shall be as you say then, Richard, but I think you are being misled by his great size."

Edward tried to maintain a bland expression and not scowl at this dark, hawk-nosed cousin.

"Nay, Warwick. He is a bright boy and has the makings of a good soldier. He might even make a statesman. Look at how convincingly he's pretending he doesn't hear us discussing him."

Edward looked at his father and smiled. The affection between father and son made Warwick uncomfortable. His disposition didn't allow for showing one's feelings so openly. "Richard, you may soon have need of all the soldiers and statesmen you can find."

"Tell me what is happening, Warwick. Your men ride in every few days, hot and tired and carrying tidings that sometimes seem to contradict each other. I haven't been able to make much sense out of some of them."

"I shall start at the beginning, then. That way young Edward will know all," Warwick replied.

Edward expected the sarcasm in Warwick's voice

to show in his face, but it didn't. York was too eager for the facts to notice innuendoes.

Warwick went on, "Finding Suffolk's body in Kent seemed to excite the people mightily. This Jack Cade, as he calls himself, stepped to the fore and said he would lead a revolt against the evil men who surround the King."

"So the rabble followed him?" York asked.

"Nay, Richard, 'twas not just the rabble, though they were part of it. His followers were weavers and bakers and monks and landholders. Respectable people, Richard. Parliament was meeting in May at Leicester, as you know, so the Cade rebels began to march slowly toward London. Cade sent a complaint to the Council in June. It was well and bluntly worded —wait, I brought a copy." He fumbled around in the folds of his cloak and, with the air of a conjurer, extracted a scrap of paper from a concealed pocket and read from it: "We say that our sovereign lord may well understand that he hath false council, for his lords are lost, his merchandise is lost, his Commons destroyed, the sea is lost, himself so poor that he may not pay for his meat and drink; he oweth more than ever any king in England and yet daily his traitors that be about him wait for whatever may come to him and they ask it from him."

"Aye, cousin, they are true sentiments and well expressed, but I doubt the Council took heed," York said.

"No, they just sent back word that the rebels were to disperse."

"But they didn't?"

"Nay, they fell back a bit, though, and the court

and most of the army headed out after them. The King camped at Blackheath. An advance guard went ahead and was ambushed at Sevenoaks."

"Were they all killed?" Edward asked. His curiosity and interest in military activity had overcome his reticence.

"All but the few who managed to ride back and tell King Henry what happened," Warwick answered curtly.

"But they wouldn't harm King Henry, would they?" Edward asked.

"No, son," York explained, "no one wishes ill for the King, but he is a . . ." York groped for a suitably objective word, ". . . a spiritual man who doesn't realize that many of the men around him are greedy and evil and doing great harm to England. The rebels only want to rid the King of that influence. That is all any of us want." He turned his attention back to Warwick. "I understand Cade's men executed Lord Say, the King's treasurer."

"Yes, King Henry had locked up Say and the sheriff of Kent in the Tower of London just to protect them from the rebels, but after the ambush at Sevenoaks, the King's troops withdrew to the north and left London open to the rebels. They stormed the Tower the first week in July and took the treasurer and sheriff out and executed them on the spot."

"What did they do next?"

"They all went out and got drunk," Warwick said bitterly. "But the Londoners and Tower guards stayed sober and ran them all out of the city the next morning."

"But you mean that the royal army couldn't deal

with the rebels and the people of London could?"
Edward was astonished.

"Yes, Edward." York smiled at his reaction. "Don't
ever underestimate London. It is the soul and heartbeat of England. No one has ever intimidated a
Londoner."

"The Council offered pardons for everyone who
turned tail and went home peacefully," Warwick continued. "Many of them did, naturally. They had enjoyed their adventure and were under the impression
that they had accomplished something. Cade is still
at large. The court and army were starting to trickle
back into London when I left."

York looked puzzled. "I had managed to piece most
of that together from your messages. But whatever
has brought you clear to Ireland?"

"There is more, and I didn't trust the messengers,"
Warwick said, leaning forward and speaking quietly.
"This man, Jack Cade, is telling people that his real
name is John Mortimer."

"Mortimer!" York exclaimed. Mortimer was his
own family name.

"He claims to be your cousin."

York was angry. "I don't have a cousin named
John Mortimer. Do you mean he is claiming to lead
this rebellion on *my* orders?"

"No, he claims only the name, though most of his
followers are under the impression that they are rally-
ing to your cause. Queen Margaret's men are busy
spreading the word among the people that Cade is an
Irishman under sentence of death for murdering a
pregnant woman. They are saying that you are behind

this rebellion and that you plan to take King Henry's place on the throne."

"Why don't you, Father?"

The bluntness of the question stunned the two men. As they stared at him in silence, he realized that he had said something wrong. He lowered his head and mumbled, "I'm sorry," though he didn't quite understand why he should be sorry. It seemed a logical question to him.

"I shall explain to you after we have heard the rest of Warwick's news," York told him.

"My only other news concerns Somerset."

"He is still in France, isn't he?" York's face had assumed a hard look at the mention of Somerset's name.

"So my spies tell me," Warwick said, "but they also say that he appears to be making secretive moves to gather his support and return shortly."

"Your spies must be more observant than mine. I was not aware of his plans to return, but I admit I'm not surprised. I suppose he'll wait until this commotion dies down. He won't want to place himself in any danger."

"You will return to England now, won't you?" Warwick asked.

"Perhaps. . . . I must think upon it."

"Richard, do you not recognize opportunity when it is served to you on a silver platter?" Warwick's voice was low and menacing.

"You know I'm not looking for any opportunity for myself. I'm only anxious to serve England. I don't *want* what you want me to go to war for," York answered. Warwick sneered at the sentiment. York ignored him. "Now I must have some words with my son. I will have you shown to your rooms and we'll talk again after dinner."

Warwick rose to go. "I wish I could stay for the explanation of why you won't be King. The boy has a good question, you know," he said and left.

York walked to one of the long, narrow windows of the tower room. He gazed out at the lush Irish landscape. "This is a beautiful country, son."

Edward said nothing. He knew that his father's mind wasn't on the view. Finally York came and sat by the boy. "I could probably usurp King Henry's place just as his grandfather usurped it from Richard the Second. But, Edward, there are reasons I shall not, and you are old enough to know them and, I hope, understand them. First, I don't want to be a king. The throne is a cage, a beautiful cage sometimes, but a cage nonetheless. I don't think it is necessary for me to be caged to help England, and helping my country is my only wish. But I would allow myself to be King if I knew it was absolutely the only way.

"King Henry is doing a poor job of the responsibility God gave him, but he can't help it. If he had wise or honest counsel, England wouldn't have the rending and upheaval that Warwick was relating to us."

"But, Father, why doesn't he have any good men around him?"

"He does have a few, but the Queen makes decisions for him and she has not chosen wisely."

"Is she a bad woman, Father?"

"Your mother says not." York smiled. "Perhaps

she isn't, but the Queen is young and not very wise. She hasn't grown up loving England as we have. She thinks she is trying to do the best for the King and herself, but she has too much pride to realize that what is good for England is good for the monarch." York rose and poured himself a glass of wine. "It would not be good for England to have another king pulled rudely to the dust like Edward the Second or Richard the Second."

Edward sat very still, puzzling over the statements his father had made. Finally he asked, "Father, the Queen has not borne a son and she's been a wife many years. Does that mean she will never have a child?"

"Son, you have pierced the heart of our present troubles. If there is no heir, or even if there is a royal son of the same stamp as the King—I shall have to be king." There was great weariness in York's voice.

"And what of the Duke of Somerset?" Edward asked.

"He is more closely related to the King than we are, but his entire line is illegitimate in origin. He has made no open move yet to contradict the law that the Beauforts are barred from succession, but I'm afraid he will eventually. I believe that Queen Margaret would favor the plan if she has no child. She has no great love for me and appears to hold Somerset in esteem. It must not happen!" York slammed the flat of his hand on the heavy table. "Somerset is the greediest of the greedy horde that is sucking at the lifeblood of England. If he were to squat upon the throne, there would be no safe corner for men who wish well for England." York leaned back and closed his eyes for a moment. "I'm sorry to overload you with my woes, Edward. Perhaps Warwick is right and you are too young."

"I think I understand, Father. My place is to stand by you and I shall be heir to your fortunes or misfortunes. I must know what they are."

"My son, you are fast growing to manhood, too fast for your own good, perhaps, but I have great pride in you."

The boy blushed and stammered, "Thank you, Father. Uh—Father, are you hungry?"

York burst out laughing. "Yes, I'm starving."

"If the Duke of York returns, certainly Charles will return with him," Ursula said, excitement lighting her pale eyes.

"Yes, and there will probably be an open outbreak of civil war," Blanche said more sharply than she meant to.

"No, the Duke of York would not rebel against King Henry," Ursula protested innocently.

"Ursula, nobody is rebelling against King Henry."

"Then what is all this about?" she asked.

How could Blanche explain that her own sister, the Queen, was mainly responsible for the danger they were all in, simply because she had flirted with the Duke of York once and consequently aligned herself with the wrong side of a deadly problem? "Never mind, Ursula, I'm not making sense. Don't worry, nothing will happen to anyone. I'm sorry I snapped at you."

Margaret entered the room with an air of suppressed agitation. "Excuse us, please," she said coldly to the other ladies, who all but fled. She took Blanche's arm in a tight grip and hissed, "Have you heard?"

"Heard what?"

Margaret threw her arms up in exasperation. "Don't be so thick-headed. You know what I'm talking about. Warwick . . . he's gone to Ireland!"

"He's not under any sort of arrest, is he? Why shouldn't he go to Ireland if it pleases him?"

"Oh, Blanche, you can be so stupid! The rebel army is ready. Warwick has gone to Ireland to get York to come back. They will try to take the throne from us."

"Meggie, there is one solution to this whole problem. If you had a son, no one could claim to be Henry's heir."

Margaret stiffened. "Blanche, you are really getting thick-headed. You know what happened the night we were married. Henry can't father children."

"All you know is that he couldn't father children *that* night. I think you should try again. Meggie, if many more years pass and especially if something should happen to King Henry, there will certainly be civil war. You must have a child."

"There will not be civil war," Margaret said, paying as much attention to Blanche's opinion as she usually did. "Only the crushing of a rebellion. Somerset can defeat York easily with the King's armies, if York rebels."

"Are the King's armies stronger than York's?" Blanche asked.

"They must be. They are the royal army."

"That doesn't mean anything. York is a rich man with many retainers to call upon. Besides, he won't rebel. I don't think he wants to be king in place of Henry."

"Blanche!" Margaret said, shaking her head. "Of course he wants to be King. By the way, Ursula's husband—what's his name?"

"Sir Charles Seintleger."

"Yes, Seintleger. He is with York, is he not?"

"I believe so," Blanche said cautiously.

"Keep close to her. She may receive some communication from her husband that would tell us if York is on his way." The thought of Margaret's regarding her as a spy gave Blanche a chill.

Blanche learned something that same week that should have alerted her to some of the tragedy the future held, but at the time it seemed merely interesting. Warwick was said to be a friend of York yet had served on the King's Council for a long time. She had often wondered how a Yorkist had gotten on the Council. In sorting rumors she learned that Warwick had not always supported York. In fact, he had thrown in his lot with York almost by default. Warwick's wife was a half-sister to the Duchess of Somerset. There had been an extremely large inheritance in dispute, which both Warwick and Somerset claimed on behalf of their respective wives. A vicious and heated argument had ensued. So, as with many political alliances, York and Warwick didn't have ideals in common; they had an enemy in common.

146

Margaret, Blanche, and Lady Alice were helping Elizabeth Woodville hem some serving napkins for Elizabeth's trousseau. Margaret had given the girl the fine linen. Even the militant Margaret sometimes liked to be engaged in mindless, relaxing activity like this, for it allowed her to forget that she was a childless queen married to a man she found contemptible. At these times she was simply a young woman, taking pride in her needlework and enjoying the ebb and flow of gentle chatter around her.

Lady Alice's eyes were beginning to fail and Margaret was helping her stitch around a corner when Lady Eleanor, the Duchess of Somerset, seemed to materialize at her side. Margaret was always disconcerted by the silent, almost invisible approach that Lady Eleanor practiced.

"Madam?" In one word the Duchess of Somerset managed to sound both critical and fawning.

"What is it, Lady Eleanor?" Margaret said. She was trying not to sound snappish, but she resented the unwelcome intrusion into her happy circle.

"Your majesty, I *only* wished to convey that my husband, the Duke, wishes audience with you." Lady Eleanor's right eyebrow had climbed halfway up her forehead.

"Very well, I shall see him in the next room. Blanche will accompany me."

"But, your majesty, I hardly think . . ." Eleanor began.

"Lady Eleanor, I am not soliciting opinions," Margaret said. "You may convey my message to your husband. Elizabeth, perhaps you could finish the part

147

that Lady Alice and I were working on."

"Certainly, your grace," Elizabeth mumbled. Her face was contorted by the effort to suppress a grin. She and the other young girls in the household privately referred to Lady Eleanor as "the bat" and were delighted on those rare occasions when someone managed to put her in her place.

As Blanche and Margaret entered the room, Somerset was critically examining a tapestry on the far wall. He looks like he's ready to ask what it costs, Blanche thought, taking note of the brightly colored hose and fur-trimmed cloak he wore. It annoyed her anew that the King's nobles flaunted great wealth and rich clothing, while the King's wife hadn't had a new dress since she was married.

"My lord, you wished to speak with me?" Margaret said in the soft, quiet voice that appealed to him.

"Why, your majesty, you took me quite by surprise." His long white hands fluttered about, illustrating, presumably, his surprise. "Pray let us sit over here," he said, making an elaborate gesture of escorting her to a chair by the window. "Madam, some information has come to my ears that I believe might be of some interest to you. There is, in Bristol, a lawyer named Thomas Young. He is a member of the House of Commons. He has, on occasion, represented the Duke of York in some legal matters."

"What has that to do with me? All the nobles have matters to discuss with lawyers from time to time." Margaret wished he would get to the point. He seemed to enjoy dispensing information drop by drop.

"But, your majesty, inquiries at the man's household reveal that he had gone to Fotheringay Castle."

"Fotheringay!" Margaret exclaimed. "That is York's castle. He isn't there. He is in Ireland."

"It would seem that Master Young had reasons, good reasons no doubt, for thinking York is at Fotheringay." Somerset gloated over the information.

"York must be stopped," Margaret said.

"But why, your majesty?" Somerset asked. Blanche was a little surprised, too. Was Margaret having a change of heart? "We are quite capable of dealing with him if he should turn up in London. I'm sure the King will accept our recommendations and send York back to Ireland in complete disgrace," Somerset said confidently.

"We underestimated York's influence once before. You were not here to witness how York manipulated the King. But perhaps you are right. We must wait and see what he intends to do." She rose to her feet and Somerset recognized his dismissal.

He picked up his green velvet hat with the long white plume and bowed to Margaret. The sisters went back to the other ladies and Margaret sat a little apart. Blanche watched her with concern, but said nothing. They went on with their sewing, but the gaiety had gone from the afternoon.

At dinner that night Margaret was pensive. Even a frenzied dog fight over a discarded bone under one of the long side tables failed to distract her. One of the knights tried to kick the dogs involved and, for his troubles, lost a piece of his ankle. Blanche noted with scorn that King Henry sent for a priest instead of a physician for the injured man. Blanche turned her attention to Somerset.

He never seemed to be still at meals except during the endless prayers and blessings that King Henry insisted on scattering throughout every meal. The rest of the time Somerset was on the move around the hall. He was circulating now. He had a large drumstick in his hand, which he used as a baton to emphasize his statements. He flitted from one group of men to another, wearing a fraudulent smile and gracefully waving his drumstick. Blanche was interested in the aftereffects of his conversations. As he left each little group, the men would either snicker or look very sullen.

They all dislike him, Blanche thought. Some of them hate him and others just think him mincing and silly, but they all dislike him to some degree. He couldn't hold these men's loyalties if York were here.

Blanche had been so deep in thought that she hadn't noticed that King Henry's chaplain, having finished giving spiritual solace to the hero of the dog fight, was intoning a final blessing on the conclusion of the meal. Margaret left the hall on King Henry's arm, as was customary. Once outside the room Henry invited her and her ladies to join him in his evening prayers, but she declined politely.

"My lord, do you pray for me?" Margaret asked impulsively.

King Henry looked surprised for a moment, then looked straight into her eyes and said, "Most fervently, my dear wife."

When Margaret and Blanche were alone later, Margaret said, "Isn't it strange? Most of the time Henry hasn't any idea of what's going on around him. Other times he seems to know the answers to questions no one else even knows enough to ask. I really want to like him, Blanche," she said in a trembling voice. "If only he would sometimes hold my hand or notice my appearance. Oh, well," she said, trying to shrug off her melancholy.

Blanche dreamed she was on a huge deserted field, a jousting field, perhaps. There were lances and banners stuck into the ground here and there, tilting and swaying at crazy angles. She couldn't move very well and discovered that she was wearing Margaret's pearl-encrusted wedding dress and over it—armor. Not a full suit, just the breastplate and helmet. The visor was down and she couldn't see very well. She tried to lift the heavy mask, but it would not move.

She looked down at her hands, but they weren't her hands, they were Margaret's. I must be Margaret now, she thought with the unreasoning that passes for logic in dreams, but part of me is still me. Just the outside is Margaret.

She could hear music, but was unable to place either the tune or the instruments. The music jingled and bounced and then a clanging element began to creep into the melody. At first it was barely perceptible, then it began to jangle and jar. More ugly sounds crept in. The music was gone. It was turning into a cacophony of horrible, rasping noises. She tried to cover her ears, or Margaret's ears—she wasn't sure whose head she had on—but the helmet prevented it.

The noises careened around inside the metal cage of the helmet.

Suddenly she recognized the sounds. It was dogs—snarling, growling, barking, yelping in pain. Then she saw them, an enormous pack of yellow dogs swirling ferociously around someone. She could catch only glimpses of the figure. It was King Henry.

He stood untouched in the middle of the mayhem. She saw him cross himself and heard him saying plaintively, "Make peace, my brothers, make peace among yourselves." Henry watched the dogs for a moment, then crossed himself again and repeated, "Make peace, my brothers, make peace among yourselves." He watched again for a moment. "Make peace . . ." he kept chanting.

In the distance there was another figure moving across the field. He sauntered along, moving between the flags and lances in an irregular course, almost as if he were dancing an elaborate dance of complex steps. As he neared, she recognized him. He was Richard of York. He was also Charles Seintleger. It didn't seem strange to her that he was both men. She simply accepted it just as she had accepted being both herself and Margaret. He seemed to see her. He swept off his hat, bowed, and smiled broadly.

It was the same smile she had seen on York and Charles first in M'antes years ago. She wanted him. She started to run to his arms, but couldn't move.

"Make peace, my brothers, make peace among yourselves," Henry still chanted. The dogs barked and circled and lunged.

Suddenly York was there in front of her, smiling. She reached for him. He stepped closer and closer still. Blanche was Margaret and he was York. She could see Charles and Blanche standing together talking over York's shoulder. She thought, incuriously, there I am—over there.

She strained against the armor to feel his body next to hers, but all she felt was the cold metal of the armor biting her flesh. She pulled him closer and tighter. She tried to kiss him, but she was trapped inside the helmet.

"Make peace, my brothers . . ."

"Richard," she cried, "oh, Richard."

His smile faded. His face came closer to the slits in the visor and he hissed, "Bitch!"

"Make peace, my brothers . . ."

She reeled back, stunned. The hateful insult echoed around inside the helmet. Then she was Blanche again, watching Margaret standing stunned, watching York stride away in the direction from which he had come. She was standing with Charles. She was wearing only a nightshift and his coarse, manly cloak.

There was a crowd standing on the field now and York had gone to join them. The people in the crowd each had a glass of wine in one hand and a drumstick in the other. They were shouting and laughing and pointing the drumsticks at Margaret; they were laughing at her sister! Cecily was there and she and Richard of York were locked in a feverish embrace.

Then, as quickly and unexpectedly as the people had gathered, they dispersed, running away, laughing at Margaret as they went.

"Make peace, my brothers. Make peace among yourselves."

Blanche tried to run to Margaret to protect her

153

from some danger she knew was about to attack her. Charles held her back. She struggled, but he grasped her hand. Then Ursula was there, too, pulling Charles away. Blanche got free of his grip and was suddenly smaller. She ran to Margaret. She yanked the visor off Margaret's head and they clung together.

Blanche looked down and saw a change in the ground upon which they stood. Something was oozing up around Margaret's feet. She took a step and it began oozing where she now stood. She began to walk frantically, trying to find a solid place to stand. Blanche followed her. Then she realized that the substance flowing from the ground was blood. Blood flowing out of Margaret's footsteps. Blanche felt the hot, iron smell attack her nostrils.

The dogs were there again. They had stopped fighting and were following them, lapping up the blood. Margaret stopped running around and clung to Blanche. Blanche looked for Charles. He wasn't there. No one was there. She called out for him, but there was no answer.

Suddenly she noticed the dogs. With terrifying precision they all looked at Blanche at once and a second later they jumped. She fell to the ground with Margaret still clinging to her and could feel the dogs tearing at their clothes, hot canine breath in her face.

"Make peace, my brothers . . ."

"Charles, help me . . ."

"Make peace, my brothers . . ."

"Blanche, Blanche, please wake up," Charles was saying.

No, it wasn't Charles. He had turned into Lady Alice. Blanche screamed and flailed her arms to fight off the dogs but there weren't any dogs. The dogs were gone.

She began to realize it had been a dream. She was in her room, not a jousting field. She had fallen out of bed in her struggles.

"My dear Blanche. Are you all right now?" Lady Alice asked. Blanche was crying. Alice brought her some wine and opened a little leather pouch. She took a pinch of powder from the pouch and put it in the wine. "This can't harm you, but it will help you sleep. There now, drink it all up. That's right. Now lie back. Don't worry, it was just a bad dream."

The King and Queen sat upon their thrones in the reception hall. The large, drafty room was practically deserted. Margaret had seen to it that there were few observers there to hear what might transpire. Blanche had no idea what was going to happen except that this was to be an official reception for the Duke of York. Blanche's thoughts were on who might be with York.

"Richard, Duke of York," the chamberlain announced. Margaret gripped the arms of her chair, steeling herself against—what? Blanche tried not to look about too frantically to see if Charles was with York. She didn't need to look far; he was right behind York, looking angry and tired. He glanced at her and she could discern a faint, very faint, smile.

"Your majesties," York said, bowing low to Henry

and then to Margaret. But in his look at Margaret, Blanche could see a hard, knowing glint. He finally hates her, Blanche thought.

"Welcome, cousin," King Henry said. "The Lord's blessing be upon you. Though we are heartily pleased to see you, pray tell why you have left your post in Ireland. Is there some trouble that has not come to our ears?"

"Your majesty, my commission to Ireland stipulates that I may reenter England if there is an emergency. I thought the recent uprising and current discontent were sufficient reason for me to come to you and most humbly offer my services to you," York explained.

King Henry nodded, still smiling. As much as Blanche hungered for the sight of Charles, she couldn't keep her eyes off the scene being played out by York and Margaret and Henry. She had a deep sense of foreboding, as if there were something dangerous in the air. It made her feel frightened and defenseless. York was angry in spite of his smiling grace. Charles was glaring about something. Margaret looked extremely nervous and King Henry . . . King Henry was beaming fatuously. He had no idea anything was wrong.

"But I believe there is trouble that has not come to your ears," York said to the King. His gaze went to Margaret for a fraction of a second. Her fingers involuntarily tightened on the chair arm.

"Pray, what trouble, cousin?" King Henry asked.

"When I landed, and at several points along my way, I was variously detained and impeded by men claiming they were ordered to prevent me from coming to London."

"By whose orders did they claim to do so?"

"By your orders, sire."

"What? I have not given any such orders. I would not have prevented you even if I had known you were on your way. How were these orders signed?"

"They were signed in your name, your majesty, but lacked your seal. Thus I was able to convince the men trying to stop me that the orders were not legal."

"Dear kinsman, I am disturbed and alarmed at this news," King Henry said. "You acted wisely to ignore this treachery."

"There is more I must tell you, sire. Along the way a man unknown to me infiltrated himself among my retainers." York made "retainers" sound like a handful of friends, though he had arrived in London with two thousand men of his private army. "One night this scoundrel entered my tent while my guards were sleeping outside. He took me to be asleep as well and approached me stealthily with dagger drawn. But I had heard him and was awake. As he lunged for me, I grabbed his wrist and deflected the weapon. The shuffle woke the guards. They were overwrought and unfortunately killed the villain before I could question him." York had told his story dramatically and King Henry was literally on the edge of his seat when York finished.

"Fair cousin, did you escape unharmed from this incident?"

"Yes, sire. God was with me."

"Let us thank our Gracious Lord for your safety. Who was the man?"

York darted a glance at Margaret. Blanche could see a flush creep up her neck. "The man was in the service of the late Duke of Suffolk, my lord. He was identified to me as a trusted servant of Lady Alice, the Duchess of Suffolk," York said.

King Henry turned to Margaret with one of his rare shrewd looks. "My lady, what do you know of this?" he lisped in an almost accusing tone.

"My lord, what do you suppose *I* would know of such matters?" she answered haughtily. "Although I do recall that Lady Alice mentioned that a longtime servant of hers had disappeared recently after she had severely reprimanded him."

Everyone was silent. Blanche knew York didn't believe her—Blanche didn't believe her and doubted that even King Henry was fooled. But no one would dare openly insult the Queen by questioning her explanation. King Henry said, "Cousin, you have a solution to our present unrest?"

"I'm not sure," York hedged. "But if you were to summon a meeting of Parliament and let the grievances be aired, perhaps a solution might be found."

"Ah—what an excellent thought," Henry said, as if summoning Parliament was a novel idea. It hadn't been suggested in his hearing because Margaret and Somerset had learned that Parliament was unsympathetic to them and gaining in power. Margaret feared the consequences of summoning the Lords and Commons. After all, the last time they met, it had meant Suffolk's death.

"If I may suggest it, my lord, I shall retire to my home at Fotheringay while Parliament is in session," York said.

"What? You will not attend though the meeting is your own idea? Pray, why not?"

"Your majesty, I have learned, to my great distress, that there are those who claim that I have some evil connection with the uprising in Kent. They claim, falsely, that I would do you harm."

"No! Who dares say such things?"

"I know not their names, my lord," York said. He didn't look at Queen Margaret this time. He didn't need to. "If I were to attend this Parliament, such people would undoubtedly give out the lie that I am trying to control its workings to some foul design of my own," York said.

"Certainly not. Men of good will could not think such a thing."

"Your majesty, your faith in your countrymen is charitable, but not all Englishmen are men of good will. The people are overwrought. They are willing to believe any manner of thing."

"Aye, 'tis sad, but I suppose I must agree with you," Henry said mournfully. "I only wish that all my countrymen were as sensible and loyal as you."

"My lord and kinsman, I am pleased that you recognize that I am your true liegeman and subject, for upon my honor, I am."

Henry was surprised. "But, my lord Richard, I never doubted it—never."

"There are many who would wish you to think me a traitor," York said.

"Then, fair cousin, let them not suggest it to me!" Henry said irritably. "I think I should make some public affirmation of my faith in you, if that is the case. I wonder how I should go about it?"

With stunning simplicity York said, "You could appoint me to the Council."

Margaret almost jumped to her feet in protest, but managed to refrain with a visible effort.

"The Council?" Henry was beginning to feel the strain of the conversation and was getting confused. "Oh, yes, the Council. But you are already on the Council, aren't you?"

"No, my lord."

"I meet with the Council so seldom I hardly know. Well, then, you shall be on the Council. I shall see to it now. I will give orders for Parliament to convene in two months' time. Are you sure you will not attend?"

"No, I cannot."

"Very well, but you must remain in London for Council meetings."

When the interview was over, York bowed again to King Henry and lingered over Margaret's outstretched hand. "Your majesty, I can't tell you what pleasure it has been to me to see you again." The sarcasm was not lost.

Blanche delayed leaving the hall so she could walk out with Charles. Her heart still pounded at the mere sight of him, but she was beginning to accept the fact that he could never be anything but a friend, the husband of a young woman who was very dear to her. She was pleased to have him as a friend if she could not have him as husband or lover.

"How does Ursula fare?" he asked.

160

"She is well, or at least better. I'm glad you didn't send for her to join you. Her health is fragile and I think a winter in Ireland would have done her great harm."

"How can I thank you for caring so well for her?"

"You cannot, for I do it for her as much as for you. You underestimate me. I am not a petty woman —to hate her for having you. I am very fond of her."

"Remember how simple life seemed in M'antes when we walked together in the town?" Charles said wistfully.

"What is going to happen now?" Blanche asked.

"To us?"

"No. Nothing is ever going to happen with us," she said firmly. "With York and the King."

"I don't know. If the Queen would send Somerset away and let the Duke of York have his rightful place in advising the King, nothing would happen."

"That will not be," Blanche said.

"Not with her consent, you mean."

"If only you and I could tell everyone else how to run the world . . ." Blanche said, trying to coax a smile from him.

He didn't seem to hear her. "She tried to have him killed, you know." His voice shook with anger.

"In a war, the object is to kill your enemy," Blanche said. "The Queen regards herself as at war with York." She knew it to be a reason and not an excuse. She also knew that deep inside she was as outraged as Charles was at the revelation of Margaret's plotting.

"How could she!" Charles nearly shouted. "He is

the finest man in England. He loves this country as she never could. She is a foreigner and a woman at that. What right has she . . ."

"Sire! You speak of your Queen. You also demean *my* origin and sex. Take care what you say." Blanche never thought she could speak to him in anger. It came surprisingly easy.

"I forgot myself. Please forgive me. I would never slight *you*. But you are an exception."

"How so?"

"You aren't French anymore. You have taken English ways and care for the country as if you were native-born. As for being a woman"—he gave her a comically leering look—"you have the body for it, but you have a man's mind."

"A man's mind?" Blanche wasn't sure whether she was being flattered or insulted.

"Yes, you think clearly and speak forthrightly. You have courage and can see beyond your immediate circumstances."

"Those are qualities of a man? Must women be stupid and timid and shortsighted?"

"No. They shouldn't be, but most are. 'Tis a pity, too."

"Come along. Ursula will be waiting for you and I must attend the Queen," she said, fearful lest this conversation lead to her saying something coy and stupid.

"Does the Queen listen to you at all?" he asked.

"Not at all. And she never will. Look, there is Ursula. Go to her."

He kissed her hand courteously and strode away.

To her disgust she realized she was trembling and her knees were weakened by the slight contact, a polite gesture, nothing more, and yet she could still feel his lips on her hand. A man's brain indeed! she snorted to herself.

CHAPTER SEVEN

Cecily Neville was in her bedchamber at Fotheringay. She had spent the morning with her maids, bringing the summer clothes out of the presses and airing them in the courtyard and on the parapets. She had washed out her long hair and rinsed it in herb-scented water. She brushed it until it was dry and shining, then twisted it into a gleaming rope to wrap around her head.

She put on a fresh summer dress and wondered once again why getting out summer clothes always made her feel so much younger. She wished Richard were at home to enjoy the balmy day with her, but he was still in London. He had kept to his original plan of not attending Parliament, but he stayed in London for most of the winter and spring, having private talks with those who were attending. She had heard little from him. Letters were too easily intercepted.

She anticipated his return and the return of her sons Edward and Edmund. Richard had taken them with him this time, saying it was time for them to start getting their "real" education. But the waiting should soon be over. Parliament had been in session for more than half a year. Cecily sat on the edge of the high bed, thinking about what sort of dress she should have made for Richard's homecoming, when there was a tap at the door.

"Come in," she called, expecting baby George's nurse.

An unexpected voice answered, "Hello, Mother."

"Edward! What are you doing here?" She ran to him and hugged him. In the back of her mind she registered how much taller he'd grown. "Is your father with you? And Edmund?"

"They are on their way. Some of our tenants were in the village as we came through. Father stopped to talk to them about some problems planting the spring crops. Father asked me to ride ahead and tell you he is on the way. Edmund is with him."

"But I wasn't expecting you at all. Why didn't you send word when Parliament adjourned?"

"Mother, Parliament adjourned rather abruptly," Edward said angrily. "Father will want to tell you all about it."

Richard of York and Edmund arrived shortly after Edward, and the whole family was together for the evening meal for the first time in many months. Cecily and her daughters commented on how the boys had grown. Richard asked about little George's progress, Edmund questioned Cecily about affairs of the manor, but no one mentioned Parliament or what had brought the family together so suddenly. Cecily could tell that Richard's interest wasn't on the dinner discussion.

He will tell me when he's ready to, she thought. But she was worried. If the news were good, he would be telling us all about it now.

As if reading her thoughts, Richard said, "If we are all finished eating, I wish to talk to your mother. Edward? Edmund? Do you wish to join us?"

166

"No, thank you, Father," Edmund replied. "If you don't mind I would rather take a ride around the grounds while there is still some light. I long for the odor of hay instead of people."

"You don't need us, Father," Edward said. "I'll get the horses saddled, Edmund."

The girls dutifully departed as well. Richard sat watching them go. "They are beautiful children, Cis," he said, giving her an appraising look. "If you keep staying so young and pretty, I may father a few more of them for you."

She smiled at him. "I'll bear all the babes you want, Richard, but you'll have to stay home more often. Tell me, what are you doing here?"

"Ah, Cis. 'Twas a waste. The Commons spent months making plans for financial reform. They labored hard and long. I helped all I could, of course. They were goodly plans. They would have worked."

"What happened?" Cecily asked.

"Henry rejected them all—every one."

"For what reason?"

"He gave no reason. He had none. Naturally he couldn't understand even the simplest of the measures. Somerset and the Queen tell him the plans are bad and he takes their word. Perhaps they don't even tell him. All the Parliament received in reply were messages purportedly from him."

"Couldn't you explain to him at Council meetings?"

"Cis, during the entire winter he attended only one meeting of the Council—the first. And then he stayed only long enough to open the meeting with a prayer. He left, saying that Somerset would apprise him of our wishes. That set a precedent. For after that Somerset just sat through the meetings watching like a fox. If the Council reached a decision, he would say he would ask the King about it. A few minutes later he would be back with the word that the King approved. If Somerset didn't like the idea, he would come back and say the King rejected it."

"But, Richard, I still don't understand why you are home early."

"Last week King Henry attended a session in the House of Commons, as has been his habit from time to time. Normally he just sat through the session— bored and glassy-eyed—but this session caught his interest."

"What happened?" Cecily dreaded the answer. She knew from the drawn look on Richard's face that the answer concerned him deeply.

"Do you remember Thomas Young?"

"Yes, he's that young lawyer friend of yours who stayed here for a few days last year, isn't he?"

"Yes, Thomas was representing Bristol in the Commons this year. He got up and recommended that King Henry, being without an heir of his body, should name his successor."

"What did King Henry say to that?"

"He didn't say anything. I'm told he just sat there blinking for a minute, then began to tremble. He suddenly got up and blundered out of the room. A little later the sergeant-at-arms came in and arrested Young."

"Oh no!"

"I had no idea he would react that way. I knew that Somerset would explode when he heard, but Young thought if the problem was brought up in public when

Somerset dared not protest, Henry might agree. Later in the day Henry sent a decree that Parliament was dismissed. So here I am—in disgrace."

"What about Thomas Young?"

"Don't worry, Cis. Warwick's spy in the Tower of London says that Young's arrest order specified that Young be released as soon as the members of Parliament are all out of London. He is in no danger."

"What now, Richard?"

York didn't answer for a moment. It was as if he was having trouble finding the words. Finally he said, "England must get rid of Somerset and I must be King Henry's heir."

"But you don't want to be King, Richard." Cecily's voice quavered.

"No, Cis, I don't. But I doubt that poor Henry will live a long life, and if Somerset should become King . . ." He shrugged. "England could not survive another reign of greed and civil dissension. Somerset is practically King now, and look at the disruption that rends the land."

"Queen Margaret is young. Perhaps she will bear a son," Cecily said, knowing she was grasping at straws.

"That isn't likely. I'm told the palace gossip is that they have not shared a bed since their wedding night. But what if she did have a child, Cis? What kind of son would King Henry father? Henry is simple-minded. His French grandfather was a lunatic. His English grandfather was an old man obsessed with hate and suspicion when he was but forty. What chance of a normal son? The Lancaster line is diseased. It is dying."

"I understand, Richard." Cecily got up from the

table. "It's getting dark and you are weary. Come to bed."

A little later, stretched out on the wide bed with a cool spring breeze bathing them, Cecily said, "What are you going to do next?"

"I can do nothing until I can build up a large force with which to attack Somerset. Force is the only way left to deal with him. It will take months." Richard turned to Cecily and took her in his arms. "But for now . . ." He kissed her with the passion borne of long months of separation.

When Parliament dissolved and Richard of York departed for his estates, Sir Charles Seintleger and Ursula went with him. Blanche was sorry to see Ursula leave. She loved her and was accustomed to Ursula's placid personality neutralizing the effect of Margaret's bad temper. Their parting was tearful, for neither knew when and if they would meet again. But after they were gone, Blanche realized that there was a certain relief. During the entire time Parliament had been in session, Charles had been frequently in Blanche's company rather than just on her mind. It had been a strain.

Nearly every time Charles was free of his duties, Ursula insisted on inviting her friend Blanche to share some of their time together. Blanche could not have turned down the invitations very often without either offending Ursula by suggesting that she disliked Charles or destroying her by admitting her love of him. So she accompanied them on walks and picnics and intimate little dinners for three.

Each meeting was agony for Blanche. They went on a picnic by a lovely little stream, and after eating, Blanche went to rinse her plate and cup in the stream —suddenly she was overcome with the memories of France and Charles. She had to grip the cup until the handle nearly cut her hand to keep from weeping. They went for a walk and Ursula said to Charles that he walked too fast and her feet were tired. Blanche had told him the same thing in Rouen when they had gone to see where Joan of Arc was burned. They all stood on the parapets of the castle one day looking out over the city. It was chilly, and when Blanche shivered slightly, Ursula asked Charles to lend Blanche his cloak. "No!" Blanche had shouted before catching herself. Ursula had been alarmed and brought Blanche a posset that evening, thinking her ill.

Toward the end of Parliament, Blanche began to fear that Ursula sensed that there was something wrong, and she prayed nightly that Ursula would never know what it was. Then Parliament was abruptly terminated and Charles left, taking Ursula with him and leaving Blanche, her emotions in tatters, to recover.

Blanche managed to avoid having a private goodby with Charles, though he was trying to bring one about. She knew that to speak to him, to feel his touch or kiss, would be unbearably painful. So she developed a headache on the day before their departure and recovered just in time to tell them both Godspeed as they left.

Jane Seintleger stayed on, a decision that Blanche was unhappy about for several reasons. She had never spoken to Jane about Charles since the first day Jane arrived at court, but this was mainly because Blanche was very careful never to be alone with Jane. But Jane watched her carefully, behaving like a self-appointed watchdog to Ursula's happiness. So their relationship was cool and just barely cordial.

Until Brithric came to court.

His name was Brithric de Bohun, and though his kinship to King Henry was distant, he proclaimed himself a staunch supporter of the King. Brithric had immediately taken a liking to Blanche. Unfortunately Jane had taken a liking to Brithric. Blanche, consumed by her problems with Charles and Ursula, had been unaware of the situation at first.

Brithric was of old Saxon stock and was named for an ancestor who had lived (and died violently) during the reign of William the Conqueror. He was striking-looking, with almost snow-white hair and an excellent physique. He had an animated manner that made the stories he told a delight. The young people at court loved to hear his tales and he was called to entertain his friends often, for he had many friends.

He wasn't extremely tall, but he carried himself with such confidence that he seemed so. He dressed beautifully, almost extravagantly, in bright colors and flashing jewels. But unlike such men as Somerset, Brithric de Bohun dressed for his own enjoyment and never seemed to care what anyone else thought of his appearance. He was polite when other young men of the court complimented him, but he didn't seem to notice the envious looks they cast at his muscular legs in tight hose that always fit and were never patched or torn. There was nothing of the fop about him, however. His face was rugged and his sun-spun hair was thick. It wasn't until Charles had left that Blanche noticed how very attractive Brithric was. He asked her to walk with him in the gardens and she found that he could be serious as well as funny and she enjoyed talking with him.

It wasn't until they came back from a walk by the river one afternoon and Blanche noticed Jane Seintleger at an upper window glaring down at her that she began to realize what was happening, at least in Jane's eyes. Blanche tried to avoid Brithric for a while that day, but she felt a great need for companionship like his—light-hearted, uninvolved—and was drawn back into his circle of friends.

Blanche could see why Jane was especially drawn to Brithric. They were much alike, popular with their peers, good storytellers. But Jane's admiration of Brithric was in itself spoiling her good disposition. There was a brooding intensity in Jane's nature, waiting for a man to bring it to the surface. Normally Blanche would have taken greater care to disentangle herself from a situation that boded harm to someone else, but she needed her friendship with Brithric to relieve her own distress. Besides, Jane didn't like her. Why should she deny herself for Jane's sake?

Charles noticed the change in Jane and was worried about it, too. "Ursula, I am concerned about my sister. She seems unhappy," he said one night.

"She is much taken with Brithric de Bohun."

"I mislike seeing her so fond of a man who is such a strong adherent of the King."

"Oh, Charles, don't say that. It sounds so—dangerous. You do not oppose the King, do you?"

"No. Of course not. I only oppose the policies of

his cousin, Somerset. I only meant that I would hate to see her align herself with a family with which I may someday find myself in conflict. If his people support Somerset, that could happen."

"Let us pray that will never happen, for it would mean I too would be aligned against my friend Blanche," Ursula fretted. "But I don't think you need to worry about Jane and Brithric."

"Why is that?"

"Because I fancy Brithric prefers Blanche."

"What?" Charles asked sharply.

"Yes, he is much in her company. I have noticed him watch her and I think he is in love with her. They make a handsome couple," Ursula said.

Charles brought the subject up later when they were with Blanche. "Nay, he is but a courteous young man," Blanche said. "I mean naught to him, nor he to me."

"I do think he is fond of you, Blanche," Ursula said.

"You are a romantic, Ursula," she replied.

"Perhaps Ursula is right," Charles said rather curtly.

Blanche's nerves were frayed and the idea of the three of them discussing this was almost unbearable to her. "What if he is in love with me?" she snapped. "Is it so impossible to imagine that a handsome young man might love me? He might even ask for my hand."

"That would be lovely," Ursula said. "I would come to your wedding and help you with your trousseau," she went on, apparently oblivious to Charles and Blanche exchanging glares.

174

Is this what it has come to? Blanche wondered. Shall we turn against one another, since we cannot turn to each other? Can there be no middle ground? She had thought once that if Margaret could not love a man, she would come to hate him instead and it had happened. Was the same thing to happen to her? Would the aching happiness she had felt years ago with Charles petrify into hate for the same man? No, it could never be. She still felt her breath catch when his hand brushed hers.

When the Duke of York asked Charles to accompany him to Fotheringay, Blanche went to Margaret to request that Jane Seintleger be sent with her brother and sister-in-law. She told herself it was for Charles's sake, to keep Jane from becoming involved with Brithric. But she didn't even believe it herself.

"No," Margaret answered, to Blanche's surprise. "The girl has spoken to me just this morning. She asked especially that she be allowed to stay here. She admitted an affection for young de Bohun, and I think since he is such a strong adherent to the King's cause, it would be well to encourage the liaison."

"Why?"

"Why? That is obvious, Blanche. Sir Charles Seintleger, your good friend, I might add, is in the pay of the Duke of York. If his sister is wed to the Lancaster side, he may not be such a strong soldier of the Yorks. Any way that I can weaken even one link in their army is to my advantage," Margaret said coldly.

"Then you care naught for Jane's happiness or her family's?"

"Why should I? *I'm* not in love with any of them."

So Margaret knew, she remembered. And still she would not agree to Blanche's request. "Very well," Blanche said with suppressed fury.

Jane stayed at court. She watched Blanche more closely than ever, but now it was in her own interests rather than to protect Ursula. The next six months went slowly for Blanche. She felt sure that a confrontation between York and Lancaster was imminent; it was spoken of almost openly at court. Brithric was kind and interested in her, but did not press for her attention. All Blanche could do was tread carefully between Margaret's tantrums and Jane's cold eye. And small wonder that Brithric's easygoing company became more and more of a refuge.

One day he said to her, "I wonder what you would say if I were to ask for your hand. No, wait, don't answer. I am not asking, I am merely wondering aloud what might happen *if* I asked."

"I'm not sure," Blanche said honestly.

"Then I shall not ask—not now. I will ask later," Brithric said and changed the subject. He didn't bring it up again.

Blanche gave the conversation much thought. Why not marry him? She liked him well enough and he would make a good husband. Margaret would raise no objections if she would remain at court. Brithric was kind and wealthy and he seemed to care for her. He was a pleasant companion. He was the one person in the world whose presence soothed her rather than distressed her. She could never marry her true love—so why not marry Brithric?

But she could not. She liked Brithric too well to

wish him a wife who loved another. He deserved someone like Jane, who would give him a whole heart. Blanche was relieved that he didn't ask again.

"But, your majesty," Somerset said, "I don't believe it is necessary for you to risk the cold to come with us."

"My lord Duke, may I remind you that the King and I are in command of the royal army?" Margaret was tired and cold and it was difficult to conceal her irritation. "If it were not for your inability to cope with Richard of York, we would not be getting prepared to go marching about the countryside in the dead of winter. Imagine, one English duke declaring a war on another! The King cannot allow that to be done. You might just as well turn your country back to the Danes. No, the King must settle this and I must be with him."

Blanche and Jane were riding in the carriage with Margaret, and Blanche wished she had the authority to speak to Margaret about her treatment of Somerset. Blanche didn't like Somerset, but Margaret was as much to blame for the conflict between York and Lancaster as he was. Although York had officially declared war on Somerset, everyone knew that he meant the Queen as well. It was foolish to offend one's allies, and Somerset must have despised being spoken to as a servant, especially in front of Blanche and Jane.

Blanche supposed that he consoled himself with the knowledge that Margaret knew in her own heart that she was to blame as much as he. Their fates had become interwoven. Neither dared abandon the other. Somerset twitched back a lock of fine hair that had fallen in his eyes. "Just as you wish, your majesty." He turned his horse and rode to his wife's side.

Blanche watched him talk with the Duchess of Somerset, whom Blanche had disliked for so many years—ever since Margaret had been forced to go to her for a loan when she was a bride. So long ago— no, it seemed a lifetime ago, but it was only eight years. Margaret had changed so much in those years. All her worst traits had become accentuated and her best qualities were gradually disappearing. But the Duchess of Somerset had changed little. She still had the same cold, superior expression—and *she* had a son.

Blanche surveyed the snowy landscape and tried to pick out King Henry. He was remarkably successful at fading into a crowd. There he was, in the midst of a group of gentlemen, staring out of newly made armor with a mournful, confused look. Blanche felt a moment of compassion for this strange, sad man, who, if he had ever done his duty on the field of battle or in bed, wouldn't be standing about in the snow sending an army out to capture one man. He had failed Margaret as much as he had failed his country. With another man she might have mellowed rather than sharpened with the years. She once had the potential to be a loving person, Blanche thought.

Finally, goodbys done and wagons loaded, the great army lumbered away from London, out to meet Richard of York. Blanche noticed that Jane had realized what it was to love a man who is going to war. She kept watching the army, trying to keep Brithric in sight. When he would occasionally ride nearer and signal acknowledgment of the Queen's carriage, Jane would beam and relax for a while. She thinks he's waving at her, Blanche thought.

The royal army camped at Blackheath. They had expected to meet York's forces before arriving. It was snowing and Margaret, still unused to the damp cold of English winters, had returned to the warm tent that had been set up for her. That was why she wasn't with King Henry when the message came from Richard of York.

He was not ahead of them in their path. His armies had circled around and were behind them. The King's army was cut off from any flight back to London and safety. York sent word to the King that he wished his sovereign no harm, that his dispute was only with the Duke of Somerset.

King Henry, temporarily unencumbered by the immediate presence of either Somerset or the Queen, sent back word that he would like to talk with York.

York replied that he would disband his army and speak with the King if the Duke of Somerset was arrested first.

Henry agreed.

Margaret was in her tent and Somerset was busy getting the camp set up for the night.

King Henry sent two knights to arrest Somerset.

Then Margaret found out what was happening. "My dear husband," she was saying to King Henry within moments, "please reconsider. You have arrested our dearest friend without even hearing a charge against him. If you must discuss this with your cousin York, then at least wait until you have heard the Duke of Somerset before you consider arresting him." She knew she had to be careful, for if King Henry became adamant, it would be awkward to countermand his orders herself.

"I suppose you may be right," Henry said wearily, "but I have given Richard a promise of safety."

"Yes, of course. He has taken a rash course, but when you explain to him that you trust your kinsman Somerset, I'm sure York will give you no more trouble. Of course he will be safe. Perhaps he would be even safer if you sent him back to Ireland. Some of your friends here might not be so tolerant of all the trouble he has caused you." Margaret stopped. Henry didn't appear to be listening to her, but perhaps the seed she had dropped would take root later. Better not push him. One thing at a time.

So King Henry ordered Somerset's release and in a short time Richard of York arrived in the royalist camp. He felt naked without his army. Warwick had argued bitterly against letting the men go, but York had insisted. After all, he had Henry's word that Somerset had been arrested and that was all he had wished. York was escorted to Henry's house (a farmer's cottage, which had the bad fortune to have been built years ago in the middle of the field where the army was now camped. It had been converted to a sort of headquarters). York bowed before his King.

"My lord King and beloved cousin," York began, "I am honored that you would see me and hear my pleas for England's welfare. I am here on behalf of many of your loving subjects whose hearts are torn by the knowledge that you are placing your faith in a man so unworthy of it."

"I place my faith only in God and His Holy Son."

"I meant your faith regarding worldly matters. Sire, the Duke of Somerset has ill-advised you many times. He cares nothing for the good of England. He cares only for what will profit him and his friends. The country is full of corrupt sheriffs and judges. The people are rebelling. This man is a traitor to you, my lord, he is a traitor to all of us who love England."

York was interrupted by a door opening from the next room. Somerset stood in the doorway. York glared at the King, who looked as startled as York was to find Somerset in their midst.

"You dare call me traitor?" Somerset raged in his high, womanish voice. "You dare that? You who would rob our King of his birthright, who would put yourself on his throne? You dare talk of *me* as a traitor?"

"I would not willingly put myself on any throne and well you know it. It is not *I* who seek a crown. It is not *I* who misgoverned in our French possessions and lost Normandy!" York shouted. He turned to the King. "And it was not *I* who gave my word to arrest this man and failed to honor the promise."

King Henry had shrunk back into his chair and was staring at them. His mouth was slack and his eyes were glistening. Tears began to trickle down his pale cheeks.

Somerset and York both realized at once that Henry hadn't understood the words of their argument, only the tone of hatred.

"Please, my cousins," he whimpered, "do not abuse one another. God's children must love one another." He reached inside his cloak and pulled out a rosary of wooden beads, polished and worn with handling. He began to pray quietly in a trembling voice. Somerset, as if incensed by the sight, went out the door, slamming it behind him.

York stood for a moment watching Henry as he had once watched the caged beasts at the Tower of London when he was a child. He felt the same pity for Henry that he had felt for the animals in the stone-lined pits.

"All for naught," he muttered to himself and slowly walked away.

Outside, the afternoon was dying. A cold, bleak sun clung to the horizon. Two soldiers approached. "My lord Duke," one said, "you are under arrest."

"On whose orders?" York asked.

"Her majesty the Queen."

"Then please tell King Henry before you take me anywhere," York said.

The soldier nodded knowingly and went into the farmer's cottage. When he came out a few minutes later, he said, "Pray forgive me, sire, there was a mistake. I am to escort you to your own camp."

182

CHAPTER EIGHT

The beginning of the devastating series of civil wars that historians would label the Wars of the Roses had been postponed. Perhaps a heavy foreboding of the mayhem they were about to perpetrate drove the principals back a step. Perhaps it was merely chance that led everyone back to his own affairs for more than a year. Richard of York returned to Fotheringay and the management of his estates. Late in the year word came to court that Richard's wife, Cecily, had given birth to another son. It was a difficult delivery and Cecily felt it would be her last child. She implored Richard to let her name the baby for him. Richard had been reluctant to pass his name along, but since it meant so much to his wife, he agreed and they named the baby Richard, mercifully unaware that England would someday call him Richard the Third and revile his name for centuries afterward.

The King and Queen went traveling. Early in life Henry had concluded that in times of trouble all the common man needed to alleviate his problems was a good close look at his sovereign. Henry believed utterly in his divine right to rule and appeared to think that the only responsibility it entailed was a duty to travel about and be seen. Margaret didn't agree with the philosophy but didn't raise any objections because it relieved the boredom of simply marking time, waiting for some fresh crisis to break. So every few weeks the court would gather their belongings, load them on carriages and carts, and ride off to impose themselves on another long-suffering peer of the realm.

And it *was* an imposition. "The court" usually consisted of scores of people. There were the King and Queen, their friends, advisors, and occasional enemies. All these privileged people required an army of retainers and servants. They took along their doctors, hairdressers, seamstresses, cooks, priests, nursemaids, musicians, scullery maids, clerks, and general errand runners. There were the men who looked after the horses and equipment. It took several people to arrange for the transportation and care of the falcons. The castles they visited were vast and largely unfurnished except for the few rooms that the residents used, so travelers took along their own furniture— beds, chests, clothes presses, and tapestries to hang as protection from the damp stone walls. Someone had to be there to move these items. There were craftsmen along to mend broken chair legs, reshoe horses, replace broken bow strings and harp strings.

And so "the court" moved on, depleting the supplies and patience of one host after another. All summer and fall they traveled. At Christmas they settled into one of the King's own castles. Margaret had learned to avoid Henry at Christmas. He observed the holiday as a strictly religious occurrence. He didn't actually forbid festivities, but managed by his frosty disapproval to cast a pall over any merriment. The day after Christmas was unusually warm and Margaret longed for the fresh air, but as she looked from the narrow windows of her room, she saw that the courtyard was a sea of mud, seething with dogs and children. Perhaps there was a peaceful place out on the parapets where she could sit in the open and write some letters.

"Come, Blanche, let us see where we can find a quiet place to sit," she said. Blanche was glad to leave the roomful of chattering ladies-in-waiting. She and Margaret were getting along well these days and the idea of a quiet visit between sisters was appealing. They found a stairway and went up. But it didn't lead outside, only into a long, dark hallway on the upper floor.

They wandered down the hall, searching for another stairway and feeling much as they had when they were girls exploring René's domain. Halfway down the hall a door flew open. A ragged woman, obviously a servant, stood there.

"You have come to see the Duchess, milady," she stated, rather than asked. "She is expecting you." The servant stood aside and Margaret and Blanche saw a woman sitting in a thronelike chair by the window. She was dressed in a coarse, homespun garment and her graying hair was in a tight braid wound severely around her head. Her face, though pale and lined, was lovely—regal and fey at once.

Both Blanche and Margaret felt fear and fascination. Who was this "Duchess" in the high, lonely room? They realized later how dangerous it might have been to enter that isolated cell, but Margaret was curious and went in and Blanche, not willing to abandon her, followed.

The woman in the chair beckoned Margaret to sit

185

on the low stool on the other side of the window and, with the same graceful gesture of her thin, ringless hand, dismissed the servant. The woman ignored Blanche as utterly as if she were invisible. She surveyed Margaret, calmly assessing her.

Finally she spoke. Her voice was low—hypnotic. "You are beautiful, Margaret—little bloodstained Margaret."

Margaret jumped to her feet. She wasn't sure whether the woman was accusing her or pitying her, but in either case she didn't like it. Besides, to address her as one would a common child, by her first name and no title! But the thin hand commanded her to sit down and to Blanche's astonishment, Margaret obeyed. Blanche would have done the same, such was the power of this strange woman.

"My doors lock from the outside," the woman said calmly. "So you will stay and listen to me. You're more comely than I had heard, but there are lines appearing. How old are you now? Twenty-three or four? Too old not to know the pleasure of a man's body. To be a virgin at your age!" she exclaimed, then sighed sadly.

"Madam, I don't know who you are, but I hardly think you should interest yourself . . ." Margaret began hotly.

"Of course I should interest myself. Everyone in England is interested. I am not so far from the world as you would imagine. Nor so far as I would like," she added quietly in a lower tone. "Has no one told you the reason for queens? A queen exists for only one reason, to bear sons—kings for her husband's country. You and King Henry cannot reign forever, thank God. *Someone* will succeed you. The world will not stop, England will not cease to exist because *you* are gone. But you shall have your man and perhaps the child you need." She got up from her chair and went to a rough wooden chest.

She got out a small leather pouch and pressed it into Margaret's hand. "Put this powder in the King's wine at dinner, then wait in his bed."

Margaret was so stunned by the entire mad conversation that she didn't know what to say. She just wanted to get away from this strange recluse. The woman was staring out the window and seemed to take no further interest in her visitors. Margaret looked to Blanche for help; then they both got up and carefully went to the door. It was locked from the outside. "Please, madam, let us out," Margaret said, trying to sound authoritative and failing.

"My dear young woman, I shall gladly let you out. People will always let you out. You need to be let in." She rose and went to the door. She tapped lightly and the outside bolt was pulled open.

With the door open Margaret felt braver. "I shall see to it that you are dealt with for locking my sister and me in like this. You will regret it."

"I have nothing left to regret but the length of the days. But you," the woman said dreamily, "you will have so much to regret—so much." She laughed softly, maliciously.

Before Margaret could reply, Blanche took her hand and pulled her away. They ran down the dim hallway like errant children, fleeing goblins.

"Who was she?" Margaret asked breathlessly when they were back safely in Margaret's rooms.

"There are rumors that the Duchess of Gloucester is imprisoned here," Blanche said. "I hadn't believed them. Here comes Lady Alice; ask her."

Alice Chaucer had bustled in with an armload of fresh linens to put away. "I just spoke to a woman in a room above," Margaret said. "Blanche thinks she may have been Duke Humphrey's widow. Could that be?"

"Yes, I just heard she was here."

"I thought the servant was just muddled when she spoke of the 'Duchess.' Why didn't someone tell me she was being kept here?" Margaret said.

"I don't think anyone knew until this afternoon," Lady Alice answered. "She's been kept in one or another of the King's castles for so long, now, I think everyone had just forgotten her. You shouldn't have gone up there, milady. She's a witch; she might have cast a spell on you. What did she say?"

"Nothing, really. Just a lot of nonsense about— about my age and such," Margaret said with a warning look at Blanche. Blanche sensed immediately that this would be another forbidden topic between them. Just another of a growing list of things they could not and would not ever discuss.

That night the servant Joan came into the Duchess of Gloucester's room. "She kept the powder, just as you said she would. It is in her jewel case."

"Nobody saw you, did they?"

"No, milady. I was careful. Why did you give it to her?"

"Because she killed my husband. If she gets the babe she wants, they will all kill each other. And I shall rejoice in the spectacle," she said with a grim smile. "I shall revel in their slaughter and my husband will be vindicated."

The court gossips got a lot of entertainment out of the Queen's unexpected meeting with Eleanor Cobham. But before long even the most fertile imaginations had wrung dry the possibilities for speculation. Oddly enough, even the most creative interpretations of what might have transpired between the Queen and the Duchess were far from accurate. Some said the Queen tried to kill the Duchess; or the Duchess tried to kill the Queen; or they conspired to put a hex on Richard of York; or that the Duchess spoke in foreign tongues and had cast a spell on Queen Margaret. Hardly a day went by for weeks that some frightened servant didn't report to the kitchens that the smell of brimstone had permeated the castle.

Nobody asked what brimstone smelled like. It was a good time of year for rumors. The first weeks of January were bleak and dull. There was little to do but try to keep warm. The nobles seldom rode out in the snow and drizzle to hunt. The days were short and the nights were long and boring. Even the minstrels and jesters were lethargic. But like even the best of rumors, interest in Margaret's adventure with the Duchess of Gloucester soon faded.

Then suddenly the gossip started up again. It had seemed an ordinary enough evening at the time, except that the Queen said she didn't care for the wine in the large goblet that she normally shared with the King at the evening meal. She insisted on a separate goblet of a milder drink for herself. She left the meal early, but asked the King to remain and finish his food and wine. By the end of the meal the King had begun to act strange. Cynics mentioned that he always acted strange, but they were ignored. The King's breathing became labored and heavy. He started fumbling with his rosary at the table and dropped it in his stewed hare.

The Duchess of Somerset, who sat next to him at dinner, claimed that he had put his hand on her thigh, but no one believed that. Gossip was one thing; fantasy was another.

The Queen was not in her room when her ladies went to prepare her for bed. They worried until Blanche told them, politely, of course, to mind their own business and go on to bed.

A drunken serving boy, who was in the habit of finishing off the remainder of everyone's wine when the goblets reached the kitchen, raped a cross-eyed scullery maid that night.

In the morning the Queen sent for the seamstress to mend her nightgown. She said it had gotten caught in the door latch and torn. But that didn't explain her bruised lip.

King Henry sent for his priest. The King always attended services in the chapel first thing in the morning. The priest had become so alarmed at Henry's babbling that he sent for the royal surgeon, who said the King must have had something for dinner the night before that upset his stomach and some of the resulting poison had gone to his brain. He advised a day's rest and a thistle-juice potion. King Henry remained in his rooms for several days, praying. Queen Margaret stayed aloof, too, but she had a smug, secretive look.

The conclusions drawn by the rumor-mongers this time were pretty close to the truth, at least regarding the effect, if not the cause, of the royal couple's odd behavior.

Blanche was willing, if not exactly eager, to be her sister's confidante, but suddenly Blanche's own problems intruded themselves into her life in the person of Charles Seintleger.

Blanche was sitting and talking with Brithric, dear, patient Brithric, whom she had come to regard as her best friend and who was able to love her without pressing his suit. "I hear we shall have visitors tonight," he said.

"Who?" Blanche said without much interest.

"The Duke of York is sending some gentlemen to present some papers . . . about taxation reform, I think . . . to the King."

"What is unusual about that? He is always making reports for the King to ignore."

"I'm told the group of gentlemen includes Sir Charles Seintleger," Brithric said.

"How nice. Is he bringing his wife?" Blanche said in what she hoped was a casual tone of voice.

" 'Tis the usual custom," Brithric said and waited

191

for Blanche to say something. She didn't and he went on, "His wife is a great friend of yours?"

"Yes."

"And Sir Charles? Is he a great friend, too?"

Blanche nodded dumbly.

"Is he also the ghost against which I joust for your love?"

"Oh, Brithric, please don't . . ."

"I'm not going to be ugly about it. I suppose you can't help it, though why I don't know. After all, I'm better-looking than he is, I'm richer, and I must love you more, for no one could love you more than I do," he said.

Blanche knew he meant it, though he said it as lightly as he said everything. "Dear Brithric," she said, holding his hand tightly and leaning against his shoulder. "You know I do love you. You are my dearest friend."

"Perhaps this time . . ."

"What?"

"Nothing."

Charles and Ursula arrived late that night. The next day Charles was closeted with the King's advisors, explaining the documents that he had been charged to give to the King. Blanche and Ursula and Jane had their noon meal together and spent the afternoon catching up on Ursula's news. She had become friendly with Cecily Neville and told them about the birth of young Richard. She tactfully refrained from asking either Blanche or Jane about Brithric, for which Blanche was especially grateful. Jane had apparently realized that Brithric would not be won over to her and she had settled into a hostile indifference to Blanche.

Blanche went down to the kitchens late that night to ask the cook to bake some extra pastries the next day for Ursula. For all her good cheer and animation, Ursula had become so pale that Blanche was alarmed about her health. Passing through a dark corridor on the way back to her rooms, Blanche met Charles leaving the meeting he had been attending. At first he said nothing; he just put his hands on her shoulders and looked at her. She felt the familiar shortness of breath and heavy heartbeat that involuntarily assailed her in his presence.

But this time there was something more, something she had not felt before. She had been holding back—refusing to admit a physical attraction for Brithric for over a year, feeling it was unfair to encourage him by kisses or caresses. She had been repressing a similar feeling for Charles for many years. Suddenly in this dark hallway the dam had broken.

Without a word, she led Charles up the stairs to an empty room. She knew what she was doing; yet it was like the dream she'd had long ago when she had felt she was merely standing aside and watching her own movements. She knew what she was doing was wrong—wrong for her and Charles at least—but she also knew she was going to do it just the same.

She led him to the room and, still without speaking, she locked the door and removed her dress. He took her in his arms and crushed her to his chest. His body was so large and warm and rough against her smooth flesh—as the cloak had been. He kissed her lips, her neck, her breasts, and she understood what the Duchess had said—too old not to have known the pleasures of a man. Blanche was learning what those pleasures were.

The next morning Blanche refused to leave her room and asked that bread and ale be sent up so that she could eat alone. She had much thinking to do. She had learned several vitally important things about herself since the day before and she had to be alone to think about them and make some decisions.

She had learned that she was a woman meant to love a man—not pine away of unrequited, unsatisfied love. She needed the physical love of a man. If it had not been for what happened the night before she might never have known. Her ignorance of her needs had saved her. But now she *did* know. In the harsh light of morning she had to face the fact that it was not Charles with whom she had made love—it was *a* man. She loved Charles, of course, but she had to admit to herself that in her ecstasy it could have been Brithric just as well.

She could not go back to living the life of an aging virgin. She was almost twenty-five. Soon no one would want her. But she could not continue this relationship with Charles, seeing him and feeling his arms around her naked shoulders once every year or two years and then being ashamed to face Ursula. For she did love Ursula, too—very much. Ursula was to her what she had always hoped Margaret would be—friend, confidante, sister.

There was another reason why last night should never have happened. She could be with child. She couldn't bear the thought of bringing another bastard into the world. She knew too well the stigma of illegitimacy. She could not do that to her own child—the child she might be carrying even now.

There was only one solution. She had known all along what it was. She dressed carefully and did her hair in a becoming fashion. She called her serving maid and asked that a message be sent to Brithric de Bohun, asking that he meet her in the great hall as soon as convenient. When she got there, he was waiting.

He surveyed her approvingly. She took his hands and said quietly, "Is there a suitable place you would like to go where I might propose to you?"

"Are you going to propose to me?" he asked.

Suddenly Blanche was happier than she remembered being for years. He was delightful. She could love him. She was anxious to be his wife. "Brithric, please marry me," she said and threw her arms around his neck and held him tightly.

Then she realized that he hadn't said anything. She drew back and looked at him questioningly. "What is the matter?" she asked. A terrible thought occurred to her. "Oh, no. It is too late! I thought you would wait—how awful of me—I'm sorry." She turned to go, horribly embarrassed.

"No, it's not too late," he said. "It would never have been too late. It's just . . . well, I wonder why, that's all. But I don't want to ask. I'm not sure I would want to know. Just be very sure, I ask that of you. Don't do this today and change your mind tomorrow. May I ask that much of you?"

"You may ask anything of me. I want to spend the

rest of my life with you," Blanche said and, to her own astonishment, realized that she meant it. She wanted to grow old with him and bear his children and laugh with him over the same old jokes. "I love you, Brithric," she said and discovered she had tears running down her face.

"You don't have to say that," he said.

"I *do* have to say it because I mean it." She kissed him so passionately that a passing scullery maid paused to watch and giggle. "Come with me to tell the Queen," Blanche said when she had gotten her breath back and chased the maid away.

"When shall we marry?" Brithric asked.

"Is this afternoon all right?" Blanche said and laughed.

Their betrothal was announced by the Queen herself that evening after dinner. Margaret had seemed pleased with the arrangement. She approved of Brithric, not as an individual particularly, but as one of those who supported the King. She was glad to have Blanche marry a man who was at court because that meant Blanche would remain with her.

Blanche's friends and Brithric's were delighted and came to them to express their approval. Ursula hugged Blanche and tearfully declared how happy she was for her friend. Charles congratulated them formally, but pain and confusion were evident in his expression. Blanche noticed Brithric's eyes narrow at Charles's approach, but she squeezed his hand in reassurance. He relaxed and was polite to Charles.

Blanche found it an odd sensation to be standing

there between these two men, knowing both of them loved her. She realized what Charles had been trying to explain when he said so long ago that he loved her but that he loved Ursula also. It *was* possible to love two people. She still had the heart-stopping passion she had felt for Charles ever since she had met him and slept curled in his cloak. Yet strangely she loved Brithric more—more? Maybe not more, but a better kind of love. A warm, comfortable love. He was not only going to be her husband, her lover—he had been her best friend, aside from Ursula, for a long time. And she suspected that the best kind of lover also had to be a friend, a good friend.

In her happiness, Blanche overlooked the fact that the only person of her acquaintance who didn't speak to her that night was Jane Seintleger.

There was only one thing bothering Blanche and it sat heavily on her conscience. Only the night before, she had lain in Charles's arms. What if she was with child? Should she delay the plans for the marriage until she knew and then, if she was pregnant, simply go away? Brithric was certainly capable of the simple arithmetic of pregnancy and would come to hate her if she tricked him.

She couldn't do that to him, nor could she delay the wedding date without lying to him about the reasons. She took a risk and told him the truth later that night. It was terrible to do so, but the alternative seemed worse. She told him that she had made love to Charles the night before and it had been part of the reason she made the decision to marry him. She told him only that and kept her eyes on the floor, afraid of seeing anger in his face, more afraid of seeing pain. There was a long silence that stretched out between them until she was forced to look at him.

He was smiling, almost laughing. "God's wounds!" he exploded. "What a thing to say of a man—that his lovemaking is enough to make you want to marry another. Thank heaven you are saying this *to* me and not *of* me."

"You're not angry?" she asked in a great wave of relief.

"Of course, I'm angry in a way. I can barely overcome a primitive urge to kill any man who has even looked at you, but—I shall be as honest as you have been—I have always thought that you and Seintleger had been lovers for years."

"No!"

"Yes, I thought so. Now I find that you spend only one night in his arms and flee from him to me. I shall never understand that, but I don't need to. I shall just reap the benefits."

"But, Brithric, you don't seem to understand at all. I'm trying to warn you that I might be with child. We must wait and find out. I can't expect you to marry me without knowing," she said.

"I have a much better idea than waiting to find out if you're pregnant on your wedding day," he said.

"Better idea? What do you mean?"

"I propose to make sure that you are. Where is that room that you mentioned?"

Blanche led the way to the room and thought, What a wanton I have become in two days and how wonderful life is.

Brithric closed the door and lithely stripped off his shirt. With his fair skin and whitish hair and the light-yellow hose that encased his shapely legs, he seemed to almost glow of his own light source in the near darkness. His chest was so broad. Blanche started to take off her dress, but he grasped her hands, then released them. She kissed him, and with expert fingers he undid her clothing while seeming only to be caressing her. He was not hurried. Her dress and shift slipped to the floor and he softly ran his hands up and down her bare arms. She pressed forward, eager to feel his body against her breasts, but he held her back ever so slightly.

Softly, slowly, he put his hands on her waist and ran them down her sides and back up, then finally cupped her breasts and kissed them gently. She put her arms around him and pressed against him, feeling the hardness of his body against hers.

Still Brithric would not hurry. He picked her up and laid her upon the bed. He stood above her, his magnificent body glowing in the moonlight, and looked down at her. He seemed to be touching her all over with his gaze and she shuddered with anticipation.

He laughed softly and said, "I love you."

She could not find words. She put her arms out to him, beseeching him to satisfy her. He stretched out beside her on the narrow bed and kissed her lightly, then harder. Then he pulled away and nibbled her earlobe while exploring her body with the lightest of touches.

She could stand no more. She clutched at him only half aware of the soft animal whimpers she was making. He smothered her with hungry kisses and entered her body. Her body became electrified and pulsed with her love for him. How could she have not known that life held such pleasure! She lay back exhausted and wept with joy.

CHAPTER NINE

Blanche was pregnant on her wedding day. She was not surprised, for she and Brithric had been together nearly every night during the three weeks between their betrothal and their wedding. More often it was at her urging than his, which pleased him enormously. Blanche didn't tell anyone but Brithric of her condition until several months after they were wed. Brithric was pleased. If it worried him that the child might not be his, he never let Blanche know. "It is my child," he said. "It will be born to my wife and bear my name. That makes it my child," he reassured her.

Queen Margaret had helped arrange the small, dignified wedding that Blanche wanted. Ursula attended and sniffled with happy tears throughout the ceremony. Charles was not there. He had left without a parting word the day after Blanche's betrothal was announced. Ursula had asked permission to stay with Blanche while Charles was traveling around England on some business for the Duke of York. Blanche was glad to arrange for Ursula to stay, for she felt that it would have been detrimental to her to be out in the bad weather getting chilled and tired.

A week after Blanche's wedding, Ursula confided in her friend that she too was pregnant. Blanche was happy for Ursula, but wondered if they might both be

carrying the same man's child. Brithric decided that
pregnancy must be a contagious disease (or so he told
Blanche) when she told him in deepest secret that she
had good reason to think that Queen Margaret was
finally with child after eight years of marriage. Blanche
was not absolutely sure, for Margaret had not confided
in her, but she knew her sister well enough to guess
the cause of her smug peacefulness, especially when
she thought back to that cold winter night of Margaret's disappearance from her bedchamber.

Queen Margaret kept her secret well and for a
long time. She thought that as long as only she knew
of her condition the child was solely and completely
hers. She would have to share him with the entire nation soon enough. But while he still lived secretly in
her womb, he belonged to her alone. Thanks to a fortunate bone structure and a fashion in full, high-waisted
dresses, she was into her sixth month before her condition became too obvious to hide.

Young Elizabeth Woodville, who had become one
of Margaret's favorite ladies-in-waiting, was now sixteen and her parents judged that she was of marriageable age. Queen Margaret gave a dinner in honor of
Elizabeth and young Lord Grey, to whom the girl had
been betrothed for several years. It was generally considered odd that the Queen should so honor the young
couple. True, the Greys and the Woodvilles were
known to be staunch supporters of the Lancaster cause,
but neither family was really important enough to rate
a special party given by the Queen herself. Only
Blanche knew why the party was being given and she
didn't wholeheartedly approve of the plan.

Margaret rose to address the company at the dinner. This was seldom a woman's place to do and would have been a shocking occurrence at any other court in Europe, but the English court had become accustomed to Queen Margaret's speaking for the King. The Queen wished luck to the young couple and then said to the guests in the hall, "My lords and ladies, we have given gifts to this young couple and now I have another gift to bestow—a gift to my King and husband—a gift to England. In October I shall be delivered of a child. Let us pray for a son for England."

There was a stunned silence in the hall for a moment while everyone absorbed the news. Then a loud cheer went up. Even Elizabeth Woodville, who now realized that the dinner in her honor was simply a stage setting for the Queen's announcement, was happy. But the cheering died down as one by one the participants noticed King Henry. He was staring at Margaret, eyes wide as if with fear. He opened his mouth to speak, but said nothing. He rose and stumbled from the room. Margaret stood for a moment not knowing what to say. A few friends stepped forward to congratulate her and cover the King's inexplicable behavior.

Margaret thanked them distractedly, then followed Henry. When she got to his rooms, there were several gentlemen standing outside the door. "Keep everyone else out of here," she ordered before slamming the door in their faces.

Henry was at his private altar. He wasn't kneeling properly. He had just dumped himself on the floor. He was praying, mumbling fervent but disjointed bits of prayers.

"Henry!" Margaret said. He flinched, but didn't stop praying. She grabbed his bony elbows and pulled him up. "Henry, how could you do this to me?"

"All my fault," he wept. "All my fault, the fruit of my sinful, filthy lust. Indecent carnal cravings. Oh, God forgive me. I am so corrupt. Do you think God can forgive me?"

"It is *not* a sin to father a child, Henry!" Margaret shrieked. "Henry, are you mad? But why should I ask? Of course you're mad. You are mad—mad!" she screamed in his face.

The King of England had gone mad.

The word spread quickly that summer morning. When his gentlemen went in to rouse him in the morning, they had found him standing where Queen Margaret had left him the night before—standing rigid like a corpse someone had propped against the wall. They put him to bed. His limbs gradually relaxed and he became like a grim infant. He let himself be fed. He didn't chew, but dutifully swallowed by reflex anything put in his mouth. He even had to be dressed in an oversized diaperlike garment, for he showed no interest in or control over his body. Though he sometimes mouthed sounds, they were not words, nor was there any inflection in his voice. Sometimes tears would stream down his face, but there was no expression there, not even sadness.

Blanche went to Margaret as soon as she heard. "I'm sorry about King Henry, Meggie," she said.

"How glad I am to see you, Blanche. What am I going to do with him? Imagine a man going mad because his wife was with child."

"That isn't the whole reason, Meggie. You know he's never been normal."

"Do you suppose he'll be like this forever?" Margaret asked.

"Who can tell? Have you seen him?"

"No. I was about to visit his rooms. I hate to do it. I would be quite content never to gaze upon him again, but his physician insists that it might bring him to his senses—as if he had senses!"

"Do you want me to go with you?"

"I would be grateful if you would. Your presence has always been such a comfort to me," Margaret said.

Blanche went with her to the King's room, but Margaret was so repulsed by the sight of the giant, mindless baby that she went away immediately and would not go back. The doctor did not press her to return, for the King had shown no sign of even knowing that she was in the room.

Even one visit had worried her for the sake of the child she was carrying. Everyone knew of cases when a pregnant woman was frightened or saw something horrible. Sometimes the baby was marked as a result. Perhaps some vapors of Henry's madness could permeate her womb and make the child's mind bad, too. Better for her and the baby to stay as far as possible from mad Henry.

Blanche concurred and they settled down to several months of companionable stitching of baby garments. Blanche and Margaret and Ursula compared physical symptoms as women have always done. Brithric was engaged in some work with the Keeper of the Privy Seal that kept him away for much of the time, Charles was in the north of England, and King Henry was a confined lunatic, so the three women had much time together.

Though Margaret would not visit King Henry, she forced herself to be dutifully concerned about his condition and care. She consulted with the doctors who examined him. She supervised his diet and insisted that he be kept clean at all times. But she admitted to Blanche that she didn't really care what happened to him. Her health was imperative, for she carried the child, the boy, pray God, who would be the next King of England. Henry's body had served its function. She was no longer interested in him.

Margaret seemed to be convinced that when her son was born, there would be no more problems. No one could then dispute who would be the next king. But Blanche wondered—the child could well be a girl. And even if it was a boy, he would not be able to govern for many, many years. If Henry's madness was permanent, who would govern during those years?

Blanche was also uneasy about Ursula. While Blanche and Margaret blossomed during their pregnancies, Ursula seemed to be sapped of strength. The size of her abdomen was accentuated by her increasing thinness. She pined for Charles, and Blanche finally wrote to Charles asking that he come to court and take Ursula back to his estates and her own doctors before the child was due. She didn't know if her message would catch up with him on his travels, but she devoutly hoped so.

Ursula's child was expected in the late part of September. The last week in August she began to have sharp pains. Blanche was at her side, comforting her.

"Don't worry, Ursula. You are just early because it is such a large babe. See, you are already of greater girth than I. You shall have a big child, no doubt a boy. Rest now and relax."

Ursula tried to rest, but she was frightened and weak, and each new contraction not only was a physical pain, but tore her emotionally. She became incoherent for periods and called hysterically for Charles. Then she would calm down and sleep fitfully. Blanche stayed by her the entire time. Jane had returned to her watchdog role and sat guarding her sister-in-law. She made no attempt to converse with Blanche, but gave her whole attention to Ursula.

Ursula was in labor all day and until early morning of the next day. When finally the babe was born, he was tiny and frail. Blanche and the midwife realized at once that he was not the only body in Ursula's womb. She had been carrying twins. That was undoubtedly the reason for her great size and early labor. The other child should have arrived in moments and they waited. An hour passed, then two. Blanche was frantic. She felt sure that Ursula and the babe would both perish if the birth was not soon. Ursula was nearly unconscious by this time and completely unaware of her peril. Finally she gave a heart-rending moan and the contractions began again. Within moments the second child was born—a girl—little and dainty and dead.

Ursula fell into a deep sleep, almost a coma, until the next day. Blanche made arrangements for a wet nurse for the boy child while Jane planned a funeral for the little girl. Jane sent for her brother, the young priest whom the family called Saint George, and he sat with them at their vigil over Ursula. Blanche kept the boy baby in the room with them so that when, or if, Ursula ever woke, the child could be given to her immediately. They agreed not to tell her of the death of the girl twin until she had regained her strength—if she ever recovered.

The next day, while Blanche and Jane and Saint George sat around the bed, all of them exhausted and nearly napping, Ursula spoke. "Is Charles here?" she said softly without opening her eyes.

"Not yet, Ursula," Jane said, holding Ursula's hand to her cheek. "He will be here soon, don't worry."

"The child—boy or girl?" Ursula asked.

"A boy," Blanche said. She had come to Ursula's bedside with Jane. Jane rudely pushed her away.

"The child is a boy," Jane said as if Blanche hadn't spoken.

"Good. That is good. Blanche?" Ursula asked.

"I'm here, Ursula."

Ursula finally opened her eyes and smiled at Blanche. "Come closer," she whispered. Blanche bent closer. "I'm dying, Blanche," she said calmly. "No. I know I am and I haven't much time. I would ask one thing of you."

"I will do anything for you, Ursula."

"Please raise my son for me."

Jane interrupted: "No, Ursula. I will raise the boy. Blanche is no kin."

"Blanche is more than kin to me. She is my heart's friend. She will raise the boy to love his father, for *she* loved his father."

Blanche shook her head wordlessly.

"I am not injured by it. I loved Charles and you so much that I could not help but see that you loved each other," Ursula said, clinging to Blanche's hand. "I didn't mind. Promise me, Blanche. Promise to keep my son and teach him how much I would have loved him if I had lived."

"I promise, Ursula. But there is no need. You will be well soon. Now rest a bit. Do you want the babe here with you?"

Ursula nodded and Blanche brought the baby from his crib to Ursula's bed. Blanche put a pillow behind Ursula so she could turn a little to the side and nestle the child in the crook of her arm. "He looks like Charles," Ursula said weakly. She put her cheek against the baby's downy head and closed her eyes. She died holding the child.

Blanche took the baby and sat holding him and weeping softly. Jane started talking to Blanche in a low growl. "Are you satisfied? You are a wicked woman—wicked! You ruined her life. She loved you and you tried to steal her husband. But you won't steal the child. I won't allow you to take him from his family. And you can't have Charles, either—you have Brithric. You took him away from me, too. You took Ursula and Brithric—give me that baby!" Jane tried to take the baby, and Blanche became aware of her for the first time. She hadn't even noticed the outburst.

"Jane, stop this. You don't know what you're saying," Saint George said, pulling her away.

"I know what I'm saying. You just don't like hearing the truth," Jane said.

"Please, George, get her out of here," Blanche said, holding the baby tightly.

George managed to get Jane out the door. She was still hurling invectives at Blanche. In a little while Brithric came into the room. "Time to leave her now, Blanche," he said. "Take the boy to the wet nurse and come with me." Blanche did so, but before she left she touched Ursula's lifeless hand and said, "Farewell, dear friend—heart's friend."

When they were back in their own rooms, Brithric took Blanche in his arms and said, "The priest told me of your promise."

"I could do no other. She was dying, Brithric. She was my friend."

"I'm not chiding you. I know how close you were to her. If you wish to keep the child, I will make no objections."

"That is generous of you. It will be up to Charles, of course. It is his child, too. He may want to take him back for the women of his family to care for," Blanche said.

"Then there is no decision to be made until he gets here and is told what happened. But you are tired. That is not good for *my* child. You must go to bed now. I'm going to stand guard and see that no one disturbs you until tomorrow."

"Brithric, I fear that God may look down and notice what a mistake He has made, giving you to someone as undeserving as I."

"I'm sure God has forgotten all about me. Now get to bed."

Charles Seintleger arrived a week later and Blanche was spared having to see him until after Saint George and Jane had told him about the death of his wife and newborn daughter. They took him to see the baby and found Blanche there, changing the blankets in the baby's crib. She went to him and said, "Charles, I am so sorry. If there had been anything in my power to save her, I would have done it."

"I know . . . I know. I only wish I had been here. It would have made it easier for her and there were things I should have told her before it was too late. But at least she had you."

He held the baby for a long time, looking him over carefully. Finally he said, "Jane, would you please wait in the hall for me? There are things I must discuss with Blanche."

Jane flared up. "I should think you had discussed overmuch with this woman ere now." He started to say something, but thought better of it and simply stared coldly at her. She stood like a little torch, thin and upright with blazing red hair, but finally she wilted under his glare. "I shall be outside the door," she said defiantly and flounced out.

"Saint George tells me Ursula asked you to care for the child," he said.

"Yes, I promised I would and I will gladly keep that vow if you wish. But the choice is up to you. He is yours now."

"I can think of no better mother for him than you, but I forfeited the right years ago to ask anything of you. I can't expect Jane to care for a baby—she is

211

too upset to make such a commitment before she is even wed herself. My mother is in failing health and her household is getting slipshod and careless without a firm hand over it. As soon as the child is old enough, I will take him with me, but that will be several years. For Ursula's sake, if not for mine, please keep the child for now."

"I shall do so for both of you."

"How cruel and unreasoning life can be," he said.

"Why do you say that?"

"Because I thought for years that if it weren't for Ursula, may God forgive me, I could have you. Now Ursula's gone and part of me with her and you are married to another and planning to raise my son for me. How could this have happened?"

Blanche could say nothing. There was no answer.

"Do you love him?" he asked.

"Brithric?"

"Yes."

"Do you recall our meeting in the gardens that first time after your marriage? You were trying to make me understand how you could love me and still feel affection for Ursula. I didn't comprehend how such a thing could be—then. Now I know. Yes, I love Brithric—more than I love you in many ways, but not instead of you. That, to me, is life's cruelty. That so many people have *no* love and we are cursed by an abundance. We cannot talk of this again. When are you leaving?"

"Very soon, I'm afraid. I'm not supposed to be here at all except to get Ursula to take home. Now

I am too late even to bury her. I shall go tomorrow. I will send word of where I am so that you can send me news of the boy."

"He cannot go on being called 'the boy.' What is his name?"

"Did Ursula express a preference to you?" he asked.

"No."

"Then he shall be named Richard Seintleger."

"For Richard of York?"

"Yes."

"That is too much name for such a tiny being. May we call him Dickon for now?"

"That would suit him," Charles said. He got to his feet and prepared to go. "I shall not see you again before I leave. There are no adequate words to express my gratitude."

"There is no need to search for words. We know each other too well," Blanche said.

"Bless you, Blanche."

The next day Blanche had the baby and his wet nurse moved into a room adjoining the apartments she and Brithric occupied. Brithric was interested in Dickon and acted as though he was a member of the family. Blanche settled into a peaceful time of waiting. The Queen was expected to deliver her child in six weeks or so and Blanche's time would be shortly after that. Blanche and Margaret went back to sewing and waiting, but it was lonesome with Ursula gone and quiet without Jane, who had gone back to her mother's home without even asking permission to leave. Blanche had explained to Margaret that Jane was overwrought over the death of her sister-in-law, and Margaret asked no questions.

The thirteenth of October was St. Edward's Day. Margaret had hoped that her son would be born that day. She went to chapel that morning despite a backache that made kneeling uncomfortable. She tried to have some bread and ale in the morning, but couldn't get more than a few bites down because of a pain in her stomach. Blanche was worried. What if Margaret were to come down with the flux when she was so near her term? It wasn't until later in the morning that they realized that the pains in her stomach were occurring at regular intervals. Margaret was suddenly frightened and excited. The child *would* be born on this auspicious day!

Just as she got into a flowing shift and ready to take to her bed, a gush of fluid announced that the baby was, indeed, on the way. And with that, the slight cramps and backache became real pain. Steady and regular, but not strong enough.

Margaret was young and healthy and the pains were not as bad as she feared. Between times she sipped a little wine and talked with her ladies. All afternoon they waited. Alice Chaucer had come to court to be with Margaret, and it was a great comfort to have her sweet, familiar face there to see and her plump hand to hold when the pains were sharpest.

By evening Margaret was getting terribly tired. Blanche and Alice were worried at the length of her labor. The pains were harder to tolerate now in her exhausted condition. "How much longer?" she asked.

"Not long now, sweeting," Alice answered. "They are close together. It won't be much longer. Just rest."

Suddenly Margaret felt herself holding her breath and bearing down. "I didn't mean to do that," she gasped in amazement. She took a gasp of air and pushed again.

"Quickly, send for the physician and midwife. It's time," Alice told one of the ladies. "Now, sweeting, push again."

"I can't," she panted.

"Yes, you can."

She pushed again—and again. Finally she took an enormous breath and pushed until she nearly fainted.

It was over.

"A boy, your majesty. A son," the midwife announced.

Margaret slept. It was several hours before she woke. "Do you want to see your son?" Alice asked.

"Please, yes," Margaret said through parched lips. Alice brought the baby in, saying what a nice big babe he was. Margaret laughed weakly, "He's tiny!"

She asked for Blanche and was told that she had gone to rest. The physical and emotional strain of another difficult childbirth had been almost too much for her, especially since she was so near term herself. Margaret didn't mind—she had her son. He was all that mattered to her at the moment.

It wasn't until the next afternoon that it even occurred to anyone that King Henry might be told about the birth of his son. "He wouldn't understand, anyway," Margaret said.

Margaret kept the baby in her room for several

days. She and her ladies admired him constantly. One of the baby's most enthusiastic admirers was little Margaret Beaufort, who had recently taken Jane Seintleger's place in the Queen's household. She was Somerset's niece, the child who had once been engaged to marry the Duke of Suffolk's son. She had been but a baby herself then and the betrothal had been broken when Suffolk had been killed by the sailors.

Though only ten years old, Margaret Beaufort was unusually mature. She openly adored both Queen Margaret and the baby. When she could not be with the Queen, she was in Blanche's rooms, playing with Dickon. "She will make a good mother," Queen Margaret said, and mentioned to Blanche several young men who would be appropriate matches. "After all, the girl will be of marriageable age in a few years and is an heiress. It is the King's right to arrange for her marriage."

After the harrowing experiences Blanche had gone through attending the difficult births of little Dickon and the Prince, she felt that her own labor was anticlimactic. It was an easy birth, and when it was over, Lady Alice announced the child was a girl. Blanche had almost forgotten her worries over the paternity of the baby until that moment. Suddenly it swept over her. She started to cry and ask that Brithric be sent to her.

In a moment he was there. He was beaming and holding a bundle. Without a word he unwrapped the blankets and held out for Blanche's inspection a tiny being with wisps of white-blond hair. Blanche looked from the child's head to Brithric's mass of whitish curls and started to giggle. He started laughing, too, and Lady Alice and the other women in the room were left to think that Brithric and Blanche had both gone as mad as the King.

"Who is this fair-haired child? Has she a name?" Blanche asked when she could get her breath.

"Naturally she has a name. She is Matilda," Brithric said.

"Matilda?" Blanche wrinkled her nose. "Matilda is so old-fashioned. Besides, it is a name for a grown woman. A baby can't be called Matilda."

"You could call her Maud."

"That's worse. She could be called Mattie," Blanche said.

"Then Mattie she is. When she is grown she can use her real name if she wants."

When Blanche had her strength back, which was a very short time, for she was of healthy constitution, she took Mattie to meet the Queen. Margaret oohed and aahed over her and called her niece. It made a noisy nursery with Mattie and Dickon and the Prince all howling at once.

Margaret finally took the baby Prince to see his father. She had to know if Henry could be jerked out of the mental bog he was in. She had always made his decisions, given his orders. But if he was permanently impaired, as she suspected, she would need official sanctions to continue to rule England. The Council would have to declare her Protector of the Realm to rule for Henry until the Prince came of age.

But Blanche convinced her that the Council would

not agree to such a plan. They would not appoint a woman as Protector, and in that case, Somerset would have to be appointed. Margaret felt sure that with a little effort she could control him. At least now the whole question of York being declared Henry's heir was settled. Henry had an heir of his body, a son.

So Margaret dressed the baby in the finest of the fancy dresses that she and Blanche had sewn and took the baby to Henry. His doctors were with him and so were his Tudor half-brothers. They visited Henry more often than anyone else, though they would have been more at home riding the Marches than visiting London. Jasper, the older-looking younger brother, seemed very concerned about King Henry's state of mind. The young men would sit by King Henry's bed for hours, talking to him in lilting Welsh accents, reminding him of his, and their, mother—Katherine of Valois. They were trying to strike a responsive note in his clouded brain. It didn't seem to do much good although Henry was a little better now. He could hold his own cup to drink from and he would occasionally sing a snatch of songs he had learned as a child.

There were a number of other people in the room, waiting to see if either the Tudors or Margaret could jar Henry back to his senses. Margaret noted with disgust that the Earl of Warwick was among them. She hated having him there—his dark, sneering look frightened her. But he was on the King's Council, so she had to put up with him. "Wouldn't it be nice to see his face if the sight of the child brought King Henry back to his mind?" she whispered to Blanche.

They had to wait outside the door for Somerset to

arrive. It was necessary to have everyone present as witnesses if Henry should show any reaction to the child. Finally Somerset swept along the hall, wearing an outrageous cloth-of-gold cape, confident that everyone had been kept waiting for him.

Margaret walked to the bed, carrying the Prince. "Henry, here is your son—our son."

No response.

She nodded to an attendant, who made Henry's arms into a cradle so Margaret could hand him the baby. Henry held the small bundle for a moment, then, when the baby cried, Henry looked down.

"This is your son, milord," Margaret said.

"This is the son of the Holy Ghost," Henry said clearly.

There was silence broken by one snort of laughter. Margaret spun around, but Warwick's dark face was as bland as if he hadn't heard the remark.

Margaret controlled herself long enough to take the baby from Henry, who had relapsed into a stupor. She handed the baby to Alice Chaucer and walked stiffly from the room.

"I shall be burdened with Henry for the rest of his life," she said bitterly to Blanche, "but I shall never, *never* forgive him for this."

"And then he said, 'This is the son of the Holy Ghost.'" Warwick laughed. Margaret would have recognized the laugh.

"He actually said that?" Richard of York asked. "I didn't think he could speak at all."

"He hadn't said anything for months. But if he had

219

to say something, denying that the child is his is the best thing he could have said," Warwick gloated.

"Don't be daft," Cecily interrupted. "You know perfectly well he didn't mean that. He was probably pondering some religious matter, as he always does. Somebody handed him a baby and the poor fool thought it was the Infant Jesus."

"You're probably right, Cecily, but that isn't what it sounds like to most people." Warwick got irritated when Cecily was present during his conversations with Richard. Cecily could always spot the weak point in any argument and never hesitated to point it out. "I have more important news than the lunatic ravings of our King," Warwick went on. "The Council met and agreed to decide next month on the appointment of a Protector. I was sorry you couldn't be there, Richard. Thomas Young is drafting a proposal for the Commons to submit to the Council, asking them to appoint you to the post. There are many on the Council who vote with Somerset on matters that don't affect them personally, but they won't want to put him in charge of the entire country for fifteen years or so."

"What about the Queen?" Cecily asked.

"The Queen's only support is Somerset and he won't support her at his own expense. No. Richard will be Protector. I'm sure of it."

CHAPTER TEN

In later years the Earl of Warwick would prove himself capable of catastrophic errors in judgment, but this time he was correct. Richard of York was appointed Protector of the Realm. Parliament demanded Somerset's arrest for treason. While Somerset languished in the Tower of London, York began replacing the men Somerset had appointed to civil office. The dishonest sheriffs, biased judges, and cutthroat tax collectors were dismissed and replaced by the most honest men York could find. Riots and civil disorder became less frequent. Parliament enacted financial reforms that were long overdue.

There was widespread, though not complete, satisfaction at the changes. York's enemies fumed and plotted for over a year. Periodically the Council sent representatives to check on King Henry. Margaret lived in seclusion with her son and attendants. She recognized that the situation was impossible for her to change. Her only hope was the possibility that Henry might recover. She refused to see it as a remote hope. She kept in frequent consultation with his doctors.

She was being forced to learn the necessity of patience. She kept reminding herself that someday her son would reach the age to rule. It would not be for a long time, but at least there was a future to plan for, however distant.

By the next Christmas, the second year of Henry's madness, the Prince was walking and starting to talk. Margaret's ladies spoiled him terribly, exclaiming rapturously over every baby syllable he uttered.

The three children were being raised together. Blanche's Mattie was widely considered to be the beauty of the court. Charles's son, Dickon, was quiet and submissive, but occasionally showed reserves of methodical determination. Dickon, for example, was a month later than the other two learning to walk even though he was the oldest. But when he finally decided to walk he just walked; he almost never fell down or ran into things. The Prince was by inclination and circumstance the dominant member of the nursery, for he was to be a king someday and was treated accordingly.

Blanche and Margaret were playing with the children one day shortly before Christmas. Blanche was wondering when she would become pregnant again and give Brithric another blond baby to spoil. There was a knock on the door and King Henry's physician was allowed in to address Margaret. "What is it?" she asked him. "Is there something wrong?"

"No, your majesty, but I think perhaps if you and the child were to visit the King today, well, perhaps he would know you. I can't promise anything, of course, but he seems to be better. He has been saying your name."

"Blanche, hurry," Margaret ordered. "Bring the child. No, no, don't bother washing his hands, just bring him along." They hurried down the halls to Henry's rooms. Remembering the last time she had presented the Prince to his father and the humiliation she had suffered, Margaret had the room cleared of onlookers before she entered. She took Prince Edward's chubby little hand and walked to Henry's bedside. Henry looked at her for a moment as blankly as he had for over a year. Then his eyes cleared. "Wife," he said.

"Yes, my lord," Margaret said, glad for once in her life to have Henry speak to her.

He looked questioningly at the small round face peeking over the edge of the high bed. "This is . . . ?"

Margaret scooped the boy up and put him on the bed. "This is your son, Henry."

Henry stared at the boy for a minute, then embraced him. The child squirmed. "What name have you given him?"

"He is called Edward. Do you approve it?"

"Entirely."

Queen Margaret wasted no time making the best of the King's recovery. By the end of the week King Henry was back on the throne again; Richard of York was preparing to go home; Somerset had been released from his imprisonment in the Tower; and York's civil appointees were out of jobs. Somerset's friends, who had slunk away to nurse their wounds during York's Protectorate, were back in London.

It was necessary to officially relieve Richard of York of his duties as Protector. King Henry, accordingly, asked York to call upon him.

"My lord, you look very fit. I'm pleased to see you

223

returned to good health," York said, sounding as if he actually meant it.

Margaret sat next to Henry on the dais, holding her child on her lap. Blanche watched the scene and was struck by the widening differences in the two men. King Henry's illness had left him paler and thinner than ever. There were bags under his eyes, and his teeth had further deteriorated. He had aged ten years in only eighteen months. But York had held his own. If anything, he looked younger. His step was springy, his eyes alert, and his smile as devastating as when Blanche and Margaret had first met him. Blanche was sorry for Margaret being tied to this feeble, prematurely aged man. Margaret was sitting very straight and glaring at York. It made her lovely features seem cold and harsh.

"We have our Merciful Lord in Heaven to thank for my recovery," King Henry said, "and I wish with all my powers to thank you for . . . for, uh . . . taking care of . . . well, everything for me during my illness."

King Henry had no idea what he'd been told to thank York for. "I was glad to serve you, my lord, and I intend to be of any further aid that I can," York said, and with a glance at Margaret, he bowed and left.

Charles Seintleger had been present for the ceremony, and afterward Blanche met him and took him to the nursery to visit his son. He was pleased to see the boy doing so well, but uncomfortable. He didn't know quite what to do or say to such a small child. He watched them play for a few moments, then left. Blanche felt sorry for him, but knew there was nothing she could say to ease the pain of a man whose own child is a stranger to him. By unspoken agreement they no longer spoke of the past, so there was very little for them to talk about.

Brithric had apparently buried any jealousy he might have felt toward Charles when Mattie, beautiful Mattie, so obviously of his own seed, had been born. He found work to do that kept him extremely busy, while Charles was at court and managed to avoid meeting him. After Charles and the Duke of York left, Blanche and Brithric settled down to enjoy the last few months of ordinary domesticity that would be theirs for quite some time.

In May of 1445 the members of the King's Council were summoned to meet at Leicester, but Richard of York was not asked to join the meeting, Warwick was not asked, Warwick's powerful father-in-law, the Earl of Salisbury, was not asked, nor were any other members of the Council who were in sympathy with York.

The meeting never took place.

The royal army, with King Henry, Queen Margaret, and the Duke of Somerset at the head, moved northward toward Leicester. King Henry chose to regard the procession as a pageant rather than as an army and no one disabused him of the idea.

Young Prince Edward was far to the rear, heavily guarded, for Margaret knew the true purpose of the move. She and Somerset were hoping once again to provoke York into a rash action which would discredit him before King Henry and allow them to dispose of York for good. For the first time, Margaret was traveling without Blanche. She had told Blanche what she was doing without any embarrassment or misgivings. Blanche had not been invited to comment upon the wisdom of the plan, but she had been given the option of coming along or staying in London. She chose to stay, even though Brithric would be with the Queen, because she was not ready to leave Mattie behind with her nurse and she wouldn't even consider taking a child along to start a war.

She begged Margaret to leave the Prince in her care, but Margaret was adamant. She was fighting, she said, for his heritage and he would grow to be a true man, not like his father, if he was exposed early to the force and hardships of war. "But he is a baby still!" Blanche protested.

"So is his father. He must not grow to be like that," Margaret said. Blanche saw that it was useless to argue with her.

The royal army had gone as far as St. Albans when they got word that York and Warwick were on the other side of the town with a large army of their own. Margaret was suddenly frightened. According to the reports she was getting, York's army was as large as the royal force—much larger than she had anticipated. Perhaps she and Somerset had goaded York too far. But there was nothing to do now but follow through.

King Henry was befuddled by the interruption of his festive little parade. He sent a message to York, asking why he had come there with such a large group. Henry said that if he didn't know better, he would think it looked like an uprising against the crown.

York sent back word that it was indeed an uprising, but not against his sovereign lord, but against the traitors who surrounded the King.

"You see, he sings the tired old song again," Margaret said to Henry. "We know that your cousin Somerset is our good friend and advisor. York envies Somerset's wisdom and the high regard you have for him. York is the traitor, my lord. Ask him to come to you and you can explain to him that he must disband the army."

"But, wife, my cousin York is a good man. Why should he do this?"

"I think we have been misled by his charm and wit. He is *not* a good man. He is a traitor. He would have your throne and mayhap our lives." Henry was looking skeptical, so Margaret switched direction slightly. "Possibly he has merely had poor counsel and is misguided. Get him here, talk to him, pray with him. Possibly he will see his mistakes, and if not, you can have him put in prison to think upon his errors."

"Oh, I should not like to put him in prison."

"Why not?" Margaret asked, trying to keep the exasperation out of her voice. "Remember, he had Somerset in prison the whole time you were ill."

"I suppose you are right. I shall send for him to attend me here."

Margaret arranged to have Alice Chaucer and a small group of guards take the Prince back to London as secretly as possible. She had changed her mind about children and battles. She also planned an escape route for herself and King Henry, just in case the battle went the wrong way.

Somerset adjourned to the local inn to partake of

some ale while the inevitable flow of messages went back and forth. These things took hours. There was everyone's honor to be satisfied before the actual fighting could begin. Somerset was eager for the fighting to start. He'd had new armor fitted just as soon as he was released from the Tower.

The new armor had elaborate jointed knees and elbows. The helmet was pointed at the top so that any downward blow to the head would be deflected. The visor hinged on golden bolts and there was ornate carving etched into the helmet and breastplate. It had been fitted to him perfectly and was remarkably light and flexible. Naturally it would take some time to get into the padded garments that went under the armor. Then he would have his squires help him pull on the hose made of hundreds of metal loops and finally he would have his head bandaged and padded so that a blow or fall could not stun him.

But there was plenty of time. The fighting wouldn't start until daybreak tomorrow. He was impatient. He knew he was impressive in his new armor. He sat over his mug of ale, imagining himself riding out in his gilt suit, cutting down soldiers, maybe even Richard of York. It was a delightful dream. Afterward, King Henry, the poor old fool, would thank him and retire even further from the decision-making. Queen Margaret would interest herself in her child and her household, as a woman should, and stop meddling in state affairs. She would see how important he was and stop being so condescending to him.

Everything would be so easy once this fight was over.

At that moment a noise erupted in the street. The door of the inn was flung open and Somerset heard the Neville battle cry echoing in the streets outside, "A Warwick! A Warwick!"

The wounded soldier who had opened the door fell to the floor, blood pouring from his shoulder.

Somerset ran for the back door of the inn. He planned to hurry to his rooms to don the new armor. He ran out the door only to discover himself in the thick of the fight. Warwick's men had entered the city through the back gardens, not by the main street. Somerset was trying to get back inside when Warwick himself rode up. He dismounted easily in spite of the bulky armor he wore and strode toward Somerset. "Well, well, what have we here? A frightened cur? The Dog of England." He sneered and spat in Somerset's face. "I hardly recognize you out from behind the Queen's skirts, or should I say out from under?" he drawled obscenely.

Somerset tried to retain his dignity, but he was terrified to face this hateful enemy without his armor. He stepped closer to Warwick. "Sire . . ." he began, but it was too late. Warwick's hand flashed toward Somerset; the glinting blade pierced Somerset's heart before he even felt the pain. He had time for only one dying thought: How extraordinary to feel one's heart burst. Warwick's men hauled his body back into the inn to be dragged back out as a trophy when the fighting was over.

Warwick's attack on St. Albans had taken everyone by surprise, including his ally, Richard of York. York had been in his tent, composing a reply to King Henry's last message, when news reached him that Warwick had taken half the army and was already battling his way through the town. York was furious. He had known there would be a battle this time, but he was dumbfounded that Warwick dared give the orders for it to begin without consulting him. There was nothing to do now but take the rest of the men and dash into the fray.

Margaret was in her rooms in the rich merchant's home that had been taken over for her and her ladies. She heard a man's heavy stride pounding up the narrow steps. The door was flung open and Jasper Tudor stood there, his freckled face red with anger and exertion. "Your majesty, come quickly. The fighting has started. Quickly, you must get to safety. They are still at the other end of town, but you have only moments."

"The King?" Margaret asked, gathering a few items to take with her.

"He will be safe. He is at the mayor's house under heavy guard. Anyway, we can't get to him now. Let me take you to the abbey."

They flew down the steps and out to a waiting carriage. Margaret knew she might be abandoning Henry to his death, but there was nothing she could do if she stayed with him. In fact, her presence would probably endanger him more than her absence.

The carriage jolted and banged as they hurried away. Two of Margaret's ladies began to whimper, but Margaret stilled them with a scowl. Margaret noticed that the only one in the carriage who had control of herself was young Margaret Beaufort. Jasper

Tudor noticed her, too. He was desperately uncomfortable in a carriage full of women when he should be back in St. Albans fighting for his half-brother, the King. But at least there were two women in the group who could keep their heads.

Jasper left them with the sisters at a nearby abbey and hurried back to join Henry. But he couldn't find his royal brother. At the doorway of the mayor's house, where he had last seen him, were the bodies of four soldiers. Jasper recognized them as the men who had been guarding the King.

Jasper searched for Henry along the choked thoroughfare, fighting off battle-weary Yorkist knights. By now everyone still alive to fight was hot and bruised and exhausted inside his armor, which was admirably designed for jousts and tournaments but a liability in this glorified street brawl.

Jasper ducked into a bakery to gather his wits. There were a number of injured soldiers there, as well as the baker's wife, a kindly behemoth who didn't even know who was fighting, much less who was winning. She was bandaging someone. When she finally moved her bulk out of Jasper's line of vision, he saw that her patient was the King. He wasn't badly injured. The baker's wife suddenly realized who he was and became terribly flustered.

King Henry didn't seem to realize what had happened. Jasper and the baker took the King upstairs to the family's living quarters and made him rest. He immediately fell to praying and Jasper went to the windows overlooking the street. The rebels had brought the bodies of Somerset and Lord Clifford out into the road. They had stripped the bodies and left them there, gruesome and bloody in the spring sunshine.

The fighting had all but stopped. As Jasper watched, York and Warwick came along the street. Warwick strutted, his eyes sparkling with victory. York, his face hard and angry, turned to Warwick and said something. Warwick shrugged and laughed, intoxicated with winning the battle. York stepped over the bodies in his way; Warwick stepped on them.

"Richard of York comes here, brother," Jasper said to Henry.

"Bring him to me," Henry ordered in a surprisingly strong voice.

In a few moments York came up the narrow steps. He had managed to leave Warwick downstairs, but Jasper was with him. "The traitor is dead, my lord," he said to Henry.

"And yet *you* stand before me," Henry said sharply.

"Somerset is dead. The traitor who has brought us all to such grief is slain," York replied.

Henry suddenly stood up straight and shouted, "For the love of God, stop this slaughter of my subjects!"

York bowed low. "I most humbly beg your forgiveness, my lord, many of my friends and kin died this day, too, but I am most grievously sorry to have caused you additional sorrow. Please forgive me, cousin. And please realize that it had to be done."

"How could this be? What are you saying?" Henry asked.

"Somerset has for years bewitched you with bad

counsel. It was necessary to rid you of him. To rid England of him."

"Perhaps so—" Henry said weakly. "But what of the Queen? She thought highly of his advice."

York thought for a second, deciding which path to follow and knowing he must be cautious. "Cousin, I have the utmost respect and love for the Queen, but she is a woman and we know how easily women are swayed." York almost laughed to himself at how angry Cecily would be if she could hear this. Henry said nothing, but didn't look convinced. "Even the Church recognizes the limits of a woman's mind," York added.

Henry nodded. That made sense. There were no women priests.

"Therefore, my lord, I shall be happy to be of service to you. Let us speak to the troops and assure them of the love I have for you," York said.

So King Henry and Richard of York went into the streets of St. Albans and declared their affection for one another. There were declarations of peace and friendship. No one said it, but everyone knew (except King Henry himself) that the King was now a prisoner of Richard of York.

That night Jasper Tudor went to Richard of York's tent and asked to see him privately. York waved away the clerk who had been working at the table over some maps. "Richard, when you came to the baker's shop today I held my dagger behind my back, ready to attack you when you tried to kill the King, but you didn't make a move to harm him." Jasper looked confused. "Why, then, did you do all this if not to murder him? You could have."

"Jasper, you are a man of honor and intelligence," Richard said wearily. "Perhaps you, if no one else, will understand. I don't want to be a king. I only want England to be ruled with justice and not evil such as Somerset represented. I have no reason to harm King Henry."

Jasper shook his head slowly as if unable to believe what he was hearing. "But you could have gotten away with it. You could have seized the throne today. You might be wearing the crown of England now."

"No doubt I could. Warwick has 'mentioned' it to me. He, too, expected me to murder Henry. He feels he has been cheated. No, Jasper, allow me to speak frankly to you from my heart. I have spent my life working for England's welfare. I have lived for years in France, receiving my only payment in insults. I have been separated from my wife and children more than I have been with them. To be king would be to spend the rest of my life serving only my country. I'm tired of this. Don't misunderstand me—I have the right to be King. The throne was wrenched from my family by King Henry's grandfather, and my father and grandfather died trying to assert that right, but to be king and to rule well is to give up everything else that a man values.

"Jasper, you must see what is to be done. Help me. Help England. I am going to appoint men to the Council who are honest and will serve England before themselves. If King Henry will retire from public life and if, more important, Queen Margaret will no longer interfere, I can do this."

"But, Richard, they are King and Queen of England. Henry may not be best suited to kingship, but he *is* the King. He must be the real ruler. To do otherwise would be to set a precedent. It would make the monarchy a joke, a meaningless trifle, an ornament."

"No. Only while Henry lives. A strong and able king would not be restricted."

"I cannot agree. Henry is King. Whatever his failings, he is still King. I have sworn my loyalty to him —so have you."

"Then we must regard each other as enemies, Jasper. I regret it, for you are a fine young man and I would have your friendship and support, but I must do what I know to be right."

"I know that, Richard." Jasper put his hand out to Richard, who took it in both his hands.

"Jasper, anything may change. I cannot promise that a strong Council will right all the wrongs that now rend England. I cannot even promise Henry's safety forever, but whatever happens, I hope that you at least will understand, if not agree, with what I do."

"Richard, I know you have not sought my advice, but this I must say—pray pay less heed to Warwick. He is a wily man seeking only for himself."

"I know him well, Jasper. Thank you."

The next day King Henry and Richard of York came to the abbey where Queen Margaret had taken refuge with her ladies. Richard of York himself had come to the gates to escort her to Henry's side. The implication was clear to everyone. York was in charge —of King Henry, of Queen Margaret, of the government of England. Margaret remained as aloof and

235

dignified as possible. She admitted to herself that she was temporarily defeated, but she would not grovel, especially not to Richard of York. She couldn't allow herself to show any weakness in front of this man whom she had made her enemy.

The combined armies marched back to London with Richard of York and King Henry at the head. Margaret had been relegated to a secondary position, as most of the men thought fitting for a woman. Word of the battle had reached London before the army.

Blanche was in an agony of suspense. Everyone in London knew of the welfare of the principal participants, but there were no messengers who could tell Blanche what had happened to Brithric. She would simply have to wait and ask Margaret.

Even when Margaret returned, Blanche had to wait until she had been officially welcomed and taken to her rooms. Finally Blanche got a chance to speak to her. "Where is Brithric?" she asked.

"Blanche, this has been the worst week of my life. Can you imagine that fool Somerset not being ready to meet the enemy? He almost deserved to be killed. Then I had to ride back here behind York, like one of the servants . . ."

"Meggie, *where* is Brithric!"

"What? Brithric . . . Oh," she said thoughtfully, "I have no idea."

"Was he hurt?"

"I don't know."

"You don't know! Didn't you even inquire?"

"Blanche, you have no idea how frantic I've been these last few days, worrying about what's happened, and I had to get most of my own belongings ready for the return. Poor Alice Chaucer isn't really as much help as you are . . ."

"Meggie!" Blanche shouted. "Brithric is my husband. He might be dead . . . or captured. How could you not even think of him? He is your brother-in-law."

"Blanche, I'm sorry. You're right. It was very silly of me," Margaret said.

"Silly!"

"Well, unkind at least. But I'll find out for you."

"Never mind. I'll find out for myself," Blanche said, running out the door. She intended to find some soldiers and simply start asking each one if he knew of Brithric de Bohun's fate. But she hadn't gotten far before she ran into Brithric himself. "Oh, thank God you're safe," she wept.

"I'm sorry I could send you no word," he said. "How is Mattie?"

"She is too young yet to understand, but I think she has sensed my fear. She has been unusually quiet. Come, let's see her and you can tell me what happened."

"By the way," Brithric said to her on the way to the nursery, "I saw Charles Seintleger today. He was not injured."

Blanche stopped walking and looked at him. "Brithric, I had not even wondered. I hadn't thought of him. All my thoughts were of you."

"I know that. But sooner or later you would have wondered. Now you need not."

"Thank you," she said and kissed him lingeringly.

Later that evening Blanche asked, "How do you come to be here? You fought on the losing side of a war only days ago and yet you are back at court. Will we be allowed to stay?"

"I'm not in danger now. The Duke of York is willing to let many of the King's adherents stay on in their positions if they are not troublesome and are not in opposition to his policies."

"And you are not?"

"No. Most of what I've been doing has to do with the colleges the King founded. There has been no corruption involving the finances largely because the Duke of Somerset took no interest in the schools. They are not a political issue and York's spies are good enough to have reported to him that I do my work well."

Blanche was puzzled. "You don't seem to have any objections to York being in control and yet you fought for King Henry."

"I have no objections to York's policies. I think he is an able administrator, certainly more able than Somerset, because he is an honest man and Somerset is not. I would not say this anywhere but in our own rooms, but I think York would be a good king."

"I can hardly believe you are saying this . . ."

"I'm not saying he *should* be king. I think any country that allows individuals to replace rulers it doesn't like ends up in constant civil war and that is worse than any bad ruler."

"And so you support King Henry. How strange men are."

"Why do you say that?"

"You could have died this week fighting for a man whom you know to be incompetent."

"I wasn't fighting for King Henry. I was fighting for the monarchy. An ideal, not a man."

"And I am more interested in a man," Blanche said, nuzzling his neck.

Queen Margaret was allowed friends at court. York had made a point of trying to publicly reunite Lancaster and York adherents, but no one was prepared to rally round King Henry again, not just yet. It was beginning to appear that King Henry would never again be normal or even normal for Henry. He wasn't entirely mad, just foggier than before the battle of St. Albans. And he was getting somewhat bad-tempered, which was a new problem.

Henry was anxious that everyone observe his own pathologically strict moral code. One warm day when he was riding with some other gentlemen of the court, they had come unexpectedly on a group of young men frolicking in a pond. The boys were naked. Henry's gentlemen watched the boys splashing and dunking one another for a moment, remembering fondly when they too had been young and exuberant. But King Henry turned pale and screamed that they must cover their nakedness. "Shameful, shameful to appear thus before God," he ranted. The boys clambered out of the pond and ran. King Henry rode home white-lipped and trembling.

One evening at a dance performed after dinner by some of Margaret's ladies-in-waiting, Henry became terribly upset by their low-cut bodices. He stopped the performance and ranted at dancers and audience alike on the sinfulness of inspiring lust by lascivious costume. Most of the girls fled in tears before he had finished.

Margaret tried to ignore Henry's ridiculous behavior—until it touched upon her son. King Henry and Prince Edward were in the courtyard one morning. Henry was trying to teach the child a bedtime prayer, an effort that didn't promise to hold the child's attention for long. As they sat on a bench, a pair of mongrel dogs at the other end of the court began to mate. The Prince pointed them out. "Look, Papa, look at the funny dogs."

Henry slapped him.

The boy's face crumpled, but before he had begun to cry, King Henry had fallen to the ground, sobbing incoherent reproaches. Blanche was nearby and whisked the boy away to Margaret, leaving the King's attendants to deal with him. Blanche told Margaret what happened.

Margaret, in unthinking fury, rushed to Henry's apartments. She found him prostrated before his private altar. "Help me, Lord, to bear this daily reminder of my sins," he was praying.

Margaret could say nothing. She went back to her rooms and sobbed bitterly. "He thinks of Edward as his punishment," she told Blanche brokenly. "He only endures him as a penance, a living hairshirt, for his great 'sin.' The sin of making love to his wife once in ten years. My beautiful baby Edward. How could anyone feel that way about his own child?"

Blanche put her arm around Margaret and smoothed her hair. "I don't know, Meggie. He doesn't know what he's saying. He's never been right in the head. He'll forget this pretty soon. Don't let him upset you."

"How can I not let him upset me? I have only one short life to live and he's destroyed it. What right has he to do this to me? Blanche, I was a pretty bride, wasn't I?"

Blanche nodded. "Yes, you were."

"I was a nice girl. I've never hurt anyone. . . ." Blanche winced, but said nothing. "I was pretty and talented and learned. Remember what I was like?" she appealed.

"But somehow I was sold to an imbecile," Margaret went on. "Father and Uncle Charles, for the sake of a signature on a treaty, turned me over like a bolt of goods to a slobbering idiot. They tied my life —*my* life—to him. Oh, my God, I can do nothing about it. How can I go on facing another day and another day and another day of this, my life simply running out like sand for the sake of a man I loathe?"

Blanche understood Margaret's desolation and felt sorry for her in spite of the many times she'd had reason to be angry with her. Margaret was selfish and thoughtless and foolish many times, but what would I be like if I had to face being married to someone like King Henry? Blanche wondered. If Blanche could have eased Margaret's distress, she would happily have done it . . . but there was no way to serve except as an understanding listener.

Gradually Margaret's sobbing subsided. "What am I to do, Blanche? I must keep him alive and sane. It's the only chance to save the throne for Edward. But I can't change nature for him. I can't stop people from having bodies or animals from mating."

"No. You can only try to control what the King might see."

"When we were girls in Anjou," Margaret said, "I dreamed of being a queen. I dreamed of a handsome husband and many beautiful children like Edward. I thought there would be days of picnics and nights of love and poetry. Oh, Blanche, what did I do to deserve this? What has happened to me?" she whimpered into Blanche's shoulder. "I sometimes wish I had married Pierre de Breze."

"Pierre de Breze!" Blanche exclaimed, remembering for the first time in years the young man in Anjou she thought she'd loved before she knew what it meant to love. "You didn't love him, Meggie."

"No, but he loved me, I think. He would have been good to me and life would have been easy, wed to him. Oh, but what use to even think upon it? I'm wed to a madman. 'The village idiot,' his own uncle once called him. Henry the Sixth," Margaret said bitterly, "Henry the Foolish, Henry the Mad."

She was silent for a moment, fighting back a fresh outbreak of tears. Finally, in a shaking voice, she said, "Blanche, what is it like?"

"What is what like?"

"What is it like to be with a real man? I can't help but wonder what it is I've missed."

How can I tell her? Blanche thought. How can I express how the rest of the world fades and disappears when two people tell with their bodies the passions they feel in their hearts and heads. How to tell someone else about pleasure so intense that it is exquisitely painful—pleasure that sweeps over a woman in waves and finally subsides, leaving her exhausted and content?

How could I say what it's like to look into someone's eyes across a noisy crowd and know instantly that you are sharing the same thought, Blanche wondered. There was no way to say what it was like to share innermost secrets and fears with another person, knowing they will be met with understanding, not criticism.

Margaret suddenly realized that Blanche was regarding her with pity, a superior sort of pity she could not abide. "Never mind!" she flared. "I don't need a man anyway. I've my son to raise and important things to do. You may go now!" Blanche curtseyed and left without a word.

The next day Margaret gave instructions that the Prince was to be kept away from the King. Henry didn't ask to see the child again. The Prince soon forgot the incident in the courtyard. Margaret didn't.

CHAPTER ELEVEN

King Henry soon went mad again. This time it was a wedding that did it.

Jasper Tudor's sickly older brother, Edmund, had come back to court after an absence. He had been in Wales during the battle of St. Albans, suffering from the cough that had plagued him most of his life. A betrothal had been arranged between Edmund Tudor and Margaret Beaufort. Queen Margaret had promoted the match, thinking that anyone who wanted to put the girl on the throne (as Suffolk and Somerset had once been accused of planning) would think twice about it with her married to a queen's bastard. The girl was sweet and sensible and admitted a preference for Edmund. Margaret had become very fond of her and had dubbed her Meg, remembering happier times when she herself had been called Meg.

Edmund Tudor, hemmed in for years by his frail health, had come to London on some minor business only to discover that little Meg, whom he had known since childhood, had suddenly grown up and, more important, grown beautiful. She had just turned thirteen, but was as unusually mature for her age as he was immature. She was very small and the tiniest bit plump. Edmund was charmed by her and asked Queen Margaret if he could marry her right away.

Margaret found welcome diversion from her own problems in helping the girl get ready for the marriage. There was feverish sewing and planning. Richard of York allowed Margaret to arrange a large wedding, presumably on the assumption that it kept the Queen occupied and therefore out of his way.

Finally the guests began to converge on London. Margaret Beaufort was a descendant of John of Gaunt, the original Duke of Lancaster, so all the Lancaster supporters came. York made sure that many of his friends came as well, for it would have been unwise to allow that many of the King's sympathizers to gather without supervision. Almost everyone pretended to forget his animosities. The Earl of Warwick was the exception. He went about glowering at all, but miraculously failed to offend anyone, which seemed to distress him.

After the wedding, there was a grand feast. Richard of York's family attended—all but baby Richard, who was only three years old. Cecily went out of her way to be pleasant to Margaret, but though Margaret had once been fond of York's wife, she could not yield to Cecily's overtures of friendship. Cecily recognized Blanche and smiled and waved at her across the crowd of guests, but they didn't get an opportunity to talk to one another. Blanche was sorry for this—she had pleasant memories of Cecily.

Richard and Cecily's oldest sons came along also. Blanche was amused by the difference in the two young men. Edmund was dull and stodgy beyond his years, but young Edward was quite unusual. He was only thirteen, a giant of a boy, towering over his father and Uncle Warwick. It was rumored that he had already fathered a bastard, but it was not only his maturity and dazzling blond good looks, but his charm, that was exceptional. Women of all ages found him irresistible. Blanche thought that even Margaret was being drawn into his net.

"Madam," young Edward had said to the Queen, "how unfair that you should be both Queen and Beauty. So few women achieve either and you are both." The words were outrageous flattery, but he spoke in a slightly mocking manner, not as though he mocked her, but as if the two of them were sharing a very private joke on the rest of the world.

Blanche turned her attention to the King. He was having a bad day. She suspected that he had no idea where he was or why. He sat still, receiving his subjects, smiling occasionally and murmuring "God bless you" at intervals. Those optimistic enough to attempt to engage him in conversation got merely a vacant smile for their troubles.

Toward evening, as the usual wedding-night jokes began, Margaret got nervous. What if Henry made some terrible outburst again? The drinking and jokes went on. The bride laughed, the groom gave every indication of suffering terminal embarrassment, but the King didn't even appear to hear what was being said. Margaret sat next to him at the head table in the great hall. She kept watching him out of the corner of her eye. As the noise level got higher, she thought she heard him say something. She leaned closer.

"Sin, sin, sin," he was chanting quietly.

"Henry," Margaret said gently. "Henry!" She squeezed his hand.

"Sin, sin, sin . . ."

She pinched his arm—hard. He didn't notice. As unobtrusively as possible she summoned two of his gentlemen, his "keepers." "Get him to his rooms," she hissed. "Quietly and fast! Don't let him say anything."

They did as they were told, but Blanche noticed that Richard of York was observing Henry being taken away. She looked across the room and saw that Warwick and York's son Edward were watching York watch Henry. An ominous network of observation—it frightened her. York's expression was deliberately bland, but Warwick and young Edward of York appeared to be ready to climb the tables and drag York to King Henry's vacant chair.

When the dinner was over, the bridal couple went before the empty place for the King's blessing on the marriage. Queen Margaret apologized for his absence, explaining that some important business had come up that the King had to attend to. She wished them happiness and long life on his behalf.

Whether they were happy, no one ever knew, but history would not forget the bride. Edmund Tudor didn't have long to live, but little Margaret Beaufort was to marry three times and see the reigns of six kings—one Lancaster, three Yorkists, and two Tudors. The Tudor kings were her son and grandson.

Word spread quickly—the King had gone mad again. The Council met and proclaimed Richard of York Protector of the Realm once more. He had been responsible for making decisions for England for months, unofficially, but with Henry mad again it had to be made legal. Margaret again had to simply accept Henry's madness and her inability to do anything about it. But something unexpected could always occur that she could turn to her advantage if she kept alert and informed.

What did happen next was not, however, to her advantage. It was an unprovoked attack on her morals. It was led by the Earl of Warwick.

Warwick was a sullen and taciturn man in private, but he had a gift for public harangue. He could, and often did, begin as though speaking loudly to a few friends, and before anyone realized how it had happened, he would be lecturing a public gathering. He loved to do it, sometimes merely for his own amusement as other men enjoyed the challenge of chess, usually with the purpose of embarrassing someone.

This morning he had been to a church service at court. Margaret was there with the Prince. She was accompanied by Somerset's widow and their son, who was now almost twenty years old. While everyone else prayed, Warwick observed the Prince and young Somerset and formulated an idea.

Later in the day Warwick was in a busy section of the city with some of his friends. "Do you recall the surprise we all felt at the news that the Queen, after eight years of barren marriage, was to give birth?" he asked loudly. "Is this not an extraordinary circumstance?" he said to a passing merchant. "Good sire, pray give me an honest man's opinion. If your good wife had not conceived in the first eight years of marriage and then suddenly was with child, what would you think?" He winked broadly. The merchant and his companions snickered.

"But I saw the young Prince Edward this morning," Warwick went on. "Does he resemble the King? No, the child is sturdy and dark-haired. The King is slight and frail. But look sometime at the Duke of Somerset's boy. Sturdy and dark. Remember Somerset's appearance and remember how much the Queen kept him about her before he was killed."

"I seen him once," a man in the crowd told his friends. "Dark, he was."

"Remember how the Queen defended Somerset in all his traitorous plans? Remember how she raised the dog Somerset to one high post after another?"

The crowd snarled its agreement at the injustice.

"This, countrymen, is the behavior of a woman toward her lover."

Cheers!

". . . and he *was* her lover. This child we see with her, this small, dark-haired boy whom we are told to call 'Prince' is not a prince; he is a duke's bastard —a queen's bastard. Are we going to watch this boy grow up to rule *us*—a queen's bastard?"

Warwick had drawn quite a crowd by this time. Londoners loved to get together and listen to someone rant at another's expense. They cheered and booed at appropriate intervals. Warwick began again for the benefit of those who hadn't heard the beginning of his remarks.

Though they listened and acted appreciative of his line of reasoning, most of the people in the crowd didn't truly believe what Warwick was saying. It was simply a diversion, an entertainment. But a few believed. And most went home and told their friends what Warwick had said and some of their friends believed. It takes only a few believers to keep a rumor alive, and this rumor lived for years to haunt Margaret.

Though Margaret steamed in frustrated fury at Warwick's accusation, there was little she could do about it. She could hardly go out in the streets of London to defend her reputation. There were several aspects of Warwick's accusation that particularly galled her. For one thing, the night on which she had conceived the Prince had been the worst night in her life. It still made her skin crawl to remember so much as a moment of her hour in Henry's bed. She had felt as much disgust at the act as Henry had, but only because Henry was the other participant. Secondly, if she had ever considered having an affair with anyone, Somerset would have been her last choice. She had regarded him with almost as much repulsion as Henry.

Besides everything else, she was wounded that anyone, even Warwick, hated her enough to spread such slander. She had disliked Warwick from the first time she saw him that awful evening when he had escorted her around the muddy little pond at M'antes. She knew that he must reciprocate the feelings, but for him to make his feelings so public hurt her. More than that, he frightened her. If he would say that the Prince was illegitimate, what else might he say? He was suggesting that her son should not take the throne when he came of age. He hadn't come out and said that the throne should go to York, but everyone who heard him knew that's what he meant. Suppose he decided to take some kind of action to insure that——

Margaret had heard that it was Warwick who had

led the attack on St. Albans without York's knowledge. What if he decided on some attack against her son? Margaret gave orders that the Prince's nursery be moved to the room next to hers. She kept him in her room at night and began to watch even more closely who was allowed near him and what he was fed. She spent most of her time with him, pampering and spoiling him.

The boy had become the only thing that held Margaret's life together, the only person she really loved, the only reason for her existence. It was for him she must fight. She knew she would never have another child, not by Henry. So all her energies to save the throne from Richard of York were directed to the boy.

In the spring King Henry recovered again and had what were probably the most lucid few days of his life. It seemed for a while that he honestly understood his situation. In fact, when he was told that Parliament was meeting under the eye of Richard of York that day, Henry called for his robes of state and marched into the House of Lords before York could be warned. King Henry thanked York for his efforts and formally released him from his responsibility as Protector. Henry told York that he had certainly earned some time at home with his family and that he could leave immediately.

York, unprepared for this, had no choice but to go home after the King had told him to do so. But King Henry's awareness slipped away quickly. Though he never went completely mad again, neither was he ever entirely lucid again. Whatever had jarred his mind into normalcy never returned.

So, for a short time, the situation stabilized. King Henry was pliable and did what Margaret told him to do. He had a particularly bad time the next winter when word came that his half-brother Edmund Tudor had died, but he didn't slip over the brink, only prayed more excessively than usual for a week or so. Edmund had died in a cold castle in Wales. He had wasted away that winter of the cough that had plagued him since he was a child. Henry hinted that it was marriage and the excesses of the flesh that had killed him. Several months later Queen Margaret received word that Meg Beaufort, Edmund's young widow, had given birth to a son, whom she had named Henry in honor of the King, his uncle. Margaret sent a messenger to Wales asking that Meg and the baby come to London, but Jasper Tudor politely refused to let his sister-in-law go. He said he was now the guardian of his nephew and would take care of him in Wales and raise him as a Welshman.

Blanche was aware of what was happening at court, but very little of it interested her. She was, however, truly saddened by the news of Edmund Tudor's death. It had seemed to her that the marriage between Edmund and Meg had been a true love match. It was tragic to think of poor little Meggie Beaufort widowed so young.

For the most part, Blanche kept apart from court intrigue. She still attended Margaret as chief lady-in-waiting, but she had done so for many years, now, and could attend to her duties and still have time for Brithric and Mattie.

Though it was a peaceful time, Blanche had the

feeling that it was only an interval. There was an aura of impending disaster and she woke nearly every morning wondering if that would be the day that the slender thread of peace would snap.

It did snap.

It happened because King Henry got an idea.

"A love feast!" Cecily exclaimed. "What in the world is a love feast?" She began to giggle.

Richard of York let his wife go on laughing. He didn't think it was funny. He could hardly believe that the Queen would allow King Henry to put something this silly over on everyone. Of course, she probably couldn't stop him. Once he got one of his rare ideas he was like a dog with a bone—he wouldn't let go of it. But a love feast!

York had been informed just this morning that he was required to be in London the first week in May to participate. The same message had been sent to all the leading peers of the Lancaster and York parties. The idea was to show solidarity of the nobility for the benefit of France. The French were making threatening gestures to the few English holdings abroad. King Henry thought it would scare the French into submission if they thought the English were united and had forgotten past animosities. Besides, King Henry felt it would be a nice Christian thing to do on general principles.

The idea was to stage a big parade that would wind its way through London. The participants were to be the peers of England, lined up in pairs, each one walking side by side with his worst enemy. Or rather, his *former* worst enemy, for Henry honestly believed that all had been forgotten and forgiven.

"I'm sorry, Richard," Cecily sniffed. She didn't sound sorry—she sounded hysterical. "It's just that I can picture you all skipping naked along the streets with flowers in your hair."

"While you're setting up that little scene, you should know that I'm to be paired with Queen Margaret," Richard said sourly.

Cecily nearly exploded with laughter.

But even Cecily had to agree with Richard when the time came for the parade. It wasn't funny. Everyone but King Henry was cranky and sullen. It was a cold, misty spring day and London was living up to its reputation for foul-smelling fog. Sir Thomas Parr's son William and the Duke of Buckingham's son got into an especially undignified fist fight while the procession was being lined up. They nearly managed to get their fathers, who were unwillingly paired, into the brawl. The Earl of Salisbury pleaded illness that would prevent him from attending. King Henry sent his own physician and a carriage to bring him. Warwick made a point of dressing entirely in black and telling everyone he was in mourning for his lost dignity.

Margaret was in the unfortunate position of having to act as though she thought the love parade was a good idea, though she hated it as much as anyone present. She especially hated the walk with Richard of York at her side.

Blanche didn't have to participate, but Brithric did. The committee who were forced to select the pairs were hard pressed to find an enemy to pair with Brithric, for he had none. In ignorant desperation they accidentally hit on the one person Brithric didn't want to have anything to do with—Sir Charles Seintleger. Blanche spared both men the indignity of being seen by her. She stayed indoors and refused to watch the parade. No words passed between Brithric and Charles, and Brithric returned merely ruffled and cranky from the experience.

Mercifully the parade was soon over without any serious damage to anyone. The wretched guests then had to endure the love feast that followed. Everyone choked down the food and went home for the night.

Many of the nobles maintained homes in London, but the most important of them often stayed with the King. Castles such as Westminster were so large that they were really cities within cities and could accommodate a number of nobles along with their entire retinues. Such was the case the night of the love feast. The King and Queen had the Earl of Warwick, among others, staying with them. Margaret hardly knew what kind of idiotic misplanning caused Warwick to be at Westminster, but she thought it best to ignore the problem rather than create a scene.

Late that night, while the kitchen servants were still cleaning up, a fight began. Warwick's servants were sharing clean-up duty with the royal servants, as was customary. John Baker, who had been a servant in the royal household for many years and felt the dignity of his position, decided to straighten out the morals of Warwick's drunken boot boy. John wasn't any more sober than the boot boy, so the method of instruction he employed featured a lot of kicking and slapping. The boot boy's lady love, a scullery maid, had been drinking the leftover wine, too, and felt that John Baker was going too far, so she prodded him with a fork in his fleshy backside. Naturally John turned on her and knocked her down. Another of her admirers (for she was a buxom, obliging girl and had many male admirers) then entered the argument with a knife in his hand.

John Baker's friends found this invitation irresistible and joined in with any implement close at hand. Knives and skewers became swords, serving platters doubled as shields. As the fight got louder and bloodier, it attracted more participants and quickly outgrew the confines of the kitchen area. The boot boy, recovering his wits, such as they were, decided the Earl of Warwick should know that a great part of his staff was being incapacitated. He ran up the back stairs toward Warwick's apartments.

John Baker saw him leave and gave chase. The mob followed. Warwick's bodyguards, finding themselves inundated by a brawling mob for no apparent reason, assumed that they had come to attack the Earl of Warwick. "My lord Warwick! Treason, treason! Run for your life!" they shouted above the din. Warwick's rooms had a concealed staircase, so he hurriedly threw on his cloak and ran. He fled through the blackened streets to the Duke of York's home.

He woke York and Cecily and told them that the Queen had tried to have him killed, but that he had narrowly escaped with his life by virtue of his superior wit and cunning. He planned to make his escape across the Channel to Calais in the morning. York said he would inform King Henry and the Council of the Queen's treachery.

But with morning came information as to the true nature of the "assassination attempt." When Warwick learned that he had made a desperate escape from nothing more than a petty argument among the servants, he was mortified. Nobody could have devised a more devastating practical joke if he had tried. He had made a fool of himself and everyone knew it. Richard's son Edward came to the noon meal with a stone crock on his head, which he said was part of his new armor.

Warwick insisted that Queen Margaret was behind the whole thing and went on with his plans for escape. Warwick was Captain of Calais, having won the post from the Duke of Somerset by means of a dagger in Somerset's heart. Calais was a vital spot to England's welfare, for most of the merchandise exported from England went first to Calais. The Captaincy of Calais was a political appointment, a lucrative and prestigious one. Though the Captain of Calais usually appointed an underling to do the actual administrative work and was not required to reside there himself, Calais made an excellent spot for plotting, gathering forces, and launching attacks against unpopular sovereigns.

Warwick's move to Calais set in motion all the political animosity that had been stilled for a while. York, sensing trouble, left for Ireland. Margaret sent word that York was to be returned, but York had made himself very popular there and the Irish were not about to bundle him up and send him back before he was ready to go.

Margaret felt sure that Warwick would invade England as soon as he had sufficient numbers of men lined up. Even Blanche, who always tried to be optimistic, had to agree. But she was very unhappy with Margaret's way of preparing for this eventuality. Margaret met the challenge by behaving in the same manner that had cost Somerset his life. She ousted a number of Yorkists from their holdings and awarded the spoils to various of her friends for promise of certain numbers of men and horses for the coming battle. She offered Brithric a sheriff's post, which he very tactfully turned down. "Why should I take a job I don't want or need and couldn't do well? It wouldn't make me any more loyal to the King," he told Blanche later.

The Earl of Warwick, having a spy network beyond compare, naturally heard of Queen Margaret's activities and stepped up his own planning in order to be ready before she was.

BOOK TWO

CHAPTER TWELVE

"Madam, the King has been captured and War-wick's men are on their way to take you back to London," the messenger announced.

"Thank you for telling me," Margaret replied.

Blanche stood at the window. She didn't even bother to take her eyes off the dismal rain outside. The messenger was only confirming what they had feared and expected to hear. She and Margaret and the children were at Coventry. King Henry had been captured a day's ride away at Northampton, where they had left him.

The Earl of Warwick had crossed the Channel to Sandwich nearly a month before. The rain had slowed him down on his march to London, but it hadn't slowed the enthusiasm of the hordes of men who joined with him on his march across Kent. Margaret and her military advisors had realized that they could not hold London against him. They left Lord Hungerford and Lord Scales in charge of defending London, but those two gentlemen had simply holed up in the Tower for their own safety as soon as the King and Queen were out of the city.

It had been a difficult decision for Blanche to go along, for she felt, as she always had, that children should not be taken along to battles as if they were picnics. In this case, however, she feared for their lives if they remained in London. Warwick's forces were sure to invade the city, and who could tell what use he might make of a hostage like the Queen's sister? She had considered taking Mattie and Dickon and fleeing in a different direction, but every man, including Brithric, was needed in the army. No one could be spared to escort a woman and two small children.

So she had packed up as many things as she could get into two boxes and got ready to go to war. When they got to Northampton, Margaret made the decision to part with King Henry and the army. Warwick's men were closing in with a huge force and a battle was sure to ensue within a day or two at the most. Margaret knew that Warwick's primary aim was to gain physical possession of King Henry and the Prince. If Warwick captured Henry, it was absolutely imperative that she and her son, the heir to the throne, be free to rally forces to free the King. She knew if Warwick captured her and her child, they would probably never see anything but the inside of the Tower for the rest of their lives, however short those lives might be. She had to be the head of the royalist party if it was ever to rise again, for she felt quite sure, with Warwick's superior force, this battle would be in his favor. There had to be a healthy, living heir of Henry's body available and free or there would be nothing to fight for.

Blanche had no part in Margaret's choice, but was relieved that they were to get away from the fighting. She was nearly faint at the thought of her and Mattie being captured. No harm would have come to Dickon,

of course. His father was no doubt fighting with Warwick's army or he might be in Ireland again with
Richard of York, but either way, he was in favor with
the Yorkists and his son would thereby be immune to
harm if captured.

Blanche didn't want to leave Brithric, but if she
had to decide between staying in the middle of a battle
and possibly seeing him killed, or taking the children
to safety, there was no question as to her duty. After
all, she could do nothing to protect Brithric, but she
could protect Mattie and Dickon. Blanche agreed with
Margaret that the Lancaster rose would almost certainly go down in the mud before the week was over.
But Margaret believed it would bloom again; Blanche
wasn't so sure.

Shortly before the battle began Margaret and Blanche
took the children to Coventry and temporary safety.
There they waited. And now a messenger had come to
tell them that Warwick was on his way to escort them,
under guard, back to London.

Amazingly enough, Margaret had quietly acquiesced.
However, the moment the door shut on the messenger,
Margaret became a whirlwind. She had brought along
a number of semivaluable trinkets for just such an
emergency. She gave a coin to one of the servants who
was with them. "I saw a cart below with a wooden
coffin on it," she said. "Go buy the cart and the coffin.
Get the body out of it and get the cart ready to go.
Hurry if you want to be alive tomorrow."

She ordered another to go into the town square to
get common clothing, the older and dirtier the better,
for them to wear. Within moments, Blanche and Mar-

garet were ready to go. They had loaded some of their things in the coffin and had the rest sent on to London as if they were headed there. When Warwick's men arrived to escort her to London, they would be told that the Queen had ridden ahead to the city on her own. Margaret and Blanche and the children rode out in that direction with their few servants at a slow, defeated pace, but as soon as they were out of sight of Coventry, they turned and set a faster pace in another direction.

They were headed for Wales. They had made every effort to make their group look as common and inconspicuous as possible, and the rain helped. By the next day they looked like any other merchant's family, mud-splattered and disgruntled, taking the body of a family member home to be buried. Margaret was excited by the escape. She had managed it well and found the danger thrilling. Blanche was merely frightened. Not so much for herself as for the children and Brithric. She knew she might not see him again for a long time—if he was still alive. She had no way to even find out if he had survived the battle.

She had known it might be this way, but that didn't ease her pain. She and Brithric had crept out of the busy military camp the night before she and Margaret had left the army. They had made love under a hedgerow, like a common milkmaid and her swain. Neither had mentioned that it might well be the last time they would ever share each other's bodies, but the passion of their lovemaking had reflected their knowledge. Now every time Blanche thought of that night, the memory caused something to twist and hurt inside.

She could not even divert her energies and thoughts to comforting the children, for they didn't seem to need any comfort. They were enjoying this greatest of all adventures. They could not know the danger they were fleeing, of course, and to them it was a game. More than a game really, for they were pampered children—they had been shielded from the world and now they were out in it, dressed like peasants' children. They loved it and Blanche could remember well enough to realize that she would have felt exactly the same way.

There was only one problem among the children. Mattie and Dickon had been taught from birth to defer to the Prince, for he was to be their King someday. It hadn't been difficult to get Dickon to go along with this, for he had an introspective mind that was seldom bothered by trivialities. Even at the age of five he seemed to realize that if he was obedient it saved time and trouble, and that left him more time for his own thoughts.

It was proving much more difficult to get Mattie to give Prince Edward his due respect. She disliked him for some private, childish reason of her own, which she would not explain to Blanche, probably because she didn't really understand it herself. Margaret had insisted that on this flight, the Prince was to be treated like any other child, for special deference to him might make them all appear suspicious.

Prince Edward didn't like the idea, but it was a dream come true to Mattie. Normally Mattie was expected to curtsey to him when entering his presence. Now she was adopting a casual style that included

draping her arm around his shoulders in false cama-
raderie and making faces at him. It drove him wild.
That, of course, encouraged her to perpetrate further
outrages. Prince Edward, or "Neddie," as Mattie insisted on calling him now, became progressively
nastier, and Blanche was forced to admit that his bad
temper was a trait she had been aware of and trying
to overlook for a long time.

Blanche tried to mention tactfully to Margaret that
Prince Edward's behavior was becoming ugly, but
Margaret cut her off. "He is to be a king, Blanche.
Kings do not have to behave as ordinary people."
Another topic that cannot be discussed, Blanche
thought.

After a few days Prince Edward developed a bad
cold and became so unbearable that even Mattie got
tired of goading him. It was too easy to make him
angry—the challenge was gone. After days of bleak,
hard travel they finally reached Harlech Castle in
North Wales. They didn't have a servant to spare—
only two had been brought along—so they couldn't
send word ahead to tell Jasper Tudor they were coming. In fact, Jasper's gatekeeper refused at first to let
them inside the castle walls. He knew perfectly well
that queens of England didn't ride around in common,
dirty clothes with a few loutish attendants, snotty-
nosed children, and a coffin! Neither did queens of
England travel around in the rain trying to get in
where they were neither expected nor invited.

They finally convinced the gatekeeper to convey a
message to his master and shortly Jasper Tudor came
hurrying across the courtyard. Blanche was surprised

to see how handsome and self-assured he had become since the last time she saw him. "Your majesty! What an honor," he said. "Come, let's get you inside by the fire. What brings you here? My bailiff just returned from business in Coventry. He told me of your plight, but he said you were being taken to London. I should have been there to help the King, but I underestimated Warwick's forces. I didn't think he was a serious threat. But how come you here?"

Before Margaret could answer, Meg Beaufort ran out into the courtyard, skirts and hair flying. "Your grace, welcome to Harlech," she said breathlessly. "The boy is with you—the Prince, I mean. And Blanche, how glad I am to see you." She and Blanche embraced. Meg immediately fell into her former role of attendant to the Queen. She saw to it that Margaret and Blanche had hot water, fur rugs, and mulled wine to warm themselves. She had servants take the children to be cleaned up and put into dry clothing.

Only then did she relax and mention her own child. She sent for the baby to be brought for the Queen's inspection. "What a fine boy," Blanche said, not really meaning it. The baby looked puny and shriveled, but his lusty voice and voracious appetite convinced her that there was nothing wrong with his health. She found it amazing that any child could survive a year in the climate. The rain, which had been merely unpleasant in London, was horrible here.

Margaret and Blanche had grown up in France, where the climate was more often friend than foe, and found living in a cold stone castle in Wales a shock. A gust of wind that would be a breeze elsewhere was an icy knife slicing through the narrow window slits at Harlech. In fact, life at Harlech was austere in the extreme. The rushes on the floor were seldom, if ever, changed. If Blanche dropped something on the floor, she would often find the skeleton of some creature in the filthy rushes before she found what she dropped. Meg Beaufort had tried to keep up the living quarters, but it was a man's household and she could make little progress against Tudor tradition. The meat was stringy, the wine gritty, and the food was always cold by the time it traveled from the kitchen to the dining hall. Jasper didn't seem to notice. It was how he had always lived except when he visited London, where he considered life to be soft.

But the cold and inconvenience was secondary to Blanche's distress. She was desperate for news of Brithric. She even considered dressing as a peasant and traveling back to London to make inquiries. But she had to admit it was a completely impractical plan. In the first place, she hadn't been near enough peasants to know how to act like one. And even a convincing peasant woman could not roam about the countryside without being either questioned or raped. So she had to be content with waiting—endless waiting.

Margaret had decided that Jasper's advice would have to be her mainstay, and he said to do nothing now. "We must wait and see what Warwick and York do next," he said. "I am sending letters to all our friends telling them that you and the Prince are alive and free. I am telling them that you are ready to do battle at the next opportunity and that you are depending on their good will and love of their rightful

King. In the meantime there is nothing to do but wait, mayhap for a long time. But you are welcome here," he added, seemingly confident that he was offering comfortable lodging, "for as long as we must wait."

"Thank you, Jasper, it is good of you to be so kind to us."

"Madam, you are my brother's wife. You are also my Queen. I am honored to serve you," Jasper said.

Warwick took King Henry to London. The King was lodged in the Tower of London. Not, of course, as a prisoner, although he was one, but as a dignified guest. Warwick spoke on the King's behalf and tried to maintain the fiction that decisions were being made by the Monarch. King Henry didn't know that decisions were being made and did not even inquire. He didn't ask about the Queen or his son. He requested ornaments for his private chapel.

In August Cecily and her children moved to London. In October Richard of York himself arrived from Ireland. He was to address Parliament on the tenth, but it didn't work out quite as he had expected.

York had made the decision that Margaret had feared for as long as she had known him. In truth, it was her idea, not his. If the Queen had not acted on the assumption that York wished to dethrone Henry, Cecily believed that her husband might never have considered it.

York entered the House of Lords and walked slowly and with a sense of history-making to the front of the room. Instead of bowing to the empty throne as was customary, he stepped up to the dais and stood next to the gilt chair. While he didn't actually sit down as if it was his, he laid his hand on the high back in a proprietary gesture. Then he waited. Certainly this was the moment for someone to cheer him or ask him in the interests of England to take the reins of government in hand. As it was, no one said anything. There was nothing but a smothering silence.

Richard of York, waiting in Ireland for the summons to come claim the crown, didn't know how much Warwick, heavy-handed and offensive, had alienated even York's staunchest supporters. It had begun to occur to York's friends that Warwick had managed York's fortunes for a long time, and if York took the throne, power might rest largely with Warwick. They didn't want Henry on the throne, but they wanted even less to be under the thumb of the Earl of Warwick. He was as self-seeking as the worst of the Lancaster toadies. He had a devious, sly intellect and was more of a master of intrigue than most of the other barons could cope with.

Richard of York stood at the front, still resting his hand on the throne, wondering what to say next. He didn't prepare a speech. It had never crossed his mind that he would need to say anything but "thank you."

The Archbishop of Canterbury timidly approached York. In a voice just loud enough to be heard by those closest he said, "My lord, have you come to visit the King?"

York glared at him, still speechless for a moment, then spat out, "I know of no one in the realm who ought not, rather, to visit me." He turned on his heel and strode furiously out of the room.

Warwick, standing concealed at the back of the assembly, hissed to a friend, "I've chosen a fool. All he needs is a pig bladder. I should have had a clerk pen the words for him. Still, it's too late to alter the course. I'll have him on the throne in spite of himself."

One of King Henry's friends visited the Monarch the next day in the Tower. King Henry was astonished at what he heard and admonished his friend that he must have misunderstood York's gesture and words. Henry said, "Since my cradle, for forty years, I have been King of England. My father was King, his father was King. You have all sworn fealty to me on many occasions, as your fathers swore it to my father." He felt certain that there had been a misunderstanding. No one would consider displacing him.

Blanche sat at the narrow window slit, gazing blankly at the courtyard below. She spent many hours this way, willing the time to pass, hoping against all sense that someone would ride in someday with a message from Brithric and knowing it would not happen. This day someone did ride in. She recognized him as Jasper's friend, Harry Percy. She watched him dismount, slip in the snow, and start talking to Jasper. The two men then hurried into the castle, which was barely warmer than the bite of December outside. Blanche knew that Percy's news must concern Margaret and wondered idly what news Percy had brought. Was the King dead? If so, were they better or worse off? Probably better. If Henry was dead, the rightful King was the child playing at Margaret's feet and this child was under their roof, not York's. Maybe Percy had come to tell them that York had simply locked King Henry up somewhere and declared himself King.

But whatever it was, it was of secondary interest to Blanche. She was becoming obsessed with thoughts of Brithric. The only thing that prevented her from becoming a madwoman was the necessity to act cheerful and normal for Mattie's sake.

It was half an hour before Jasper and Harry Percy came to Margaret's rooms. Percy had a nervous stutter, and in an effort to avoid stuttering, he spoke with maddening slowness.

"Your majesty, I'm—glad to see you so—well."

"Please, my lord, what is your news? What is happening in London?" Margaret asked.

"Jasper tells me you—knew of York's attempt to take the—throne in October."

"Yes, that was the last reliable message we had. No doubt later messengers were held up by the bitter weather."

"After that day York took his claims again to—Parliament. This time someone—Warwick—had told him what to say. He said that he was of an—older family of Edward the Third than the—Lancaster kings. He said that he had better right to the throne."

Blanche was taken back for a moment to a night many years ago when she was a girl listening to Alice Chaucer explain the family tree to Margaret. Margaret had seen immediately that York appeared to have a better claim to the throne. That, and other considerations, had poisoned Margaret's mind against the King's handsome cousin from the beginning. Now, so many years later, so many deaths later, York was pressing that claim. "What did the Lords say to that, sire?" Margaret asked.

"They said that his claim—was true." Margaret's expression hardened, but she said nothing. "But, your majesty," Percy tried to assure her, "the members of —Parliament said that they had sworn their loyalty to —three generations of Lancaster kings and could not displace Henry."

Blanche could hardly believe it—a Parliament crammed with York's supporters refusing his claim. "So they disallowed it?" Margaret asked.

"They suggested a compromise. York—agreed to it."

"Compromise? What sort of compromise?"

"King Henry is to rule for the rest of his life, since the peers have—pledged their loyalty to him, but Richard of York is to be his—heir."

"His heir! That cannot be. The King's heir is his son! My son!" she cried. "The King will never agree to such an arrangement."

"He *has* agreed," Percy said sadly.

"He cannot!" Margaret shrieked. "He must have been tortured."

"I'm sorry, madam. He was not. I was with the—deputation that took the suggestion to him." A note of contempt crept into Percy's voice. "He—read it. I'm sure he understood what it meant and he—agreed. He didn't seem to mind. I said to him, 'But, your grace, this will—disinherit the child of your blood,' and he answered, 'He will be happier if he is not weighed down with this burden. Perhaps he will take the cloth.' "

"He wants my child to be a monk!" She slumped

back in her chair, trying to maintain her control. "My lord, this will not be. I promise you on all that is sacred that my son *will* be your King. I know your loyalty, sire, and I appreciate your honesty. When the time comes to move against York, I shall look for you at my side."

"I will—be there, madam. Would that I could lay down my life for you and King Henry!"

"Pray don't lay down your life. I need you whole and breathing," Margaret said.

Blanche could wait no longer. "My lord Percy, have you any word of my husband?"

"I could not—stay in London long enough to make many inquiries. I found out nothing. I'm sorry," he answered.

When Percy had left, Margaret and Jasper sat for a long time in silence before she spoke. "Jasper, how could they do this? How could Henry do this to his own son?"

"Madam, it is useless to speculate on my brother's reasons for anything. He has none, or none that make sense to anyone else. As for the peers, they had no single reason or principle to act on, though they would tell you they have. They are a group of individuals, each acting simply on what he thinks will profit him most. The ideals they choose to cloak their decision in follow the decision. They are reluctant to abandon a king to whom they have sworn loyalty, no doubt, but that is only a minor consideration. They fear Warwick's power if York were handed the crown. This is just a method of putting off a decision. When

Henry dies the whole problem will be fought out again without regard to what they decide now.

"I think, too, if I may be frank with you"—Jasper hesitated, afraid of Margaret's possible reaction—"I think the barons may fear your son."

"Fear Edward—why?"

"Fear for his inheritance. I believe that they think he may turn out with a mind like his father's."

"How dare you! How dare anyone suggest such a thing?" Margaret lashed out. "The boy is entirely normal. I have been told that the King has been odd since he was a child. My boy is quite sane."

"I'm sorry, madam, this is a time for honesty between us. The boy is not entirely normal. He has a cruel streak in him. I've seen it myself."

"How can you say such a thing? He is the soul of kindness."

"Last week one of my grooms reported something to me that I didn't intend to tell you, but I think now you should know. One of the stable bitches had whelped in the barn and young Edward asked to see the pups. The groom showed him where they were, then left him while he attended to his own work. When he got back, the Prince was gone and the pups were dead. Their necks were broken."

Margaret was stunned. "But you have only a servant's word for it. You cannot accuse the King's son on such flimsy evidence," Margaret objected, sick for fear that it was true. She had caught him once pulling the feathers off a live bird, and Blanche had hinted that there was something wrong with him.

"It's not a question of taking anyone's word. It is simply something that happened. I have watched the boy myself. I know what he is like, as do you, I believe."

"What would you have him be—all sweetness and simplicity, like his father? His father is mad most of the time, and when he is not mad, he is stupid."

"Lower your voice," Jasper said sternly. He didn't know a lot about women, but he recognized hysteria when he saw it coming. "Those are treasonous words even when spoken by a king's wife to a king's brother."

"What would you have, then?" Margaret hissed. "Do you too want to see my son removed and the Yorks wear the crown?"

"You must know that no matter what happens I will fight for my brother's right to the crown—and his son's right to it. I am merely trying to tell you what your enemies think, and you must realize that some of it may be true. You cannot fight something without understanding it, and every soldier learns early to recognize weaknesses in his own defenses."

Margaret saw the sense in that. She thought a long moment and said, "Jasper, you are right. I have been thinking like a woman, not like a soldier, and I must now be a soldier. A woman has no power in a situation like this by the mere fact of her womanhood. I can no longer be just wife and mother. I must be a commander of forces." She glanced at the icy courtyard. "Forces! What forces? You and me and Harry Percy."

"Nay, madam, you have a great deal of support. I

have been sending and receiving messages since your arrival. Many of your friends are standing by, ready to come to your aid, but this is not the moment. They will be ready when you are."

"When will I be ready, brother?"

"I don't know. We will keep in touch with events in London and see what happens. You will recognize the time when it comes—or at least I will. If you are still willing to rely on my judgment?"

"Of course I am, Jasper. While we wait, then, you must teach me to be a soldier."

"The first thing is to let word get around that you are going to France to recruit support to free the King."

"I am going to France?" Margaret exclaimed, excited at the prospect.

Jasper looked at her in surprise. "Of course you're not going to France. We are going to Scotland."

Cecily and Richard were enjoying their noon meal together. It was the first time they had been alone for a meal since Richard's arrival in London. Everyone seemed to want Richard's time; he was busy from dawn to late at night. His official installation as King Henry's heir had been impressive. The sword of state was carried before him as if he were already King. He was dressed in his finest robes, and with Cecily and young Edward and Edmund beside him, he was cheered madly by the common people who lined the route. Though he had vehemently denied wanting to be King, he was obviously enjoying the honor of pseudo-kingship.

The meal was interrupted by Warwick. "Richard,

news from Scotland. It is as I thought. The Queen is not in France, but has gone to Scotland to enlist James the Second's support."

"Yes, I thought that is what she would do. I was hoping that she really would go to France. Her chance of success was less there. James would welcome an invitation to invade England and he has the forces to do it," York said. "Why are you smirking like that, cousin?"

"Because I have more news," Warwick said. He grabbed a chicken leg and chewed it thoughtfully, making his audience wait for the rest of what he had come to tell them. "James the Second of Scotland is dead."

"Dead?"

"Yes, my spies tell me that he was besieging one of his castles that refused to acknowledge his authority. He had some new cannon he planned to use against the rebels. The first shot blew up the cannon and killed everyone standing near it, including the King.

"Then his wife, Mary of Gueldres, is carrying on for him," Cecily said. "An alliance between two queens . . ."

"Do not underestimate Mary," Warwick warned. "After James was killed, Mary of Gueldres took command, finished the siege, captured the rebels, and marched to Edinburgh for the funeral of her husband and the coronation of her young son as James the Third."

"Is Queen Margaret in Edinburgh also?" York asked.

"No, Queen Mary left Edinburgh to visit Margaret at Lincluden. Margaret was received with great honor,

I'm told. Queen Mary has announced that they have much to discuss and she will be staying with Margaret for a fortnight. This is all I know at the moment. But I think I can guess what they have to talk about."

"They are both mothers of young royal sons," Cecily mused. "That is a powerful bond. Will Queen Margaret get Scotland's support?"

"I think she will," Richard said. Warwick nodded agreement. "And if I know Jasper Tudor, they will march straight for London to capture King Henry. We cannot allow that to happen. Cis, I'm afraid it's going to be another Christmas apart. We will have to start north and try to destroy as many of the Lancaster strongholds as possible before Margaret starts south."

"But, Richard, it's November already. She won't start until spring. Can't you wait?" Cecily asked.

"You forget that the Queen is being guided by Jasper Tudor," Warwick said. "Winter doesn't stop a Welshman. They like fighting in the snow, especially since their adversaries usually aren't prepared to fight in cold weather. It is necessary to move as quickly as possible."

"I'm sorry, darling, but he's right. I must leave as quickly as I can. I will take Edmund with me. Warwick will stay here in London to guard Henry in case the Queen's armies get past me. Edward will make the season jolly for you, Cis."

On the day Richard and his armies departed, he said to her, "I don't like this, Cis. I have never led an army against a woman. But, pray God, this will be the last time. If we can capture the Queen and the Prince and get them safely locked up with King Henry in the

Tower, their support will evaporate. So long as Margaret is free she is a threat to the peace of England. I shall, hopefully, be at our castle at Sandal by Christmas. I will send word to you from there." He kissed her long and hard. Cecily had never been so reluctant to see him go. She watched until long after he was out of sight.

CHAPTER THIRTEEN

Two sleepy sentries stood guard at the gates of Sandal Castle. It was a waste of their time, they agreed. It was the day after Christmas and armies always stopped fighting for the week between Christmas and the New Year. Not that they hadn't seen enough fighting in the previous two weeks. They had come with York from London. York's son Edmund had moved toward Wales, and York toward Yorkshire, to destroy all the Lancastrian strongholds they could before Queen Margaret made her move. They had done well. Several castles along the way had been surrendered with little resistance, but when they got to Sandal, York stopped and Edmund rejoined him.

They had information that Queen Margaret was at Pontefract Castle, a mere ten miles ahead. She had a large army with her, and since Christmas was only a few days off, York ordered that they stop and rest during the holiday. The sentries agreed that it wasn't much of a rest. It was cold and everyone was hungry. The fall and winter had been harsh and Sandal Castle was not very well stocked with provisions. York's army had moved in and consumed most of the grain and ale in a matter of days. Now they were having to send out hunters every day to kill game to feed the men. Today more men than usual would go out, for the makeshift Christmas feast the day before had left nothing to eat today.

The sentries sat shivering and complaining until dawn. They noted without alarm that there were several of the Queen's soldiers standing on a rise to the north, observing them. There was nothing unusual about that. York had soldiers watching Pontefract Castle, too.

It was hard to tell when dawn came. It was a foggy, overcast day with a cold mist and occasional snowflakes. Finally the hunters began to assemble at the gates. The men were bundled in their warmest furs and were complaining about the chances of killing something that they couldn't even see in such weather. York himself was with them, though he wasn't going hunting. He gave them instructions to be very careful and listen for any call to return. The sentry in the tower high above signaled that the soldiers on the hill to the north were still there and doing nothing suspicious. The hunters left through the heavy gates.

They had barely gotten out of sight when the tower sentry sent word to York that the Queen's soldiers had disappeared behind the hill. York wasn't really alarmed about it. They were probably just changing shifts, but to be safe he ordered that the gun be fired to signal the hunters back. It might clear up enough later in the morning to make it safer to be outside the castle walls. York went up to the tower to see if he could pick out the hunters returning. He squinted into the foggy air. He could hardly see the ground. The signal was fired again, and just as York saw the first of the hunters nearing the gate, the sentry grabbed his arm.

"Look, my lord, they are attacking! There, to the north."

York looked to the hill where the soldiers had been a moment before. Thirty or forty horsemen were galloping over the rise. They had been concealed behind the hill.

York's son Edmund came running up the steps with Warwick's father, Salisbury, panting behind him. "Father, can you see them? Only one of our men reached the gate."

York spoke quickly to one of his aides: "Get horses saddled as fast as you can."

"Richard, you're not going out there?" Salisbury wheezed.

"I have to. I cannot just stand here and watch my own men slaughtered. There aren't many of the Queen's men."

"And how many more do you think are still behind the hill?" Salisbury asked.

"I doubt that there are any more. This is probably just a small force sent to harass and demoralize us."

"I'm coming too, Father," Edmund said.

"Very well, get your horse saddled. Hurry."

"If you are determined to do this, I'm with you," Salisbury said, already on his way down the stairs.

The tower sentry stayed at his post. He saw York and his son Edmund and old Salisbury ride out the gates with a force of fifty men. He could hear the fighting going on below, though he couldn't see it very well. When next he looked to the sinister hill to the north, he saw another group of the Queen's soldiers

285

coming over it, and another and another. Hundreds of men, it seemed.

The sentry couldn't see the soldiers take Salisbury. They intended to take him back to the Queen to use to get ransom from Warwick, his son. But Salisbury, though old, was spirited and he fought back. They killed him.

The fog obliterated the sentry's vision. He didn't see Edmund try to escape, only to be caught by young Clifford, whose father had been killed at St. Albans. "Your father killed mine and now I'll kill you and all your kin," Clifford shouted at Edmund before he plunged a sword deep into his abdomen.

The sentry in the tower didn't see the Queen's soldiers kill Richard of York. He didn't see them chop York's head from his body and cram it onto a spike.

The sentry slumped into the corner and wept as the Queen's forces swarmed through the gates of Sandal Castle.

Margaret was intoxicated with victory. She knew of York's death, but had only had time to think of it as a political fact, not a personal one. Jasper Tudor had stayed at her side, advising her every step of the way, but insisting that she make the actual decisions. He was teaching her to be a soldier, a general.

After the rout of Sandal Castle, she gathered her army to march into the city of York. She rode beside Jasper at the head of her army. It wasn't until she was almost beneath the gate into the walled city that she looked up. There on spikes stuck into the archway were three heads. On one side, the grizzled countenance of Salisbury, on the other side the tragically youthful head of Edmund, and in the center, lips drawn back from gleaming teeth in his death agony, the head of Richard of York. His dead eyes stared down at her. His hair was matted with his own blood and on his head was a paper crown.

Margaret had seen death many times before, but not *this* death. She involuntarily reined in her horse and stared back at the face above her. She felt herself about to faint and knew that she could not allow herself to do so. She averted her eyes and drew a deep breath. Suddenly she doubled over sideways and vomited. Jasper grabbed her to keep her from falling.

" 'Tis a vulgar sight for a woman," he said to his aide, "though I thought she was less frail than that. Blanche," he said, looking around for her. She was riding to the rear, talking with frantic animation to the children to keep any of them from looking up. "Blanche, take the Queen into the city. I have sent ahead orders that rooms are to be prepared for her."

Blanche hurried the children along, but not quickly enough to prevent them from noticing the heads. Prince Edward acted as though the heads on spikes were simply part of the scenery, but Dickon and Mattie burst into tears. Blanche tried to soothe them and Margaret at the same time and ended up nearly in tears herself.

Margaret had sent word to Alice Chaucer to attend her in York, and that night Alice arrived. Instead of bowing formally, Alice took one glance at Margaret and folded her in her arms. "Ah, sweeting, what have they done to you? You're so thin and pale," she said.

"Come here and rest. I'll get you some light supper and ale. While the servants are preparing it, you get yourself into a warm shift and let me brush your hair for you."

Margaret began to sniffle.

"Now, now. You get warm and fed and then you can tell me all about it," Alice ordered. Blanche had never been so relieved to see anyone as she was to see Alice. Blanche knew that it was a moment of trauma for Margaret, but she couldn't have coped with it herself. She was too wrung out and upset over the children and her own worry. She *had* to find out about Brithric. She had decided that Hell must be like this —not a place but a state of mind of constantly not knowing what had happened to a loved one. She couldn't even begin the process of getting over his death, for she didn't know if he was dead. She thought he probably was or he would have found a way to get word to her, but suppositions were not the same as knowing for sure. The town of York was full of soldiers. Certainly she could find someone who knew of Brithric's fate. She would get the children to bed and then set out to ask questions. Alice Chaucer had freed her from her duties to Margaret so that she could do so. She would always be grateful for that.

Blanche had just gotten the children settled when there was a knock on the door. "Madam, there is a man to see you," the servant told her. Blanche hurried into the anteroom and for a moment didn't recognize the man who stood waiting to see her. His clothing was dirty and ragged and he stayed in the shadows as if unwilling to be seen. "Charles!" she cried. "Is it really you?"

"Quietly," he whispered. "My life is not safe here. I must go immediately, but I heard you were here and I had to see you before I left."

"Come with me," she said. "Dickon is sleeping in the next room. You want to see him, don't you?"

They crept quietly into the children's room and Charles stood looking down on the boy he had fathered. Tears came to his eyes and he brushed them away with embarrassment. He looked then at Mattie. "Your girl?" he asked.

"Yes."

"She is beautiful," he said softly. "I must speak to you and then I have to go before I am caught." When they got back to the anteroom, he said, "Have you word of Brithric?"

She shook her head, suddenly afraid that she was going to find out he was dead.

"He was with King Henry when Warwick captured him. I was there. I saw a soldier try to strike the King. Brithric struck back in the King's defense and was set upon." He spoke hurriedly, anxious to be gone. "Brithric was injured but not killed. I have no idea how badly he was hurt. Then I lost sight of him. I inquired later and was told that he had been taken to the Tower of London. I was not able to see him, but I used what influence I had, which is small, to get him put into a healthy room above ground rather than the wet cells underground. The last time I heard, he was still alive. I know nothing more of his condition and I cannot say for sure that he is alive now."

"Charles, how can I thank you for risking your own safety to tell me this? You can't imagine what I've been through not knowing." She began to weep in spite of her firm resolve to take whatever he told her calmly.

"The Queen has won for the time being. She will undoubtedly march for London and you may see for yourself what has happened to him."

Even in the grip of her emotions she could not over-look his. "Charles, I am terribly sorry about the Duke of York. I know how you admired him."

"It's not just that I admired him. He was right and your sister is wrong. She will destroy our country."

"I won't argue with you. You are too good a friend to have taken this risk for me. I can only thank you."

"It was a small thing to do. You would have done the same for Ursula, and you are raising my son. Would that I could do more for you."

They stood staring at each other, their own self-imposed rules preventing them both from saying what they were thinking, that there was still a great love at rest between them.

Without speaking, he kissed her lightly on the cheek and was gone.

Margaret and her forces stayed at York for several weeks, waiting for additional support to reach them. They were weeks of exasperating impatience for Blanche. She tried to send a message of inquiry to Lon-don, but the city gates were barred and still under War-wick's control, and the messenger returned without any additional information. If it hadn't been for her great need to get to London, Blanche might have enjoyed her stay in York. Queen Margaret actually had a court again. After the long months of dreary isolation in Wales, it was nice to have other people around to talk with. Lady Alice Chaucer stayed on and was joined by Lady Grey, nee Elizabeth Woodville. Blanche remembered with some resentment how the Queen had used Elizabeth's betrothal as an excuse to give a dinner announcing her own pregnancy. But Elizabeth hadn't seemed to mind and she was happy now, so it didn't matter. She and Lord Grey were well matched and content with each other. Lord Grey had come to fight on the Queen's side and Elizabeth had persuaded him to let her and their two little boys come along with the Queen. The boys were very young, their innocence giving a sweet, domestic touch to the warlike court.

Finally in February Queen Margaret and her forces began to move southward toward London. It was an ugly march. Not only was it cold and muddy, but her army was out of control. They were leaving a path of destruction that even Margaret couldn't condone. As they neared St. Albans, the town where the Duke of Somerset had been killed long ago, they got word that the opposition was facing them. Somerset's son, a pimply faced young man named Henry Beaufort, begged the Queen to put him in charge of the armies on the field. "The Earl of Warwick killed my beloved father here, your majesty. As a boy, I saw his body stripped and thrown out into the square. I must avenge his death and there is no better place," he said.

Although Margaret found Henry Beaufort as unappealing as his father, he was a good soldier and so she agreed to his request. Jasper Tudor moved some of his forces west to try heading off York's son Edward, who was still in Wales, but reported ready to move to Warwick's defense.

Margaret and Blanche didn't see the battle, but stayed at a safe distance with the children. Blanche suddenly felt old. She was only thirty, but the same fight that Margaret had nurtured as a girl was now being fought by the next generation. Henry Beaufort, fighting for the Lancasters, was a boy of five or six when she first saw him. Blanche remembered Edward of York as a chubby-faced little boy showing Margaret a toy, a boat or soldier or something, and saying proudly, "My father made this for me." Now his father's head rotted on a spike over the gates of the city, and Edward, no longer a child, was moving in with an army against them.

One of the first reports from the battlefront touched horribly on this second generation of victims. Lord Grey, Elizabeth Woodville's young husband, had been killed. Elizabeth said nothing when the news was brought to her. She clung tightly to her little boys. Margaret tried to comfort her, but Elizabeth retained a dry-eyed, stony silence. Blanche waited for the first shock to sink in, then went to Elizabeth and said softly, "I'm sorry."

"I'll never be the same person as I was yesterday," Elizabeth said. "I begged him not to make this his fight. Yesterday we were a happy family. Now I am a widow, my sons are orphans. I loved him, you know."

"I know."

"The Queen killed him. . . ."

"Hush, you mustn't say that."

"But she did. It wasn't his fight, it's hers. I didn't care which side won—now *I've* lost."

"Elizabeth, when this is over, take your boys and go back to your people. You have a big family to go home to, don't you?"

"Yes."

"Then go back to them. Stay away from court. Stay away from the Queen," Blanche said, wishing she could take the same advice herself. Margaret's preoccupation with the destruction of the Yorks was destroying many lives, perhaps Brithric's as well as Lord Grey's.

Throughout the day reports came to Margaret. Some good, some bad, but on the average the Lancaster cause seemed to be winning. When night began to fall, word came that Warwick and his men had fled, leaving the King behind. Queen Margaret hurried into St. Albans. She was delighted to see Henry alive and well. As husband and father he was a total loss, but as a political pawn he was absolutely vital to her. She found him sitting under a tree, dressed in a full set of armor and attended by two of Warwick's men. "Arrest these men," Margaret ordered.

"Nay, madam, I promised them their safety when they stayed to protect me. They must be released," Henry begged.

"Send for the Prince," Margaret ordered and stood glaring at Henry until Blanche brought the boy. Blanche thought she was bringing the child to see his father and was surprised to find what the true purpose was. "My son," Margaret said, "I ask you, what

293

shall be done with these men you see wearing the badge of York?"

The boy's eyes glittered. "They shall die, madam. Their heads shall be cut off," he piped.

"So be it," Margaret said.

Blanche was too shocked to speak and she knew her remonstrance would do nothing but further anger Margaret. But to ask such a decision of a child!

Sir Thomas Kyriel, one of the sentenced knights, stepped forward. "May the wrath of God fall on those who have taught a child to speak such words," he said boldly.

"Behead him," Margaret shrilled.

King Henry put his face in his hands and wept.

Queen Margaret moved toward London. She and Blanche had carefully avoided speaking to one another in the days since the two knights were beheaded. Blanche had faced something she had been trying to keep in the dark, unacknowledged places in her mind. The Prince, the boy she had tried to help raise, was vicious. Already at eight years of age his mind was as warped as his father's but in a different and much uglier way. From that time on, she did all the small inconspicuous things she could to keep Mattie and Dickon away from the Prince and talked probingly with them, trying to detect if anything of his character had come off on them. She reassured herself that they were healthy-minded, curious youngsters. But they were growing up much faster than Blanche liked to see. They knew too much of the harsher sides of life than anyone should know at such an age.

Dickon was almost old enough to join his father. In peaceful times he would have done so several years ago. But Blanche kept hoping against hope that the next battle might be the last. But many men had twelve- and fourteen-year-old sons with them in battle. Edward of York was leading armies and upholding his father's standard, and he was but eighteen.

Blanche began to consider also her own appearance. It hadn't mattered to her for a long time what she looked like, but now she tried to see herself as Brithric would see her if she found him alive. She had lost her girlish plumpness and her hair wasn't as glossy as it had been once, but all in all, she didn't think she looked her age. She was fortunate in having had good health and hadn't yet lost any teeth. There were wrinkles of worry and concern that had become permanent around her eyes, but she was pleased to discover that she didn't look nearly as bad as many women did at her age. If only they could hurry to London.

Just as they got under way they got word that Jasper Tudor had run into young Edward of York's forces. There had been a brief, fierce battle, which Edward had won. Jasper had escaped, but his old father, Owen Tudor, whom Blanche had never met, had been captured and beheaded. Edward of York was now moving toward London from the west and Margaret was moving her army in from the north, but Margaret was only a day's march from their target and Edward of York was several days away.

When they reached the city wall, Margaret sent an envoy in to speak with the mayor, Geoffrey Boleyn. Boleyn was a friend of hers and sympathized with the

Lancaster cause personally, but he regretfully sent word that the population was so against her armies entering the city, after all they had heard of the devastating march to St. Albans, that it would be unsafe for Margaret to try to enter London. He would send provisions out to her army, however.

Blanche asked permission to go in alone to see if her husband was still in the Tower, but Henry Beaufort told her to wait. The city gates would not be opened for a single individual, certainly not a woman. Just wait a few days, he advised, London would change its mind. Blanche was frantic, to have come so far only to be thwarted so close to her goal.

The carts carrying the provisions were waylaid long before they got outside the city, and Margaret's troops got hungrier while they waited for London to relent. The army was disintegrating. The foot soldiers, the common men, were needed at home. It was one thing to go off and fight during the winter when there was nothing else to do anyway, but spring was coming and who would feed their families for the next year if the planting weren't done on time? So they began to drift away during the nights. Every morning the camp had shrunk a little more. Then came the rumor that Edward of York was only two days away and moving quickly toward them.

Margaret realized that she would be in trouble if she allowed herself and her dwindling forces to be trapped between a hostile army and a hostile city. She withdrew. She had the King with her, after all, and London wasn't that vital. She could set up court and run the government from anywhere she chose so long as she held on to Henry.

It wasn't that easy for Blanche. She had gotten this far and couldn't go back without getting into London. She hit on a plan, worked it all out in her mind, and asked Margaret if she could stay behind. Margaret didn't want to leave her behind. "What are you going to do? You can't stay here alone," she protested.

"I will be all right. It's very important to me. If Brithric is well, I will join you as soon as I can get him out of the Tower. If not, I will follow you as soon as I can."

"But how can you accomplish either?"

"I have Charles Seintleger's son. Charles is in favor with the Yorkists. He will help me," Blanche explained, not mentioning that she had no idea where Charles was or how to find him.

"I don't like it, Blanche, but you seem to have your heart set on it and I can't deny you anything that means so much to you. But I do think you are being foolish."

"Thank you, Meggie," Blanche said, feeling some of the old affection she had for Margaret.

Edward, Duke of York since his father's death, held his mother in his arms. Cecily was weeping in another's presence for the first time since her husband's death. Edward was still young enough to be a little frightened by his mother's tears. He had never seen her cry before. But he was the man of the family now, eighteen years old and a peer of the realm, and as he saw it, rightful heir to his father's claim to the throne of England. "Come, now," he said to Cecily, offering her a silk handkerchief. "Where are the young ones?"

"I sent them to friends across the Channel as soon as I heard about your father. I thought they would be safer there."

"You were right to do so, but you should have gone, too."

"I had no need to worry. Queen Margaret doesn't hurt women; she only kills their husbands and sons," Cecily said bitterly.

"Actually I'm glad you're here, Mother," Edward said. "I'll take good care of you."

"What can I do to help you?" Cecily asked.

"Just keep your ears open to anything I should know and come to St. John's Field tomorrow and see what happens."

In the morning there was a great crowd at St. John's Field. They were mostly Yorkist, since most of London was Yorkist in sympathy. Cecily hardly knew what to expect, but watched the milling crowd for a hint of what was about to happen. Suddenly there was a hush for a moment and then loud cheers broke out. Cecily could see her son approaching, tall and handsome, a head above everyone else. He was dressed regally and the gold in his cape picked up the gold in his hair. He was really the handsomest man in the kingdom, Cecily thought, and apparently the crowd agreed with her. Men cheered and fought each other to pat his shoulder. Women swooned and young maidens giggled and blushed at the sight of him.

He had Warwick with him. As Edward neared his

mother, he flashed the smile that so reminded her of Richard, and he bowed low over her hand. Then he turned to the crowd, which Cecily noticed had filled out with a great many of the nobility in among the commoners.

"My friends, my countrymen—and women," his voice boomed out. The people cheered and laughed at his inclusion of women. It was well known how much he liked the ladies. "There are questions that should be asked of you. I am here to ask those questions."

There was a deep, significant silence. The people sensed that they were about to alter history.

"Is King Henry the Sixth worthy to remain your King?"

The answer was deafening: "Nay, nay, he is not!"

Edward held up his hand for silence. He waited; he must have full attention. "Would you have me be your King?" he asked.

The crowd went berserk. "Yea, yea, yea!" they shouted. They wept and flung themselves forward to touch him, to kneel to him, to kiss his hands.

"I must admit I am perplexed," Cecily said later that night to Warwick. There had been celebrations all day long and Cecily was tired. "Why is it that my husband, a man of proven judgment and ability, only months ago offered himself as king and was rejected? Now my son offers himself and is all but devoured. What is the difference?"

"There are two differences, Cecily. One difference is that when Richard offered himself we had the King in the Tower under our control. He was good enough as a figurehead, but now that she-wolf Margaret of

Anjou has King Henry, there is no way to be loyal to our party without committing treason unless the Yorks have their own rightful king on the throne."

"What is the other reason?"

"The other is the nature of the men. Don't bristle like that—I mean no criticism. Richard never wanted to be king. You know that as well as I. And no matter what he said, it showed. But this son of yours—he wants more than anything else in life to be King of England. And the people know it. He will be King of England when he is crowned in three days' time."

Edward's coronation was magnificent. Edward was magnificent. There was a service at St. Paul's Cathedral and then he was carried in state to Westminster. He took his seat on the throne, his enormous physique dwarfing the gilt chair. It symbolized to Cecily that it was Edward, not the throne, that was really important to England.

"I have come, my lords, to take my place on the throne of England. It is my rightful place, my right by inheritance as the true heir of my ancestor, Edward the Third. I am now to be Edward the Fourth, your King, and I shall do all that God and my own powers can for the good of our beloved country."

As Cecily listened, a long-forgotten scene flashed through her memory. It must have been fifteen years ago when Cecily first met Queen Margaret. Margaret had said, "Perhaps when God wills, I shall have a son, too, and name him Edward. He will be Edward the Fourth. Our Edwards will be fine friends."

At that time Cecily had felt pity and understanding for the girl who had the misfortune to be married to

King Henry. Now, with her husband and oldest son dead at the hand of Queen Margaret, Cecily Neville felt only hate.

Blanche had finished explaining to Cecily about Brithric. "So you see, I had to ask for your help. I know you have no reason to do anything for me, but I remembered how kind you were and I thought you would understand," Blanche said.

"I'm glad you came to me. I, too, have pleasant memories of you and the time we met and you played with the children. You were so good with them. Are these yours?" Cecily asked, looking at Dickon and Mattie, who were standing behind Blanche's skirts.

"The girl is mine. The boy is Sir Charles Seintleger's son."

"Sir Charles's son! He and his wife stayed at Fotheringay with us for a while. I was sorry to hear of her death. She spoke so highly of you. So this is her child. Come here, young man. Let me look at you. He favors his father, does he not? I have a boy a little older than you. His name is Dickon."

"That is my name, too, madam."

"He is named for your husband," Blanche told Cecily.

Cecily's eyes misted over. "What a proud tribute. I will arrange for you to be taken to the Tower to look for your husband. Do you wish to leave the children with me while you go, or do you have friends here?"

"I have no friends here but you. I appreciate your thoughtfulness."

"After the noon meal I will have someone escort

you to the Tower and the children can play with my Dickon. How did you get into the city?"

"I paid a farmer to let us hide in his cart when he was allowed through the gates to take his baskets to market to sell. For enough money he was willing to leave his baskets out in a field where he can pick them up tonight and bring them back tomorrow."

"You are a clever woman."

"I am a desperate woman."

"Haven't you anywhere to go?" Cecily asked.

"No, but I will find something. I still have a little money left."

"No, you will stay here until I can make arrangements."

"How can I ever repay you?" Blanche asked.

"You can't. But someday you will do what you can for someone else who can't repay you. You see, I am working out old debts now."

Later that day a man arrived to escort Blanche to the Tower of London. She rode in a carriage emblazoned with the arms of York and felt only a momentary guilt. The carriage drew up before one of the many imposing gates of the fearful old fortress. Her escort dismounted and went to speak to the gatekeeper. She held her breath. Any moment now the man might come back to tell her that Brithric was not there, that he had died or been executed. The men talked endlessly.

Then her escort came back and remounted his horse. It was only partial relief for her. Perhaps the gatekeeper didn't even know their errand. Maybe he had only been questioning their credentials for entering the Tower. The great doors swung open and the carriage rolled into the central courtyard. Blanche had been here before, but only to the Royal Apartments, never near the prisoners' quarters. The carriage stopped and she got out. She was afraid to ask any of the questions that were tearing her heart. She followed Cecily's servant through a stone archway and up some wide steps. He seemed to know where he was going and she followed docilely. At the top of the second flight of steps the man stopped in front of a sturdy locked door. He tapped lightly, and when it opened to reveal a manservant, Blanche's escort said nothing.

It was up to her now. "I seek Brithric de Bohun," she said breathlessly. The manservant bowed and backed into the room, pulling the door open for her. She entered a large, cold room. There were windows, but heavy curtains were drawn tightly against the cold, and in the dim light she could hardly tell where she was. She blinked owlishly in the semidarkness.

"So you have come?" a venomous feminine voice said out of the gloom.

"Jane?" Blanche asked of a shadow that was materializing into a distinct form.

"Yes," she answered coldly. "You were not here and someone had to care for him. Naturally you would not. I should have known you would get here before the end to reclaim him."

Blanche wasn't listening to her. Her eyes were adjusting to the lack of light and she could see, in the corner of the room, a bed set into an alcove. Under the heavy layer of covers a figure stirred. "Brithric!" she cried and ran to him.

His white-gold hair was unkempt and fanned out

303

like a limp halo around his head. His face was flushed and wet with fever sweat. She sat carefully on the edge of the bed and took his hand. She held it to her face and kissed it and wept. "Oh, Brithric, I found you. Thank God, I found you."

His eyes opened slightly, then closed, then opened again with the full realization that she was there. "Blanche? You're here?" His voice was so weak she could hardly hear him.

"Yes, I'm here. I'm going to stay with you until you are well, then we'll go away."

"No—I'm dying."

"No, no, you're not dying. You're just tired and I'll make you well," she said.

"Dying . . ." he said matter-of-factly.

"Don't talk," she said. "I shall talk now, and later, when you're rested, you can tell me what has happened. Mattie is well." He smiled wanly. "She has grown tall and is becoming very beautiful."

"Hair?"

"She has long white hair," Blanche said, almost laughing and feeling hysteria bubbling dangerously near the surface.

Brithric smiled in acknowledgment of the memory of how happy they had both been that the child had hair like his. "I shall bring her to see you tomorrow," Blanche said.

"No tomorrow . . ." he whispered and shook his head, though the effort was visibly painful.

Blanche had forgotten Jane's presence until she spoke. "Blanche, you must go now. You are tiring him."

"Go!" Blanche said indignantly. "I shall not go at all. This is my husband and he needs me."

"He does not need you now. Get out of here," Jane hissed. They were both trying to talk quietly so Brithric would not hear them. But he did.

With great effort he raised his head and turned to Jane. "Would you leave us?" he said to her.

She stepped back as if he'd struck her. She stared back at him and then walked stiffly out.

Brithric lay back, exhausted from the effort of lifting his head. Blanche studied his sleeping face—so thin and drawn from illness. It was hard to believe that once she had known him and not known she loved him. How could she ever have lived without his love? How would she do so now if he died? The manservant entered the room with a basin of warm water and a lint cloth to bathe his face. Blanche took the cloth and spoke to the servant. "Has he been like this long?"

"Not this bad. But he's been sick ever since he got here. He had a wound in his shoulder. It seemed to be healing, then got worse again. There was great swelling."

"Was it drained? Was he cared for?"

"Yes, madam. And he was better again for a while; then the poison started growing again in his chest."

"Can he live?" Blanche asked, knowing and fearing the answer.

The man shook his head sadly.

Blanche sat by Brithric's side for long hours. Sometimes he moved slightly in his sleep, then groaned with the pain it caused. Night fell, but Blanche was unaware of it until the manservant came in to light the candles.

He brought her some broth and bread. He meant it as a kindness and she tried to eat, but could not. Blanche held Brithric's hot, dry hand and felt his pulse grow so feeble that sometimes she could not feel it at all for moments. The candles burned down and sputtered as their life ran out, eaten up by flame.

A faint sliver of light penetrated the heavy curtains when Brithric stirred again. He opened his eyes suddenly—startled at something that was happening to his body. "Blanche!" he cried out. Then he shuddered violently and blood gushed from his mouth and nose. He lay still. Blanche took the lint cloth and, with the now cold water, carefully cleaned his face. Tenderly she brushed the hair back from his forehead. She put her hands to his pale, lifeless cheeks and said softly, "I love you, Brithric."

She went to the windows and pulled open the drapes. She stared down with detachment at the busy people below and wondered how they could go on with Brithric dead. How could she go on? The manservant came to the door and looked at her questioningly. "He's gone," Blanche said. "Please ask Lady Jane if she would like to see him."

But there was no need to call Jane; she was just outside the door. She ran in and threw herself down beside the deathbed, sobbing violently. Blanche stood by the window, trying to keep Jane's ostentatious grief from infecting her. Finally she could stand no more. She went to Jane and tried to speak kindly. "Jane, come now, that is enough." She took Jane's arm to help her up.

But Jane shook off her hand and stood by herself. Her face was ugly and blotchy, her eyes red with previous hours—days—of weeping. "Of course it's enough for you. He's dead. Now you're free of him and I—I who loved him—wasn't even allowed to be with him at the end." She was screaming.

Blanche tried to remain calm. It was not seemly to behave thus in Brithric's presence even if there was no longer life in his body. "It was not your place to be with him, Jane. *I* was his wife," she said firmly.

"Your place!" Jane shrieked. "What place should you have? You stole him from me, just as you tried to steal my brother from Ursula, poor, dead Ursula, who loved you. You stole Ursula's love from me, too. You are evil and wicked."

"That's not true, Jane. Calm yourself."

"It is true. You know it is so. You have even stolen my brother's child. My own nephew."

"That is enough," Blanche said and briskly slapped her as hard as she could. Jane quickly gathered her skirts and ran from the room. Blanche resumed her place by the side of the bed and sat quietly, unable even to cry. After Jane's ugly outburst it would have seemd sacrilege to weep. She knew that she must look forward now. She had a child to raise by herself and another child to care for until his father could reclaim him. She had only one place in the world now, with her sister, the woman who was responsible for Brithric's death. She suddenly felt the full impact of Elizabeth Woodville's accusations against the Queen. But Elizabeth was free to resent the Queen—to turn away and rebuild her life. Elizabeth was still young and beautiful and had a large, loving family to return to. Blanche had no one but Margaret.

Blanche called the manservant and asked for pen and paper. She sat down at the table near the window and wrote a letter to Brithric's family, telling them of the manner of his death, and then set out to arrange that his body be taken with haste to his family's estates. She would not go with him. She didn't know his family. They had never shown any interest in her or Mattie, and she felt it best to sever her connection with them. She had already said goodby to Brithric and that was all that mattered.

Blanche went back to Cecily's house that night. Only then did she allow herself to cry. Cecily cried with her. "You shall stay with me here," Cecily said after they had both wiped their eyes.

"I cannot."

"Why not?" Cecily asked.

"My lady Duchess, you must be forgetting. I am the Queen's sister. I am your enemy," Blanche said.

"You and I could never be enemies. We are widows who have lost fine men and have chlidren to raise. I am not trying to make you stay with me forever, though it would please me. I know your loyalty to your sister"—only then did her voice have a tinge of acid—"but there is no way for you to go to her. You have no idea where she has gone and you cannot simply roam around the countryside looking for her."

Blanche recognized the truth in this. "But I must go to her immediately."

"And you shall. As soon as her whereabouts are

known, I will try to arrange transportation for you, but for now, stay with me."

"I don't know. . . ."

"Blanche, please stay. I need comfort, too," Cecily said, suddenly looking as lonely and helpless as Blanche felt.

"Certainly," Blanche said, once again feeling that someone needed her and glad to feel the need.

CHAPTER FOURTEEN

Blanche had feared that Cecily's son Edward, now King Edward the Fourth, might be a frequent visitor and it would be awkward for the new King's mother to be harboring the fugitive Queen's sister. But Edward took no account of Blanche's presence. He wasn't even interested in her as a hostage. Apparently he knew enough of Queen Margaret's psychology to realize that she would gladly sacrifice her own sister to her ambitions and so Blanche as hostage was valueless. Besides, King Edward was far too busy to spend much time visiting his mother. He could not just sit back and enjoy his position.

There were small Lancastrian uprisings all over England and Edward couldn't locate King Henry and Queen Margaret. They had seemingly just disappeared. Blanche realized that King Edward was King only in London. Most of the north of England favored King Henry and didn't credit the validity of Edward's claim. So King Edward dashed about like a dog with fleas, defending one town after another, always in the hope that the next battle would deliver the ousted King and Queen into his hands.

Palm Sunday of 1461 found the York and Lancaster forces drawn up face to face at the town of Towton, near York. Both sides had marshaled enormous forces, with the principals of both sides present.

As the fighting began, so did a late snow. It was the most savage battle that any of the participants were ever to see.

The snow was blinding—great fat flakes swirling into everyone's eyes. It no more than fell than it turned crimson with the blood of the dead and mutilated soldiers on the ground. The earth was soaked with blood. When night came the Lancaster forces tried to turn and flee. There was a bridge behind them and the hundreds of men in bulky armor tried to get across the narrow passage. Quickly it became jammed. Desperately other soldiers tried to wade the river and drowned in their armor. So many died that their bodies washed downstream forming dams of flesh encased in steel, over which the rest of the soldiers retreated.

Many thousands died that day. The mass burial pits formed mounds that were to remain visible centuries later. Edward and his Yorkist army won, but at terrible cost, and they failed to capture any of the former royal family.

Margaret, Henry, and Prince Edward awaited news at York. When the fleeing Lancaster soldiers reached York with tales of the horror behind them, Margaret took her men, her child, and her idiot husband and fled northward toward Scotland and safety. King Edward entered the city of York after ordering the heads of his father, brother, and Warwick's father removed from the gate where they still rotted. He immediately sent forces after Margaret, but with little hope of catching up with her.

Margaret and her small band made a zigzag course

to their objective. They went north to Alnwick Castle, but upon receiving word that Edward's troops were close behind, she decided not to go straight north to Edinburgh. Instead she went west of Kirkcudbright. By that time King Henry was in poor health and his reasoning seemed again on the edge of sanity, so she left him at an abbey there. She felt sure his presence would be kept a secret. Even if Edward of York did find out where he was, he could hardly risk invading Scotland and violating sanctuary. There was Henry's mental state consider, too. Though Margaret had tried to keep from him what had happened at Towton, he had heard enough to be terribly upset and this was no time for another complete breakdown.

Margaret got Henry settled at Kirkcudbright and headed back east and north to Edinburgh to meet again with her sister queen, Mary of Gueldres. Margaret kept her son with her. Jasper Tudor was on his way to meet her at Edinburgh.

"Dear sister," Mary of Gueldres said to Margaret when they were alone after the court ceremonies welcoming Margaret back to Scotland, "we have much to discuss."

"I have much to thank you for and more to ask of you," Margaret said. "The soldiers you provided me in our last battle against the usurper were of great help to me, but I'm afraid there were just not enough to win our cause."

"You're going back to try again?" Queen Mary asked.

Margaret looked at Queen Mary with affection. "I have come to know you well, and you me. If one of your subjects tried to displace your son from his rightful place, I have no doubt that you would fight any odds for him. We are more than sister queens; we are mothers. You know what I must do."

Mary said, "It is time for a long and completely honest talk. There is a great deal to be settled. First, I must admit to you that our interest in your cause is not entirely personal sympathy. There is another consideration. England and Scotland have long been at war; for centuries our people have fought against one another. During your husband's reign there has been less fighting. Henry is not an aggressive man. Edward of York is. He is, from all reports I get, young and military-minded. If he remains on the throne, he will almost certainly renew the war between our countries.

"So while I, a woman and mother," she continued, "support your cause for personal reasons, my barons are somewhat inclined to support you for their own reasons."

"Somewhat inclined . . . ?"

"Yes, somewhat. There are many men in Scotland, as anywhere else, who are by nature warlike. Some would like to see the fighting resume in the hope of gaining back some of our towns that have been in English hands for years."

Margaret began to understand.

"You are a perceptive woman, Margaret. You must see the solution to this. The peaceable will fight for you to keep King Henry on the throne and avoid a larger war in their own country. That is enough reward for them. But the others have nothing to gain from peace with England unless . . ."

"Unless I promise them the gain they want," Margaret finished for her.

"Yes, I'm afraid that's the only way."

"Just what is it that they want?"

"They want Berwick back," Mary said.

"Berwick?" Margaret said. She should have known that would be the price. Berwick was a border town between England and Scotland over which there had been bitter and bloody fighting for centuries. The English had lost many lives in capturing and holding Berwick. Margaret had never been able to see why anyone wanted Berwick so badly.

"That shall be the agreement, then," Margaret said.

"No, I'm afraid we are not yet agreed," Mary said, to Margaret's surprise. "If we are to join you in this fight, we must assure ourselves of your victory. Do you know where Edward of York gets the thousands of extra soldiers to fight you? He buys them in Burgundy. They are paid mercenaries. There is no reason you cannot do the same. France hates Burgundy and you are a daughter of France. Louis the Eleventh is a kinsman of yours and with sufficient—encouragement, let us say—he would no doubt come to your aid. Then we could launch an attack on Edward of York from two directions at once."

"What do you suppose this 'encouragement' would amount to?" Margaret asked, beginning to wonder slightly at Queen Mary's knowledge of these matters.

"It so happens I have had recent communication with Louis on the subject. He knows that you have no money to pay in advance to hire his armies. He would wish only some considerations after you won."

315

"What, exactly, does he want?" Margaret asked.
"Calais."

"You have promised Calais to the French!" Jasper Tudor paced the room, wringing his hands.

"I haven't actually promised yet. Henry Beaufort has gone to France on my behalf to discuss it with Louis."

"To promise Berwick was folly enough. You *have* promised Berwick, haven't you?"

"Yes, I sent the agreement to Henry. He signed it. I didn't think it would make that much difference," Margaret said defensively.

"It will make the English dislike you all the more," Jasper said.

"The English already hate me. And I do not care. I have no wish to be loved—I want to be Queen."

"But Calais, Margaret! How could you? Calais is the jewel of England."

"I do not care!" Margaret said.

"You *will* care," Jasper came close and said in an ominously quiet voice. "If you should win this battle, then what? Do you suppose that King Louis will simply congratulate you and go about his business? Why do you suppose he wants Calais? If you win and he gets Calais, it will be just a matter of time before France invades England by way of Calais and then what will you do? Ask Scotland for help again? Scotland and France are traditional allies—they will simply squeeze England between them and you have offered them each a first step—Berwick and Calais. I understand you have also made a betrothal agreement between your son and Queen Mary's daughter?"

"Yes. Was that the wrong thing to do as well?" Margaret snapped.

"No," Jasper said absently. "Betrothals can always be broken. That was a harmless agreement." Jasper stood thinking for a while. Finally he asked, "Was it Queen Mary's idea that Henry Beaufort represent you in France?"

"Well, yes, I suppose she did suggest it first. Why do you ask?"

"Do you know that Henry Beaufort is Queen Mary's lover?"

"What!" This was an aspect of her sister queen that Margaret hadn't even considered. "I'm shocked. But I can't see that it makes any difference to us. Does it?"

"I don't know. Maybe it won't matter at all. But it is a fact to keep in mind."

When Cecily heard what was happening, she told Blanche. To her credit she did not gloat over Margaret's stupidity or express her fears for what might happen to England. Neither did Blanche say what her reactions were to the news. They managed to speak of these matters impersonally, as though neither of them were involved. It was a mark of the depth of their friendship that they were able and willing to do so.

Blanche was convinced that what Margaret was doing was both wrong and foolish, and she was sorry that Margaret had gone to Scotland. Blanche could not possibly ask Cecily to arrange transportation for her to go there. Even if Cecily were willing and got King Edward's approval, it would be impossible. No group coming from Edward's capital could hope to gain safe access to Scotland, not even if they were escorting Queen Margaret's sister.

Blanche's days would have been unbearably long if it hadn't been for Cecily and the children. Mattie was growing fast and would soon be a young woman. She had taken her father's death quite well, which was probably because she had seen little of him since outgrowing babyhood. Young Dickon was becoming more enigmatic, more tightly controlled than ever, but without losing his amiability. The high point of that year for Blanche was hearing from Charles. She felt that she should keep track of him for Dickon's sake—at least that's what she told herself. Actually it was more than that. He was now her only tie to a happy past and she longed for news of him.

With Cecily's help she made inquiries and finally learned that he was acting for King Edward as a special envoy to France, to King Louis's court. She wrote to Charles, telling him of his son's whereabouts and progress with his education. She said nothing of her own situation, but he knew what had happened, for he wrote back a short, polite note thanking her and expressing his sympathy on her husband's death. There was nothing personal in his letter, and yet she took great comfort in hearing from him at all.

Charles said nothing about what he was doing in France. Blanche heard about what was happening there from Cecily.

Henry Beaufort was still at the French court on Queen Margaret's behalf, but negotiations such as he was engaged in took time, especially since King Louis felt that the longer he delayed in agreeing to help, the more he stood to gain in the final agreement. He allowed Beaufort to live at his court and started a leisurely progress around the country. It was a full year before Beaufort was ready to return to Scotland, and then he was in disgrace before he even arrived.

"He has bragged all over France of our intimacy," Mary of Gueldres stormed. "He has made me sound like a common slut."

Mary had been ranting about Beaufort's behavior for days. The sister queens had been too much together of late and each was becoming irritating to the other. "Please try not to excite yourself," Margaret tried to soothe her. "We are only hearing rumors from far off. I'm sure when he arrives, you will find that he has not spoken ill of you."

"Rumors! How naive of you, dear Margaret. Do you think I listen to rumors? I have spies in that court. I could quote you his exact words, were it not so shameful to me. You wish to defend him only because he is the son of your own lov——" She caught herself and stopped.

"My own lover!" Margaret exclaimed. "Is that *really* what you think? Those old rumors about Somerset. So you have been thinking all this time we have been discussing our love of our sons, I have been trying to promote a bastard son of mine!"

"I spoke in haste. Please forget this," Mary said.

"How can I forget such slander from one whom I

have loved and esteemed for so long?" she said, warming to the subject. "Perhaps you have reasons of your own to suspect *my* son's legitimacy. Perhaps there are doubts about *your* son." Margaret knew as she said it she was being unwise, but her vanity was so wounded that she could not keep from lashing out.

"Madam," Mary said coldly, "you have been in my country at my mercy and my hospitality for a long time to speak to me thus."

"Too long, I believe," Margaret said.

"Exactly."

A month later Margaret was at Kirkcudbright, getting ready to depart for France herself. Beaufort had arrived in Scotland and narrowly missed being killed by an unknown attacker. Margaret had accused Queen Mary of arranging the attempt on Beaufort's life. Mary denied it. More heated words followed and Margaret decided that she should leave before she lost all the men and money that Mary had promised earlier.

One of the Frenchmen who had accompanied Beaufort back to Scotland was Pierre de Breze. Margaret had always thought of him as the man she might have married if she hadn't wed King Henry. Margaret was surprised at the change in Pierre. She remembered him as an ordinary-looking man of thirty or so. At nearly fifty he was red-faced and bulbous-nosed. He had a belly that preceded him and he did an excessive amount of throat-clearing before he spoke. He never hinted at the love he'd once had for her, but treated her very kindly. She appreciated it, for few of her associates went out of their way to treat her nicely anymore.

Margaret was delighted to see him. It was the first time in many, many years she had seen anyone from her former life in France. He had followed her misfortunes and took a great interest in her welfare. When the opportunity arose to help her, he had volunteered. He agreed to take her and the Prince away from Scotland to France and help her plead her cause to Louis the Eleventh. "Ma petite," he said, "your papa will be glad to have you back in France if only for a while. He pines for you." This was a lie, but a harmless one, Pierre thought.

"I haven't heard from Papa for years. Is he well, Pierre?"

"Time marches, petite. He is older, but spry. He still paints and dances with les belles."

"I can hardly wait to see him," Margaret said, in English. It had come as a shock to her that there was a great deal of her native language she would have to relearn. I have become English in spite of myself, she thought resentfully.

She visited King Henry before she departed, but only briefly. He had completely immersed himself in the religious life at the abbey and he wasn't quite sure who she was.

So on the first day of April 1462, Margaret, her son, Pierre de Breze, and Jasper Tudor set sail from Scotland, where she had worn out her welcome, to France, where she hadn't been invited. Within days of Margaret's departure the Earl of Warwick arrived in Scotland to offer Edward the Fourth of England as a husband to the widowed Queen Mary of Scotland. She turned him down—with regrets. She'd heard of his lusty nature and good looks and she was sorry to miss the opportunity to wed such a man.

"Blanche, can I help you pack?" Cecily asked.

"Nay, I have little to pack, little of my own, that is. Most of what I possess is because of your generosity and I should be embarrassed to have you see how many of my belongings are actually yours."

Cecily waved her hand, dismissing the concept of personal property. "That is silly; you have been my guest and friend. I would have done more for you if it had been in my power."

"You have done so much for me," Blanche said, holding her hand. "I shall miss you sorely."

"And I you. But you are going to France, to your homeland. You will be with your sister again. You will get to see your father again and old friends. Perhaps Dickon will get to see his father."

"You have word of Sir Charles?"

"Yes, I thought I'd told you. I must be getting forgetful. Sir Charles has been summoned to my son's court to make some sort of report. But with the weather so uncertain in the Channel, you might get to France before he starts back."

I hope so, Blanche thought. I dearly hope so. I have such need to see Charles, just to reassure myself that the happy times in the past actually happened.

After tearful farewells, Blanche and Mattie and Dickon set sail aboard a crowded ship for France. They made excellent time. There were a great many people at the docks when they arrived and Blanche watched idly, not expecting to see anyone familiar, for who would be there to greet her? But as the plank was lowered for the passengers to begin disembarking, a man pushed through the waiting crowd and dashed aboard.

"Charles!" Blanche shouted and waved frantically. "Over here — over here! Look, Dickon, 'tis your father."

"Blanche, you made it in time," he said, and in his enthusiasm he hugged Dickon. "Son, how big you've grown."

Dickon, shocked at being treated so affectionately by a father he hardly remembered, pulled back in embarrassment.

"In time for what, Charles? What is happening?" Blanche said, suddenly alarmed. Had something happened to Margaret?

"Why, in time to sail back with me," he said. "My ship leaves in the morning. There will be time to get your trunks moved aboard." He said it as if there had been some prior arrangement worked out that she had simply forgotten for the moment.

"What are you talking about?" Blanche asked. "Go back? I just came from England. I must join Margaret. I sent word to her that I was coming."

Charles stared at her, not understanding. "Queen Margaret? But—but, I thought——"

"Thought what?"

"Come, we'll find you lodgings for the night and straighten this out."

They found a room for Blanche and the children and sat down to talk after sending Mattie and Dickon out to explore the neighborhood. "Charles, there has been some misunderstanding," Blanche said.

"Yes, but we will clear it up right now. You see, I got word that you were coming to France. I thought you were coming here—well, to be with me. Jane wrote to me about Brithric, you see. I'm sorry."

"I'm sorry too, Charles. Sorry you were misled."

"No, 'twas my own fault. I should have spoken formally to you of the matter and not just assumed that you would come to me without my asking."

"But, Charles . . ."

"So now I *am* asking. We are free, you and I, and we've had a great love for each other for many years. Will you marry me now and come back to England?" he asked with apparent confidence in an affirmative answer.

"Charles, I can't . . ."

"Don't worry. I can get your trunks taken care of and you can write to your sister to tell her you're not coming after all."

"No, Charles. It's not the trunks. I just can't go with you."

"What do you mean?"

"I can't go with you. Not now. I must go to my sister."

"But why? Your sister doesn't need you. You have great gifts of love and wisdom to give and she has never appreciated either."

"But it is my duty. I must remain loyal to her. I always have been. It is my place in life. I made a promise."

"Are you trying to tell me something else? That your love for me is gone?" Charles asked.

"No, of course not. I fell in love with you nearly twenty years ago and I still love you and I want to go with you. Really I do, but I need time to think."

"There is little time."

"Then you must leave me to sort this out in my own mind. My loyalty to Margaret is too much of a habit of mind to be broken in a matter of moments."

"This may be our only chance," Charles said almost angrily. "You have lost a husband, I have lost a wife. These are perilous times. We may never see each other again if you don't go with me in the morning."

"Please, Charles, go away and let me think."

He left without another word. She went to the window and watched him come out of the door below and walk across the courtyard. She turned away and changed her dress for dinner, hardly aware of what she was doing. Mattie and Dickon came back, wanting to eat. She said nothing to them of what she and Charles had discussed, but they seemed to know that she had something important on her mind and they were unusually quiet.

After dinner she went back to the window to watch for Charles. She had made her decision and was anxious to see him. She was still waiting when there was a knock on the door. She rushed to open it, but it was not Charles. It was the innkeeper. "This came for you," he said, handing her an envelope.

She tore it open and at first didn't recognize Margaret's handwriting. The note had obviously been written hastily:

Dearest Blanche,
    Please come quickly.
        M.

What had happened? Oh, no, what am I to do? Blanche thought. She paced the room with the note crumpled in her hand.

At first she didn't even hear the second knock on the door. Then the sound penetrated her disturbed thoughts and she rushed to fling it open. This time it was Charles. She began to cry. "Oh, Charles, I'd decided . . . I'd made up my mind and now this . . ." She thrust the note at him.

He read it and said nothing.

"I can't go with you," she said, spreading her hands in a gesture of despair. "You do understand, don't you? She must be in trouble. Look how it's written . . . as if she didn't even have time to explain."

"Very well," Charles said coldly.

"Oh, Charles, please say you understand."

"I do understand, but I think you're doing the wrong thing. You can't expect me to be happy about this, can you?" Blanche shook her head. "What about Dickon?" Charles said, motioning the boy to come to him. "Dickon, I am going back to England and Blanche is staying here in France. You are eleven years old now and are of age to make your own decision. I would be pleased to have you with me and you may come along if you like or you may remain with Blanche and Mattie. Think very carefully, but I must ask you to decide very quickly nevertheless."

What a decision for a child, Blanche thought. A decision I myself am incapable of making intelligently. She watched the boy. As usual, his thoughts were not reflected in his square, handsome face. He glanced at Mattie, who was standing at his side, clutching his sleeve as if to physically prevent him from going. "No, Father," Dickon said, "I will stay here. Blanche and Mattie need me more than you do." He said it so matter-of-factly that there was no way to know if he was implying any criticism of his father's long absences.

"Then it is settled," Charles said. "Blanche, will you change your mind?"

"I cannot. I wish I could, but I cannot," she said.

CHAPTER FIFTEEN

Margaret embraced her tearfully. Blanche felt a surge of the old affection and tried to magnify it in order to justify her decision not to go with Charles. "I was afraid you had abandoned me and I couldn't have stood it," she said.

"What is the matter? What did you need me for?" Blanche asked.

"Your husband," Margaret said. "Where is he?"

"He died," Blanche said, amazed that such a heartbreaking fact could be reduced to two such simple words. "But what's wrong? You wrote to me to hurry."

"Yes, I was so anxious to see you. It's been such a long time."

Blanche sat down heavily. "Do you mean to tell me that's the reason you wrote to me? You just wanted to see me?"

"What's wrong with that?" Margaret said in an offended tone.

"Oh, Meggie, how could you have done this?"

"What have I done? I was eager to see you and I wrote to tell you so. What right have you to be angry with me for that?"

"Never mind. You're right, it's my own fault. I should have known."

"Known what? What is the matter with you?" Margaret asked.

Blanche sighed. "Nothing. I've just made a mistake, that's all."

"Oh, Blanche, look. Here comes an old friend. You do remember Pierre, don't you? Pierre de Breze."

Blanche looked at the man who was approaching them. But he was old and portly. Where was Pierre, handsome Pierre, figure of romance from her youth? Could this be Pierre? Certainly not. But this man's eyes . . . yes! This wheezing old man was Pierre. Blanche had a mad urge to laugh or cry, she didn't know which. She controlled it and said, "Yes, of course I remember. It is good to see you, Pierre."

Seeing him lifted her spirits. There was no malice in her pleasure at finding him aged and unattractive. It was simply that she hadn't laughed at herself for a long time, and seeing how her dreams of the past had fooled her struck her as enormously funny. She was surprised to find that she could still laugh at anything. Now that she could again find humor in herself she felt as though a cloud had lifted and she was ready to begin living life and not just waiting to be tossed about by circumstance. She had been wrong in choosing to come to Margaret, but it was too late to alter that. She would just have to make the best of things the way they were.

France was as beautiful as Blanche remembered it. Even though she loved England and had never particularly wished to return to France, the air was somehow warmer and fresher than she recalled. The trees were greener and the spring blossoms held more scent. Margaret sent a message to King Louis at Bordeaux, asking to visit him. A message was returned. Louis would be honored to have the Queen of England join him. Margaret was worried about her clothes. Even in Scotland her wardrobe had looked old and faded, but here everyone was so stylish, and she looked even worse in her own eyes.

She went to court in her wedding dress. It was still her best gown, though the blue skirt was worn and there were discreetly patched places. She had removed the golden discs from the daisy centers while she was in Scotland. They had paid her passage to France. She had sewn new centers with silk thread.

She was in her thirties and looked older. The last years of worry and fighting had aged her. There was gray threading through her hair and lines in her face that had not been there before. One day she said, "I look ten years older than you, Blanche." Then she laughed as if she were joking, but it was true.

When they reached court, Margaret was even more depressed. Her rooms were warm and rich, the furnishings beautiful, the food was tender and flavorful (especially after Scottish winter fare). There were delicate pastries and honeyed fruits at every meal. The ladies of the court were glittering, well-dressed, and frivolous and they let her know in subtle ways that she was merely a poor relation who had lost her crown.

Margaret's biggest disappointment was her father. Blanche feared it would be so, but could do nothing about it. Margaret recalled clearly her parting with René and the tenderness between them. When she learned that she was to see him again, she was nearly sick with excitement. "Father!" she shouted, throwing herself into his arms like a child when he arrived.

"Ah," he said, carefully extricating himself from her grasp. "So this is my little girl, all grown up."

"I'm so happy to see you again, Father," she said.

"And I you, my dear. I'm planning a feast in your honor tonight. Will that suit you?" René said.

"I suppose, but I thought maybe we could dine quietly together and catch up on all the years we have been apart."

"No, no, we shall have plenty of time for that sort of thing. Do you have something a little nicer to wear?" René asked absently.

"No, I haven't," Margaret said, fighting back tears. "Perhaps I could borrow something."

"Well, I imagine I can find you something. I shall have an escort here to pick you up tonight. Au revoir, ma chérie."

"Please, can't you stay a while?"

"Mais, non, I have much to do, plans to make for tonight." As he ambled out the door he noticed Blanche standing there. "Ah . . ." He scratched his head. "Blanche," he said and absently kissed her hand. "How nice to see you." He strolled out.

After René left, Margaret allowed herself a full half-hour of self-pity. "He has forgotten the love he once had for me, Blanche," she whined.

"You should have expected it. He was always shallow and fickle in his affections," Blanche said.

How alike they are, Blanche thought. She weeps because he no longer loves his own daughter, yet I am as much daughter to him as she and he could hardly think of my name. But Margaret didn't notice that because she is like him. Blanche was angry with both of them for being so hugely concerned with themselves and so oblivious of others. As for René, Blanche didn't really care if he remembered her or not. She had realized, even as a girl, that when she left for England, he would forget her existence.

"Now I am nothing more to him than a relative who provides him with an excuse to arrange a party," Margaret went on complaining. "I have been helped during all my troubles in England by knowing that somewhere there was someone—at least one person—who cared very deeply for me no matter what happened. I now know it wasn't true. Father no longer loves me," she finished melodramatically.

"What about me?" Blanche said, trying to keep the cattiness out of her voice.

"What? Oh, I know you love me, Blanche. I meant only that I am disappointed. And of course I have my son . . ."

More than ever before, Margaret poured the hungry love and devotion of which she was capable on her only hope, her son. It appeared to Blanche that the boy was beginning to chafe under the load of his mother's love and there was some disillusion on Margaret's part as well. Margaret was often annoyed with him lately. He was inclined to brag and strut, and whenever he was reprimanded, he resorted to whining and threats. Still, better he be a little bit of a bully, she thought, than be anything like his father. Yes, the boy was a little moody, but all children were sometimes. That didn't mean he was harboring his father's madness.

Margaret was forced to wait weeks to be presented to Louis and she was surprised to find, when she finally met him, that he had not merely inherited but exaggerated his father's ill looks. King Louis was really grotesque: a mound of flesh, a badly arranged face with little piggy eyes staring out, taking in everything. He welcomed Margaret to his court with the same fervor that he applied to everything he did. He knew she was penniless and had a dressmaker and hairdresser do what they could for her before she appeared at court.

"This is my most honored and honorable kinswoman," he announced to the court, "the true Queen of England. I bid you all make her welcome. And this is her son, the next king of England," he said, casting a porcine eye over the boy.

"Alas, he may not be the next king, your majesty, unless you . . ." Margaret began.

"Allow me to present my wife," Louis cut in smoothly.

Margaret tried again later to bring up the subject of the reason for her visit. Louis said, "We are to have a grand hunt tomorrow. You will join us, of course?"

After the hunt the next day Margaret said, "If I might have a word with your majesty on a matter of some importance . . ."

"In good time, madam," he replied.

Margaret was forced to realize that Louis would discuss her situation with her if and when *he* chose. He knew why she was there and would not be hurried. Pierre de Breze helped her fill the time. "Do not sorrow yourself, ma petite. King Louis will speak with you when he decides to, no sooner, no later. For now, let us play some chess."

So they waited. The court moved from palace to palace, hunting, dancing, partying, and Margaret followed the court, always alert for the summons to meet with Louis. It was months before he condescended to speak to her privately and then it was to drive a hard bargain. He would lend her 20,000 livres, only a fraction of what she had hoped for. Moreover, he stipulated that she must pay back twice that amount in one year. She must also turn over Calais to France. Margaret agreed to it all. She had no choice but to accept his terms or give up the fight, and she could not do that.

King Louis lent her a few ships, the sailors to man them, and her old friend, Pierre de Breze. She hired a small army with the 20,000 livres. They set sail in October to head up the eastern side of England. They were within sight of Edward of York's ships several times, but managed to avoid getting within firing range of them.

They landed on the coast of Northumberland. There were three castles in the area that were currently held by sympathizers of the Lancaster cause. She planned to set up court as soon as she could safely bring King Henry out of hiding. In the meantime she stayed with Blanche and a few of her ladies in a rich merchant's house. As soon as it was safe, she would simply rule

England from there rather than from London. But within a few days rumors began to circulate that Warwick and the usurper Edward were on their way north to oust the borrowed French army and capture the Queen and Prince.

Lady Alice Chaucer came to see Queen Margaret. She had become infirm and it cost her dearly to make the trip. She was closeted with the Queen for a long time in an upstairs room. When she came downstairs, looking bewildered and defeated, she asked to speak privately with Blanche.

"What is wrong, Alice?" Blanche asked.

"You must make her listen to reason."

"Margaret?"

"Yes, I have pleaded with her, but . . ." She spread her hands in a despairing gesture. "Warwick's army will be here soon. They may be coming now and I fear so greatly for the children — the Prince and yours."

"But what is there to do? We have faced danger before."

Alice leaned forward and whispered, "There is a woman in the village near my home. They say she is a witch, but 'tis not true. She knows things that are going to happen. She has told me many things that have come to pass as she said. She told me that a great duke would move against the Queen and there would be children's blood spilled. I know she meant Prince Edward or your Mattie or Dickon." Alice was wringing her knotted hands. "You must get the children to safety."

"But where is safety?" Blanche asked, feeling the fear trembling in her own voice.

336

"There is a convent a few miles from here. The sisters take in orphans and some well-born children to educate, as well. If you were to send the children there, no one would ever know who they are. I will take them there for you and say they are relations of mine. You could leave them until this is settled and take them back out whenever you wish. Please, Blanche, I'm so afraid the prophecies will be true. I have known the Prince and Mattie and Dickon since they were babies together and I would as soon die as see harm come to them."

"What did the Queen say to this?" Blanche asked.

"She said you may do as you please, but that she must keep the Prince with her."

Blanche thought for a moment. How seldom she had important choices to make, and when such occasions arose, they always seemed to demand instant decisions. "I think the Queen is right about the Prince, Alice. She must keep him with her. She dare not become separated from him. But for Mattie and Dickon . . . If Warwick should take the town, I would be in danger of capture, for he wouldn't believe that I am a worthless hostage." She was talking to herself rather than to Alice, but it helped clear her thinking to put it into words. "They would be safer apart from me, where their identities are not known . . . yes, I will send them to the convent. Can you take them there for me?"

"My carriage will be back in a few moments. Can they be ready?"

Blanche called the children and ordered servants to pack their things quickly while she had a few words with them. "But, Mama, when will you be able to come back for us?" Mattie asked after Blanche had explained the plan to them.

"I probably won't have to hide from Warwick at all. If his forces are turned back, I will come for you in a few days. But you must not count on that. The Queen will retreat to Scotland if there is no other choices and if this area is taken by Warwick, it may be months before I can get you back."

"Why can't we just leave now, Mama, before anything happens?" Mattie asked.

"How could we, darling? We are stuck on a corner of England without any way to escape. We cannot acquire a precious warship just for the three of us. We couldn't possibly ride through the advancing army. If it were possible to leave now, just you and me and Dickon, I would carry you away in a second," she said, hugging them both. "Besides, you will have fun. You both like pretending. You can go to the school with the other children and pretend to be someone else. Lady Alice will make up an imaginary name for you on the way and you can make up brothers and sisters and adventures that really haven't happened."

"I don't need to make up adventures. I have had too many adventures already," Mattie said.

"Don't worry," Dickon said, "I shall take care of Mattie for you."

"I shall count on that, Dickon," Blanche said seriously. "I will either come for you or send a message as soon as I can."

"Mama . . . what if . . . well, what if you are captured?"

"If I should be captured and you hear of it, you must somehow get word to Dickon's father and to Cecily Neville."

"And——" Dickon began.

"If you should hear of my death—no, Mattie, don't cry, you are nearly grown now and you must listen to me—if you hear of my death you must write to the King, Edward of York, Dickon, and explain who you are and ask that your father come for you. There is something you can't understand yet, but you must remember: Do not let Mattie be taken into your Aunt Jane's house no matter what happens. Can you remember all this?"

The children nodded and Mattie wiped her tears away with the hem of her skirt. Instinctively Blanche started to correct her, then thought better of it. "Now you must go. I promise you this: If I must leave here I will do everything I can to take you with me, but if I can't I will move mountains to get back for you at the very first opportunity. Now go. Lady Alice is waiting in the carriage.

It was barely an hour later that the Prince ran into the Queen's room, where she was sitting with Blanche discussing the children's move. "They're running away, the cowards!" the boy shouted. "I'll have them all beheaded. Please, Mama, catch them and let me behead them."

"What does he speak of?" Margaret asked Breze, who had come puffing into the room after the boy.

"The soldiers are deserting. We cannot stay. The Earl of Warwick's men are only hours away. Hurry, I have a boat waiting."

"A boat?"

"Yes, we must catch up with them."

"Good. I shall behead them," the Prince joined in.

"No, you shan't," Breze said sharply. "We cannot defend ourselves without them. We must escape with them if they insist on going."

"But I can't leave my few friends to face Warwick alone," Margaret objected.

"What good can you do without your army? You would only be caught, you and the boy, and your cause would be dealt a death blow in truth."

"I suppose you are right. When are we leaving?"

"Immediately. Put on all the warm clothes you can wear and hurry."

"What about my ladies?"

"They will be safe here, except Blanche. There is not room or time to take anyone else."

"I am coming, too," Blanche said. "Then hurry," Pierre said without argument.

One of the women with Margaret helped them into extra petticoats, hose, and an extra dress for each over the ones they were wearing. "You and the others go to your husbands," Margaret said. There were protests, but Margaret insisted. "Do not worry, we shall be safe. Is the Prince ready?"

They all but ran to the dock. An undignified spectacle—a boy, an old man, a tired queen, and her sister all dressed in several layers of clothing. They could see the fleet still in the harbor. They piled into a small boat and began rowing out to the closest ship. The wind came up and it began to rain. Breze's face was redder than ever and his breathing was labored.

"Please, let me row. You rest a moment," Margaret said to him.

"Nay, madam," he panted, "you are a queen."

"If I were frail, I would have died ere now, sire," she snapped. "Let me row."

It was harder than she thought. She was fighting not only the water but the wind as well. She and Blanche took turns with the oars, but it did no good. The wind was blowing them back to shore, but far to the north of where they started. The fleet got farther and farther away and finally disappeared in the thick fog that was rolling in. The waves got higher, the wind stronger. Breze made them stop rowing and they all huddled in the bottom of the boat to keep from overturning. The icy rain cut through the layers of clothing they wore.

"Look out!" Breze suddenly shouted, pointing at a huge wave that was almost upon them. "Jump—get away from the boat!" He grabbed the Prince and flung him out of the boat. Margaret's scream hadn't even reached her lips when Breze grabbed her and threw her in after the boy. Blanche jumped rather than let herself be thrown in.

As she came sputtering to the top of the cold, salty water, she saw the boat picked up and flung into pieces by the wave. Edward was beside her, choking and sputtering. She could hear Margaret shouting, but couldn't see her. She tried to help hold the boy's head up out of the water, but she was so heavy and water-soaked that she could hardly keep herself up.

"Here, hold this," came a voice behind her. It was Breze. He had hold of one of the larger pieces of what

341

was left of their boat. It was large enough to push the boy onto.

"Get out of those clothes; they'll pull you down!" Breze shouted. "I'll help the Queen," he said, and disappeared.

Blanche had seen a cat thrown into a pond once and had marveled that the cat, who had never been near water, could swim. Now she understood how: it was swim or die. She began pulling off layer after layer of wet, clinging clothing. She could hardly stay up in the water to use her hands, her legs were so tangled in wet skirts and petticoats.

Finally she developed a method. She decided which hook or button to work on next, then, taking a deep breath, she let go and frantically worked under water to get free. She always came up a few feet from the chunk of boat and had to thrash her way back. Then she would get her breath and start over. Eventually she got loose from everything but her undermost shift. It wasn't until then that she realized how terribly cold she was.

Her teeth were chattering so violently that when Breze asked if she was all right, she couldn't answer him. Every muscle in her body was trembling.

The boy was blue with cold and appeared drowsy and numb, but was alive and breathing. Pierre had Margaret pulled over to the wood Blanche was clinging to. She was in as bad a condition as the Prince.

They clung there for—how long? An hour, maybe; it seemed like months to them. They were blown around and tossed in the waves, but could not see shore or boats. Suddenly Blanche felt a sharp pain in her foot and realized that it was a rock. Her foot had hit a rock! They were in shallow water.

Then they could see the shoreline—a bleak stretch of rocks and bare trees. They paddled madly, shouting for help. An old man appeared at the edge of the beach. "Mon, there's someone oot thar!" he shouted to a younger man. "Help me here."

They waded in and helped pull Margaret, Pierre, Blanche, and the boy out. The younger man took off the extraordinary-smelling fur outer garment he wore and wrapped it around Margaret. The old man wrapped his coat around the Prince. Blanche and Pierre had to stumble along over sleet-slick rocks in bare feet.

Blanche didn't remember what happened next. She never was sure whether she fainted or simply wiped it out of her mind, but the next thing she knew she was sitting up on a lumpy straw pallet, and a toothless old crone was pouring something sticky and warm in her mouth. She immediately looked around the dark, smoky room for the others. The boy was asleep on a pile of skins in the corner. Margaret was napping by the fire. There was no sign of Pierre. The room was small; it appeared to be a single-room structure, a peasant's hut. The floor was earth packed hard by years of use. There was a scooped-out area in the center where a fire had burned low.

There must have been a hole in the roof for the smoke to escape, but it didn't work well. The room was stale with smoke and the smell from the fish-oil lamp in the corner. Blanche looked into the bowl from which the woman was feeding her. It was a broth of turnips and grass to which some sort of rancid fat had been added. Blanche found it disgusting, but went on swallowing it, for she was starving.

She felt awful, numb and stupid from sleep. Her hair was a tangled mess and her face was sticky, apparently from the old woman's previous efforts to feed her. She looked down at her hands; they were chapped and cracked. Her nails were broken. She thought first of getting clean and changing into fresh clothes, only to remember that she had torn off all her clothing in the water. All she had was the wrinkled, dirty shift she wore.

"Meggie," she said softly, not wanting to startle her. "Meggie, wake up."

Margaret was suddenly alert and hurried to her side. "Blanche, I've been so worried. How do you feel?"

"How long have I been unconscious?"

"Since yesterday. You didn't even toss as with a fever. I suppose the accident and the cold water was a shock to your mind and body."

"Are you all right?" Blanche asked her.

"Yes, I suppose. Though I still can't get warm and I have no clothing but my underwear."

"Where is Pierre?"

"I don't know. When I awoke he was gone." Just then there was some activity at the door and Pierre came in dragging something. "Where have you been? What are those?" Margaret asked.

"Some of your things. I bribed the boy, the one who helped pull us out of the water, to go to your lodgings and steal your clothes chests before we were missed."

"Did he also bring any news?"

"Yes, but not good news. Warwick arrived on our

heels. Edward of York was not with him. He was taken ill with measles on the way and had to stay behind."

"Measles! Is he very ill?" Margaret asked hopefully.

"Nay, he had the body of a plow horse. He will certainly recover."

"What did Warwick do?"

"The fleet, our fleet, that was trying to get away was captured. It was a good thing we did not catch up with them. Warwick has laid siege to two of our castles. He has them surrounded."

"Two of our castles, but we had three fortresses," Margaret said.

"I know we had three, your majesty, but . . ." He hesitated, unwilling to tell her. "Henry Beaufort turned Bamborough over to Warwick for a promise of a pension from Edward of York."

"Henry Beaufort?" she said, stunned by the information. "Henry Beaufort turned Bamborough over to Warwick! How could he do a thing like that? His father died for our cause. He has been our friend since he was a boy."

"We cannot dwell on the motives of traitors, milady. Will you be well enough to travel by tomorrow? We are practically under Warwick's nose here. He has patrols out all over the countryside looking for you. We cannot be safe here for long. You are already a curiosity in the neighborhood. I've asked these people to keep quiet. They don't know who you are, but they know that you are a great lady, and when they hear that the Queen is being searched for, they may be willing to sell information."

"You are right. We will leave at daybreak. Can you get horses for us?"

"If you are willing to part with some of your jewels," Breze said.

"I can't think of any better use for them." Margaret laughed a little hysterically.

"Then get a few more hours' sleep and we will go."

"Pierre, you could turn me in to Warwick, you know. You would be amply rewarded," Margaret said.

Pierre looked horrified. "Do you think I am a dog? A cur who would do thus?"

"No, I'm sure you wouldn't. I didn't mean that. I just don't understand why you are willing to do so much for me."

Pierre didn't answer.

By daybreak they were entering the forest, thick and menacing. They did not dare travel by road until they were well within the safety of Scotland. They had given some villagers trinkets of Margaret's for four very elderly horses. Margaret had her two small chests of clothes and belongings strapped to the horse she rode. None of them knew his way through the forest, but it was a bright day and they were able to follow the sun in the general direction they knew they had to go. Around noon they came to a road they had to cross. Breze went ahead to see if there was anyone on the road. He came back stealthily, leading his horse.

"There are thieves ahead. They are robbing some people on the road. We could try to work our way around them, but we don't know which way they will go. I think we had better wait here until they are gone."

"Should we just hide here like any commoner?" the Prince asked haughtily. "Sire, you and I should go ahead and kill them."

"I think it wiser to wait here," Breze said. It was difficult to control his temper with this boy, but Breze had to remember that he was trying to put the child on the throne and slights to the boy would be recalled by the man.

"Our friend is right, son," Margaret said. "He is more knowledgeable in the ways of the forest than we."

"Oh, very well, but I should like to kill them," the boy said sullenly.

They ate the dry bread and drank the stale, watery ale that they had brought along and rested for a while. Breze went back to see if the road was safe. "There is no sign of anyone near now," he reported. "But this has served as a warning to us. The woods are full of brigands. If we should be attacked, you three must escape. I shall try to lead them away. Your majesty, it would be best if you not wear your rings or any other jewelry."

"But I haven't anything valuable with me. I have left all my best jewels in France."

"Just the same, you should wear nothing of any value. These brigands don't know the difference and would as likely attack you for trinkets."

Margaret took his advice and hid her rings in her bodice. They traveled on. Late in the afternoon they heard someone riding near them. They stopped and listened, but could no longer hear anything. "It may be our imagination," Breze whispered, "but I think it best if we stop here and not make any more noise."

Quietly they dismounted and sat listening for a long time. At last they agreed that they must have imagined the sounds, but it was too late to go any farther. They finished the bread and ale and spread out their cloaks to sleep on. Night had fallen quickly and Blanche was exhausted. It seemed only a few minutes after she had gone to sleep when Breze shook her gently and said, "Come quickly. There is someone in the woods. I heard them. Mount your horses, and when I signal, you ride that way." He pointed in the darkness of the forest. "There should be a river a mile or so ahead. Wait there for me."

"What are you going to do?" Blanche asked, her mind still not quite clear.

"I will try to take them by surprise. If I am not there to meet you by noon tomorrow, you must try to make your way on your own."

"Margaret won't like leaving you," Blanche said.

"I know she won't, cherie, but you know that she must—for the boy's sake."

Blanche woke Margaret and told her what was happening. Then she woke the Prince. In the darkness he was not so anxious to attack the robbers and he went quietly to his horse.

"Be careful," Breze said when they were mounted. "Go now."

They rode away quickly and heard Pierre behind them making a great deal of noise, presumably to cover the sound of their escape. In a moment they heard shouts and the clash of weapons. They rode on.

Blanche's heart was pounding with fear and the exertion of riding so quickly in unfamiliar territory. Her horse stumbled several times, but recovered itself. Shortly they came to the stream that Breze had said was ahead.

Blanche tied their horses to a tree and they struggled upstream a little way. She was afraid that if the horses made noise, it would give away their location.

They spread their cloaks on the grass and lay down quietly to wait for Pierre. It was not very long before they heard voices. Someone had indeed found the horses, as Blanche feared they would. She took the Prince's hand and gestured to Margaret to try to slip away from the men. In the dark every twig snap sounded like a cannon shot, and they had gone only a few steps when someone grabbed her. She found herself looking into a leering face with bloodshot eyes and foul breath. "Lookee here, what's this?" he said loudly. He dragged the three of them back to where his friends stood with the horses. "That one's a bit over the hill," he said of Margaret, "but this one's not bad-looking. A fine lady, I'll wager." He cast lecherous eyes over Blanche.

A young man was busy building a fire. He kept stopping and listening for sounds in the woods. He seemed extremely uneasy, but said nothing. "Say you, ox brain!" their captor shouted to the young man, who started guiltily, "get them boxes off the horse and let's see what the fine ladies has got in them. Yessir, them's fine ladies and good gels in the grass, I'll wager." He made a grab for Margaret around the waist with his hammy hands. Margaret turned her face away and struggled to get free. He slobbered all over her neck.

Suddenly he yelped. Prince Edward had prodded him in the back with the small knife he carried. "Unhand my mother, sire," he said in a strong voice. "You shall meet your death for this rashness. This is the Queen of your country and I am your next King."

The bandit roared with laughter. "Got a lot of spirit, ain't ye? So this is the Queen of England, is it?" He grasped the boy's cheek and banged his head back and forth. "Well, I'm the King of France, what ye think of that?"

"Let him go, please," Margaret said, trying to pull the bandit away from her son.

"Aw, now I'm awearying of this," the bandit said and flung the Prince to the ground. Margaret struck the man in the face. It was a stupid thing to do, but she had lashed out instinctively like an animal whose young are endangered. The bandit snatched Margaret's hair and spun her around. He held a knife against her neck.

"Let her be," the young robber said. He had abandoned the fire.

"So she's got a champion, has she?" the leering bandit said to the younger one.

"No, but we got better things to do. Come see what's in the boxes."

The older man discarded Margaret, throwing her to the ground as casually as an old coat. They went to work on breaking into Margaret's chests, which they had taken off the horses. Margaret and Blanche and Prince Edward were together near the edge of the circle of light cast by the campfire. They started creeping away from the firelight and into the protective darkness of the surrounding forest. They stayed on the ground and began to silently hitch themselves along, inch by inch. The older bandit and the one who had been busy getting the chests were sitting with their backs to their captives. The young man was facing them and glanced at Blanche.

She froze.

He looked away and they began sliding along the muddy ground again.

He looked at them again. Blanche's heart stopped. Certainly he would notice that they had moved. But he seemed not to. He looked away.

Inch by muddy inch.

The young bandit looked at her again. This time he was sure to notice. Blanche looked at him, her terrified gaze locked with his. Slowly, almost imperceptibly, he shook his head from side to side.

He was signaling her not to go farther. He was aware of what they were doing and he wasn't going to give them away. He glanced at his companions and, sure that his attention was on the chests they were rummaging through, back to Blanche. He inclined his head slightly to one side and closed his eyes for a second.

He was telling them to feign sleep. Or it seemed that must be what he meant. Blanche knew that even if they got outside the little circle of light, there was practically no chance of escaping these men in their own familiar territory, so they had to take a chance on doing what the younger man seemed to be telling them to do. Blanche whispered to Margaret, who after her own burst of courage, had decided to let Blanche take charge.

They pretended to sleep. They had no idea what time of night it was. It seemed like days since they had escaped their first camp, but it was probably only an hour or so. They could hear the rumble of the bandits' voices, but couldn't distinguish what was being said. They had no idea what had happened to Pierre de Breze.

Blanche pretended sleep and was so tired that once or twice she caught herself dropping off. The robbers talked and drank together around the fire for a while. They seemed to have forgotten their hostages, for they flopped down on the ground themselves and shortly they were snoring the loud, sloppy snores of drunks.

The young bandit wasn't asleep, however. When the older men were out soundly, he got up and crept toward them. "I be Willie. I'll help you," he said loudly. Margaret put her finger to her lips. "Never you mind them, ma'am. They sleep like dead boars when they be drinking," he assured her. "You go on downstream, quiet. I'll come behind with the horses."

His word was good. He caught up with them downstream and led them through the forest, guided them up a hill, and told them to dismount. "We're here now. You can get warm and rest a bit."

Blanche looked around. He seemed to be talking about his home, but there was no building in sight—nothing but a craggy hill face. "Come on in," he said, pushing his way through the bushes to a cave opening. "Maudie, we got folks," he said. A pretty girl appeared in the opening. Blanche couldn't tell if she was sleep-confused or simple-minded, but she gave them warm, ragged covers and built up the fire. Blanche could hardly give any more thought to her situation. She made sure Margaret and young Edward were settled, then she dropped into a deep, dreamless sleep.

In the morning Willie, the young bandit, was gone. Maudie was crouched by the fire, nursing a baby and humming to herself. She didn't speak, but smiled and offered Blanche a handful of something that vaguely resembled bread. Then, satisfied that her hostess duties were done, she went back to nursing the baby and humming.

There was nothing to be gained by questioning the girl, and the Prince was still sleeping. Blanche shook Margaret awake and motioned her to come outside and share whatever the foodstuff was in her hand. Yes, it must have been some sort of bread. They went cautiously to the cave entrance and peered out. No sign of Willie or of the bandits he had been with last night. They sat by the entrance for a while, savoring the sun's warmth after the cold dampness of a night in a cave. What were they going to do? Blanche wondered. Two fugitive women and a child lost in a forest. But somehow the beauty of the sun shining down through the forest made them feel less desperate.

They heard someone coming and quickly darted back into the cave before they recognized the voices.

It was Willie and Pierre!

Margaret ran to them and threw her arms around Pierre. He was astonished. "This young man found me in the woods, your majesty. He told me he had you safely hidden," he said.

"What happened to you, Pierre?" Blanche asked.

"I rode into the midst of the bandits. It took them by surprise. They unhorsed me and went after you. I lost my sense of direction in the fight and was going the wrong way, trying to find you, when Willie found me. Are both of you and the boy all right?"

"Yes, we are safe. Willie, why did you help us get away?" Blanche asked the young man.

"They didn't want *you,* they just wanted to steal your jewels, but they was so drunk I was afraid they might hurt you. I went back and got your things. They won't even remember it when they wake up. I got to go now. I got to get back to them. You'd best go, too. Your horses are tied right down there."

"Thank you, Willie," Margaret said. "I'm sorry I have little to give you in thanks for your help."

"There's nothing I need, ma'am," Willie said, with every appearance of meaning it.

"Then wake the Prince, your majesty, and we shall be on our way," Pierre said.

CHAPTER SIXTEEN

King Edward the Fourth leaned back in his chair, assessing the mother and child who stood before him. The woman, Meg Beaufort, was a cousin of his and he remembered her wedding. She had been a coquettish child then. Now she was a woman of twenty and quite a beautiful woman at that. The boy with her was five or six years old and was thin and solemn. He had a strangely unchildlike demeanor. Edward had the uncomfortable feeling that the child was judging him and finding him lacking. "It is good to see you back in London, madam," Edward said.

"I wasn't sure, when your men stormed Pembroke, whether I was being captured or freed, my lord," Meg Beaufort said with a laugh. Jasper had been good to her and she loved him, but she had hated the dismal castles that had been her only homes for the past seven years. She noticed the child at her side stiffen. Jasper had trained him well. He was Welsh and resented his mother's implications that there was anything wrong with Wales. The cold, austere life there had suited him well.

"You were being freed, cousin. When Lord Herbert took advantage of Jasper's absence to storm Pembroke, he had no idea that you and the boy were there," Edward said. He enjoyed talking to this lovely contemporary of his. He was usually surrounded by older people, like his cousin Warwick and his friends.

Meg Beaufort, or rather Margaret Tudor, as he reminded himself she was now, was nice to talk to. She would no doubt be nice to sleep with as well. She was pleasant, intelligent, and had been without a man in her bed for several years. He had given some thought to an alliance between himself and his cousin Meg when he heard that Lord Herbert had found her. But Meg was a Beaufort, more closely related to Henry the Sixth than to Edward himself. He didn't want to further complicate the relationship between the two branches of the Plantagenets. When he married, it would be either to a foreign princess or to a country-woman of his own who was outside the vast family feud.

The thought of bedding Meg Beaufort was certainly tempting, just the same. "What do you wish to do now, Meg? You are free to go back to Wales if you wish, but, of course, I cannot let the boy go."

"I know that," she said. She realized the importance of her child. He would have been next in line for the throne if Henry were King and anything should happen to Henry's son. With King Henry still at large, anything could happen. "For myself, I wish to marry, my lord."

"You do?" Edward was glad she was so direct. The coyness she had shown as a girl was gone. "Why is that?" he asked, thinking he had been right that she needed a man in her bed.

As if reading his thoughts, she said, "That isn't the reason." She stood for a moment as if forming her sentence. Suddenly she said, "Edward, I'm tired. May we stop being King and subject so I may sit down and talk to you?"

"You are a breath of fresh air," Edward roared. "Sit and have a glass of wine with me. Let your maid take the boy back to his rooms."

"I need a husband's protection," Meg said when they were seated. "I cannot go on being Jasper's charge. He is a good man, as you know, and he has done well for me by his standards. But I don't wish to grow old stuck away in Wales. I want to be in the middle of things. I am not an intriguer, but neither am I simple-minded."

"Very good. Do you know Henry Stafford?"

"I met him years ago before I left for Wales. I remember very little about him. His father is the Duke of Buckingham, is he not?"

"Yes, Buckingham is King Henry's man, but Stafford is his second son and has always been a faithful friend to me. He is a good military leader and a good man."

"That is enough."

"He is also comely," Edward said slyly.

"That is even better." Meg smiled.

"Then I shall see what can be done. He is eager to marry and deserves a good wife. In fact, he has asked me about you."

"I am grateful to you for taking this affair into your hands. I would like it arranged as soon as possible."

"Why, are you afraid I won't be King long enough to carry it out?" Edward asked.

"Oh, no, Edward. I didn't mean that at all. I could-not make any such judgment anyway. I have been kept in such ignorance of England's affairs. Jasper felt that the less I knew, the better. He said I was to rely entirely on his judgment and he would take care of me."

"I think you are well able to rely on your own judgment," Edward said.

"I think so, too. Please, Edward, since you have already taken this much time with me, pray tell me what has been happening. Where is Jasper now?"

"Alas, I don't know where Jasper is. I don't really know where *anyone* is. It's like fighting spider webs in the dark. I stab here and again there and hit nothing. Queen Margaret—I shouldn't call her that, but I don't know quite what else to call her—Queen Margaret captured three of our northern castles and Warwick recaptured them. She fled and stories filtered back about her nearly drowning, then being set upon by thieves. There is probably no truth in it, but it was a good story. She and her sister and that French friend of hers, Pierre de Breze, turned up in Scotland again. Jasper joined them there. I don't know where he had been. About a year later they came tearing down with a Scottish force and recaptured the same three castles. This time they had King Henry with them. They set him up in one of the castles as King—issuing lots of harmless edicts in his name and making much of setting up a royal court.

"We have been at a stand-off for a long time now. Queen Margaret cannot get any farther than her three strongholds and I can't be secure on the throne until I have Henry and his son in my keeping."

"Poor Queen Margaret," Meg said thoughtfully, without realizing that it was not the best thing to say to Edward.

"She is a formidable opponent because she doesn't know what she's doing," Edward said, unoffended by Meg's sympathy for his adversary.

"What do you mean?"

"Every time I figure out what a military leader's next move would be and expect her to do it, she does something else. It's usually something stupid, but it's also unexpected and sometimes works for that reason alone."

There was a scratch at the door. "Come in," Edward shouted. Henry Stafford came in, looking embarrassed at having interrupted Edward and Meg. He hoped that they had been discussing him.

"Stafford, this is my cousin Margaret Tudor," Edward said courteously.

"Greetings, sire," she said, suddenly shy. "Meggie, this is my constant friend Stafford. I hope, Henry, that you will have time to show Meg the city of London. She has been gone a goodly time."

"It would please me," Stafford mumbled.

"Now, what news have you?" Edward asked.

Stafford looked questioningly at Meg. Did the King really intend to discuss state business in front of her?

"Get on with it, Stafford. Meg is my new advisor. You'll find her to be that rare thing, an intelligent woman."

All Henry Stafford cared about at the moment was that she was a beautiful woman. "Sire, a messenger has arrived with word from Warwick. He says that Queen Margaret has taken her son and Breze and sailed."

"For what destination? Did he know?"

"Yes, sire. The sailors said that the ship was bound for Flanders."

"Flanders? It may be a ruse, but I have expected her to go in search of more help. Has she left King Henry behind again?"

"Warwick did not know. He has had his men watching the three castles closely and has not seen King Henry removed."

"That doesn't mean anything, does it?" Meg interrupted. "If he were watching closely enough, he would have noticed Queen Margaret leave."

"True, Meg, but the three castles are fairly remote and it is difficult to see everyone who comes and goes."

"Warwick says that he intends to launch an attack on Bamborough and see if he can capture King Henry," Stafford said.

"Yes, with Queen Margaret and Breze gone, we stand a better chance of taking the castle. Did Jasper sail with them?" Edward asked.

"Warwick did not know, my lord. He thought not, but said he couldn't be sure."

"See, what did I tell you?" Edward said to Meg. "I never really know where anyone is unless they are outside my grasp. Then I never know when they may turn up behind me. Well, there is nothing to be done until we hear more from Warwick. You two go take a tour of the gardens."

It was several weeks before King Edward heard the

results of Warwick's attack on Bamborough Castle. He got the message on the way to have supper with his mother and young brothers.

"He took Bamborough, then?" Cecily asked.

"Yes, he took the castle, but Henry was gone."

"Did anyone know where he's gone?"

"No," Edward said unhappily. "Henry had apparently been there when Warwick started the attack, but when Warwick entered the great hall, he found Henry's bodyguards there, dead. They had all been killed in the battle. If they were there, Henry must have been with them and escaped on his own. I can see how he could do it. He is so good at fading into a crowd, so undistinguishable, that he probably just walked away from the fight without anyone taking notice of him. Most of the young soldiers have never seen him. They wouldn't recognize him." Edward sat down and stretched his long legs out in front of him.

"He could go unnoticed anywhere for as long as he wished," Cecily said. "Even in his robes of state he always looked to me like a farmer who was dressed in someone else's clothing."

"That's right. He could be in some little village passing as a freeman or a common laborer."

"Isn't it more likely that he is at a monastery?" Cecily asked.

"Yes, I suppose so, if he found his way to one. But the religious orders revere him. I wouldn't dare go up and violate the sanctuary of every monastery in the north of England on the outside chance of finding him. It is also possible that some Lancastrian noble found him wandering around and took him home. He could be called anyone's half-witted cousin and be kept hidden without exciting curiosity."

"Do you think you'll ever find him?" Cecily asked.

"I think so. No matter where he is hiding, sooner or later somebody will wonder who he is and find it profitable to turn him in. I just hope he doesn't die first."

"Why? It would solve one of your problems if he *were* dead."

"Yes, dead—but identified. If he dies nameless in some forest, I will never be able to prove that he is dead. I will spend the rest of my life with feeble old men being hoisted up and proclaimed the rightful king."

"Maybe he's dead," Margaret said coolly. "Of course, if he is, we need to know for sure. Doesn't anyone have any idea where he is?"

"No," Pierre answered. "Jasper's letter said he had spies scouring the countryside along with everyone else's spies and no one has even a hint of where he's gone."

"That attack on Bamborough was in December. If the weather was as bad as it usually is up there in the winter, he might have died of exposure." Margaret had given up trying to pretend that she cared what happened to Henry. He was to her, as he was to the opposition, merely an object—important to have control over, impossible to care about.

Even Blanche, who was normally rather soft-hearted about poor, stupid King Henry, had lost interest in his fate. She was back with Mattie and Dickon and that was the only thing that mattered to her. She had been able to send them word that she was well, and learned through a letter from Alice Chaucer that the children knew of her situation. She had nearly smothered them with affection when she finally went to get them from the convent. It was astonishing the difference a year had made in them. They had both grown, of course, but it was more than just size. Mattie wore her hair up now in sleek, pale braids around her head. Dickon had profited by a year with other children, and though he seemed more mature than ever, there was a sparkle in his personality that Blanche had never seen before.

Life seemed like a lovely dream to Blanche. She had the children and they were all safe again. They were back at the French court. Margaret had received nothing but empty promises in Flanders. Now, in France, Louis the Eleventh was refusing to talk to her again, but allowed her to stay and wait. She had been through that before and had learned to subjugate her pride to her needs. She would wait until he felt like discussing money and troops with her. She told Blanche she felt as if she had spent her life waiting for one thing or another.

In fact, she had decided that waiting was perhaps the best course. Her son was not old enough yet to put on the throne in his own right. He was developing a strong, militant personality and would be ready when he was fifteen or sixteen to rule—with his mother's advice, of course. If only she could get possession of Henry or be certain that he was dead, she could bide her time, building strength and money for a few more years.

She had given up her youth. There was nothing she

wanted for herself. She was thirty-five and looked older. Peering into a looking-glass in dim light, she could still pretend to see herself as she had once been —pretty and glossy-haired—but she knew it was illusion. The years of flight and worry had taken their toll. Her hair was graying and her health had not been good since she had faced death in the icy waters off Berwick. There was nothing really wrong with her, but she got tired easily and was depressed most of the time. Blanche found it more tiresome than ever to get along with Margaret, but the children were her form of compensation.

Even the company of the Prince failed to cheer Margaret these days. He had been all the joy and comfort she had needed when he was small, but he had grown away from her. He wanted to spend his time with men, military men. He liked to listen to tales of war and bloodshed. Though war and death and treason had been Margaret's constant companions nearly all her adult life, she never liked to discuss them, and the boy could talk of nothing else.

He was her son and she loved him more than herself, but it hurt her every time she saw him, for he did not love her in return.

". . . and should arrive tomorrow," Pierre was saying.

"I'm sorry. Who should arrive tomorrow?" Margaret asked.

"Haven't you heard what I've been saying?" Pierre asked a little snappishly. As much as he had always cared for Margaret, the years of conflict were beginning to tell on him, too. "I said that Warwick is coming here. He should arrive tomorrow."

"Warwick here? What on earth for?"

Pierre sighed. If only she had listened the first time. "It is rumored that he is coming to arrange a marriage between the sister of the Queen of France and Edward of York."

"The Queen's sister, the Lady Bona! Oh, no! If that usurper is married to King Louis' sister-in-law, Louis will never be able to give me his support. Warwick would do this to spite me, even if it were not to York's advantage." She clenched her hands and paced the room. "Is there nothing we can do to stop him?"

"I see nothing to do. Louis may not agree to the match, but he probably will. It would be to his advantage."

"You think that Edward of York is firmly on the throne and my son will never be King?" Margaret asked sharply.

"It is not a question of what I think. But it seems that King Louis believes it."

The Earl of Warwick was at the French court all spring and into the summer. Louis seemed to be amused by the machinations of Margaret and Warwick trying to avoid meeting each other. Margaret kept to her rooms as much as possible, but couldn't risk being completely forgotten by Louis. She spent a great deal of time with the Queen of France and her ladies, including the Lady Bona, but the subject of Warwick was carefully avoided. It was obvious that the needlework that the ladies were engaged in was for the Lady Bona's trousseau, but no one admitted it in front of Margaret. And not knowing officially what it was for, Margaret had to help them.

One day when they were thus engaged, a knight

came to the ladies' chamber. "Your majesty, the King sends his love and greetings," he said to the Queen of France. "He is returning from the hunt and requests that the ladies join the gentlemen for a picnic feast. The tents are being set up now. You are all invited."

The ladies set aside their needlework and hurried to get ready. Margaret tried to fade out of the room, but the Lady Bona caught her. "Nay, madam, do not leave. You are invited. You must join us. The fresh air would do you good." She had been hoping to see these two English enemies together even since Warwick's arrival and hadn't had the opportunity of bringing about a confrontation. She wanted a little excitement. Waiting for the marriage settlement to be agreed upon was so boring.

There was no way out of it. Margaret had to join them. The ladies strolled in a group, with the two Queens a little ahead, out to the edge of the castle grounds. There were huge multicolored tents erected like monstrous flowers that had bloomed there overnight. The breeze rustled and blilowed the silk, and hordes of people roamed across the lawns. King Louis was inside the largest tent with his favorite nobles and Warwick.

The women entered. "There you are," Louis said to his wife; then he noticed Margaret beside her and could not conceal a slight frown. "Madam, you have decided to join us. You know the Earl of Warwick, of course." He talked on, happy to have avoided the question of what title to assign to the exiled Queen in whose place he was planning to put his wife's sister. It was so awkward with them both there. What was he going to do to get Margaret out from under foot? He was getting tired of having her around, giving him sad, pleading looks.

Margaret nodded curtly to Warwick and walked on, but she had directed a look of such venom at him that even the great Warwick, the kingmaker, as he now liked to be called, was taken aback by it.

"Kingmaker, indeed," Margaret had snorted to Blanche when she first heard the nickname. "Does young Edward the usurper know that his cousin calls himself this?"

"I don't believe he actually calls himself kingmaker. He just allows and encourages others to do so," Blanche had answered.

Kingmaker! Now the French court referred to him that way, too. Not deliberately within Margaret's hearing, of course.

Kingmaker. Hideous term.

Finally the venison was done and the tables laid with linen cloths and gold knives. The King and Queen took their places. Warwick was invited to sit on the King's right and Margaret, not to be outranked, managed to sit at the Queen's left. She noticed the raised eyebrows that greeted this maneuver, but ignored them.

Halfway through the meal a servant appeared at the King's elbow and handed him a piece of parchment. Louis glanced at the message, stared out across the tent for a few moments, then read the message through again. His plump face became red, and with elaborate care, he began to fold and refold his napkin. The tent became quiet. All eyes were on him.

"My lord Earl," Louis said loudly to Warwick. Warwick looked confident. Whoever was in trouble, it wasn't he, he thought. "Are you acquainted with an English-woman named Lady Grey—Lady Elizabeth Grey?"

Elizabeth Woodville? Whatever would King Louis know about Elizabeth Woodville that could so anger him? Blanche wondered.

"Lady Grey?" Warwick was perplexed, too. "Yes, I have met her on occasion. Her mother was Jacquetta of Luxembourg."

"Regardless of who her mother was, Lady Grey is now the wife of Edward of York," King Louis said, pointedly not referring to him as King Edward.

Warwick stared at Louis. Never before at a loss for words, he could say nothing.

"While we have enjoyed your visit with us," Louis said with heavy sarcasm, "we are at a loss to understand the purpose of this visit. Edward of York has announced that he married this, this . . . person several months ago. It seems strange to us that you, who claim to be representing his suit, would not know this. It seems that you have tried to make a fool of us. Either that or you are not what you *think* you are." Louis stood up abruptly and left the table. His Queen trailed obediently after him. Margaret was left staring across the gap they had left into Warwick's angry eyes.

Margaret was smiling. Warwick stared back at her, unseeing for a moment. He finally noticed her and his look grew speculative. Then, astonishingly, he smiled back at her—the dark, sinister grin she remembered from the first time she had met him.

His expression frightened her and yet was exciting.

What if—it was no use thinking about—but what if Warwick himself decided to change sides? Edward of York had insulted him grievously, made a fool of him in public. What if Warwick's look meant he might throw his support to Margaret's side? What else could it mean? Warwick hated her as much as she had always hated him. Why else would he smile at her, of all people, when he had no cause to smile at all?

Warwick left court that night. He did not communicate with Margaret or anyone else. King Louis didn't bother to tell him goodby. The Lady Bona retired to her rooms in an orgy of self-pity. Margaret began to talk to Blanche and Pierre constantly about Warwick. Warwick might swing his support to her, but there was another possibility, she said. He might decide to be King himself if he were sufficiently out of favor with Edward of York. He might consider it a short step from kingmaker to King. Instead of two factions in the fight for the throne, there might be three. That might be to Margaret's advantage, too. It would at least split up the opposition.

There was still no action she could take right now. As valuable as Warwick's help might be, her pride would not allow her to court his favor. He had done her too much damage. He had said malicious things about her. In the meantime, she was sure he would step up his efforts to find King Henry, so she would have to do the same. Henry was the key to everyone's cause. Whoever held him had the advantage.

Margaret had learned the virtue of patience, but so had Warwick. He was content to wait for the best opportunity and try out various combinations of plans in the meantime. He was rumored to be on very cool terms with King Edward, but so far there had not been an open break.

A year after his humiliation in France, Warwick came riding into London one summer day with a valuable trophy.

Warwick had captured King Henry.

He wouldn't say where or how he found him. Warwick brought Henry into London as a prisoner. There was no doubt about that. He had the sad, confused man tied to his saddle as if he had some idea of escape. But the people of London, who were generally Yorkist in sympathy, did not cheer at the sight as Warwick had expected. They stood in silent knots along the streets, watching Henry ride through. They didn't want this befuddled being as their King, but he had been King once, and to their minds, no king of England, present or past, should be so degraded. They felt pity for the prematurely aged and incompetent old man. After all, he *had* been their King.

Warwick took Henry to the Tower of London, where he was lodged in comfort but not splendor. He was treated as a guest, not a favored guest, but a guest nevertheless. Henry asked for nothing but a rosary; Warwick's men had taken his. He seemed content with his lot; he spent his time in prayer and meditation and sometimes would sit for an hour with the guards, chatting about inconsequential matters. They treated him gently, as one would a well-mannered child.

He would not say, or perhaps did not know, where he had been for the past year and a half.

CHAPTER SEVENTEEN

For four long years they waited to see who would make the first overt move. Margaret—Warwick—Edward—they all waited. They were like strange cats circling cautiously in laborious slow motion, each afraid of lacking sufficient power to win, afraid to attack, afraid to retreat.

And they grew older and impatient to have it settled.

All but Blanche. She had found contentment with Mattie and Dickon in France. She knew that danger and death would touch her life again, but she was able to push it to the back of her mind for weeks at a time. She was a woman meant to love a man and she often wondered where she would be and what she would be doing now if she had married Charles Seintleger when he asked her. But she was through with regrets for the past. There were nights when her longing for a man in her bed to warm her and love her was almost painful. But she couldn't have everything, and she *did* have the children and had peace and relative harmony in her life, even if it was only temporary. She did hear from Charles at intervals. He always sent gifts to her and the children on their saints' days and New Year's and she heard, through Cecily, that he was part of King Edward's trusted circle of advisors.

King Edward was seemingly the least affected by the waiting. He was young and handsome and male. He made the best of it. The solemn and unhappy court of Henry the Sixth was replaced by a court of gay young people, spending the days at picnics and hunts, the nights in ballads and rendezvous. But another part of Edward brooded and worried. He knew that more war would follow. He had Henry in his keeping—that helped. But he didn't have it in him to order the murder of a man who was, in himself, harmless. Henry had done Edward no injury, not directly. Besides, Henry's death would not eliminate the cloud hanging over Edward's reign. So long as Henry's son lived, King Edward of York was not secure.

But in the meantime King Edward enjoyed himself. He had his family at court. They were close and he liked having his mother and brothers and sisters near him. The only problem was his younger brother George, Duke of Clarence. Clarence was headstrong, sly, and nasty-minded. Edward pampered him and put up with his unattractive behavior and considered him a nuisance.

But in this, Edward was wrong. Clarence was more than a nuisance—he was a danger, a danger to everyone. He was pathologically addicted to plotting. It didn't matter who was plotting what, Clarence was in the middle, stirring up discontent on all sides. Until the spring of 1469 Clarence's plots did no more than cause some hurt feelings and irritation, but that spring Clarence proved to be the catalyst to the beginning of the final episodes of the long war between York and Lancaster.

The Earl of Warwick had two daughters—Isobel, a girl of eighteen, and a younger girl, Anne. Clarence had gone to visit Warwick and his family. There was nothing strange in that and Edward was glad to have Clarence away from court until he discovered *why* Clarence had gone.

Clarence had married Isobel. The implication was clear. Warwick would not have arranged for his daughter to marry a man with no future, and no girl in her right mind would marry Clarence for love. Warwick would use his daughters as he would any other capital, to invest in a future.

Warwick, the kingmaker, was getting ready to make a new king. Edward had proved to have his own mind. Clarence was sufficiently stupid to be a figurehead king, controlled by his father-in-law.

In France, Queen Margaret observed the situation and, with the advice of Jasper Tudor, who was now in France with her, did nothing.

"Let them fight it out," Jasper advised. "When they are tired and have wasted the best of their armies on each other, we shall return and defeat whoever has won."

"But that's the coward's way," the Prince said.

"That is the smart way," Jasper corrected.

"When I am King, I shall not wait for others to fight my battles," the boy said sulkily.

"*If* you are King," Jasper said.

"That verges on treason, sire," the boy said with all the huffy dignity of a spoiled sixteen-year-old.

Jasper shrugged. He had come to dislike this boy more than he thought he could dislike anyone, but

Jasper was a man of honor and could not forsake Margaret after promising his help. He had forfeited his lands on her behalf and his only way to regain them was to put this nasty child on the throne. He was beginning to fear that he would probably get little for his efforts in either case.

"We cannot afford to argue among ourselves," Margaret warned both of them.

The next March Warwick made his first move. He attempted a rebellion against King Edward. It failed, primarily as a result of Clarence's treachery. Clarence decided at the last moment to offer his support to his brother Edward even though Warwick was supposedly fighting to put Clarence on the throne. Warwick was not captured, but embarked immediately for France. He took his daughter Isobel along, but left Clarence behind with King Edward, who didn't really want him, either. Isobel was pregnant, and as the ship tossed and lurched toward France, she gave birth. The child died within moments and Isobel barely held on to her own life. When Warwick landed in France, he was given the same kind of reception that Margaret was so accustomed to—tolerant but not encouraging.

Margaret felt sure that Warwick had come to gain the support of the King of France. She was also sure that he would not *get* the support unless he had something better than Clarence to back him up—Clarence who had proved himself an imperfect puppet.

Warwick would have to come to her. She was his last choice, but he would have to ask her help. And he would ask on *her* terms. She had much to settle with him. He had wounded her pride, her vanity. He had deliberately besmirched her good name.

He would be made to pay for it.

Richard Neville, Earl of Warwick, kingmaker, stood in the antechamber of the room where Queen Margaret was to receive him. His normally dark face had a reddish hue and he paced angrily while he waited. He had been waiting an hour already. He knew she could have seen him long ago and was deliberately making him stand out there like a peasant calling on his master.

His aides had tried to make small talk, but his answers had been so fierce that they had taken the hint and subsided into uneasy silence. As he paced, he thought over the conditions under which he was allowed to call on Margaret. He was to bow upon entering her chamber and bow again every three steps as he approached her throne. Where had she found a throne? Maybe she borrowed one from King Louis, he thought nastily.

When he reached the throne he was to kneel in an attitude of complete submission. He had prepared a speech of apology for all past wrongs he had committed against her. The prepared speech had been checked and rejected by her aides three times before it was judged to be satisfactorily abject.

He was nearly choked with humiliation, but he had no choice. He was now officially a traitor and had forfeited all his lands and revenues in the abortive rebellion. He could not go back to England while Edward was King. He had to align himself with someone who had a claim to the throne. He could never hope to gain enough support to openly put himself there.

Margaret was his only hope and he would grovel as much as necessary to win her over. At last the door opened and Pierre de Breze stepped out. "Her gracious majesty, the Queen of England, will see you now."

Warwick entered the chamber and executed the prescribed bows. He reached the makeshift throne and knelt. The cold floor burned his knees.

"I am most grateful that your grace has generously consented to take time to see me and hear my unworthy appeal."

Margaret nodded curtly for him to go on.

"I have come to beseech you to come to England's aid and restore our beloved King Henry to the throne, his rightful and God-given place. I beg for the welfare of the nation and our subjects and I come to most humbly give whatever help I, your most undeserving subject, may offer." Warwick swallowed the bitter taste the words were leaving in his mouth and went on: "I know that I have mightily sinned against your honor and good name and I swear before God that I have seen my error and would tear out my heart before I would fall back into my evil ways."

"This falls sweetly upon my ears, my lord, but sour on my soul," Margaret said. " 'Tis pity that you can't mean even part of your exalted words."

"Nay, majesty, every word is truth."

"This has been a pretty charade. Now let us conduct our business. What are you really here for?" Margaret said coldly.

"I wish to offer whatever friends and powers I may possess to restore your husband to his throne and your son to his place as heir."

"And what do you wish in return?"

"Nothing but the opportunity to serve my King and country."

"Nothing else?" Margaret said sarcastically.

"Only the return of the lands that have been taken from me by my usurping kin, Edward of York."

"I might consider such an arrangement."

"There is one other thing I beg your gracious majesty to consider," Warwick said quickly. "I have a daughter . . ."

"I know of your daughter. She is married to the usurper's brother Clarence. At your instigation, I understand. Does she fare well?"

"She is recovering from her recent loss, but Isobel is not the daughter I refer to. I have another daughter, Anne, who is sixteen, just the age of your son. Anne is comely and obedient and would make a most excellent wife for your son."

"For *my* son? My son is the Prince of Wales, the next in line to the English throne, the child of kings and queens. Your daughter may be comely, but she hasn't the noble blood that my son will require in a wife. Perhaps she hasn't even your blood," Margaret said, digging at Warwick's wife in the same way that Warwick had insulted Margaret so many years ago.

Warwick's face became a deeper shade of red. He must let it go by. This was not the time to tell the bitch what he thought of her. "You need only to see the girl to know that she is mine."

"No. You know how important to a king a royal marriage alliance can be. Prince Edward must save himself for a more profitable marriage."

"Madam, I can think of no more profitable marriage than one that can put him on the throne," Warwick said coldly. Enough was enough. Margaret needed him as much as he needed her and it was time she be reminded of it.

"I will consider your apologies and your suggestion, my lord. I will summon you when I am prepared to discuss it further. You may go now," Margaret dismissed him.

Warwick said his farewells and rose to walk away.

"Are you in the habit of turning your back on your Queen?" Margaret shrilled.

Warwick turned back. "I did not think. Please forgive me." He backed out of the room. He closed the door behind him and hit the page standing beside it so hard that the boy fell to the floor. It did no good, but he had to hit someone.

Blanche stood near the doorway, watching Warwick. "It has begun," she murmured to herself.

"I should have known that Warwick wouldn't help to gain the crown for someone over whom he had no control. That is what happened with Edward of York and Warwick learns quickly," Margaret said as she paced madly back and forth across the room. Blanche sat in front of the fireplace, trying to sew and act interested in Margaret's harangue at the same time. "But he is mistaken this time. He couldn't hope to have the same hold over a son-in-law that a mother has over

378

her own son. Since he cannot be King, he wants his daughter to be a queen."

"Are you considering the marriage?" Blanche asked.

"Naturally I'm considering it, but I must first think out all the possibilities. Who can say what might happen once we were back in England and secure on the throne? Warwick might die of natural, or less than natural, causes. This girl, his daughter, might die, too. I hear she is frail. Frail young women often die of childbed or fever. Then, you see, Blanche, I would be free to arrange another more suitable marriage for Edward."

"I see. Have you ever met this girl or even seen her?"

"No, of course not. What difference would that make?"

"None. I just thought you were bargaining rather carelessly with the life of a stranger."

Margaret looked at her coldly, but refused to be baited. "Look, Blanche, I have only two choices—I can accept Warwick's terms or I can remain here, waiting out the rest of my life for another opportunity. Anything would be better than our situation here. We are nothing but poor exiles, with very little money and even less of the respect that should be due the Queen of England in a foreign court."

"Are you really that unhappy here?" Blanche asked.

Margaret stared at her incredulously. "Aren't you?"

"No."

Margaret shook her head in saddened disbelief. "Well, I have to take the chance. There is no question of joining our interests with Warwick's without the marriage. He made that clear. Now do you wish for me to see the girl?" Margaret said with a playful coquettishness that ill became her years.

"Nay, 'tis nothing to me," Blanche said.

"Oh, but it is," Margaret said. She went to the door and spoke to her serving woman. "Send for Anne Neville. I wish to speak with her."

When Anne arrived it seemed to Blanche that the child was the typical daughter of an overbearing father. She was pretty, but painfully timid. Her wide-spaced eyes were a deep, clear, frightened blue. Her pert little nose practically quivered with fright. She looked to Blanche as if she might, at the slightest provocation, bolt for the closest thicket.

"Come here, Mistress Neville; let me see you well," Margaret said. Anne came a little closer. "Pretty figure —delicate for childbearing, though," Margaret whispered to Blanche. Blanche involuntarily shivered. "Do you know your father is planning for you to wed my son?" Margaret asked Anne. The girl nodded shyly. She looked desperately near tears. "Would you be pleased to be wed to Prince Edward?"

"I would be honored," Anne answered.

"But would you be happy?"

"If that is what you wish, majesty."

"What would *you* wish?"

"It is not for me to say."

"You are a pretty girl, Anne. Is there someone else? Do you fancy yourself in love with another?" The girl's lower lip trembled and a glistening tear slipped down her cheek. "Who is it, then?" Margaret demanded.

"It is nothing, your grace. I shall be honored to

make whatever marriage my father should decide upon." Her voice was so quiet that Blanche could hardly understand her.

"Only the lowliest of peasants are privileged to marry for love, you know," Margaret said. "It is not a requirement in the high-born. Occasionally loves comes later with us. You must not count on it."

"I know." The girl was so pitiful Blanche's heart hurt for her.

"Yes, I think you do know," Margaret said. "If obedience were all I think you would be a perfect wife for any man. But if you marry my son you will have to be strong as well. You will have to temper him, soften him, advise him without appearing to do so. What kind of ruler he will be will depend on what kind of queen you are."

"Yes, your majesty. If it be your will that I marry the Prince, I will do as you have said," Anne said miserably.

"Then go, and please do not be so mournful in his presence," Margaret advised.

When the girl left the room Margaret seemed to sag and age visibly. "Anne Neville is fortunate. At least she has seen her future husband. She has some idea of what to expect. I was happy at my betrothal because I didn't know Henry. Do you remember that day, Blanche, when we sat in my room after the tournament and talked about Henry and wondered what life would be like?"

"I remember. It was long ago."

"It wouldn't have made any difference if I had known, I suppose. The choice to marry or not was not my choice any more than it is Anne Neville's. Knowing what I was getting into would not have changed what happened. It's been a long time since I've allowed myself to think of those times. Do you ever just sit and think of what we were like then?"

"Sometimes. Not often anymore."

"I remember . . . but the past is past," Margaret said, trying to shake off memories. "Will you return to England with me?"

"Meggie, you asked me to recall the day of the tounament when we wondered what the future held. Do you remember also what I told you then?"

"No."

"I promised to stay with you. I will come with you, Meggie. I don't know how to do otherwise."

"I have thought over your proposal, sire. I have interviewed your daughter and found her acceptable. I believe our mutual cooperation may be beneficial to us both," Margaret said to Warwick. The scene was familiar—Margaret seated at her "throne," Warwick on his knees before her. This time the room was more crowded. Warwick's wife and daughters were there and so were the Prince and his attendants.

"When shall we proceed with the marriage?" Warwick asked.

"The sooner this is settled and we can proceed, the better."

"I quite agree. Shall we have the banns read this Sunday and hold the wedding in three weeks' time?"

Blanche noticed that Anne Neville was looking at the floor, as if it were not her fate that they were deciding. Prince Edward was picking at a hangnail. He wasn't at all interested in the arrangement. For his age he had remarkably little interest in the opposite sex. "Three weeks would be fine," Margaret said. "But there is one stipulation that must be made. They are still but children—their marriage will only be legal, not actual, for the time being. It is not to be consummated. They must maintain separate establishments until we have displaced the usurper."

Warwick looked surprised, then thoughtful. He knew why she made the stipulation, of course. If the marriage were not consummated, an annulment later would be easier. She intended to dislodge Anne as soon as she was back in power. But there were two sides to the question. If they should lose the next battle and Margaret and the Prince were to flee again, Warwick might be able to seal a new bargain if he had Anne free and unspoiled, ready to marry more advantageously. An annulment might be desirable from his point of view as well as hers. He had no other daughters left to bargain with and Clarence had ruined Isobel's value. She was damaged goods now. Yes, perhaps it might be best for him. And if Margaret tried an annulment that he did not want, he could count on Anne to swear that she had had relations with the boy. Anne was a good girl; she would do what she was told. "They *are* very young, your majesty. I agree. But I do think that once the usurper is displaced, it would look better if they lived together as man and wife."

"Very well." Margaret had won some time. "Pierre, Jasper, let us join the Earl in the small chamber now and discuss the details."

383

Blanche hurried back to her own rooms. "Mattie," she said, "do you know where Dickon is? Please fetch him."

"Mama, what is wrong?"

"Nothing—yet. Please get Dickon."

In a few moments he was there with Mattie hanging onto his sleeve as she had the day years ago when Blanche had asked him if he wanted to go with his father. But now she wasn't going to *ask* him. "The Queen is going to invade England, as you must have guessed by now, Dickon. You are no longer a child and it is time for you to go to your father."

"No!" Mattie cried.

"Yes," Dickon agreed. "You are right."

"But why? Dickon . . . Mama . . . why?" Mattie asked frantically.

Blanche put her arms around the girl, now grown to woman. "Because he is a man, Mattie. If he went with us he would have to fight with the armies for Queen Margaret. He might be fighting against his own father. This cannot happen."

"No . . . no, but why should he have to fight at all? This is all so silly. This is Aunt Margaret's battle, not ours. I have never even understood why there are two sides to fight at all."

"I hardly recall anymore, but the fact is, if Dickon went with us, a healthy young man in the Queen's entourage, he would be expected to join in battle."

"I suppose you are right," Mattie admitted and started to weep.

"I would like to ask something of *you* now," Dickon said to Blanche.

"Yes?" Blanche said, half knowing what he was going to ask.

"When this is over—and it will be soon, Mattie," he said, putting his arm around her and continuing to address Blanche—"may Mattie and I marry?"

"I can think of nothing that would please me more," Blanche said.

"Very well. When do I leave?"

How can Mattie and I, in our different ways, love this matter-of-fact boy so much? Blanche wondered. "Immediately. I have letters from your father that should be proof enough of your identity to allow you to travel safely. When you reach England, go first to Cecily Neville. She can find your father."

The Prince and Anne Neville were married in July. Anne looked terrified; Prince Edward was bored. Isobel Neville wept throughout. Whether she wept for herself or her sister was questionable, for sitting beside her was her husband. Clarence had popped up unexpectedly. His brother, King Edward, had run him out of the English court, where he had been trying to disassociate himself from Warwick, Isobel, and the recent rebellion. He swaggered into Isobel's rooms one day and prepared to resume his marital duties and privileges.

Margaret and Warwick were both embarrassed at his presence, but there was nothing to do about it. They were both only guests of King Louis' court and weren't in any position to specify who else might be a guest. If Louis was willing to tolerate Clarence, so must they.

Mattie alternated between weeping and giggling. She was soon to be a bride and wanted to enjoy the ceremony of someone else's wedding, but she was also a perceptive girl and knew Prince Edward as well as anyone in the world. She had become attached to Anne Neville and despaired on her behalf at the thought of anyone having to spend her life with the selfish, cruel boy Mattie had grown up with and knew all too well.

There was no celebration after the ceremony. There was no time. They were all involved in feverish plans for the coming invasion. They felt it was necessary to attack immediately. Warwick reported that Edward of York's troops were no match for the combined force of Margaret and himself, but they dared not let Edward have time to gain strength over the winter. They had also obtained help from Louis. He had been unwilling to help either of them singly, but he thought that together they could win. He would provide money and troops, though they would pay dearly in interest and trading agreements advantageous to France.

They also had to settle the matter of Clarence. He was not the least useful as a friend, but he could be dangerous as an enemy. His turncoat personality had already cost Warwick a great deal. Finally an agreement was reached. When King Henry was back on the throne, his son, Prince Edward, would naturally be his heir. But if the Prince and Anne Neville should not have a son, Clarence and his descendants would be next in line. Justifying this was difficult, since, if Clarence was eligible, then his older brother Edward was even more eligible. But the eventuality was unlikely and something could be thought up in the meantime, if necessary. It satisfied Clarence and that was all that was necessary for now.

The plan for the invasion was simple, or at least as simple as a battle plan for such high stakes could be. Warwick, along with Jasper Tudor and Clarence, would invade England in September. They would send ahead messages to their manors to have troops waiting. Pierre de Breze would come with them in charge of the French troops that Louis had loaned. As soon as Edward of York was killed or captured, they would send for Margaret and the Prince. In the meantime Warwick would have Henry recrowned.

Margaret didn't like the idea of staying behind and letting Warwick have unsupervised control of Henry, but she dared not risk her son's safety if the battle should not go in their favor. If Warwick should lose this bid, she would be safe in France with the boy and no worse off than she had been before. But she was optimistic. She felt sure that they would not lose. They had a far superior force. Edward of York had the support of Burgundy and Flanders, but if they could attack quickly enough, he would not have time to call them in.

It would work. It would have to work.

CHAPTER EIGHTEEN

Elizabeth Woodville stayed in her chambers waiting for her mother, Jacquetta, to return with news of Edward's whereabouts. All London had been in a stir for two days. The King had gone north to suppress another of the endless rebellions a week before when news reached London that Warwick and Clarence had landed in England with a large army and were marching on King Edward. Jacquetta had hurried to join her daughter and granddaughters. Queen Elizabeth was in no state to endure the worry and suspense without family support. For the Queen was about to have another child, perhaps a boy this time. King Edward's position would be far stronger if he had a male heir instead of just daughters.

A messenger had arrived a few minutes before and Jacquetta had gone down to the courtyard to hear whatever news he might have. Elizabeth paced the huge room, waiting impatiently. She was no longer the lithe, gentle-eyed girl who had served and loved Queen Margaret. She was in her late twenties now and had borne several children—two sons for Lord Grey and three daughters for the King. Aside from her pregnancy, she was heavier. She had become a deep-bosomed woman, mature and attractive in a voluptuous way.

But her once gentle eyes were hard now. She had

seen and done much since she was a girl at Queen Margaret's court. She had made her way nicely in the world and pulled her family to the top with her. Her father and brothers, who had once devotedly served King Henry, were now important men in England and served King Edward.

Jacquetta came breathlessly through the door. "Elizabeth, quickly, get your things together."

"Mother, what has happened? Is Edward all right?"

"He has fled the country. Warwick nearly captured him, but Edward narrowly escaped. The man I spoke to says Warwick and Clarence are now marching on London. They are only a few hours from here. You must go to sanctuary at Westminster Abbey. It is the only place you can reach now where you will be safe." Jacquetta summoned Elizabeth's ladies and ordered that the necessary packing begin. "Don't forget the clothes and furniture for the new baby. He will likely be born at Westminster."

"Hasn't Margaret done enough to me?" Elizabeth raged. "She has already been responsible for my first widowhood. Does she wish to kill Edward, too? I think she would destroy all the men in England if she could. All for the sake of that crazy old idiot she's married to." Within two hours Elizabeth, her mother, her daughters, and most of her household had taken up quarters for a long stay at Westminster Abbey.

"Where has he gone?" Margaret asked Pierre de Breze. Pierre had returned to France immediately after the invasion of England.

"It is rumored that Edward of York is in Burgundy.

His sister is married to the Duke of Burgundy and it is a logical place for him to take refuge."

"Then we have not yet won this fight. So long as Edward of York is free to return we are not secure," Margaret said. But she was not unduly distressed. It was a disadvantage that the usurper had fled rather than been killed, but her situation had improved so vastly that it seemed only a minor problem. "I am told that you have brought back most of the French troops you led, Pierre."

"Yes, they are still under my command. King Louis commissioned them to us for a period of one year, not just for the duration of the initial invasion, you remember?"

"When are we to go to England, then?"

"I don't think you should go yet."

"Should not the Prince be showing himself to the people?"

"It might be good, but there are other considerations now. Warwick will have many small pockets of resistance to clear out before it is safe for you and the boy to travel in England. Let him spend the winter routing them while you stay in safety. After the new year begins, you can take the boy and go to London," Pierre suggested.

"You fancy the fantasy that Warwick will *invite* us to join him?"

"Mais non, it is certain he will never ask you to come to England. He has control of the rightful King, King Henry. It is what he has always wanted—to hold ultimate power in England. This is why I brought my troops back with me. When we go, we will be ready to show force. But it is best to wait until the first flurries of rebellion are over."

"I believe you are right," Margaret admitted. More waiting, a lifetime of waiting for something. But this time she was waiting for something worthwhile, something positive. She would go back to England a victor, not a poor guest tolerated and laughed at behind her back, as she had been at the French court all these years. This wait would not be long. "What of Jasper?" Margaret asked.

"He has gone to Wales to reclaim his estates and find the boy."

"The boy? Oh, yes, Margaret Beaufort's son. I had almost forgotten him. He was under Lord Herbert's care, was he not? What has become of little Meg?"

"She has been twice widowed, your majesty. Young Stafford succumbed and now she is to marry Lord Stanley. There were no children of the second marriage. The boy, Henry Tudor, is hidden away in Wales somewhere. Jasper hopes to find him," Pierre said.

"You know, Pierre, if I did not know well Jasper's devotion to my husband and myself, I might be suspicious of his intentions. He is much concerned with his nephew. And the child is my husband's nearest relative aside from our own child. The boy must be—what ... thirteen or fourteen by now?"

Blanche had been sitting quietly, not wanting to interrupt Pierre's recital, but she could not hold her tongue any longer. "Meggie, that is a terrible thing to say! After all Jasper Tudor has lost and suffered for your sake."

"Blanche, don't be angry. I didn't mean I don't trust

him, just that if he were anyone else I might not. Do you see what I mean?"

"I think I see exactly what you mean," Blanche said sourly, but didn't elaborate. "Pierre, is there any news of Dickon?"

"I was fighting, not talking, with the enemy," he said. Pierre had not approved of Blanche's raising the boy, then sending him off to the other side, even though it was where his father was.

Margaret had been ignoring this exchange. "Still, the boy is Margaret Beaufort's child and she is of royal blood . . ."

"What?" Blanche said.

"Little Henry Tudor. His grandmother was a queen of England and his mother is a Beaufort. Jasper might have something in mind for him . . ."

Blanche stood up and walked stiffly to the door. "Meggie, I simply will not listen to such slanderous talk, especially when you are questioning the motives of someone who has shown his loyalty to you to the extent that Jasper Tudor has." She swept out indignantly and slammed the door.

"Blanche is showing her age," Margaret said carelessly. "She is getting touchy."

"You may find the King strange in his ways, Henry," Jasper warned the solemn youth at his side. "You must remember that he has borne much and he was always a man of gentle disposition."

"I know, Uncle."

"He has spent many years now in the Tower and has lost touch with the things of this world."

"I can understand that, Uncle. I too have been out of touch," young Henry Tudor said somewhat con-descendingly.

If Jasper noticed the tone he wasn't offended. He loved his nephew as if he were his own son. Henry Tudor could do no wrong in Jasper's eyes. They had arrived at the King's chamber. Jasper was shocked at the sight of his half-brother. Warwick had brought the old King out of his cell in the Tower and had him dressed in his former robes of state, but they hung even more loosely on his angular frame than before. He was fifty years old now, but looked seventy. His skin was like dusty old parchment. He sat on the raised chair, moving his lips soundlessly and staring blankly around the room.

"Your majesty, greetings," Jasper said and was somewhat surprised when King Henry looked directly at him. "It is I, Jasper, your brother." Did the King recognize him? Perhaps. "I have brought your nephew to meet you." He pulled the boy forward. "This is Edmund's son, your brother Edmund. Edmund has died; this is his son." King Henry continued to stare at the boy.

Henry Tudor bowed to the old man. "Dear Uncle, it has been my greatest desire to meet you and tell you of the great love and respect I have for you." The boy sounded as if he meant it.

"You must not fall into lewd companionships while you are here," King Henry admonished. What is he talking about? Jasper wondered. "You must take care that your robes are clean and your mind devoid of sin and lust. You have been granted a great honor, but you must not give in to vanity. Your father and mother must be made proud of you. You shall attend Mass twice daily and keep an altar in your own cell. You must not be out on the streets at night. You must study diligently, for the masters will beat you for your own good if you do not."

Suddenly Jasper realized what was going on in the King's mind. He was back when he had founded Eton. He thought Henry Tudor was one of the new students brought to the King for instructions. In the old days, Jasper had heard this lecture delivered many times.

"I shall, your majesty," Henry Tudor said. It seemed not to matter to him what the King was talking about.

A trumpet blast startled Jasper. On the tail of the sound, Warwick entered the King's chamber and strode to the throne. He stood beside the dusty old man and placed a hand on his shoulder. "Ah, Jasper, I see you found the boy. He is thin and pale. You must keep him here and feed him on good London fare for a while. That will fill him out. Now if you don't mind, I have some papers for the King to sign." Warwick dismissed them.

When they were out in the street, Henry Tudor said, "Where am I to live, Uncle, with you?"

"No, you are going back to Wales. I like not the look on Warwick's face. He is called kingmaker, you know. He is a dangerous man and you are the closest relative to the house of Lancaster. You will be safer in Wales."

"As you say, Uncle. I would like to talk to you about the financial status of some of your estates before I go, however."

By that evening Jasper knew more about the condition of his holdings in Wales that he had ever known before. The boy certainly knew money.

The first Parliament since King Henry the Sixth's "readaption," as it was called, met in November. The customary bills of attainder were passed against the losing side. The Lancaster holdings that had been turned over to victorious Yorkists years before were now snatched from them and returned to the Lancaster supporters. Warwick regained his holdings, as well as grasped those of Lancasters who were no longer alive to regain their former properties. Next, the matter of the justification had to be settled. Warwick could not have Edward of York proclaimed an out-and-out usurper without its reflecting on Warwick's own part in putting him on the throne. Also, he had to reward Clarence for behaving himself this time with a promised place in the line of succession. It was the only way to keep Clarence from changing sides again.

Finally Warwick hit on an idea that would take care of the problem very neatly.

"Blackburn?" Cecily fumed. "I never even heard of anyone named Blackburn."

"They say he was an archer in your husband's army," Cecily's friend said. "The Parliament says that you had an affair with him, and King Edward is the illegitimate son of that union."

"I know what they're trying to do, but why must they attack me so foully to do it? And Clarence allowed it. Clarence! My own child! And Warwick, my nephew, my own kin. How could they? So, I suppose

Warwick claims that he did not know until now that Edward was a bastard and that clears the way to add Clarence to the line for the throne?"

"Yes, as next in line, legitimately."

"Well, at least they aren't trying to make me a whore for all my life. They grant that Richard was the father of *some* of my children. What colossal filth! I shall see to it that Warwick pays for this. He shall pay. Wait until Edward hears of this."

"Just a few more minutes, now. Push harder. Just once more," Jacquetta said.

Elizabeth Woodville gasped for breath and bore down again. Her tangled hair stuck to her neck and face. Sweat stood out on her forehead. She took another deep breath and pushed.

"That's it, my dear. Now rest. Get me another cool cloth," Jacquetta ordered a servant. "Just rest. It's all over."

Elizabeth breathed shallowly for a few minutes, eyes closed, hands unclenched. "Mother," she whispered, "is it another girl?"

"No, darling, it is a fine boy. A healthy boy, a son for the house of York. Your husband's heir."

"Thank God," Elizabeth whispered before falling asleep.

Pierre de Breze had been correct when he told Margaret that Warwick would have to spend the winter putting down rebellions. Edward the Fourth had been in the north, routing out nests of rebels, when Warwick took him by surprise the previous fall. Now Edward

397

turned the tables. Warwick was in the north when Edward landed at Ravenspur in March. Edward was met by cheering countrymen who had eagerly awaited his arrival. They joined him on his march to London. Their ranks swelled as they crossed country. Warwick was caught unawares. Edward took London without a fight. He took control of poor addled King Henry, who was glad to get back to his comfortable, solitary state in the Tower.

Elizabeth Woodville emerged from Westminster with her new son. She was Queen of England again. Edward spent two weeks playing with his new son, making love to his wife, and conferring with his generals. Warwick was said to be moving south—slowly, cautiously.

Unfortunately for the Lancaster cause, none of this news reached France. There were spring storms playing along the coast of England, churning the narrow Channel between England and France. Edward's ships had been among the last to cross safely and no news had come back.

Margaret knew nothing of Edward's invasion. So far as she knew, he was still in Burgundy. She had waited out the winter. She had not heard from Warwick. She and Pierre and their borrowed French army had arranged to sail in April with or without an invitation from Warwick and now they sat in the harbor, waiting for the water to calm and the storms to abate enough to cross.

Finally a clear day dawned and Margaret set sail. She thought she was going to meet Warwick. But she would never see him again.

Margaret landed at Weymouth on April thirteenth. It wasn't until then that she heard that Edward was in England. Rumor was that he had moved out of London that very day to attack Warwick. Jasper Tudor was rushing from Wales to meet her. She could not turn back before she knew what was going to happen to Warwick.

If Warwick were the victor in this clash with Edward, her arrival would be perfectly timed. She could march to London as if it was she and not he who finally dispatched the usurper. If Warwick lost . . . well, she was ideally situated on the coast to flee if necessary.

The next day, Easter Sunday, Jasper arrived from Wales with some of his troops and some important news. Richard Neville, Earl of Warwick, great king-maker, was dead.

Edward's troops and Warwick's had battled at Barnet. The details of the battle were unclear, but one thing was certain: Warwick was dead.

Margaret nearly panicked. Her impulse was to turn back and plan a new attack. Jasper Tudor, however, was encouraged. "We have not lost an ally, madam— merely a temporary friend. Edward is certain to have lost men and strength in this battle even though he was the victor. This is the perfect time to attack."

"We haven't enough men to attack him," Margaret objected.

"Not here, but I have reserves waiting in Wales. If we move north and west into Wales quickly enough, we can get together a substantial army."

"I am accustomed to things moving so slowly, with months and years between to make decisions. But you are right. I shall, however, send the Prince back to France, where he will be safe."

"No, Margaret." Pierre entered the conversation for the first time. "You must not expect more blood to be shed for a boy who is never present at battles fought on his behalf."

"He is right, your majesty," Jasper agreed. "The people have not seen him since he was a baby. They will not fight for a young man who still is kept hidden behind his mother's skirts. They know he is of age to be fighting for his own rights. If he goes back to France, we might as well all go back."

"But he is my son. He is all I have. He is the only heir. I cannot risk his safety," Margaret pleaded. She looked to Blanche for support, but Blanche's only concern was whether Charles and Dickon had been in the battle and whether they had survived.

"You must," Jasper said sharply. "He is a man now, not a child. If he cannot stand for himself now, he will never be able to. Thousands of lives have been given for him—English lives and Scottish and French. He must be at the head of the army."

Margaret closed her eyes as if to shut out logic. They were right, of course, but they were not mothers. How could she subject her son to such danger? After all the years of agony and humiliation she had endured for his sake, how could she willingly put his very life in danger? But it must be. Margaret knew this campaign was the last chance; she must take it. "Yes, he will lead the army," she said. "How soon do we leave?"

"Tonight. We will have to go north along the river Severn to a crossing point. Then we will move west into Wales. I will get the troops ready to move," Jasper said, already on his way to the door.

It was not easy. The troops were reluctant; the men had not been paid for some time and could find very little food in the area. Lancasters were not favored here and the farmers had used great imagination in hiding their stores from the hungry army. The soldiers dragged their heels, and at the end of each day (since they had not made enough progress), their leaders kept them marching into the night. The result was that each day they were more tired, more footsore, and moved even more slowly than the previous day. The terrain was wet and muddy and it was too early for spring crops to line the sides of the road for pillaging.

As far as Blanche was concerned, the only good thing to come out of the maneuver was what she learned about her own daughter. Mattie was only sixteen, about the age Blanche had been when she first came to England, and Mattie was a strong-minded girl. Blanche remembered first love and the giddiness she had felt at the very thought of Charles Seintleger, but if Mattie was giddy and shaky-kneed over Dickon's safety, she did not show it. Mattie would have been justified, especially at such a tender age, in doing a great deal of worrying and railing against the circumstances that were endangering her future. But she did not. She did not even question, not aloud at least, why she and her mother had to stay with Margaret.

What have I brought her to? Blanche wondered. I made a vow of loyalty to Margaret and have remained true to her even when no one could have blamed me for doing otherwise, but had I the right to impose that vow on my daughter? But Blanche told herself that she was not to blame . . . Margaret was to blame. In various ways Margaret had killed Richard of York and Elizabeth Woodville's first husband and so many thousands of others. Even Brithric—dear, long-dead Brithric, who had given Blanche so much happiness and this beautiful, sensible daughter—he would not be dead if it were not for Margaret's ambitions.

So, for the first time, a true bitterness began to well up in Blanche's heart. Not for her own sake—she had accepted her own losses and learned to deal with them years ago—but for Mattie's sake.

While Blanche pondered these new realizations and shivered and starved with the Lancastrian army, Edward of York's army moved slowly toward them. Edward's army was also slow. They, too, were tired and hungry, weary of marching. They had suffered great losses in the battle of Barnet against Warwick. But they moved on. The two armies lumbered on like two sides of a triangle nearing a common point, the first crossing over the river Severn into Wales. If Margaret's armies could get across before Edward's armies reached them, they would have fresh reinforcements waiting in Wales. If not, the two armies would meet.

Margaret and Jasper herded the army like slow, stupid cattle. Farther east, Edward pushed his men. Blanche spent one evening during the march laboriously removing the pearls from Margaret's wedding dress —the pearls that had formed the daisy emblems. She made no attempt to replace the design with threads, as when the gold centers had been removed. Margaret needed the pearls to pay the soldiers. The pearls on her wedding dress were the last thing she possessed of any value. If she won this battle, she would have everything. If she lost—nothing, not even a good dress.

Finally Margaret's army reached the city of Gloucester, the first place where an entire army could be taken across the Severn. "Send a party to the city gates to greet them and ask permission to pass through," Margaret ordered.

Within a half hour the advance party came back. "They fired on us, your majesty," the leader reported. "They will not allow us to pass through. They have barred the gates to the city and set archers and guns on the walls."

"Jasper, can we force our way through?"

"We could if we had several days to spare, but Edward of York's troops are only hours away. We will have to go on."

"How far is it to another crossing point?" Margaret asked.

"Another ten miles or so at a place called Tewkesbury."

"Then we must move on immediately."

The men grumbled, nearly rebelled, and, minus a few deserters, moved north again. It was well after dark when they reached Tewkesbury. There was no resistance. The bridge was clear.

"Why have we stopped?" Margaret asked Jasper.

"The men are exhausted. We cannot get all the soldiers and horses and supplies across quickly, and if Edward of York should attack before we are all across, we would be leaving a part of the army to be slaughtered."

"But what if he attacks while we are still on this side of the river?"

"Then we fight, and I'm afraid that is what is going to happen. My scouts tell me he is but a mile or two away and still moving. Madam, the battle will be in the morning, I fear, and on this side of the river."

"Send my son to me," Margaret said.

Margaret had her priest say Mass for her and the boy, but he fidgeted throughout. She wanted to sit with him and talk of her love for him. But he was eager to be gone. He was to lead a division in the morning and wanted to get back to polishing his armor and talking strategy with the other men over stolen ale. She could not hold him to her. She wanted to wrap him in her arms and soothe him as she had when he was a child, but he didn't want to be soothed. She hugged him and he cracked his knuckles while enduring her embrace. He wanted only for morning to come so he could fight. He didn't have time for a sentimental woman.

Margaret tried to understand. She kissed her son good-night, gave him her blessing, and then went to a convent nearby to wait. Blanche and Mattie and a few other ladies, who had accompanied their husbands to battle, joined her there for the long wait ahead.

Blanche was awake all of what remained of the night, and in the early morning she went to a high upper room of the convent. Margaret was sitting there by herself. No doubt she had sat by the window all night. Blanche wondered if Margaret had been in need of comfort during the long night, but Blanche was all out of comfort. She had none to spare for Margaret, who had brought them all to this.

Blanche pulled a stool to the window and sat next to Margaret, waiting. Neither of them spoke. Then they heard the trumpets announcing that the battle had commenced. There was a wooded strip of land between them and the area that would henceforth be called Bloody Meadow. They could not see anything of what was happening, but could hear the battle faintly.

The whinnying of injured horses, the piercing screams of wounded men came through to them occasionally. They could hear the cannon being shot and the trumpets being blown. No one came to the convent to tell of what was happening. No one could be spared from the fighting.

Blanche knew that when someone could take time to send a message to Margaret, the battle would be over and the message would tell them the victor.

They watched the woods, looking back and forth across the horizon. When a rider came, they must see him. They grew hungry and thirsty and their eyes throbbed with pain, but they could not leave the window. They must watch for the messenger.

The sounds of death and slaughter went on and on and on. For hours the sounds of destruction came muffled and obscene through the forest barrier. A nun brought some food. They tried to eat, but it stuck in their throats. Margaret drank a little wine, but it gagged her.

They waited. They watched.

Were Blanche's ears failing, or was it getting quiet?

She listened more intently. There were only infrequent cannon shots now. The underlying rumble of battle had stopped.

They caught a glimpse of movement at the edge of the forest. She squinted her eyes. Someone was coming.

There! A rider. Closer and closer.

Not one rider, a group—six or seven men on horseback. Blanche couldn't identify them. They carried no banner and they were too away for the women to see if they wore any insignia on their clothes.

They moved closer and both women peered intently to see who they were. One man was clearly the central figure. The rest rode apart from him in a circle.

Just a little closer.

"Jasper!" Margaret exclaimed. It was the first thing she had said all day.

The man in the middle *was* Jasper. He was dirty and his clothes were torn and bloody, but it was certainly Jasper. "Thank God," Margaret said.

One of the other riders turned to say something to the man behind him and Margaret and Blanche could see the back of his cloak. There on the back was the emblem of the white rose. The *white* rose—the emblem of the house of York.

Jasper was not coming as a victor; he was a prisoner, escorted by a Yorkist guard.

So the victory was not Margaret's. Edward of York had won.

Margaret almost slipped to the floor, but caught herself. "I do not know anything yet. I must wait and receive Jasper. This is not the end, even if we have lost this battle," she said against all reason. "Perhaps Jasper changed his mind and sent my son into Wales before the fighting started. That might be . . . mightn't it, Blanche?"

Blanche said nothing. She tried, but no words would come.

"Even if he was captured, we will get him free somehow," Margaret went on. "It may take a while, but I will find a way." She straightened her pose and smoothed back an errant lock of graying hair. "I must compose myself. Jasper will be here in a moment."

She was standing proudly erect when Jasper entered the room. The defeat etched in his face spoke for itself. "It is over, your majesty."

"And the outcome, my lord?" she asked, as if she did not know.

"We have lost. Our men fought valiantly, but against stronger forces."

"And my son, Prince Edward?" she asked.

Jasper stood mute. He opened his mouth, but words would not come out.

"My son," Margaret snapped. "Is he hurt?"

"He is dead," Jasper said.

Later there was a plaque marking the place where the boy was buried. It said, "Here lies Edward, Prince of Wales, cruelly slain while but a youth . . . you were the sole light of your mother, the last hope of your race."

They were taken away later that day. Blanche silently packed Margaret's few meager belongings while Margaret sat at the window staring out as she had all day. Edward of York sent an escort to bring the Queen and her attendants to London, where they were lodged in the Tower. Mattie and the few other ladies went along. Margaret did not speak during the long ride, nor did she look back or cry.

Blanche felt the weight of memories press upon her as she entered the Tower of London by the same gate she had entered when she last saw Brithric. They were lodged in the royal apartments and put under heavy but unobtrusive guard.

"Meggie, Henry is here in the Tower," Blanche said as she helped Margaret prepare for bed the first night there. "I'm sure they would let you see him if you wish. Shall I ask?"

Margaret shook her head. "I never want to see him again."

She got her wish. The next morning word was brought to them that King Henry the Sixth had died in his sleep during the night. The guard told Blanche that the old King was thought to have died of grief over the news of his son's death, but Blanche didn't believe it for a moment. The guard turned to go, then remembered something else. "You are to come with me. There is someone to see you," he said to Blanche.

"Who is it?"

"Sir Charles Seintleger." He led her down a steep stairway to a waiting room.

Blanche stood uncertainly at the doorway. Charles looked at her for a moment and memories flooded over her. He wasn't really so different from that night in France when he had given her his cloak. Older, of course, but still handsome. He still had kind eyes and broad shoulders. A smile spread across his face.

"Charles," she said and threw herself into his arms. He kissed her with the passion of a young man and she returned his kiss, though she felt her lips bruising. Finally she tore herself away from his embrace and said, "What of Dickon? Mattie . . ."

"He is well. He was at Tewkesbury and was knocked unconscious, but he has recovered. He wanted to come with me, but I thought it best for him to rest for another day or two."

"I must tell Mattie."

"In a moment. There are other things we must settle first."

"It's all over now, isn't it, Charles? All the years of fighting and death."

"Your sister has nothing left to fight for. Her husband and son are dead. King Edward is secure on the throne."

"What will happen to Margaret now? Will Edward execute her?"

"He should, but I think he is averse to having a woman's blood on his hands. She will be sent back to your father, if he will have her."

"He won't have her back unless he is paid to do so," Blanche said with brutal honesty.

"Then I suppose he will be paid," Charles said. "I don't think Edward even wants her in the same country."

"And me?" Blanche said.

"It is up to you—it has always been up to you. I spoke to King Edward this morning. His mother had already told him that you are her friend and asked that you go free. He has agreed."

"Dear Cecily. She has done me so many kindnesses."

"Blanche, I've loved you for as long as I can remember. Our children are to marry and we shall soon be grandparents, no doubt. Will you marry me now?"

"I made the wrong choice when you asked me before. I can't afford to make the same mistake again."

"I was afraid you would choose to stay with your sister," he said, embracing her.

"No, I have paid for the promise I made her. I have not been able to do anything for her. She had no need for my love or advice and she has nearly ruined my life. I'm almost forty years old and I've earned the right to live my own life now and seek my own happiness. I want to go tell Mattie that Dickon is safe; then take me away from here, Charles."

EPILOGUE

Edward the Fourth could not bring himself to execute a woman, not even one whose actions had cost him so much. Margaret of Anjou was shuttled as prisoner-guest from one castle to another, including that of her old friend Alice Chaucer, for several years. Finally her father, René of Anjou, was persuaded to take her back and she died in France eleven years after Tewkesbury. She was a broken, forgotten woman.

Anne Neville, once free from her marriage to Prince Edward, married Richard of Gloucester, Edward the Fourth's youngest brother. When Richard became Richard the Third, Anne Neville was Queen of England for a short time before dying of consumption.

Three years after Margaret of Anjou's death, Henry Tudor, with the help of his uncle, Jasper, defeated Richard the Third in battle and became Henry the Seventh. Thus ended the Wars of the Roses and three hundred years of Plantagenet rule.

Long before dawn of the following day the castle-folk were astir. The sleepy murmur of voices quickened and rose to the angry humming of a disturbed hive as the first pink streaks stained the sky. As if the coming of the sun was a signal, the castle erupted into violence with morning. Men bellowed, women shrieked, horses whinnied, oxen lowed, and asses brayed. Cart jostled loaded cart, wheels locked, the carters cursed and occasionally came to blows. Between them, men-at-arms threaded their overfresh horses, adding confusion when the more spirited animals took exception to a chance blow or sudden movement to lash out with their heels or begin to buck.

The scene in the courtyard where the nobles were assembling was very nearly as confused. Most of the Queen's ladies traveled in great, well-cushioned wagons, but Alinor, the two Isobels, and a few of the younger ladies-in-waiting, as well as the Queen herself, planned to ride. Maidservants ran back and forth with small items of comfort that had been left behind—a pomander for Lady Leicester, an additional veil to ward the dust for Lady de Mandeville. The mules stamped and snorted; pages darted about.

At last the Queen came from her chambers. Simon hurried across to lift her into her saddle. The great white palfrey moved forward, and behind it the whole disorderly mass was galvanized into action. Because there was no danger, there was little discipline. By and large the ladies rode somewhere near the Queen, but

Isobel of Clare fell back to ride beside the litter that carried William Marshal. Alinor teased her a little about that, saying that she went to determine whether her orders had been obeyed. William had intended to ride and had yielded to Isobel's tears after all of Simon's logical arguments had been pooh-poohed.

Alinor had ridden back too at one time to talk to Beorn Fisherman. She had had virtually no contact with her men since she had been at Court, and she wished to know whether all was well with them. Beorn had a few complaints. Most of the troop had been quartered in Alinor's house, and there had been some trouble about a woman. Alinor shrugged and laughed and approved of Beorn's disciplinary measures. It was bound to happen when the men were idle, she thought. She must either send most of them back to Roselynde or find duties for them.

Soon after, she was riding well ahead. A young squire, who was vaguely familiar but whose face she could not place, had fallen in beside her as she was about to return to her position near the Queen. He had admired her handling of her fresh mount, and Alinor admitted to being accustomed to the saddle. From this they had passed on to talk of hunting, which was a favorite sport for anyone who could ride well. That brought sighs and a confession that she had missed that pleasant activity sorely since being at Court.

The squire shook his head. "And I fear you will continue to miss it. Lord Richard is no passionate huntsman as his father was. He is more inclined to war. But even if he had been, he is like to be too busy with affairs of state to go ahunting."

If Alinor thought it doubtful that any ardent hunter could be diverted from that pastime by mere affairs of state, she had no time to express the idea. The talkative young man's tongue was still busy.

"And in Winchester," he said teasingly, "we will all

2

be pent like prisoners, so that we may make a brave show for Lord Richard's arrival. It would not do to have half the noblemen scattered over the countryside when he comes." He cast a look around at the disorderly mob. "I do not think the Queen would mind if some of us rode out a little." His expression turned roguish. "If I can start some game—will you follow?"

"What?" Alinor laughed, "without dogs?"

The young man shrugged. "We cannot ride far— that, the Queen would see fault in—so dogs would do us no good. Will you come?"

"So close along the road and with this rout, I doubt if you can start even a hare," Alinor said.

She had a momentary doubt that the squire desired a little dalliance behind the first bush he could find, but he was some two or three years younger than she and did not look in the least amorous. In fact, some minutes later he had started a hare. Alinor would not have ridden off alone, but some two dozen ladies and gentlemen saw what the squire had and went hallooing off after him. It seemed safe enough, and they all coursed it for ten minutes or so, as long as it would run, for the sheer joy of galloping over the fields. When the creature had found a thicket impenetrable to the horsemen, although one or two gentlemen even dismounted to try to poke it out, the group turned back. Alinor found the pleasant young squire beside her and held in her mare to thank him for the sport.

"You should thank me," he said ruefully, "for you will get back scot-free, but I will be whipped for laming my horse."

And, as they moved slowly forward, it was obvious that the poor beast was limping. Alinor watched the halting gait for a moment. "Have you looked to see if he has picked up something in his shoe?" she asked. "It looks like trouble with the hoof rather than with the leg."

3

The boy dismounted at once and Alinor held the reins while he examined the stallion's hoof. "You are right," he exclaimed, "but I fear the damage has been done. There was a stone here I think. It is gone now."

Alinor glanced around. The other riders were nearly out of sight. "Come," she said, "you may ride pillion behind me. Without your weight, he will do better."

With a word of thanks, the young man sprang to Dawn's crupper. Alinor reached back to give him his horse's rein, but instead of taking it, he seized her about the arms and breast with one hand and about the mouth with the other, loosing a wild hunting halloo. In spite of his youth, he was very strong. For one moment, Alinor sat in stunned, paralyzed stillness. Then she began to struggle. She bit the hand across her mouth with all the energy that affronted rage afforded her; she dropped her reins, throwing them as well forward as she could with her fingers so that her captor would not be able to control her horse; she raised her sturdy legs and slammed the hard heels of her riding shoes into her mare's sides.

At that final indignity—added to the loud noise in her ear, the loose rein, and the double weight—Dawn rose on her hind legs and pawed the air. She was as anxious to get rid of the strange weight on her crupper as Alinor was. The bite had brought a shriek but no loosening of the boy's hand. Instead of leaning into her mount's rise to force Dawn down, Alinor threw herself backward. The boy uttered another shriek and started to slide, but he still did not relax his grip. Dawn came down with a thud that threw her riders even more off balance and loosened Alinor's feet from her stirrups. Indifferent to anything beyond her need to free herself, Alinor twisted and tossed herself back and forth. Dawn lifted again. Now Alinor could not have leaned into the rise even if she wanted to. As she toppled backward, her captor cried out again and fell, dragging her with him.

4

The fall finally broke the squire's grip. He had hit the ground first with Alinor atop him. Although slender, Alinor was a sturdy young woman, and though half stunned, she was able to roll away. She was not frightened. There was no one in the world who wished her ill, and her death would profit no one but the King, who would gather in her heirless lands. The only thing any man could desire was her broad acres and, perhaps, her person. To obtain either of those—or both—she must be unharmed. And no man would hold her long enough for that. Simon would come for her, leading every vassal she had. No keep would hold out long in the face of so angry and determined an army.

Alinor scrambled to her feet, her hand on her knife. The boy would not dare use his, but there was nothing to stop her from using hers if he tried to take her again. She gave a passing thought to killing him then, but he was already stirring and she would not trust herself to be quick enough to avoid his grasp.

As her head cleared, the more practical notion of catching Dawn arose. Alinor glanced about and uttered a most unmaidenly oath. The mare had taken fright in earnest and was well away and running hard. At least, Alinor thought, she was running in the right direction. If she sensed the other horses in the cavalcade, Dawn would head for them.

That hopeful idea was what brought fear upon Alinor. If Dawn should not reach the group or if the mare was not recognized as hers, no one would know she was missing until they reached Windsor Castle. Actually, it might be hours after they arrived before her absence was noted. The confusion of finding the correct quarters, unpacking and setting up furniture, cooking and serving a meal would be no less than the confusion of departure. Certainly the Queen would not be writing letters, and Alinor had no other specific duties that, remaining undone, would betray her absence. In those hours, she might be taken anywhere.

5

How could Simon come for her when he did not know where to go—or even who had taken her? Alinor realized with a shock that she did not know herself. The boy was someone's squire; she had seen him accompanying someone at Court, but she could not remember who. Now she understood why. He was not wearing the colors of his house. That was why the face was only vaguely familiar. One looked at the master, not at the man.

Run, Alinor thought. But run where? There was no place of concealment for her among the open fields; she was no hare to creep in among the low thickets and find a hole in the ground, and the woods were too far. She could not outrun the boy in her full riding skirt. Outrun the boy! That was the least of her troubles. She could hold him off with her knife, but he could not be alone in this. That hunting halloo that had so startled Dawn was to summon those who would really take her. Soon there would be men and horses.

Alinor cursed herself for not slitting the squire's throat at once, but it was too late now. He was sitting up and shaking his head. Hopeless as it was, Alinor took to her heels. On the other side of the thicket she would be out of sight, at least temporarily. She drew her wimple up across her face to shield it as much as possible from the branches and brambles and plunged in where the brush seemed thinnest.

The eye of youthful love is very keen. Although he rode close behind his master, as was his duty, Ian de Vipont was never unaware of Alinor. He knew where she rode, to whom she spoke, and how long she had been away from the Queen's vicinity when she went to talk to Beorn. Even though the distance was considerable, he knew the gray mare and her green-habited rider when they careened off in the chase. Thus Ian was also aware that Alinor was not among the laughing group of hunters who returned.

6

For a few moments he hesitated, staring over the fields, hoping to see her merely riding more slowly than the others. For a few moments more he delayed because he feared to bring punishment upon her. Then he reproved himself. Lady Alinor was no Lady Greensleeves. She would not ride apart to use a ditch or a hedge like a common whore. Perhaps she had fallen and the others had not noticed!

"My lord," he called.

Simon finished what he was saying to Lord de Mandeville and dropped back so that Ian could come alongside. "Yes?"

"My lord," Ian swallowed, "Lady Alinor is no longer with us."

"No longer— What of that? Doubtless she has ridden back to speak to Lady Isobel or—"

"No, lord. She went to speak with Beorn Fisherman, but then she rode off with a party that was coursing a hare for sport. They have returned but not Lady Alinor."

"Are you sure?"

"Yes, lord, I am sure."

Simon was about to ask sharply how Ian could be certain about one girl in such a rout of riders when he caught the intent—and unmistakable—expression in the young man's eyes. He shut his mouth, feeling decidedly uneasy. Alinor might be infuriating, but she was no fool. She had not ridden off alone and—Ian was right—she would have returned with the others. Simon pulled his helmet up over his mail hood, swung his shield forward, and reached out to take his lance from Ian.

"I will murder that girl if she has stopped to pick wildflowers," he growled. "Go and summon my troop and Beorn and his men and follow me. Which way did she ride?"

Ian pointed. Simon clapped spurs to his horse and took off across the fields. They were open except for the dividing hedges and at first he saw nothing. Just out of sight of the road, however, his heart rose in his throat when he saw, off to his left, a riderless gray mare stumbling now and again on her hanging reins. He turned his mount in that direction, and Dawn came toward him, whinnying a welcome, for the loose rein and the empty saddle frightened her. Simon spurred on more frantically, only seeing with the corner of his eye that the mare was shining with sweat but not really lathered. Alinor could not be far—but how to find her, one small girl in a green dress, lying in a green field?

Before she won through the thicket, Alinor's wimple was in shreds, her dress had several rents, and her face and hands were trickling blood from scratches. Despite her hurts, she had considered staying in the brush; but if she moved, the sound would betray her and, if she did not, her pursuers would find her and pick her out in minutes. Confined by the brambles, she would not even be able to use her knife. She had heard, as she struggled, the renewed hallooing of the squire, and when she looked around, the result of his calls began to show. By twos and threes, men were riding from the distant woods.

Her roving glance had caught something else previously hidden by the thicket—a low mud and wattle hut, perhaps a shepherd's shelter. It was no safe hiding place, but perhaps it had a door she could bar, which would delay her captors making off with her. The few minutes it would take for them to break in might be worthless, but one could not tell. It was possible someone would notice the riderless mare. Alinor lifted her skirts and began to run. Behind her she could hear the boy thrashing his way through the brush. Ahead, the riders were closer; they too were hallooing. It was a clever device. Even if some trick of wind should carry the sound to the Queen's cavalcade, it would not arouse any interest. A petty baron hunting with a party of friends would utter just such cries in excitement or to keep the party together.

When Simon first heard the hallooing, he thought just that and uttered a heart-felt thanksgiving. There would be others to help him search and probably others who knew these fields well. He turned toward the sound, roweling his horse unmercifully, because in his mind's eye he saw Alinor weeping with the pain of broken bones or stunned, helpless, and frightened. He was indeed so immersed in his mental image that even when the riders were in sight, he did not at once perceive the oddity of the fact that there were no hounds. Only the long-ingrained habit of danger, which had made him put his shield on his arm, saved him from being cut down when he came upon the first pair.

The truth burst upon him when he saw the glitter of a lifted sword, so that he was able to ward off the stroke of one man with his shield. The other, however, opened a nasty gash along his ribs as he threw down his lance, useless for such close work, slipped his wrist through the loop of his morningstar, and freed it from his saddlebow. The morningstar was not a weapon Simon favored. It did not make clean wounds like a sword but crushed and tore. Now, however, he sought it instinctively. Clean wounds or death were too good for those who threatened Alinor.

The sick, wet crunch, the choked-off scream, the thud of a man's fall when the spiked steel ball at the end of the brutal, barbed chain connected were sweet music. The backswing caught the top of the other rider's shield with such an impact that it forced the metal edge back into his face. His sword stroke, aimed at Simon's head, fell awry on his shoulder. There was enough force left in it to cut the surcoat and drive the mail through shirt and tunic and open the flesh. Another trickle of blood began to stain the gray surcoat. Simon laughed and swung his arm. The ball flew wide. The barbs of the chain caught the nape, below

9

the helmet, pierced through the links of mail hood. Simon pulled. Jaw and neck tore away. The man fell without crying out, gagged by his own blood.

The horse hardly needed spurring now. Melee-trained, it charged toward the oncoming riders. Simon swung the morningstar forward, caught it by the short steel handle to which the chain was attached. Blood dripped down onto his gauntlet and glistened redly wet on his stallion's hide. He regretted the loss of his lance now. He could have slain out of hand two of the three who had turned aside from their original target, which Simon could not yet see.

Accustomed to fighting in larger groups, the men-at-arms rode bunched together. Bred to tourney fighting, where each knight fought for himself, Simon swung wide, turned his destrier sharply, and took on the man on the far right. His shield went up to block a wild sword thrust. The morningstar swung up and then straight ahead, as a man would thrust with a sword. At the point of greatest momentum, Simon released the handle. The steel ball shot forward, struck the helmeted face, thrusting the man sideways. Instinctively his arms swung out to seek support, and the shield on his left arm struck his horse in the side. The beast shied, fouling the mount of the middle rider.

Simon rode on past. His horse could not have checked in time in any case. As he turned his beast, he whirled the hanging morningstar. A trail of red droplets followed it, but its charge was soon renewed at it took the middle rider, who was struggling to control his startled horse, in the back of the neck. This was no game of knightly endeavor in which men politely circled each other to meet face to face.

The third rider had managed to avoid the plunging horses of the other two and was circling also. He thought he had taken Simon's measure, but he had erred in failing to take account of Simon's destrier. On

10

signal, the battle-trained stallion reared upward and turned short. The sword cut, aimed to take off from behind the arm that wielded the morningstar, struck the bottom edge of Simon's shield, slid down, and scored his calf. Perhaps that sight was a brief comfort before the morningstar came down again.

Bereft of opponents, Simon looked about for more. He was breathing hard but more with fear that Alinor had been, or would be, carried away while he was thus occupied than with effort. He had fought many better skilled and more dangerous opponents in the past. First, far in the rear, in the direction from which he had come, he saw his own troop and Alinor's, Ian urging his flying horse to still greater effort and Beorn thundering along just behind. His intent was so fixed that he did not register them either as help or hindrance. There was only one thing Simon sought.

Then Simon found his objective. He did not yet see Alinor, but from various directions the horsemen were converging upon one spot. Simon clapped his spurs to his mount's already sore sides and it leapt forward, even breasting the thinned spot in the brush where Alinor and the squire had forced a path. Down beyond he saw her at last, her back to the wall of the shepherd's hut. It had no door. Four men ringed her, but not too close, for one was nursing a hand from which blood dripped. Another held the five horses. He was the first to die there. He did not even have time to cry a warning. He had not looked around, expecting more of his companions and finding the scene before the hut of more interest. The morningstar caught him full in the chest. Blood filled his lungs and burst from his nose and mouth. The horses, suddenly freed and affrighted, galloped away.

Startled at the sound of pounding hooves so close, one man turned from Alinor and shrieked a warning. He was the second of that group to die. None of the men had drawn a weapon. Perhaps, had Simon seen,

11

he would have held his hand, but his eyes had only taken in Alinor's bloody face and hands and torn clothing. When the man-at-arms fell, he had no face. The third, Simon brained with a single downward thrust of his shield. The man had not pulled his helmet on over his hood. What was there to fear from a single girl?

The fourth and fifth fled without even drawing swords. They were not cowards. Two men afoot were no match for a knight mounted on a war-wise destrier. Across the field those who had been coming slowly began to spur their horses onward, but the shouts of Ian and Beorn and the men who followed made them pause. When they saw the size of the troop, most of the men riding with lances fewtered; they did more than pause. They turned their horses and rode away at the best pace they could make.

Simon pushed the loop of the morningstar off his wrist, flung himself from his mount, and caught Alinor to him, gasping between rage and fear for her.

"Let me go!" she cried, her voice high, hysterical, terrified.

Alinor did not fear the man who seized her—she feared for him. She had recognized Simon as soon as the man-at-arms screamed a warning to his comrades. But the blood! Her love was covered in blood. It seemed to Alinor—who had seen men hacked to pieces—that she had never seen so much blood in her life. Simon misunderstood. He thought she was dazed by fear and did not know him.

"Alinor! It is I, Simon. Beloved, do not struggle so. No one will hurt you now. You are safe. My love, my love, when I find who has done this to you, it will take him ten years to die."

"My God, my God," she sobbed, "no one has done me aught. But look at you! You are covered in blood. Where are you hurt, dear heart?"

"*I* am covered in blood!" Simon exclaimed, relaxing his grip, so that he could look at Alinor. "*You* are

12

covered in blood." His face turned ugly, but his voice was soft as to wheedle a frightened child. "Beloved, tell me who beat you. I swear on my life that man shall take no revenge upon you."

"No one. No one," Alinor assured him and threw her arms around his neck and kissed him.

Simon's mind could hold no more at the moment than the bloody fight, his terror for Alinor, the pain that was beginning to press upon him. Overriding all when Alinor touched him came a wave of unthinking passion. He tightened his grip again and his mouth responded to hers, hard and dry at first with the thirst of battle, then softening as his blood answered to this new demand and left the fighting muscles to course through groin and mouth.

Alinor had kissed the lips of many men, young and old. She had kissed then in greeting and parting in her grandfather's day, and she gave the kiss of peace to her vassals and liegemen. A kiss to her had been a physical contact little more meaningful than a pressure of the hands. Occasionally, as when she kissed Sir Andre, she had felt a stir of affection. Nothing had prepared Alinor for the sensations that enveloped her now. It was as if her flesh had developed nerves in new places. Her breasts rose and the nipples filled; her loins grew warm and soft. Regardless of the fact that Simon was crushing her to him so hard she could scarcely breathe, she attempted to press still closer. His lips parted; hers followed. His tongue touched hers; the tip of hers slid under his, caressed its roots.

In his life Simon had had many women, willing and unwilling. There had been the greensleeves and the prizes of war, the serf girls who had fulfilled a sudden animal need and the castle ladies who had wished to taste a new delicacy. But before he had seen Alinor, Simon had loved only one woman deeply and devotedly—the Queen—and he had never, even in dreams, associated her with sexual passion. Topping the physical stress of battle and fear, the onslaught

13

of combined love and lust nearly felled him. His knees trembled and tears filled his closed eyes and oozed under the lids to mingle with the sweat of exertion on his face.

Through mail and clothing, Alinor felt him shake. New to passion, she did not associate the trembling with desire. The last image fixed in her mind was the bright, wet blood on Simon's gray surcoat. The trembling of a wounded man meant weakness to Alinor. Anxiety drowned passion. She disengaged her lips gently.

"Beloved, beloved," she murmured, "sit down here. Let me tend to you. You are hurt."

Simon opened glazed eyes that slowly began to fill with horror. "What have I done?" he said faintly.

Alinor understood. "Nothing," she soothed, "nothing. A kiss to comfort me." She stroked his cheek. "Come. Sit. Let me see to your hurts. No one saw. We are alone."

"Alone?" Revulsion thickened his voice. To take advantage of a frightened girl was disgusting. Simon bit his lips, still soft and warm from her kiss, and stared at her. Perhaps he had not been the first to take advantage. "Who has torn and bloodied you?" he cried.

"No one. Simon, love, listen to me. I ran through the thicket to escape the boy and the branches and brambles scratched me and tore my clothes. That is all. No man laid a hand upon me." Alinor looked at the three bloody corpses that lay so near. "And you have paid them well already who only threatened me."

She took his hand to lead him around the hut, suddenly remembering how bitterly he had spoken about blood and terror. Alinor knew that some men were taken with a sickness after battle and could not, for a few hours, bear to remember or look upon what had been done. And the blood was still welling from his right side.

"Come, beloved, come away from this abattoir," Alinor urged gently. "Let me stanch your bleeding."

"Oh God!" Simon put up a hand to his face. "Do not use those words to me."

"What words?"

"Do not— You called me 'beloved,'" he choked.

Alinor bit her lip. She had not realized. It was indeed necessary that she be more careful. "No, no," she agreed quickly. "I will call you 'my lord' or 'Simon' when we are among others. Do not fret my lord. Only come with me and let me attend to your hurts."

He searched her face and found there only a desperate anxiety. "I am not hurt," he assured her, a little relieved.

Those warm lips, opening so readily, that little tongue—she had only been aping his practiced caress. She did not understand. The words of love—only relief. He had done no irrevocable harm, he told himself, yielding to her pull and following docilely around the hut, out of sight of the carnage he had wrought. There was no need for him to tell the Queen he was no safe guardian. No need to yield his trust to another who would not really care for her.

"Sit," Alinor bade him, ignoring the silly remark that he was not hurt. She found to her relief that her knife was still in her hand, and smiled a little, thinking how the body responded to need without real thought. When the strange man-at-arms had reached for her, she had stabbed his hand before she even thought of doing so. Yet she had held her knife carefully atilt all the while Simon embraced her and she him.

Simon was glad enough to rest for a while. The succession of violent exertion and violent emotion combined with loss of blood was taking its toll. He sank down, propping his back against the wall of the hut, lifting his scabbard out of the way, and making sure his sword was loose in it. Although he made preparations for defense automatically, he did not fear attack. His men and Alinor's would not go far. He closed his eyes.

A sound of tearing cloth jerked them open again. "What do you do?" he asked, seeing Alinor with her skirt above her thighs, busily slitting her shift to pieces.

"For shame," she laughed at him, "look away or you will see me naked. It is the only clean cloth about me. I am all muddied from crawling about through hedges, and I must have something to bind you with."

"Bind me? Tush! I have fought half a day with worse hurts. It is naught but a slit in my skin. Do not trouble yourself. A leech shall see to me when we return to the Queen."

Alinor had had wide experience of the wounds of war and the filthy leeches that attended the wounded men in the year during which her liegemen had fought, sometimes bitterly, to keep her safe. Perhaps the leeches who served the Court were wiser and cleaner, but Alinor was not about to chance Simon's well-being on such a hope. She met his eyes.

"You are mine, to me," she said fiercely, "and none but I shall see to you." Then seeing how startled he looked, Alinor smiled and told him what she would say to others to convince them that she did no more than her duty. "I have tended Sir Andre and Sir Giles and Sir John and many others when they were hurt for my sake. Shall I do less for you who are the warden set over me? Would you have men say that I hate you and wish you ill?"

Simon looked away and Alinor went back to cutting up her shift. It was reasonable enough, he thought, but that passionate "You are mine, to me" disturbed him. Then he remembered when he had heard Alinor say that before, and he began to laugh. God pity the man or woman who tried to interfere with Alinor's inordinately powerful sense of possession; Simon understood that he now belonged to her—just like her castles, her lands, her vassals, and her serfs. For any and all of these she would work and fight. In a sense she loved them all. Doubtless in that sense, she loved him too. It was safe to let her tend him.

By the time Ian and Beorn and the men returned, Alinor's work was also done. She had removed Simon's belt, lifted his hauberk and undergarments, tsked over the gash, which needed stitching but which she now saw was not serious, and bound it firmly with pads and strips from her shift to reduce the loss of blood.

"We could not catch them, my lady," Beorn lamented, growing quite red with anger when he saw his mistress' disheveled condition.

"I think it is just as well," Alinor remarked calmly.

"We cannot hide this from the Queen," Simon sighed, then brightened. "Yes we can. We can say you had a fall from your horse."

"Ah, yes," Alinor agreed very gently, but with a sarcastic lift to her brows, "and doubtless you were so enraged at my bad riding that when you bent to lift me up, you burst. That is clearly why there is a rent in your hide."

Simon guffawed with laughter, then gasped and clapped a hand to his bandaged side. "Well, if you do not like my explanation, think of a better one yourself. The Queen has no need to know of my bruises. If I do not approach her until after we reach Windsor, a clean gown will cover all."

Alinor took his hand. She had made him remove his gauntlets when she saw the marks they made upon her gown and his own face. "My lord, my lord," she reproved him mischievously, "to save me a scolding you are prepared to perjure yourself before your liege lady."

"It was not your fault," Simon said defensively. "You did not ride off alone. If you were taken by surprise—" His voice faltered. She had not ridden off alone, but perhaps she had separated from the group willingly, not understanding what was really meant by whoever arranged the tryst.

17

"Oh, no," Alinor said, her voice echoing her disgust at her own gullibility. "I was tricked." She related the entire sequence of events, adding, "The reason I am glad we took no prisoner is that I fear it would be an embarrassment to the Queen to have proof of this wrongdoing. Someone with the power to hold me and hide me planned it. If there were proof, the Queen would be constrained to act. This way she may drop a hint of reproof or not as it seems best to her. Thus, she must know of it, and she may scold me or punish me for being a fool so easily taken in. I have well deserved it."

Simon shook his head. "The trick was well played. If it had not been for Ian's quick eyes to see you were missing—I doubt if wiser heads than yours would have seen the trap. But, indeed, it is well that the Queen should know. Thus, I can set a watch upon you—"

"And I will keep that watch," Beorn burst out, his respect for Simon overwhelmed by his wrath. "And I will pray that another attempt be made. You need not fear, my lady. The Queen will not be embarrassed by it. There will be such small pieces remaining of the men that try that none will know them."

"I am sure I will be safe" Alinor soothed her outraged master-at-arms, then turned toward Ian. "So I have your quick eyes to thank for my rescue," she said. "If I have a gift in my power that would be to your liking, I wish you would name it."

Stricken mute, the young man shook his head. Simon watched his squire's face, then lowered his eyes. He had not been mistaken. The only question now remaining was whether it would do the boy more harm to keep him where he would see Alinor or send him away where he could only dream of her. I am better off than he, Simon thought wryly. At least I am "hers, to her!" He is nothing, a passing glance and smile, a gift of armor or a horse. Thank God she did not offer me a reward.

18